JOSEPH WAMBAUGH is a former LAPD detective,
multiple *New York Times* bestseller, and a Mystery Writers
of America Grand Master. He is widely recognised as the
father of the modern police novel. He lives in LA.

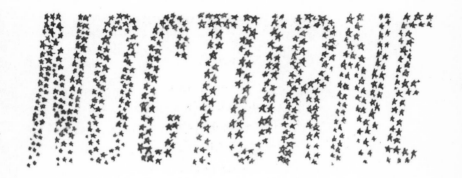

A CRIME NOVEL

JOSEPH WAMBAUGH

A Mysterious Press book
for Head of Zeus

First published in the United States in 2012
by Mysterious Press, an imprint of Grove/Atlantic, New York.

This edition first published in the UK in 2012 by Head of Zeus Ltd.

9 7 5 3 1 2 4 6 8

A CIP catalogue record for this book is available from the British
Library.

ISBN (HB): 9781908800558
ISBN (TPB): 9781908800565
ISBN (E): 9781781850534

ACKNOWLEDGMENTS

As ever, special thanks for the terrific anecdotes and great cop talk goes to officers of the Los Angeles Police Department:

Randy Barr, Jeannine Bedard, Jennifer Blomeley, Adriana Bravo, Kelly Clark, Pete Corkery, Dawna Davis-Killingsworth, Jim Erwin, Brett Goodkin, Jeff Hamilton, Brett Hays, Craig Herron, Jamie Hogg, Mark Jauregui (ret.), Rick Knopf, Rick Kosier (ret.), Fanita Kuljis, Cari Long, Rich Ludwig, Al Mendoza, Buck Mossie, Thongin Muy, Julie Nelson, Scarlett Nuño, Al Pacheco (ret.), Victor Pacheco, Bill Pack, Helen Pallares, Jim Perkins, Robyn Petillo, Kris Petrish (PSR ret.), Brent Smith, Bob Teramura, Rick Wall, Evening Wight

And to officers of the Los Angeles Port Police:

Kent Hobbs, Ken Huerta, Rudy Meza

And to officers of the San Diego Police Department:

Michael Belz, Matt Dobbs, Mike Fender, Doru Hansel, Fred Helm, Jeff Jordon, Charles Lara, Lou Maggi, Adam Sharki, Mike Shiraishi, Merrit Townsend, Steve Willard (S.D. Police Historical Association)

And to Debbie Eglin of the San Diego Sheriff's Department

And to Erik Nava and Ken Nelson of the San Diego District Attorney's Office

And to Mike Matassa (ret.) of the Bureau of Alcohol, Tobacco, Firearms, and Explosives

And to Danny Brunac, longshoreman of San Pedro

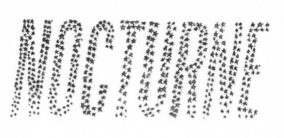

ONE

"So now I'm like, a hottie hunk on account of my fake foot, is that what you're telling me? I'm all irresistible or something?"

"It's not that you're irresistible," the young sergeant said. "It's what your prosthesis represents to certain people, those who suffer from a kind of paraphilia. Specifically, their disorder is called apotemnophilia."

"And what's that mean exactly?"

"The manifestation of a desire so intense that therapists have a hard time even explaining it, possibly a desire with a powerful sexual component. It's a fascination with amputation that sometimes goes so far that the person wants to *be* an amputee."

Sergeant Thaddeus Hawthorne was a twenty-eight-year-old UCLA graduate who, like thousands of Angelenos before him, had learned that his BA degree in the liberal arts had very little practical application in the job market of the twenty-first century. He had tested for, and joined, the LAPD just shy of his twenty-second birthday because of the good pay and job security. He had a very high forehead, and a sparse dark mustache crowded the limited space between his long, bulbous nose and upper lip. He anxiously looked from one blue uniformed cop to another as he spoke, both sitting across the table from him in a booth farthest from most of the bustle on this Friday evening at Hamburger Hamlet.

The recently appointed sergeant, who had just finished his probationary period at Van Nuys Division as a patrol supervisor before transferring to Hollywood Division, knew he should use "college talk" sparingly, if at all, in the company of street cops, especially this pair of weathered surf rats with their doubtful smirks and sea salt stuck to their eyebrows and lashes.

They were several years older than he, both being divorced womanizers, and they unnerved him with their reputations for sneaky get-back when it came to supervisors they didn't like, especially young supervisors.

"You mean there's nobody else but him that can do it?" the taller one said, nodding toward his partner.

Sergeant Hawthorne knew that this tall one had been driving during the fateful pursuit a year prior where his partner had suffered a hopelessly smashed foot in a traffic collision. It had ended with the pursued killer in a stolen van being shot to death by Officer Britney Small, then a probationary boot, currently working Watch 5 along with these two.

The sergeant said, "Your partner happens to be one of the few law enforcement amputees in all of California. It would be greatly appreciated by everyone in the Hollywood vice unit if we could eventually get the guys bankrolling their operation, and I'd certainly write you a glowing commendation that would look good in your personnel package."

Sergeant Hawthorne looked uncertainly at his massive burger, wishing he could cut it in half but not daring to, not when the tall cop across from him was effortlessly mashing his with one big paw and tearing into it like a wolf.

The taller of the suntanned cops scoffed at that lame enticement of a written attaboy but flashed a grin at his partner, saying, "See, dude? I told you when we got our new foot, fame would follow." Then he told the sergeant with pride, "You should see when this crusher catches a juicy at Malibu. He can even, like, hang three inches of our fiberglass foot and rip that kamikaze just like always. My pard's got a *pair* hanging on him!"

The sergeant was trying to figure out exactly what the hell the tall one had just said to him when the shorter one said, "Carbon, not plastic.

2

The surfing skate is made from carbon and polyurethane, not fiberglass."
Then he told the sergeant, "I got two models. The on-duty foot is way
different and fits real good in my boot, and it's pretty easy to run on."

The tall one said, "You should see all the Emmas in butt-floss bikinis
start jiggling their chesticles when they ogle the robo kahuna with the
bionic hoof. It's all beer, bubble baths, and blow jobs for him. Me, I'm
happy just to get his leftovers."

"He's always pimping me out at Malibu," the shorter one said dryly.
"He, like, tries to sell them on sympathy disrobing for a handicapped
kahuna."

Bewildered by the surfer-speak and opting instead for flattery, Sergeant Hawthorne said to the shorter one, "I think it was pretty gutsy
of you not to take a medical pension and retire when the accident happened. A lot of officers would have."

That didn't work. Both cops shot the sergeant a snarky look that
said, "We don't quit, dude," and the shorter one said, "What you want
me to do is way twisted. Even for Hollywood, this is sick shit."

"I can't deny it," Sergeant Hawthorne said, taking the first bite of
his cheeseburger and sadly watching a dollop of ketchup squirt out
onto the yellow L of the sky-blue UCLA sweatshirt he wore when
working vice to make himself look less like a cop. The troops around
Hollywood Station said he was so lacking in copper machismo that he
could dress in an LAPD raid jacket and still nobody would ever make
him for Five-Oh.

"Whose idea was this, anyways?" the shorter cop asked.

"Sort of my idea, I guess," Sergeant Hawthorne said. "I talked to
your watch commander as well as your midwatch sergeant about it before I decided to invite you here for a bite to eat."

The shorter cop said, "Lemme lock in on this. Are you telling me
that Sergeant Murillo actually thought I should do this demented shit?"

It was Sergeant Lee Murillo who'd pointed out that the young vice
sergeant resembled the nineteenth-century writer Edgar Allan Poe, and
had begun referring to him as "Sergeant Edgar."

"Well, no," Sergeant Hawthorne admitted. "Your sergeant said it was completely up to you and that nobody should try to influence you one way or the other."

"Does the croaker who does the kind of freaky swashbuckling surgeries you talked about still practice around here?" the tall cop asked, starting on the second burger he'd ordered because, what the hell, little Sergeant Edgar with the big vocabulary was sponsoring the meal, wasn't he? In fact, the tall cop had ordered the burgers with fries, plus a side of onion rings, and was even considering a piece of cherry pie with a double scoop of ice cream.

The vice sergeant said, "Not anymore. He's a burned-out crack addict now. He was fairly notorious for doing various kinds of edgy operations in a certain Tijuana clinic. It's an abattoir."

"A what?" the tall one said.

"A slaughterhouse." Sergeant Hawthorne instantly regretted using a word they might not understand. He was aware that everyone at Hollywood Station knew this pair by their surfing monikers of "Flotsam and Jetsam," and he noted that Flotsam always referred to Jetsam's prosthesis as *our* foot, so it appeared that these two were Velcroed. He began to think of possibly including the tall partner in the deal as a way to persuade Jetsam to accept the assignment.

Jetsam said, "He probably got one of those craigslist doctor degrees where they treat all ailments with leeches."

"No, Dr. Maurice Montaigne's medical degree is legitimate," Sergeant Hawthorne said. "But his license to practice was pulled long ago."

"What was that word you used to describe this creepy crap?" Jetsam asked.

"Apotemnophilia," the sergeant said, this time leaning over the plate before taking a second bite of his burger. "I've been reading up on it."

Flotsam said, "That's the biggest word I've heard since 'pica and pagophagia.' We got a call about a dude from his momma. He used to get all weirded out when he got drunk, and he'd eat red clay and ice cubes. She got scared he was gonna clog his colon. He told his momma it was for an iron deficiency. I told her it was just fucking Hollywood."

Sergeant Hawthorne stared at Flotsam for a moment before saying, "That's very interesting."

Jetsam asked the sergeant, "Why would anybody go all off the hook with fantasies of doing something like that to himself?"

"I told you, it's truly incomprehensible," the sergeant said, after chewing and swallowing a modest bite. "There aren't many people in the entire world who have this condition."

"And they all live around here, probably," Flotsam said with a head shake. "Fucking Hollywood."

The sergeant had been assigned to the station long enough to know that in these parts, cops always uttered the mantra "This is fucking Hollywood" to explain anything inexplicable, so he merely nodded and said, "It's illegal to amputate a healthy limb in Mexico as well as the U.S., but of course it's a lot easier to get it done across the border. So that's why I've prepared a cover story for you about a place in T.J. called Clínica Maravilla."

Jetsam said, "How could I fool anybody? Wouldn't the quack see my amputation was, like, done by skilled surgeons?"

"No doctor will be seeing you at all. We've been told that Dr. Maurice is effectively retired, holed up somewhere smoking crack twelve hours a day. He's harder to find than John the Baptist's head."

"Who the fuck's looking for that?" Flotsam wanted to know, and Sergeant Hawthorne cursed himself again for using an obscure metaphor.

"Who's the freak you're dying to pop?" Jetsam asked.

"We're not really dying to pop the Russian with paraphilia. He's just a very important client being serviced by the collector and the big boss. The collector is the guy who takes the money and pays all the bills, and sets up the special dates, and arranges for the girls to get medical care when needed, and—"

"With the weird croaker we're talking about?" Jetsam asked.

"At one time." Sergeant Hawthorne nodded. "But now that the dangerous doctor's a hopeless crackhead, they no doubt use somebody else these days. What we're hoping you can do is to get enough info that we can jack the collector for a few felonies and use that to persuade him to trade up for his boss. The collector's name is Hector Cozzo. The girls call him Hector the collector, and he's got a minor rap sheet for identity theft, forgery, and possession. The most time he's ever done is sixty days in county jail. He's a small-timer who somehow got this pretty good gig of collecting from massage parlor girls and from dancers working at a nightclub in east Hollywood that I'm sure you know about, Club Samara."

"In other words, he's a pimp," Flotsam said.

"More or less," Sergeant Hawthorne said.

"So who's the boss?" Jetsam asked.

"That's what we want to learn from Hector Cozzo. Our source said that massage parlor where Cozzo collects, is partly staffed by Asian girls who we now think were brought into the States as part of a human-trafficking ring, possibly with the help of Asian and Armenian or Russian gangsters. This could turn into a RICO indictment. You probably heard about the federal prosecutors indicting seventy members of Armenian Power last February?"

Both uniformed cops looked at each other with blank expressions, so Sergeant Hawthorne said, "No? Well, Armenian Power was working with Eurasian gangs here in Hollywood, Glendale, and other places, doing everything from identity-theft scams to kidnapping for ransom. The particular massage parlor and nightclub girls we're interested in have to pay their masters for travel expenses from their home countries, plus room and board and living expenses. Not to mention the stiff prices they have to cough up for drugs, so they can tolerate their pathetic lives. They're never able to pay back what they owe, and eventually, they either run away or just get cut loose with the clothes on their backs and a few bucks in their purses."

"You mean, after they're all thrashed and shot out?" Jetsam said.

"Exactly," the sergeant said. "Some of them are underage, too, but they get supplied with good ID and Social Security numbers and the rest of it. It's hard for ICE to prove they're in the country illegally, and besides, the feds are more concerned with Department of Homeland Security task force jobs these days, especially anything that remotely smells like terrorism. They're not much worried about illegal immigrants who get pimped out in Hollywood. We're working this mission on our own."

Flotsam said, "This here collector, how do you know about his client with the . . ."

"Apotemnophilia. One of the older Korean girls who ran away and now lives in Las Vegas got busted, and she's trying to cut a deal on a possession-for-sale she's facing there. She did a lot of talking to the Vegas police, and they phoned us because the crimes she talked about are going down here in Hollywood Area. I had a long conversation with her on the phone. It was very enlightening."

Flotsam was not surprised that a young top spinner like Sergeant Edgar would refer to their bailiwick using the now politically correct LAPD designation of "Hollywood Area" instead of the more militaristic-sounding "Hollywood Division," by which all of the older coppers still called the unique real estate policed by the officers of Hollywood Station.

The tall cop said, "So is the hooker that dimed the collector willing to testify if you bust him for pimping or whatever?"

"I had to promise her that we would never subpoena her into a Los Angeles courtroom before she'd talk to me at all. Besides that, she doesn't know anything really specific. What she does know she learned one night last year when she got an outcall job to a house in Encino that's occupied by Hector Cozzo, though his name is not on the deed. There she was ordered to service a big middle-aged guy with a streak of white running through his dark hair. "

"Like a fucking skunk," Jetsam said sullenly.

Sergeant Hawthorne said, "She guessed he was Russian, from his accent. She was told that he was the collector's wealthiest and most

7

important client. She did her job that night and got well tipped out, and was allowed to sit around for a few hours afterward, doing some blow that Cozzo gave her while he and the Russian talked in an adjoining room. She got a peek at some photos from an album the Russian brought with him and saw that they were looking at shots of amputees and amputated limbs. Arms, legs, hands, feet."

Flotsam said, "Goddamn! She's lucky the freaks didn't do a little amputation on her that night. Just for the fun of it."

Sergeant Hawthorne said, "Anyway, at one point, she overheard Cozzo mention to the client, that yes, he'd heard of a surgeon the big Russian knew a lot about. A surgeon that charged twenty thousand for taking an arm and fifteen thousand for a leg, on otherwise healthy people in a Tijuana clinic."

Jetsam said, "Did your snitch say if those two mutant deviates had all their own body parts intact?"

"Yes, they did. And by now I've read enough about that kind of paraphilia to know that most of these people are obsessed with the *idea* of amputation but don't necessarily try it out on themselves. They probably like to hear horror stories about some of the more gutsy people who allegedly went the distance. But Hector Cozzo is not one of them. He was only trying to please the Russian."

"Why don't you, like, *operate* the goddamn massage parlor with an undercover copper and get a violation for prostitution and be done with it?" Jetsam said. "Why fuck with this sick Russian at all?"

"We've tried UC operators without success," the vice sergeant said. "These people are super careful and highly suspicious, and besides, we're looking beyond a masseuse turning tricks. I know you've heard a lot lately about the LAPD cracking down on so-called erotic massage parlors, but we're aiming higher. We want the money guys behind this one. So after we got the intel from Vegas and I learned about the collector's rich Russian client with paraphilia, well . . ."

"Dude," Flotsam said to his glum partner. "Don't push the off button. Let's air this out. I wish they'd send *me* in as bait to chum up the water. I could handle whatever some Bangkok Bessie might wanna spring on me besides a back rub." Then he leered at a buxom waitress and said, "And I could totally bring game to this here breast-aurant."

"Keep your mind in *this* game, bro!" Jetsam said. "They're trying to shanghai me here!"

"Funny you should say that," Sergeant Hawthorne said. "The name of our primary target is Shanghai Massage."

"See?" Jetsam said. "There's all, like, bad juju going on here. I'm not down with this program."

"Don't go aggro, dude," Flotsam said to his partner. "He ain't asking for a kidney."

"And we're not looking for a misdemeanor prostitution arrest on an individual masseuse," Sergeant Hawthorne said quickly, pleased to have Flotsam as an ally. "This is an intelligence-gathering mission, nothing more. We're hoping that any masseuse who meets you will gossip about you to the collector, about an amputee client who tipped well and talked about having had his foot surgically removed in Tijuana by Dr. Maurice. We hope the collector might get curious enough about you to wonder if you could be a brother-in-fantasy to the big Russian. You being a somebody who had actually gone the distance with an amputation of a healthy foot. And if so, his very important Russian client might be burning with curiosity to meet you and hear all about how your Tijuana amputation went down. And if that works and you get inside, who knows what information and evidence you might be able to gather from these people?"

"That's a lotta ifs you got going here," Jetsam said.

"What's Cozzo look like?" Flotsam asked.

Sergeant Hawthorne produced a six-year-old mug shot, put it on the table, and said, "White male, thirty-two, five-six, a hundred forty soaking wet, black hair cut in a mullet, brown eyes, teeth like a ferret, and flamboyant in the clothes he wears."

The surfer cops barely glanced at the photo, and Jetsam said dismissively, "Everybody in fucking Hollywood's flamboyant, so what's that mean? Half the male population uses Johnny Depp guy-liner, for chris-sake. And who the hell but the lamest of low-life skateboarders that wear their baseball caps sideways would have a mullet haircut in the twenty-first century?"

"How do you know this ain't just get-out-of-jail-free bullshit from your Vegas snitch?" Flotsam said, piling on.

"We've been able to corroborate some of it," Sergeant Hawthorne said. Then he added, "I'll bet I could get your watch commander to let me borrow you both for the occasional nights we'd be needing you."

"What the hell would I do?" Flotsam said.

"Maybe you could kind of act like security for your partner, sort of like his muscle. If he gets a foot in the door."

"It's my stump that's gonna get me in the door," Jetsam reminded him.

Sergeant Hawthorne managed a polite guffaw at the amputation humor and said, "Maybe a good cover story would be that you're a seller of illegal video poker machines, the kind that's springing up in residential casinos all over L.A. They're brought from Arizona and can rake in between one and two thousand per machine per week, no problem. With your highlighted blond hair and permanent suntans, you resemble each other enough for you to claim you're brothers, and I think Hector Cozzo would buy that. If he accepts the amputee, he'll accept the brother with no worries that this might be a police sting."

"First of all, we don't use tanning parlors," Flotsam said, his eyes narrowing.

"And we don't highlight neither," Jetsam said, equally resentful. He touched his lightly gelled hair and said, "These streaks're what the sun does to hard-core kahunas that surf year-round."

"I didn't mean to suggest anything untoward," the sergeant apologized.

Flotsam grunted and turned to Jetsam, saying, "Untoward?" Then, to their host: "If we work for you, Sarge, we might need a translator."

Sergeant Hawthorne, who was thinking exactly the same thing about *them,* said, "You can ask any of the night-watch vice officers about me. I'm a forgiving supervisor, and I'm easy to get along with. Maybe I don't look or sound the part, but I'm a pretty good street copper as well."

Doubting that, Flotsam told his partner, "Dude, it could be nectar-neat to catch an occasional break from these bluesuits and, like, go all *Mission Impossible* for a night or two."

"Easy for you to say, bro," Jetsam said. "You ain't the one that'd have to get your mind into a ghoulish game of show-and-tell where some psycho pervert wants to hump your stump."

Sergeant Hawthorne said, "It's not like that. Cozzo is basically a grifter with a rich foreign client who has a very strange Achilles' heel, that's all."

"If he ever decides to go the distance himself, the geek won't even *have* a heel," Jetsam reminded them with a perceptible sneer.

"We could try it once and see how it goes," the vice sergeant said. Then: "Whoops!" as another dollop of ketchup obliterated the A in UCLA.

Jetsam shook his head. "Sarge, your sweatshirt now just says UC, as in 'undercover,' with two blobs of red beside it. So you just managed to out yourself. Any denizens of the dark out there can read that you're UC, and you did it with your own ketchup."

Sergeant Hawthorne managed an embarrassed smile and began wiping ketchup off the sweatshirt and off his face, until scraps of shredded napkin clung to his chin.

Jetsam looked at the vice sergeant and said, "What's the thread count on these things anyways? You got pieces of it hanging off your face."

Flotsam said, "Sarge, if we let you dial us in, you gotta learn how to eat a fucking hamburger. You're making us, like, way nervous here."

TWO

"THE FIRST THING you gotta learn is, forget classroom Spanish. It's not San Pay-dro. Around here everyone pronounces it San Pee-dro, or just Pee-dro most of the time."

Dinko Babich was conducting a late-morning tour for Tina Tomich, his mother's first cousin, and her husband, Goran, who had arrived two days earlier for a brief visit to the Babich family home. Tina and Goran were in San Pedro to take one of the cruises to Hawaii being offered at Great Recession prices in the third summer of the Obama presidency. Dinko was conducting this private excursion at the request of his mother, Brigita, as a way to kill the last few hours until their ship was ready to board. All they had done since their arrival was sleep, eat, and gossip incessantly with Dinko's mother, who'd said her good-byes to their Cleveland relations that morning while Dinko loaded his forest-green Jeep Grand Cherokee with their luggage.

Dinko was still bloated from the food orgy of the last thirty-six hours. Of course, there was the inevitable *mostaccioli* and sauerkraut, staples of San Pedro Croatians, but his mother had worked for days prior to the visitors' arrival and had prepared spicy pork meatballs and boiled Swiss chard with olive oil, garlic, and potatoes. And not just any olive oil, mind you, but Dalmatian olive oil. Dinko's grandfather had always said that even a dish of sardines and mackerel tasted like Mary

12

the Mother of God had prepared it, if you had Dalmatian olive oil and local, brick-oven French bread for the dipping.

Dinko's mother, whose parents had emigrated from a village near Dubrovnik, had apologized to Tina and Goran because she had no way to purchase Adriatic fish, which everyone in her family believed to be the best in the world. But she presented a main course of the Croatian version of shish kebab and, if that wasn't enough, another main course of beef in tomato sauce. And somehow fearing that her Cleveland cousins would leave her home unsatisfied, she served with their breakfast a plate of *burek,* pastry made of cheese, apples, and more meat, just in case their cholesterol had not spiked yet. And she packed them some thin fried pastry, to take with them in case they got hungry after boarding, but mostly to prove that the old-world way of cooking was alive in San Pedro.

Goran was sixty-four, one year older than Dinko's mother, and forty years ago he had almost left Ohio for Los Angeles to apply for a job as a longshoreman, hoping to work alongside Dinko's late father, Jan. That was until the call came from another cousin, offering an apprenticeship as an electrician. And so Goran stayed in Cleveland, married Tina, and had four children with her. They were extremely proud of their grandchildren and had bored Dinko with family history to the point of his almost wanting to smoke some grow in front of them, which he figured would induce cardiac arrest from both senior citizens, if his mother's feast didn't do it first.

While he was driving them on their brief tour, Dinko said, "You can also call the town Speed-ro if you want to. Sometimes I think half the population under fifty are tweakers. It's like Zombieland. You're afraid they'll bite you and you'll turn into one."

"What's that mean?" the older man asked. "Tweakers?"

"Crankheads. They smoke their crystal, mostly. Pedro will never be what it was back in my grandpa's day or even my dad's day. Nowadays it's sorta where the ocean meets the ghetto. Definitely not a southern California beach community, that's for sure. You can get hit over the head with a beer bottle and robbed. We call it being robbed at beer point."

"So sad," Tina said.

"The town is just overrun with Mexicans," Dinko said. "Gaffey and Pacific are our main streets, and Pacific is full of Mexican shops and dollar stores and people selling junk right out on the sidewalks. There's a street gang culture now, and tagging everywhere by baby gangsters. You stand still too long, some little BG might come along and tag your ass within an inch of your life."

"It's a shame what's happened to America's towns," Goran said.

"Of course, Pedro is not really a town," Dinko said. "It's part of the city of L.A., but it's far removed from the rest of the city by that skinny strip of land between Normandie and Western that takes the L.A. city limits way down here to Pedro. We're here because L.A. needed a port, so they took that strip of land and stuck the Harbor Freeway in the middle of it."

"I'll never forget coming down here the other night on the freeway after you picked us up at the airport," Tina said. "All those lights from the Port of Los Angeles. Thousands and thousands of those tall orange lights, and the crazy pattern of storage tanks and cargo containers stacked up as far as you can see!"

"Those're low-pressure sodium lights," Dinko said. He'd brushed up on port stats when he'd learned that his mother would make him tour the relatives around Pedro. "The port handled eight million containers last year. More or less."

"And those huge cranes out there at night!" Tina said. "From the freeway they look like scary monsters from a *Star Wars* movie or something."

"Good call," Dinko said. "George Lucas and his crew loved those big cranes. They look sorta like the giant white Imperial Walkers in *The Empire Strikes Back*."

"How many people work at the port, Dinko?" Goran asked.

"The December report I just read said over nine hundred thousand jobs and thirty-nine billion in wages and taxes were generated by the Port of Los Angeles last year. Of course, we refer to the rest of the city

up north of here as Los Angeles. We say, 'I'm driving up to L.A. today'
even though, technically, we *are* in the city of L.A. See, we always think
of Pedro as a town, not a part of the big city. It was always *our* town,
but now it's becoming *their* town—the Mexicans, I mean. Us Croatians,
and the Italians too, we're all way outnumbered by the Mexicans, and
there's also plenty of blacks nowadays. The Mexicans have taken over
the flatlands. The old-time families that're left mostly live up on the hill,
west of Gaffey. You won't find many blonds like me at San Pedro High
School these days."

"You aren't blond, Dinko," Tina said. "More like light chestnut now.
But you used to be blond when you were a kid. Your mother sent us pictures. A little towhead with big blue eyes. Now look how tall you are."

"How many Croatians you still got in the union?" Goran wanted to
know.

"For years I always heard there were forty thousand people of Croatian ancestry living somewhere close to the harbor, but I think there's
maybe only a few hundred longshoremen left here in Pedro from the old
Croatian families. In fact, the area across from your cruise-ship terminal
is a housing project full of greaser street gangs that shoot people and
sell drugs. You can drive through it and smell pot." He paused and then
said derisively, "Welcome to the harbor, where the sewer meets the surf.
Where the debris meets the sea."

"And you, Dinko? You would never touch any dope the hoodlums
sell, would you?" Tina asked him with worry in her voice.

She was even fatter than Goran, and her jowls bounced from her
vigorous nod of relief when Dinko said, "Not me, Tina. You think I
could operate a crane like my dad did if I was a freaking doper? Pardon
my language."

Dinko was lying twice: first about operating a crane and then about
his claim to sobriety. Although he had a pretty good job driving a utility
tractor rig, he'd twice in the past year spilled containers from a chassis
he was shagging around the container yard, and he'd tested positive for
drug use following the accidents. The second offense had resulted in a

thirty-day suspension for being under the influence of marijuana, which is why he had time to take his visiting relatives on a tour.

"How much you get for driving a crane, Dinko?" Tina wanted to know.

"Crane operators get about four hundred a day," Dinko said, and that much was true.

"You hear that, Goran?" Tina said. "You coulda been a longshoreman. Dinko makes all that money and he's only, what? Thirty-two years old?"

"Thirty-one," Dinko said. "But don't forget, I been a dues-paying member of the ILWU since I was a teenager. I didn't make the big bucks till I earned my A book and worked my way up."

"Please, Tina," the fat man said with a sigh. "I done pretty good as an electrician, didn't I?"

"We coulda lived in California and had nice winters," she said. "We coulda lived here in San Pedro next to the harbor and . . ." She corrected herself: "I mean, San Pee-dro, and we coulda watched the big ships come and go."

Goran just sighed again and looked at Tina's young relative as if to say, You see, Dinko? You see the cross I carry?

Dinko thought if he had to live with Tina for a week, he'd need to rip a bong twice a day just to cope. While he talked, he drove them to the San Pedro landmarks, including the parks at the south end by the mouth of the harbor, heading first to Angels Gate, where the Korean Bell of Friendship was a must-see. He also drove them by the Point Fermin Lighthouse and Museum, but they said they were too tired to go inside.

It was a clear, sunny day, so they parked and looked out to sea. Goran said, "What's that big island, Dinko?"

"Santa Catalina," Dinko said.

"But it's so close!" Goran said. "The old song said it's twenty-some miles to Catalina Island."

"On a clear day like this, it looks a couple of miles away," Dinko agreed. "Like you could row there in a dinghy, but you'd have to row for twenty-two miles."

Without getting out of the car they took cell photos of the American Merchant Marine Veterans Memorial, a striking bronze depicting two merchant seamen climbing a Jacob's ladder during a rescue, a tribute to the men who'd suffered the highest U.S. casualty rate in World War II.

Dinko said, "The L.A. and Long Beach harbors make these the biggest ports of entry in the country for container ships. They say that everything you're wearing and everything in your closet, two-thirds of it came in through one of these two harbors in cans we unloaded."

"Cans?" Goran said.

"That's what we call the containers," Dinko explained. "We unload the cans with cranes for the independent truckers that wait in lines four blocks long. The containers're stacked five high on the ships, and sometimes we gotta get on top and unfasten the locking device by hand. I don't like that. A crane could knock a bunch of cans over real easy. When a can falls, it sounds like an earthquake, and it can pancake the cab of a truck. We lose maybe six or eight people a year. One time I saw a ten-ton boom come out of its stay and crash down and slice a guy in half."

"Maybe it's a good thing I became an electrician after all," Goran said. "Money ain't everything."

"How much does a longshoreman like you make a year?" Tina asked.

"A night-shift crane operator can make a hundred seventy-five grand a year," Dinko said. "The day-shift crane operator can make up to a hundred fifty. Back in my grandpa's day, you had to have sponsorship to join the union. The union books got passed on to a longshoreman's kids. It had your name and ID number on it and the hours you worked. Most were Italians and Croatians then. Cops, firemen, even doctors and lawyers sometimes were allowed to work part-time on the night shift to make extra money."

"What happened to change it?" Tina asked.

Dinko said, "There was a big lawsuit to break up the nepotism, and the union lost and got forced to open things up to a very bad element. It was a shotgun wedding that never worked out. If there aren't enough registered longshoremen to work a job, the casuals come in, but it takes the casuals eight hours to do the work we can do work in two hours. They're the grunts of the waterfront, and they work like Frenchmen."

"I guess that's when the other *kinds* of people came in?" Tina said.

"For sure," Dinko said. "We got some blacks, but Mexicans make up at least half of the entire union. We got thugs that won't break away from their street gang culture, no matter how much they make. Nepotism was good. We replaced it with dirtbags."

"It's a different world, Dinko," Goran said, "and it ain't a better one."

They declined to shoot cell-phone photos of Fire Station No. 112, an award-winning building designed to shelter a 1925 classic fireboat that could produce more than ten thousand gallons of water per minute. Ditto for no photo op when Dinko stopped in front of the Warner Grand Theatre, a 1931 Art Deco beauty, one of three remaining, designed by the architect B. Marcus Priteca, who was commissioned by Warner Bros.

They did take some pictures when Dinko drove them past Croatian Hall, where the words above the door said, "God Bless Croatia."

Dinko said, "In my dad's day everybody called it Slav Hall, but no more. Not since the big war over there with the Serbs. Now we're Croatians, not Slavs. Back in the day, lots of Slavs, including Serbs, came to work in the fishing business and on the docks. Back when the canneries employed maybe thirty thousand women, mostly illegal Mexicans."

"Could we drive by your church again, Dinko?" Goran asked. "I oughta take a picture."

Dinko parked in front of Mary Star of the Sea Catholic Church, and Goran got out and snapped a few cell-phone shots of the words on the façade: "Maria Stella Maris Ora Pro Nobis."

"I remember your father's letter saying you were baptized here," he said to Dinko. "He was a proud man that day, I can tell you."

"I went to school there," Dinko said. "My grandpa stood with me when I made my confirmation in that church."

"Back way before you were born, your grandpa, he used to always write about the tuna fishing to my father," Tina said.

Dinko said, "In my grandpa's day, the Croatian fishermen would go out, twelve on a boat for maybe three months in Mexican waters. They'd come back with a hundred fifty tons of tuna in the hold and unload at Terminal Island. You used to almost be able to walk from one boat to another, there were so many. But then the superseiners came here. They could easily go to Costa Rica to fish. And just like that, it was over. There's still shabby old gill net boats around, manned by Asian fishermen catching squid for local markets. We say the Asians eat everything in the water except submarines. Anyways, we still have Croatian and Italian Masses here at the church, along with Spanish, of course. You can't get away from Mexicans, no matter what."

Both Goran and Tina were more than ready to call it a day by the time Dinko drove them to Point Fermin Park, the southernmost tip of the City of Angels. The Cleveland cousins actually got out of the Jeep and walked a short distance across the shady lawns and gardens, and saw people picnicking and jogging and playing with Frisbees.

And then Dinko said, "Lotsa people jump off the Vincent Thomas Bridge, or they come here to Point Fermin and hop over the barrier there, and do a dive off the cliffs. Pedro is a popular place to come to if you're of the jumper persuasion. Once I saw the Port Police hauling a floater with a rope around his torso. The dead guy's arm kept waving at the tourists every time the body hit a little ripple."

The suicide talk was too much for Tina, who said, "Maybe we should start heading for the ship, Dinko."

When they passed Ports O' Call Marketplace, Dinko pointed to the sign reading, "Home of the Proudest People on the Coast." He said, "That used to be a great place for tourists to go and have a bite to eat right on the harbor and browse in the shops. Now it's just a place where the Mexicans go on Sunday to get drunk and slap around their women. Look there. He's spun."

He pointed to a raggedy, toothless man standing on the curb near the intersection where Harbor Boulevard turned into Front Street. While Tina was trying to admire the Pacific Electric car that served as a trolley, the raggedy man waved a cardboard sign in her face that said, "Will work 4 meth."

When they arrived at the World Cruise Center berths, Tina gasped. There were two cruise ships docked there, just south of the mile-long Vincent Thomas Bridge, looming in the background. The nearer ship was so enormous from this vantage that it was hard for Tina and Goran to take it all in.

Tina said, "That ship. It looks like a big white building that got knocked over and is laying right there by the dock."

"Raise your gaze," Dinko said. "Look behind it. You're seeing two ships, not just one. Sometimes they load and unload up to thirteen thousand people in a single day."

And then the cousins realized there was an even larger ship docked behind the nearer one. It soared higher, and Goran said, "How do they get things that big to go so fast on the ocean? And how the hell do they park them?"

"The port pilots who go out on boats and bring in the big ships are the highest-paid city employees," Dinko said. "They deserve it."

"It makes you feel real small just looking up at them," Tina said to her husband. "And to think, we'll be on one."

Goran said, "Well, Dinko, I'm glad to hear you done so well in life, even with all the changes in your union."

"I hope you're saving a lot for your golden years," Tina said. "Are you planning for the future?"

Dinko, who never planned past the current day, just grinned and said, "Time to go aboard for your second honeymoon. Have fun, but don't do anything naughty. Everybody's got cell cameras, and you might end up on YouTube!"

THREE

Sᴇʀɢᴇᴀɴᴛ ʟᴇᴇ ᴍᴜʀɪʟʟᴏ, seated at a table in the front of the roll call room, was easily the most popular supervisor at Hollywood Station. He was conducting roll call for Watch 5 and, as usual, wanted to get officers of the midwatch in an upbeat mood before turning them loose on the streets at sunset. Sergeant Murillo was the son of Mexican farmworkers and had spent much of his formative years in the public libraries of the Central Valley while his family worked the fields. He still got most of his entertainment from books, and was a whippet-lean long-distance runner who had competed twice in the police Olympics. Although he was not yet forty, his hair was pewter gray, and he could look quite professorial when wearing his round wireless bifocals.

They were fielding seven cars, and all fourteen officers sat at long tables in fixed chairs with framed movie posters behind them, this being the only police station on the planet with one-sheets hanging on walls around the station. Many of them were from old cop movies or famous films that featured specific locations policed by the cops of Hollywood Station. On the wall by the door was a framed photo of a beloved senior sergeant they called the Oracle. He had died of a heart attack five years prior on the pavement in front of the station, where stars bearing the names of station officers killed on duty were set in marble and bronze, just like famous movie stars were remembered on Hollywood

Boulevard's Walk of Fame. And being a superstitious lot, every officer would touch the Oracle's picture for luck after roll call, before heading out to the streets.

The brass plate affixed to the frame around the Oracle's photo said:

THE ORACLE

APPOINTED: FEB 1960

END OF WATCH: AUG 2006

SEMPER COP

Sergeant Murillo was doing his Kung Fu impression on this particular Thursday's roll call while he read the lineup of names and car assignments. "And you, Grasshopper," he said to Officer Francisca Famosa with the appropriate accent and lilt, "you will be working Six-X-Forty-six with the Unicorn tonight . . . if you can find him."

Fran Famosa was an attractive thirty-five-year-old Cuban-American with thirteen years on the Job. She had a dusting of tan freckles on her nose and cheekbones, freckles a bit darker than her hair, which she wore pinned up off her collar, per Department regulations. And like all female uniformed officers, she wore a pale and subtle shade of lip gloss. She was a divorced survivor of a bad marriage to a now unemployed television sportscaster, and the mother of a four-year-old daughter.

Fran shook her head in dismay. Her partner for the remainder of the deployment period was Chester Toles, who was fifty-eight years old with nearly thirty-five years on the LAPD. The midwatch coppers tended to be divorced or never married, making it easier to work a shift beginning at 5:00 P.M. and lasting until 3:00 A.M., at the height of the street action. Chester was one of the few at Hollywood Station who'd been married to the same spouse for most of his life, and he had three children and four grandchildren. He was notoriously lazy and would try to kiss off any call he could, but since he "owned his pink slip," due to having been a cop since back when Gerald Ford was in office, he was fearless in the face of official reprimands or even short suspensions. He considered himself, administratively speaking, bulletproof.

When it came to handling an end-of-watch call or an unpleasant job of any kind, nobody could ever find Chester, so Sergeant Murillo had dubbed him "the Unicorn." He said that Chester Toles was like a mythical being that didn't exist. Fran Famosa had gotten stuck with Chester as a partner when his assigned partner contracted a staph infection and was ordered off duty for at least three weeks.

Earlier in the week, Fran had taken Sergeant Murillo aside to whisper that everyone was happier when the Unicorn was a "house mouse," working the front desk in the station lobby, instead of being on the streets in a black-and-white. She asked why Murillo couldn't keep him assigned there.

Her sergeant had said, "The captain thinks Chester will be more likely to pull the pin and head for Idaho to drink beer and fish his life away with old cronies if he's forced to work the streets for a while. And by the way, he could manage to vanish for long periods of time even when he was a house mouse, so that was no picnic for us, either."

"Why me?" Fran had persisted, but Sergeant Murillo had replied, "Because you're just about the most mature and sensible officer on Watch Five, Fran. We know you can manage him." And what could she say to that?

"So, Chester, are you with us in body and spirit this afternoon?" Sergeant Murillo called out, looking directly at Toles, who sat at the back table beneath a movie poster depicting Gloria Swanson and William Holden in *Sunset Boulevard*.

Next to that one was a poster showing Barbara Stanwyck in *Double Indemnity*, wearing the worst blond wig ever inflicted on an actress. Most of the more noirish one-sheet selections had been placed there by "Hollywood Nate" Weiss, LAPD's only card-carrying member of the Screen Actors Guild.

Chester Toles hadn't responded, so Sergeant Murillo said, "Yo, Chester! Time to wake up."

Flotsam, who was sitting on Chester's left, looked over and saw that behind the aviator eyeglasses that Chester believed made him look more macho, the pudgy cop's eyes were closed.

The surfer cop said, "Don't disturb him, Sarge. Climbing the stairs took its toll, and he needs his narcoleptic nap. When Chester retires he'll die of terminal bedsores."

When Chester heard his name that time, his little blue eyes suddenly popped open, but everyone knew he'd been snoozing. In addition to being Hollywood Station's invisible man, Chester was also the king of non sequiturs. He scratched the blotchy pink skin on his shiny bald dome while suppressing a yawn and said, "I wasn't sleeping, Sarge. I was just deep in thought about something from back in the day. I been trying real hard to remember the name of the sergeant we had here on the midwatch before you transferred to the station." He looked around earnestly at the other troops and said, "Any of you old enough to re-member? The supervisor that looked like Luca Brasi, but was a girl? The one we called B.P., for Big Panties? *That* one? An old boyfriend of hers told me that when she wore her thong underwear it produced a real camel-toe effect down there, if you catch my drift."

The entire assembly was speechless after that, especially the three women officers on Watch 5. Then Sergeant Murillo broke the silence by saying, "Too much information. Let's go to work."

Fran Famosa's heavily lashed brown eyes rolled back in her head as she sagged in her chair and mouthed to the ceiling, "Why me?"

She was so disgusted that when she got up and left the roll call room she almost forgot to touch the Oracle's picture for luck.

The sun was not close to setting at 5:30 on this warm summer evening, as the midwatch cops loaded the trunks of their black-and-white Crown Vics, called "shops" because of the "shop numbers" on the doors and roofs. The numbers allowed any observers, as well as the police heli-copters they called "airships," to identify individual patrol units. Radio car 6-X-72 frequently was the final one to leave the parking lot because of last-minute trips back to the women's locker room by Officer Sophie Branson.

She was forty-two years old with twenty years on the Job and had been a blonde for so many years that only her academy classmates remembered her as a brunette. Her career with the LAPD had added a dozen pounds or so to her five-foot-nine frame and produced lines around her mouth and creases at the corners of her eyes, but otherwise she felt she'd looked acceptable when, recently, she'd attended her class reunion at the police academy. She had been married and divorced three times, twice to other cops, and was the mother of a six-year-old son.

About her most recent husband, she'd told her partner, "As a cop, he's solid. As a husband, he was a spawn of the devil."

She was partnered with Marius Tatarescu, a Romanian-born cop who was close to her age but did not have her experience. He'd joined the LAPD a decade later in life, after mastering English well enough to pass the civil service exams. At age forty-three, he only had eleven years on the Job. He was big and burly, a jolly jokester with a heavy accent, extremely dense black hair, and matching winged eyebrows. The first night they'd worked together, Sophie had told him it was a good thing the LAPD no longer required patrol officers to wear hats on duty, because he'd never find one big enough to accommodate his hair.

He explained his bachelorhood to Sophie and the other much-married coppers of the midwatch by saying, "I am fourth-generation vampire from Transylvania. I suck too much blood from all girls I date, so nobody likes to marry me."

When citizens 6-X-72 encountered would inquire about his accent, Marius would say, "Texas is my home estate." When people would grin and say, "Dallas?" Marius would answer, deadpan, "Austin. I was long-time neighbor pal of Georgie Boosh."

The reason it took 6-X-72 so much time to leave the parking lot was because Sophie Branson would often remember something that was missing from her war bag. Marius's war bag was just the regular black nylon model that most of the seasoned male cops carried.

Sophie's war bag was the kind many women coppers preferred: a suitcase on wheels, such as airline flight attendants pulled to and from their boarding gates.

It wasn't that she didn't have enough gear on her Sam Browne, including a Glock .40-caliber pistol, a Taser, OC spray, a rover radio, handcuffs, and extra ammo. There was other gear to be hauled: a Remington 870 shotgun, an Ithaca beanbag shotgun, a helmet, and, in her war bag ticket books and notebooks, pet treats and chew toys. It was the absence of enough pet food in the war bag that usually made her return to the locker for extra treats. Sophie Branson was a dedicated animal-rights advocate who firmly believed that the meanest pit bull they encountered on their beat was more worthy of kindness than any man she had ever married.

Sophie was well known by everybody at the station for rescuing things: birds, cats, dogs, hamsters, the lot. Whenever anyone found animal hair or bird feathers in one of the shops they'd say, "Sophie was here." She was a dues-paying member of PETA, the Humane Society, the ASPCA, and other animal-welfare groups. She had been admonished several times for picking up a stray dog while on duty and leaving it in the cot room with a sign on the door saying, "In use" until she could take it home after end of watch.

She had caught feral cats with humane traps set in the Hollywood Station parking lot and fostered them until she could find them homes. Her own house in Van Nuys was a veritable menagerie. And once, while patrolling in the Hollywood Hills, she'd spotted a mother possum that had been killed by a car. She'd pulled the three babies out of the mother's pouch and had taken them home, where she'd bottle-fed them, releasing them back in the Hollywood Hills when they were old enough to fend for themselves. She'd taken photos of her carpeted cat house at home, with rescued kittens and possum babies peeking out the little windows, and she'd taped the photos inside her locker at the station.

There'd been a noteworthy moment in the roll call room a few months earlier when one of the midwatch coppers had been about to mash a huge centipede crawling across the floor. Sophie Branson had let out a yell and scooped up the insect on a page from her notebook.

She'd admonished the cop, saying, "They keep spiders away! It's a sin to kill a centipede!"

After she'd returned from releasing the insect outside the station, Sergeant Murillo had said to her, "Sophie, maybe that's true of mockingbirds. But centipedes?"

It was Marius's turn to drive, and Sophie was happy to "take paper"— that is, to write reports and fill in entries on the Daily Field Activity Report, aka "the log," and tend to the onboard MDC computer mounted between them. Marius was driving westbound on Melrose in what was still heavy traffic, because "rush hour" could last until darkness on these summer days in the most traffic-clogged city of North America.

"I'm grateful to ride shotgun tonight, partner," she said to the big Romanian. "I had to get up early and go to Lance's day care center to watch a production of *The Wizard of Oz*. It was adorable, but I didn't get enough sleep."

"Is very good you got a mother to help take care of your boy," Marius said. "Too bad his father is such a slice of turd."

"Piece of shit," Sophie said. "The expression is 'piece of shit,' and that fits him perfectly. Never marry a cop, Marius."

"I am thinking that I am too old for getting married anyways, Sophie," Marius said.

"Anybody's too old to marry a *male* cop, I can tell you that," Sophie said. "They're all little boys looking for a mommy. Every goddamn one of them."

"We got business, Sophie." Marius pointed to the MDC as the computer beeped.

Sophie opened the message and saw that it was a family dispute in a primarily Latino neighborhood in east Hollywood, and that sometimes meant that domestic violence would be involved. Then again, there could be immigrants from anywhere in the world in east Hollywood these days, Los Angeles County being a place where more than two hundred languages were spoken, not including dialects. She acknowledged the message and hit the en route button.

Marius had to find a break in the traffic to make a U-turn and head back east, while Sophie lamented, "Where the hell's Six-A-Forty-nine? And how about A-Seventy-nine? Watch Two doesn't go end-of-watch for another thirty minutes, and here they are, kissing off their calls to Watch Five. The lazy bastards. It's like a whole squad of Unicorns. Like cloning Chester Toles times twelve."

Marius didn't say anything. Sophie Branson was always complaining about something, but she was smart and gutsy and had much more police experience than he did, so he figured he could learn a thing or two from her.

When they arrived in the residential neighborhood of old cottages and cheaply constructed newer apartment buildings operated by slumlords, Marius parked and Sophie hit the at-scene button and grabbed her baton. Marius followed her to the cottage door as salsa music blared from the apartment building directly to the south. Windows were open and somebody was cooking enchiladas and it smelled good, causing Marius to sniff the air like a bird dog.

The Salvadoran woman who opened the door had a swollen bruise under her left eye. She was in her mid-forties, her hair hanging sweaty and lank to her shoulders. She was nearly obese, and wore a black cotton dress that was torn and bloodstained. She reeked of stale beer.

"Uh-oh," Sophie said sotto to Marius. "Looks like Papa's going to jail."

But when they got inside the messy little cottage, they saw her Salvadoran husband sitting on a kitchen chair held together by duct tape, holding a wet dish towel to his nose. The front of his T-shirt was bloodstained, and there were two empty beer cans lying on the cluttered kitchen table.

"Who you were saying is going to jail?" Marius whispered to Sophie, who shrugged, muttering, "It's a toss-up."

"Who called you, her?" the man demanded, pointing to his wife.

He was inked full-sleeved on both arms with tats from his youthful affiliation with MS-13, the largest street gang in the world. He also had a newer L.A. Dodgers tattoo on his neck, the kind so many gang members were sporting these days for their home-game trips to Dodger Stadium to kick the shit out of visiting fans. His head was shaved and he looked to be at least fifty years old, although guesses were tricky with aging *veteranos*. Drugs and booze and prison had taken their toll. Cops could overestimate homeboys' ages by as much as ten years.

"I din't call them," the woman said belligerently, more to the cops than to her husband. "I can take care of business my own self." Both she and her husband were American-born and spoke English unaccented, except for the old homie speech mannerisms he affected.

"What's the problem here?" Sophie said.

"Him," the woman said. "He thinks he can push me around."

The husband took the towel away and looked up, revealing a cut lip in addition to the nosebleed, and said, "I did all the pushing, huh?"

"Okay, ma'am, you step into the other room with me," Sophie said, taking the woman by the elbow and guiding her toward the bedroom, where she closed the door for privacy.

When Marius and the husband were alone in the kitchen, the man stood unsteadily and said, "I work fifty hours a week at a fucking car wash and gotta come home to her bullshit."

Marius nodded from time to time, listening to the husband tell him in speech slurred and boozy that he'd merely asked for sex before supper.

"Asked?" Marius said.

"Absolutely," the man said, sitting down again, since he was really blitzed. "And the bitch hit me with her fist or an ashtray or something, and broke my nose, I think."

Sophie was getting a very different story, of course. The woman acknowledged that a dispute had started over sex, which she was going to give him, until he got demanding and crude. She wasn't quite as drunk as he was, but admitted that the fighting took place after each had guzzled two forties and polished off three six-packs of Corona.

29

When the bedroom door opened, Sophie took her partner aside and told Marius the only detail that surprised him. The husband had managed to shove his wife into the closet during the struggle and had locked the door. It was her screams for help that no doubt had triggered the call from a frightened neighbor.

"I'm too tired today to deal with this bullshit," Sophie said sotto to Marius. "You handle it, okay? Whatever you wanna do is okay with me, but let's try to leave here without any bodies coming with us."

Marius nodded and stood in front of the husband and wife like a referee in a prizefight and said, "Look at us. What do coppers do? We drink coffee and eat doughnuts and take people to jail. I got no solutions inside my head for your problem. You got to settle your problems your own selfs. Or maybe you like to start punching each other again so I can take someone to jail?"

They were both quiet for a minute. The husband took the dish towel from his face and said to Marius, "Am I still bleeding?"

The woman said, "Officer, he locked me in the fucking closet! What if the place caught on fire? I coulda died in there!"

"Yes, madam, I am seeing your position," Marius said. "Maybe is not a tie. Maybe your husband wins the guilt game by few points here."

"All I wanted is the sex I got coming as a husband!" the man cried, and a trickle of blood flowed from his right nostril.

"In my country," Marius said, "we can have sex with a goat, but then you got to set the goat free. You cannot lock her in a closet like you do to your wife here today."

"I coulda died in there," the woman said. "This man is basically evil."

That caused Sophie to open the door and prepare to leave, but the man rocked sideways and would have fallen if Marius hadn't caught him by the arm.

"Do not drink no more tonight," Marius said. "If we come back and are finding you lumped up again, we got to take actions."

"He'll fight you if you come back," the woman warned. "He's fought cops before."

"He will not fight with us," Marius said with a frown, his heavy, winged eyebrows nose-diving. "When anybody fights with us, we got to tenderize them."

"What the fuck's that supposed to mean?" the husband said.

Before closing the door behind him, Marius said, "I work for eight years at the meat counter in a big supermarket. You do not want for us to tenderize you. Trust in me, you will not like it."

When Marius and Sophie were back in their shop she typed a short disposition of the call on the keyboard, and they quickly headed west at twilight. The sun was preparing for its nightly plunge into the Pacific Ocean, but on this relatively smogless day it was giving off a blinding, slanted light that caused them both to flip down their visors.

Ever the concerned animals advocate, Sophie said, "Marius, you never had sex with a goat back in Romania, did you?"

"I was only making a pointer to the drunk man," Marius said.

"Point," Sophie said.

"Pardon, Sophie?"

"Point. A pointer is a dog."

"With you, is always animals, Sophie," Marius said, puzzled by her correction.

And as though on cue, as they passed a seedy auto repair business that was closed for the day, Sophie said, "Pull over!"

Marius cut the wheel to the right. "What? What do you see?"

"There!" she said, pointing to a Latino boy in a ragged blue T-shirt, tan shorts, and tennis shoes. He was about ten years old and was standing next to the eight-foot chain-link fence that protected the business from passing thieves.

"The kid?" Marius asked. "What is he doing?"

"The little fucker's abusing a dog!" Sophie said, and she leaped out of the car while it was still rolling to a stop.

When he saw the two cops coming at him briskly, the boy looked frightened, and he paused with a rock the size of a lemon in his right hand. Inside the fence a large dog, probably a rottweiler mix, growled at the cops.

"Drop that," Sophie ordered, and when the boy did, the dog bared his teeth and snarled at them. "Are you throwing rocks at that dog?"

"No," the boy said, trembling. "I was throwing the rock way to the back of the yard by the cars. It's his rock."

"Whadda you mean, his rock?" Sophie demanded.

"It belongs to him. I throw it for him every day after supper. He waits for me with the rock in his mouth. He drops it and I reach under the fence and pick it up. I toss it for him till I get so tired I gotta stop. Then I scratch him through the fence for a while and then I go home."

"And what does he do when you throw the rock?" Marius asked.

"He plays," the boy said.

"Are you saying he fetches?" Sophie asked. "He gets the rock and brings it back to you?"

"Yes," the boy said, his lower lip quivering. "Every night he waits for me to play with him. His name is Barney."

Still doubtful, Sophie said, "Let's see him fetch. Throw the rock."

The boy picked up the rock and, backing away from the fence, threw it in the direction of the metal doors that were rolled down and locked for the night. Sure enough, Barney barked happily and ran for the rock, retrieved it, and brought it back to the fence, where he dropped it at the feet of the boy, who reached under the fence and picked it up.

Marius suppressed a snicker at Sophie, who reddened and said, "I'll be right back."

She ran to their car, opened the truck, rummaged in her war bag, and came back with a brand-new yellow ball constructed of hard rubber that was safe for dogs to chew. "Here," she said to the boy. "This is a gift for you and Barney. I want you to continue coming here every night to play with him."

"I will," the boy said. "I like to play with him. He's a good dog."

"That's fine," Sophie said, "because he's a working dog and he needs exercise, understand? Now let's see how he likes a real toy."

The boy took the ball from her and dropped the rock on the ground. He backed up a few paces and threw the rubber ball over the fence, and they watched it bounce toward the garages. Barney watched it, too. He trotted after it, and when it came to a stop he sniffed it suspiciously. He picked it up for a few seconds, then dropped it on the ground near a pickup truck parked by the garages. He ran back to the boy, barking excitedly.

The boy nodded to Barney, reached down and grabbed the rock, and threw it as hard as he could toward the garages. The dog, deliriously happy, ran and retrieved it, his docked tail wagging furiously.

Marius maintained a noncommittal expression as they walked back to their shop, leaving the twelve-dollar dog-safe rubber ball in the yard, but after they were in the car he said sympathetically, "Barney very much loves his rock, Sophie. Sometimes you cannot teach old doggies the new games."

"Tricks," she said with an exhausted sigh.

It was a rather uneventful Thursday night for the officers of the midwatch, but just before end of watch, at 3:00 in the morning, 6-X-66 caught a "possible jumper" code 3 call from the hotel at Hollywood and Highland.

The driver of 6-X-66 was twenty-four-year-old Britney Small, who had only two and a half years on the job and was by nature shy and reserved. She had light brown hair, pale soulful eyes, and was slender enough to be called "the ballerina" of Watch 5. As young as she was, Britney was entitled to unusual respect for having shot and killed an armed murderer whose pursued van had caused the crash in which Jetsam's foot had been crushed. By facing the killer's gun and putting him down, the then rookie cop had become an authentic gunfighter in the eyes of the crusty Old Guys at Hollywood Station who were often critical of female officers, and always critical of *young* female officers.

Her partner in 6-X-66 for this deployment period, Hollywood Nate Weiss, might be considered an OG by now, but he was so different in temperament from most of the Old Guys that the women officers never thought of him that way. Moreover, he was hawkishly handsome, with dark hair going silver at the temples, and he was ripped from almost daily workouts in the weight room. It was hard for Britney to think of Hollywood Nate as an OG. Chester Toles, the Unicorn—now, there was an OG.

Hollywood Nate Weiss, divorced and childless, was thirty-nine years old with eighteen years on the LAPD, and he was absolutely dreading his next birthday, fearing that his hopes and dreams of making it as an actor were fading with each passing year. Forty was frightening. He'd be middle-aged! Nate spent much of his time fantasizing about catching an acting job that would lead to a new career and allow him to retire from police work in two years. However, since earning his SAG card he'd managed to get only half a dozen jobs as a day player on short-lived television cop shows, and only three of them had provided a few words of dialogue. He wouldn't have gotten any of them if he hadn't used his badge as an inducement. The best job came when he stopped a has-been features director for a DUI but drove the guy home instead of taking him to jail.

Britney always preferred to work with seasoned women officers, but she did not mind working with Hollywood Nate because he treated his women partners the same as the men, except with a bit more defer- ence. She chalked that up to his artistic nature as an actor. Britney was aware that before she came on the Job, Nate had lost a woman partner named Dana Vaughn in a gun battle and had killed the man who'd mur- dered her. There were whispers that Nate had carried feelings of guilt for a long time over that incident, and that perhaps his relationship with Dana Vaughn had been more than just radio car partners. But that was only locker room speculation.

Though Britney was long past her eighteen months of probation now, she wanted to learn as much as she could, and she had encouraged Nate to let her know if she ever performed in a way that needed improvement. So far, he'd seldom offered tactical advice of any kind.

But when, a block from the jumper call, she cut the siren's wail, he did have a tip for her. He said, "You know, Britney, I'll never forget what my field training officer said to me when I got my first jumper call. A very distraught guy was sitting on a tenth-floor window ledge, and there was nobody there but us to talk him in or try a rescue. My FTO said, 'Before you do anything at all, I want you to take out your notebook and write down the names of everybody in the world you're willing to die for. When we get up there and see our jumper face-to-face, you might feel a tug at your heart and get an urge to rush forward and save the person. But first, check your list. If the jumper's name is not on your list, let the fucker go it alone and not take you along for the ride.'"

When he was finished, Britney said, "So what did you do on that one?"

"I never had to check my list. The guy jumped just as we were getting out of the elevator, and when we got back down to the sidewalk I could see that his name was not on my list, and his face didn't resemble anyone I knew, or even a human face. What used to be his head looked like somebody had mixed dozens of eggs and raspberry jam in a bucket and dumped it on the sidewalk."

"I'll make my mental list now," Britney said.

As it turned out, Britney and Nate's jumper turned out to be a mannequin that some drunken college students had hung out of a hotel window for laughs. The pranksters were gone by the time the police arrived.

FOUR

THE DISPATCH HALL of the International Longshore and Warehouse Union was sacred ground for longshoremen, and the dispatcher was a minor deity. Dinko Babich remembered when district attorney investigators, trying to arrest a dispatcher on a warrant, had invaded the hall. A mini-riot ensued when thirty longshoremen surrounded the lawmen, who had to call for LAPD reinforcements. On Friday afternoon, as Dinko pulled up in front of the hall and parked, he began stewing about his thirty-day suspension for drug use on the docks, and regretted that it would be another twenty-two days until he could get back to work.

He couldn't stand sitting around the house with his mother, and it was even worse when one of his mother's friends would come to visit for the day and spend half of it trying to persuade him that he needed to attend Narcotics Anonymous meetings because of the suspension, which he thought was ridiculous. He was a recreational pot smoker, not some spun-out tweaker who couldn't run his own life. If he hadn't been persuaded to smoke a doob with another longshoreman during their lunch break, he never would've been suspended. He'd never said he was perfect.

There was the usual token force of black men outside the hall, sitting at picnic tables, playing cards. These longshoremen did not have the A book, which usually implied connections and was as good as gold. With that book a longshoreman could sometimes work a six-hour shift and take a two-hour lunch break at the end of the shift, arriving home before the wife had even started cooking.

Dinko figured there was no use asking the guys outside the hall if they had any grow. The blacks mostly smoked rock. They could buy a piece of rock for five or ten dollars, or even a tiny chip for as little as two bucks. They liked to fire up a cookie of rock and shatter it into pieces. The Mexican rock was more like a tortilla, and they'd cut it thin with a razor blade until it resembled a communion wafer, but that wafer offered a very short trip to heaven with lots of purgatory to follow. Dinko did not trust rock. He'd seen too many crackheads get hooked behind it.

Today's young longshoremen mostly smoked crystal, and Dinko was a third-generation longshoreman, but powerhouse medicinal weed was his drug of choice, along with any decent Scotch. Crystal meth, particularly the really good ice that was popular on the docks these days, was an unpredictable drug. He'd seen guys freaking and twitching and sweating when they'd come unspooled on meth. Those guys could get you hurt on the job, and he'd seen several get sent home when it was obvious they were all tweaked out. He'd heard of a longshoreman who, while spun out on ice, had chewed a hole in his own arm, clear to the bone, "to get the demons out." Dinko had been told that while the paramedics were driving the guy to Harbor General Hospital, he'd perfectly mimicked the radio transmissions, including the static.

When he didn't find anybody around the hall from whom he could score, he decided to go looking where he'd made some connections with street dealers over the years. That territory belonged to the West Side Wilmas, the rivals of the East Side Wilmas. The commercial streets had lots of bargain shops and discount stores. Signs announced, "Food 4 Less" and "Checks Cashed Here." He saw that the car wash had at least twenty young people out there flagging down motorists, trying to raise money for a street gangster who'd been shot and killed by some other banger. An enlarged photo of the guy had been mounted on an easel, with pots of flowers placed on the asphalt in front of it.

There were gang tags on every corner, on street signs and on walls, with arrows pointing up or down to mark the territory. Many of the tags said "WW," for West Side Wilmas, and the recent news reports Dinko had read claimed there were eleven local Latino and black street gangs, with twenty-five hundred crew members, in Wilmington, Harbor City, and San Pedro. Dinko's late father had always railed about third-generation gang members being hired as longshoremen. While the homeboys were busy working on the waterfront, San Pedro and other local areas were quiet, but on weekends, when they were back with their homies, the shootings and other violence would rage.

Dinko had heard LAPD cops say that the longshoremen had the biggest gang in Pedro, but they were wrong. It was obvious to Dinko that true gang loyalty to the WW trumped job loyalty to the ILWU. His father used to wonder how this was seen by the politicians who maintained that good employment opportunities would solve the street gang epidemic in the Latino and black communities.

Dinko drove past Saints Peter and Paul, the old Catholic church with the tall bell tower that claimed 1865 as the founding date. His grandfather had told him that he remembered when almost the entire congregation was composed of people he knew. Now there was nobody Dinko knew on any of the street corners, or by the liquor stores, or in any of the other locations where he hoped to spot somebody familiar who might have weed to sell.

As a last resort, Dinko decided to try the strip bars in the industrial area of Wilmington where the independent truckers hung out, most of them Latinos and lots of them crackheads. He wasn't comfortable entering a low-life strip bar even in broad daylight, but he felt he had a good chance of finding some weed like Silver Haze, which sometimes got sold in medical marijuana dispensaries.

When he got to the first strip bar he saw that the outside looked crappier than usual, if that was possible. The joint featured nude strippers, but because of that it could not legally serve alcohol. Every time Dinko had been there at night he'd found longshoremen he recognized, along with truckers and college kids from Long Beach looking for hookers. The strippers he'd seen there were Latino and black, and once he'd seen a Samoan. The girls were either tweakers or crackheads and appeared toasted while they danced.

Dinko saw that somebody had just tagged the building with an array of symbols and initials, meaningful only to the tagger, as well as other barrio bullshit in Spanish and English—all of it misspelled, of course. For that reason alone he pulled up in front of the one farther down the road that featured topless dancers in G-strings and was allowed to serve alcoholic beverages. Dinko parked, locked the Jeep, and went inside, hoping to find someone, anyone, who might have some decent grow.

The last time he'd been here, Dinko had bought some pot from a car mechanic who worked in one of the many chop shops and wrecking yards in the area. Wilmington had a subculture of junkyards crammed right next to residential properties, as though no one had ever written or enforced zoning ordinances. And in this old part of Los Angeles, it was even possible to find obscure roads that had never been paved.

He stood in the doorway for a moment, allowing his eyes to adjust to the dark, and was surprised by what a good business the titty bar was doing, even though it was even seedier than he'd remembered. There were plenty of "border brothers," Mexican nationals in cowboy hats, boots, and hand-tooled leather belts with silver-and-turquoise buckles as big as a fist. And there were other Latinos who Dinko figured for undocumented gardeners and wrecking yard employees, drinking at the bar and flirting with the B-girls, who nearly outnumbered the customers. At least a dozen truckers were sitting around the stage, as well as maybe ten other guys, whom he figured for longshoremen, but he recognized nobody he knew.

He watched the listless, overweight black stripper onstage come close to a violation by simulating a crotch grind into the face of a customer. The stripper and the manager could be cited if there was an undercover vice cop in the place or an agent from the Department of Alcohol Beverage Control. Both vice cops and ABC agents often checked out the many saloons in the Avalon Corridor, and he'd seen plenty of citations given out in the bars around Pedro during the ten years he'd been old enough to drink in them.

Dinko ordered a beer, tipped the chubby white bartender a buck, and turned to scan the room, where he spotted Hector Cozzo, an old classmate from Mary Star of the Sea elementary school, and high school as well. He used to run into Hector occasionally after Hector dropped out in his junior year, but he had not talked to him in at least six years. Hector was fourteen months older than Dinko even though they'd been in the same grade, and he'd been the class clown who got in frequent trouble with the cops at Harbor Station. Even as a fourth-grade kid, Hector had had vulpine features and a sly grin permanently locked in place. You half-expected his irises to be yellow.

Dinko saw that Hector still had a taste for the retro, now comical Al Pacino look from *Scarface:* a big gold watch and rings on both hands, bling that Dinko figured he bought from Mexicans in places like this. He had Here I Am shades on top of his head, and he still wore his black hair in a mullet, short on the top and sides but hanging down over his collar in the back. Some things never changed.

"Yo, mullethead," Dinko said, sitting down uninvited at the small table near the bar where Hector Cozzo was nursing a bottle of beer. "That haircut is way nineteen nineties. You gotta evolve more."

"Dinko!" Hector said. "Hey, brother!" They bumped knuckles, and Hector looked genuinely happy to see him, the shorter man's crooked teeth shaded purple from the stage lighting.

"Where you been hiding out, Hector?" Dinko asked. "I don't see you around town no more, but I sometimes see your mother and dad when my mom drags me to church for the vigil Mass."

"I'm cribbed up in Encino," Hector said. "That's so I can stay close to all the porn producers. I'm always looking for talent, dawg. They call me Hector the selector."

They both laughed at that because in high school they'd called him "Hector the pimp," not just for his flashy clothes but because he'd once shown up at school in a T-shirt that said, "I will pimp you out." Of course, he'd instantly been sent home for that stunt, and Dinko recalled that Hector had wound up with some minor facial bruising after his father got through with him.

"You musta set your sights low if you're looking for talent in this joint," Dinko said, taking a swig from his beer bottle.

"Is this one of your hangs?" Hector asked.

"I'm looking to score some grow, is all," Dinko said.

"Me, I'm only here to do a little transportation job." Hector Cozzo gave a deprecatory flip of the hand. "Whadda you do for survival? Still on the docks with the rest of the Slav slobs?"

"There haven't been Slavs around here since the end of their wars over there," Dinko said. "We're strictly Croatians now, or do you get your news sixteen years late?"

"Guess working on the docks is all you *iches* can do," Hector said, referring to the suffix on the surnames of many Croatians, like Dinko Babich. Hector had always thought that the way the old Slavs did their lettering reminded him of hieroglyphics.

"And how about an enterprising Eye-talian dude like you?" Dinko said. "You found something where you can make more than your old man did back when us iches and you dagos ran the docks together?"

"I ain't doing too bad," Hector said. "I got a new red Mercedes parked out there."

"Yeah, which model? The C-Class?"

"Nope, the SL," Hector said, and he saw that get Dinko's full attention. So he lied and added, "And it's not leased. I own it outright."

"They start at a hundred grand," Dinko said. "Did you win a lottery, or what?"

"I ran into some dudes in Hollywood that hire me for miscellaneous work. It pays good."

From Hector's coy grin Dinko figured he must be running drugs, so he asked, "You wouldn't have any Silver Haze or hydro you'd be willing to sell to an old classmate, would you, Hector?"

"Not a chance," Hector Cozzo said. "I don't touch weed no more. I do powder cocaine only. And the best booze I can buy to keep my mind clear. You still a Scotch drinker?"

"Yeah, I'm surprised you remember," Dinko said.

"I remember because I was a Scotch drinker back then. I still like it after a steak, but only eighteen-year-old single malt at nearly two Franklins a bottle. The rest of the time I drink very premium vodka. I got used to it hanging with all the former iron curtain socialists that're taking over Hollywood."

"What kinda job you got, Hector?" Dinko asked, and Hector displayed that coy, snaggletoothed grin again.

"I do this and that for some guys who own various businesses in Hollywood. I'm sort of a collector. In fact, they also call me Hector the collector. That's why I got a crib in the valley, so I can be closer to my work. The drive down the Harbor Freeway to Pedro is a bitch these days."

"Well, I see you're not gonna tell me nothing, so I guess I better go look for somebody that's got some weed."

When Dinko started to get up, the shorter man grabbed his arm and said, "Don't go, brother. I got some outstanding vodka in my car. As soon as I finish what I got to do here, I can meet you somewheres and we can get juiced and gas about the old days."

"Well, I do love a mystery." Dinko sat back and took another swig from the beer bottle. "Can you at least tell me why a guy that drives an SL is sitting in this shit hole?"

"I'll be glad to answer that, Dinko," Hector said. "Because of her."

He pointed up to the stage, where a stunning new dancer had just replaced the black stripper. She didn't appear old enough to be lawfully employed there, and she looked like she'd rather be just about anywhere else. Her glossy dark hair tumbled to her shoulders in natural waves, and she had large, wide-set amber eyes. She was slim and rather tall, and she had booty. He figured there was no blanket-ass Indian blood in this girl, so he wondered what she was doing in a Mexican joint. Her silky pale mocha flesh gleamed under the light from the ceiling spots. Dinko couldn't take his eyes off her.

"So, you like her, Dinko?" Hector asked, with that smug, patronizing grin that was beginning to really irritate Dinko.

"What the hell's she doing in this dump?" Dinko asked.

"It's her first week here," Hector said. "I only heard about her last night and thought I'd come down for a look. I like what I see." Then he added, "The whole fucking world's turned nonsmoking on me, even a dive like this. I gotta run outside and grab a cig."

Dinko said, "She can't be Mexican."

"Yes, she can," Hector said. "Recently arrived from Guanajuato. Before you arrived I spent an hour talking to her and to the proprietor of this joint. She speaks English pretty good. I bought her."

"Whadda you mean you bought her?"

"I bought her dance contract, which wasn't binding in the first place, so it didn't cost much. I offered her a job dancing in a Hollywood nightclub owned by some criss-cross dudes I know, where she'll make ten times what she makes here. They're always looking for new talent, and I'm kind of a talent scout, among other things."

"What's criss-cross mean?" Dinko asked.

"You know," Hector said, "the kind of guys that cross themselves like this." And he made the sign of the cross, touching his forehead, heart, right shoulder, and left shoulder, instead of moving his hand left to right, as the Roman Catholics did it.

"You mean Eastern rite," Dinko said. "So your employers are Russian or maybe Armenian or . . ."

"Could be Serbs," Hector said, winking at the mention of the ancient enemy of the Croatians.

Dinko figured Hector Cozzo had to be working for Russians. Everyone knew that Hollywood was full of them, and they were into all sorts of crime and owned most of the nightclubs. But he couldn't stop staring at the ravishing girl. She had small breasts, but they were perky and they were real.

"She's so young," he said. "And she can't dance worth a shit, but who cares?"

"My sentiments exactly," Hector agreed. "She'll make tips beyond her dreams when she gets to Hollywood, with those bucks-up Armenians, Russians, and Georgians. All those rich old ex-commies jist love the club I'm gonna put her in. I'm letting her finish a couple sets here, and then off we go to Hollywood to let my employers see what I bought for them. She can easy get a Franklin for a special lap dance up there."

"She's just a kid," Dinko said. "She looks kinda . . . lost."

"Now I'm trying hard not to roll my eyes, dawg," Hector said. "She's a fucking Mexican whore!"

Hector's cell rang. He pulled it from his pocket, looked at the number, and said, "Gotta take this, Dinko." He got up and walked to the front door and out to the street, while Dinko stayed and watched the girl shuffle through a dance, her smile frozen, seeming vulnerable and forlorn.

When Hector returned, he seemed tense. "A Harbor City homie I been waiting for ain't gonna show up. The dumb motherfucker got stopped for running a red light, and the cops found a gun in his car. Stupid fucking silverbacks—I hate doing business with them."

"I thought you were down here because of the girl," Dinko said, pointing to the stage.

"She's part of it. I also had to set something up with somebody I got involved with in a weak moment."

Now Dinko's curiosity made him want to grab Hector by the front of his stupid pimp shirt and make him talk. He said, "Hector, what the fuck're you doing messing with Crips and Bloods? Whadda they got to do with your new life in Hollywood and all those dudes that cross themselves backwards?"

Hector signaled to a waitress for two more beers. He thought for a long moment before speaking, then said, "Did you hear about the robbery last year where a posse did a takeover of the security guards at the container storage facility down the road? The one where they

44

pistol-whipped and taped up the guards, then brought a stolen tractor in and jist hooked up to the chassis under a huge container and drove off with a can full of imported goods?"

"Yeah," Dinko said, "I think it was booze in the can they stole, wasn't it? All the longshoremen on the docks figure they fucked up and got the wrong chassis. The can on the chassis next to it was full of flat-screen TVs."

Hector said, "They probably had a bought-off trucker tell them, 'It's in row ten, space thirty-nine,' only that would be way too hard for a nigger to handle since they ain't got the brains of a dead squid. But they're willing to go in like a wolf pack with Tec-9s if somebody on the inside sets up a deal for them. They can bring it when it comes to blue steel and muscle."

Hector stopped talking and looked at his drink. Dinko nodded to encourage his classmate to continue, but Hector thought better of it and said, "Look, Dinko, I'm glad I ran into an old friend here. I need you to help me out. I need you to take that Mexican chick to an address in Hollywood and wait for her. She'll only be there for a half hour, to meet the boss. Then I need you to take her home to East Wilmington, where she's staying at for now." He pulled two hundred-dollar bills from a money clip and put them on the table with a business card from a nightclub on Hollywood Boulevard. He wrote his cell number on the card.

"That's all I gotta do?" Dinko said. "Take her and bring her back, no problems?"

"No problems. That's all you gotta do. I need you to help me, brother. This other thing with the silverbacks . . ." He stopped and shook his head, the bravado gone, making him look more like the goofy high school kid Dinko remembered.

"Man, you're not the violent type," Dinko said. "If you're fucking with the Bloods or Crips you might end up in the harbor, caught in somebody's gill net with crabs eating your face."

"I can finesse this," Hector said. "I jist gotta go talk to a dude. Will you do the job for me?"

Dinko certainly could use the two hundred dollars, but it wasn't the money that made him scoop the bills off the table. He wanted this job because he'd seen the girl.

"Thank you, dawg," Hector said, producing another business card. "I gotta run back to the dressing room now and tell her what's going on. Gimme your digits."

"What's her name?" Dinko asked, using Hector's pen to write his cell number on one of Hector's business cards, under where it said, "Hector Cozzo, Facilitator and Entrepreneur."

"Lita Medina," Hector said, standing up. "You won't have no problem with her."

"No worries," Dinko said. "I'm locked on."

Dinko felt his excitement grow as he sat alone at the table and watched the dark corridor leading to the dressing room. A few minutes passed before Hector emerged, rushing toward the front door with a thumbs-up for Dinko. Then Dinko saw the silly fucker blow him a kiss before he breezed out with a very serious expression on his goofy face.

After another ten minutes, she came from the darkness at the back of the bar and approached Dinko's table. She struck him as incredibly demure and, well, respectable. She looked even younger with her stage makeup replaced by only a little eye shadow and lip gloss. He stood, and she held out her hand. It was a delicate hand, but her fingers were long and her nails had recently been done with French tips. When he shook her hand, it felt cool and dry; his own felt hot and moist. Her lustrous dark hair, a shade lighter than Hector's, was swept back to one side of her face and fell to her breasts. He remembered how those breasts had looked when she was onstage. Now she was wearing a long-sleeved red shirt, blue jeans, and inexpensive flat shoes—dressed more for a trip to the *mercado*, he thought, than to a meeting in a Hollywood nightclub.

She nodded politely and included her matronymic name when she introduced herself, saying in heavily accented English, "I am Lita Medina Flores. I am very happy to meet with you, señor."

"I'm Dinko Babich," he said. "Just call me Dinko."

"Deenko" was how she said it, smiling slightly, revealing a tiny chip at the corner of a front tooth that made her look even younger. Then, apologizing for showing amusement at his name, she said, "Is name I never hear before this. Is good name. Very nice."

"It's Croatian," he said. "You know, the country that used to be in Yugoslavia?"

"I know," she said. "We learn about the Europa countries at my school in Guanajuato."

"Would you like to go now?" he asked.

"Please," she said. "I am very happy to go from this place."

"I don't blame you," he said, and he held his hand out, palm up, beckoning her to precede him to the door.

The summer sun, now barely resisting the ocean dive off the coast, was still bright enough that she put on drugstore sunglasses and stood beside the Jeep while he unlocked the passenger door for her. He waited until she was seated and then closed the door, running around to the driver's side. He couldn't remember the last time he'd been so courtly with a woman, and this one wasn't even a woman yet. She was a kid. And a freaking Mexican!

She held a small hand-woven purse on her lap and looked straight ahead while Dinko headed for the Harbor Freeway. He figured she would not speak at all except to answer questions.

As they were driving west on Pacific Highway, Dinko spotted a new red Mercedes SL parked just off the intersection with Bayview Avenue, facing north. The smog-laden twilight made it impossible to see more than the back of the driver's head, but what really piqued Dinko's interest was the big Asian in a dark suit, white shirt, and necktie standing on the curb, bending down and leaning in the passenger window to talk to the driver. There weren't many Asians in business suits around those streets, and there sure as hell weren't many new SLs. Then Dinko saw that the driver was smoking a cigarette, and he almost turned the car around and went back to be sure that it was Hector.

Dinko figured he was getting two Franklins to be with a chick he'd *pay* two Franklins to be with, so maybe he should mind his own business. It probably wasn't Hector, anyway. Maybe, but maybe not. Hector Cozzo *never* would've had the balls to be directly doing business with silverback street gangs, Dinko thought, not back in the day, and not now. He wished he could've seen if the driver was a mullethead.

He was almost to the freeway and still considering a U-turn to satisfy his curiosity when he remembered Cozzo's other nickname from back in school: Hector the prevaricator. They always said you could pour a quart of Sodium Pentothol in his soup and still not get Hector to tell the truth. Some things never changed.

When they were heading north on the Harbor Freeway in moderate Los Angeles traffic, which would be deemed horrendous in most other U.S. cities, Dinko said to Lita Medina, "How long have you been here from Mexico?"

"Three month," she said, facing straight ahead.

"Do you like it here?"

"Is very nice," she said.

"Do you get homesick?"

She said, "I am sorry. I do not know what . . ."

"Do you get sad and feel lonesome when you think of your home?"

She thought it over. "My home?"

"Yes," he said. "Do you have a mother and father and sisters and brothers?"

"I have my mother and two brothers," she said. "My brothers are very young and my mother does not possess good health. She has the diabetes and a weak heart and is very 'spensive to get her medicine. I must make money here and send to them."

"How old're you, Lita?" he asked abruptly. "Tell me the truth."

She faced him with a look of apprehension, opened her purse, and said, "I am twenty-two. I have Social Security and driver license. I can prove for you how old I am and—"

He held up a hand and said, "Relax, I'm not a cop. I just don't think you're twenty-two years old, no matter what your phony ID says. But don't worry, I won't tell nobody."

After another long silence she looked down at her purse and said, "I am age nineteen years and four months."

"I thought so," he said. "You're just a kid. A child."

"I am no child," she said.

He said, "I felt like I wasn't a child either when I was nineteen, but now that I'm a man, I know better."

"I am no child," she said more firmly, and this time she looked at him. "I quit the school and I work for my family almost four years in Guanajuato. I do the work what I must do. I am no child, Dinko."

He looked at her and thought he saw her eyes moisten. He decided not to press her further. He punched the CD button and played some soft rock while they rode in silence.

Smoggy darkness had fallen by the time they were close to the Hollywood nightclub, and the boulevard traffic was worse than Dinko remembered. He hated coming up to the city at any time, but weekend nights were beyond awful. The ceaseless headlights were unbearable, and sometimes it could take thirty minutes to travel a mile and a half in the bumper-locked madness. An hour of this could make him long for San Pedro, even with the Mexicans turning it into a barrio slum. There was a saying among the generations of Croatians and Italians of San Pedro: "Go ahead and leave, but sooner or later, everyone comes back to Fish Town."

After he parked in the only space he could find, nearly two blocks from the nightclub, he got out and walked with her to the door of the building. It was a typical east Hollywood commercial setup, having had several identities and business uses over the years, before becoming a nightclub. The lighted sign saying "Club Samara" was surprisingly subtle, and Dinko figured that must have something to do with zoning restrictions rather than good taste. He didn't equate Russian and Armenian hoodlums with good taste.

When they got to the door she said, "Please, Dinko, wait for me at the car. I will not be in there for very much time."

He nodded and let her go in alone. He found himself thinking about Hector. He felt like calling him and asking what the hell he was doing parked by Pacific Highway with some dressed-up Asian, but there was always a slim chance that it had not been Hector's SL. Yet he knew in his gut that the SL must belong to Hector the selector.

Dinko stood on the sidewalk looking at the endless lines of head-lights on the boulevard. At times like this he wished he had a cigarette, but he hadn't smoked one in four years. He smoked weed occasionally, but never cigarettes, not since his father had died from lung cancer, a terrible death that had made Dinko swear to his mother that he'd never smoke a cigarette again. Being her only child, Dinko was all she had left, and she never stopped reminding him of that.

One of these days he was going to get out of the comfortable Babich family home on the hill west of Gaffey, where Croatians and Italians didn't have to be surrounded by beaners, but he couldn't seem to hold on to enough money for a start. The biweekly poker games with other longshoremen were sucking him dry, and he didn't really enjoy gam-bling. After ten minutes of loitering on the sidewalk inhaling exhaust fumes, Dinko said, "Fuck it," and he entered Club Samara.

The place was very dark and more upscale than he'd expected, way above the dump where he'd found Lita. The bar itself wasn't long and wel-coming, probably because they wanted people at the tables or lining the stage, which would mean more tip money for the dancers. There were some faux-leather booths along the far walls, and the stage was first-rate, with lighting that followed the blond dancer, who straddled the pole and waved to a hooting male customer seated stageside. Dinko noted that some of the tables could accommodate four and several only a deuce, and he was sur-prised to see half a dozen youngish couples at the tables for two.

Then Dinko noticed a waitress bringing a tray of tapas to one of the tables—to be expected, because they had to serve food in these clubs in order to get a liquor license. He was surprised that so many lounge lizards actually brought girlfriends to watch other girls show their tits, but then this was Hollywood, where every kind of freak hung out. In a little room on each side of the main room, a girl was giving a geezer a lap dance. He knew that the seating there faced outward toward the main room per legal requirements, so that any vice cop or ABC agent could see into the room to determine if lewd conduct was occurring. It was the same in the titty bars down in Wilmington.

He took an empty bar stool and ordered a draft beer, just pointing to the closest of the three beers on tap they offered. When the bartender brought the brew, Dinko said, "Is Samara the name of the owner here, or what?"

The menacing bartender, with dark hair slicked back and pointing down his forehead in a widow's peak like Count Dracula, said in heavily accented English and a voice fathoms deep, "Is a great city on the bank of the Volga. Better city than this one."

His lip curled as he said it, so Dinko replied, "No offense, man. My geography's a little rusty."

The bartender turned and walked to the other end of the bar, where a customer was holding up two fingers for him and his buddy. No tip for you, Russkie asshole, Dinko thought.

Other than the ethnicity of the male customers here, most of them being white, he thought they weren't a lot different from the bar customers he saw around the L.A. harbor. Nobody was dressed upscale except for a few guys in suits, who were probably downtown stockbrokers hoping for a short-lived erection before going home to momma and the kiddies somewhere on the West Side.

Dinko felt appropriate in his skinny-fit jeans and blue cotton half-zip pullover, the right style, he'd been told by a cute salesgirl at the Gap, for a guy as tall and slim as he was. The deal was sealed when she said the blue pullover enhanced the blue in his eyes, but she'd only given him a noncommittal smile when he'd asked if she'd like to meet him for coffee sometime. The outfit had cost him a Franklin, tax included, and he figured he looked okay anywhere in Hollywood, which itself was looking tackier than he remembered it from when his dad, on special occasions, would drive them up to catch a first-run movie.

He saw Lita Medina walk into the main room from a corridor leading to the restrooms and a back office. A man was walking beside her, an older man in a double-breasted, pearl-gray business suit who was definitely not a downtown stockbroker. When he got into the light Dinko saw that his dyed black hair was swept up and back like an ancient rocker's. Christ, it even looked like he combed it in an old-time ducktail.

Dinko slid off the bar stool and scurried to the door, not wanting Lita to know that he'd come inside. As he was striding briskly along the sidewalk, he wondered why he didn't want her to know he'd gone in there. Why should he care where this Mexican kid worked, or what she did with her life, or what she thought of him? It was none of his business. He told himself she was nothing to him, nothing at all. L.A. was full of Third World tramps like her. She'd probably be fucking those old communists the first night she showed up for work.

Dinko was seated in the Jeep by the time she reached the car, and he got out, feigning boredom, and opened the passenger door for her.

"Everything okay?" he asked.

She nodded and said, "Mr. Markov says I shall begin my work on Tuesday."

"Dancing?"

She nodded.

"Lap dancing?"

"I shall do anything to get the *propinas* . . . I mean, the tips."

"Have you ever lap-danced?"

"No, but I shall learn."

"This sucks."

"Pardon?"

"Nothing. Let's get the hell outta Hollywood."

They didn't speak until they were cruising south on the Harbor Freeway, and then Dinko said, "Isn't there some other kind of work you can do here in L.A.? You got any skills?"

"I do not know that word," she said.

"Talents? You got any talents?"

"I dance," she said.

"You're no dancer," he said, feeling unaccountably angry. "You can't dance worth a damn. I saw you, remember?"

"I am sorry." She stared straight ahead. "I shall learn better."

"For chrissake!" he said, his anger growing.

"Please," she said, now looking frightened and confused. "I do not wish you to have anger. I am sorry."

"You're too young!"

"I do not understand."

"You're nineteen years old. You shouldn't be working in a place like that, hustling drinks. First of all, it's against the law."

"You promise not to tell my age," she said, and when he looked over at her, the oncoming headlights revealed tears in her amber eyes.

"Goddamnit, don't get weepy on me," he said. "I won't tell nobody, but nineteen? You're a child!"

"I am no child," she said.

"Tell me something," Dinko said. "Did Hector buy you out of a contract with that bar owner in Wilmington?"

"How you mean?"

"Did you sign a paper promising to work at that bar for a period of time?"

"No," she said, puzzled. "I do not sign nothing."

"How did Hector find you?"

"He come and see me one day and then he bring a man on other day when I am dancing. A man I think is from China, but Hector say he is really from Korea."

"Which one was the boss?"

"For sure, the big man from Korea. He say he look for girls to work in Hollywood. He tells me how much they pay me to work at Club Samara."

"Was the Korean dressed in a suit with a white shirt and necktie?"

"Very much businessman," she said. "How you know that?"

"Shit!" Dinko said. The guy standing beside the SL. Hector wouldn't tell the truth if you took his mother hostage.

53

They were silent again except for Dinko's exasperated sighs, and then she said suddenly, "And you, Dinko? How old?"

"Thirty-one."

"I am maybe older than you," she said. "In many ways."

"You'll get old real fast," he said, "working in that place."

"I work at more terrible one in Guanajuato," she said.

His anger and frustration mounted again, and he asked impulsively, "Were you a hooker down there?"

She clearly did not understand the word, and she looked at him until he said, "A whore? A *puta*? Did you peddle your ass in that miserable country? Is that what you did? Is that what you wanna do in Hollywood? Work for freaks and thugs in a sleaze joint and sell your body and get diseases?"

After a very long silence she said quietly, "I must make money how I can. I am for sure not virgin, Dinko."

Still boiling over, Dinko said, "Nobody is these days, the Virgin Mary included. Our fucking archbishop paid out more than six hundred million to cover his pervert priests. Those good padres busted a bunch of virgin cherries, I can tell you."

She started to speak, then gave up trying to work out the meaning of the angry and ugly words he'd just uttered. Whatever he'd said, she didn't want to understand it.

Dinko went on: "I don't care what you had to do in a place where the cartels slaughter people by the thousands and cut off their heads, but now that you're safe in this country, you shouldn't be taking that slimy job in Hollywood!"

Lita Medina looked straight ahead again and said, "Please do not have concern for me."

"Do you got a cell phone?"

"No, but I shall buy one very soon."

"I'm gonna give you my cell number. Call me if . . . well, just call me if you want me to pick you up and take you somewhere else."

She turned her face toward him and said, "Take me? Take me to where?"

He thought about it for a moment. "Don't you have relatives in L.A.? You know, cousins maybe, or family friends?"

"No," she said. "I live now with two girls from Guanajuato that clean the houses for the rich peoples in Long Beach."

"Can't you clean houses too?"

"For sure," she said, "but I must make more money very fast to send to my family. They have great need, 'specially my mother."

"Promise me you'll keep my cell number and call me if . . . well, call me when you feel like you gotta escape."

"What is that word?"

"Like when you gotta run. When you gotta get away from Hollywood. Call me, okay? I'll try to help you."

They were quiet again until she said softly, "I am no child, Dinko."

FIVE

SATURDAY NIGHT IN Hollywood was always an adventure, but on a night of a full moon, which the coppers of Hollywood Station called a "Hollywood moon," anything could happen. After calling roll for six car assignments, Sergeant Lee Murillo told the midwatch, "You'll be pleased to know that there is not anything even resembling a Hollywood moon tonight. Now I'll allow time for applause."

Fran Famosa clapped lethargically. She was not eager for busy nights of police work with her slacker partner, Chester Toles, watching her back. Sophie Branson, the oldest of the women officers, offered a few claps, but her partner, Marius Tatarescu, looked disappointed. With only half as many years on the Job, he was not as burned out as his senior partner, and he still craved the action.

The midwatch sergeant then said, "You're not going to like this, but I have some minor roll call training to discuss with you. It has to do with constitutional policing and cameras in cars, which will soon be installed citywide."

That brought groans from almost everyone. Sergeant Murillo waited for it to subside before saying, "What has been learned in pilot studies where they've been used is that you must not turn off the sound on the cameras, not for any reason. If the cameras don't work, then get another car. Think of the camera's visual and audio capabilities as a tool for your protection."

Ever the movie buff, Hollywood Nate said, "Come on, Sarge! When South Bureau put them in cars with that little pinhole camera facing the backseat, you know what kind of movies got produced? The kind of cheesy bombs that go straight to video. D. W. Griffith silent flicks. Nobody says a word all the way to the station with prisoners for fear of being criticized for something. All the banter between copper and suspect that used to elicit admissions is gone, baby, gone."

Sophie Branson said, "The inspector general is just looking for someone to hang for biased policing. It's still killing them in the IG's office that they had two hundred and forty-three racial-profiling complaints in a year and couldn't sustain a single one, no matter how hard they tried to screw with the coppers named on them."

"This is not a biased police department," Fran Famosa said. "Can't they get that through their heads? How come when some fool off the street comes in with a racial-profiling complaint, you gotta cut paper no matter how psycho the guy is? We get dumb questions like 'How many people of that race do you stop?' When the obvious answer is, As many as is necessary to do my job!"

Sergeant Murillo let them ventilate and then said, "Just remember that you truly do profile, but you do it based on the characteristics and behaviors of bad guys, not based on race or ethnicity. But, of course, if you're on Hispanic gang turf in east Hollywood trying to curtail gang activity, you probably aren't looking to stop and interrogate a Japanese sushi chef."

Hollywood Nate piped up: "Even if they do drive like students at the Braille Institute."

"That's an ethnic stereotype, you ham actor!" said Officer Mel Yarashi, of 6-X-76, a third-generation Japanese-American. "You just offended me and made me not so sorry for Pearl Harbor and fifty-dollar sashimi appetizers."

Sergeant Murillo waited until several cops hooted at Mel Yarashi, who subtly flipped them off; then the sergeant said, "Remember to use proper expressions, like 'reasonable suspicion' and 'probable cause.'

These things give you a perfectly legal right to stop people. And there's case law on making the driver and passenger alight for officer safety. There're lots of subtle reasons you can use. For instance, a car can have an obstructed forward view, can't it? Maybe one of the Eighteenth Street crew might hang baby shoes or those retro fuzzy dice, that sort of thing. It can be a reason to stop a gang car."

"Seriously, Sarge," Mel Yarashi said, "look at the crap that was said when the Rampart copper killed the Guatemalan drunk that was threatening people with a knife. They said the Hispanic copper shoulda told him to drop the knife in the guy's specific Guatemalan dialect. Now Spanish is like Chinese? There's a bunch of dialects we gotta learn?"

Sophie Branson said, "After that shooting, the reports were stacked so high you could stand on them and paint your ceiling."

"If it ain't the PC media, it's the hug-a-thug race racketeers!" Anthony Doakes said.

Doakes, Mel Yarashi's wiry twenty-eight-year-old partner, was a U.S. Army veteran of two combat tours in Iraq and Afghanistan, with five years on the LAPD. He was the only African-American on the midwatch, in a police division with a small number of black residents. But on weekends like this, Hollywood would see a large number of young black males on the boulevards, many of them gang members from south Los Angeles who'd arrived by subway. Because he was a garrulous talker, Anthony Doakes's sobriquet was "A.T.," for "Always Talking Tony."

A.T. took a breath and continued: "Look how the Department caved when it comes to unlicensed illegal aliens on the sobriety checkpoints that impound cars of unlicensed drivers. Whoops! I shoulda said 'undocumented immigrants.' So we can't impound *their* cars now because, being undocumented, they have a harder time getting a legal driver's license and they need their uninsured cars to drive to work. At a vehicle kill rate five times higher than licensed drivers. Do I got it right?"

Hollywood Nate was surprised when his young partner, Britney Small, politely raised her hand. When Sergeant Murillo nodded to her, she said, "The LAPD had one point eight million contacts with citizens last year. Exactly two hundred and forty-eight complaints of biased policing were filed. That comes to point oh oh oh one thirty-eight. Statistically speaking, that's virtually a zero."

Sergeant Murillo said, "Very interesting, Britney. I'm impressed."

Even Hollywood Nate was impressed. "How do you know that, partner?" he asked.

"I'm taking a couple of day classes at UCLA, and I wrote a paper on the subject," she said, smiling self-consciously.

"One other thing," Sergeant Murillo added. "We're all supposed to be using the Pelican flashlight our former chief authorized and insisted on. I know some of you are using Streamlights, but make sure they're the correct weight and size."

"Right," Nate said facetiously. "So small you couldn't concuss a cricket if you gave it a dozen head strikes with one of them. When're we gonna be required to trade our Glock forties for twenty-two target guns in order to give the dirtbags a *real* edge?"

After they stopped snickering and grousing, Sergeant Murillo said, "One last thing: our esteemed surfing duo happens to be working a special detail tonight. So if you see them out on the boulevards dressed in soft clothes, pretend like you don't know them."

"What're they doing?" Sophie Branson asked.

"Something with the vice unit," Sergeant Murillo said, and that got a few hoots and catcalls out of some of the younger male cops. *Those* two? As vice cops?

Chester Toles said, "I don't think any of the curb creatures'll take Jetsam for a copper, not if he shows them his plastic foot."

"I think that's the general idea," Sergeant Murillo said, "but I don't know the particulars of their mission. Anyway, if you see either him or his partner, don't acknowledge, unless they're yelling for help."

He thumbed through his papers, remembering that there was something about drag queens and transsexuals being victimized by vandals, and when he found it he looked at Hollywood Nate and Britney Small, who patrolled the area in question. "A note for Six-X-Sixty-six.

Somebody was shooting trannies and drag queens with paintballs last night while the victims were cruising for tricks on Santa Monica Boulevard."

Hollywood Nate said, "Boss, I can account for my whereabouts at all times. Britney is my witness. Besides that, I'm an actor, and that's a very gay profession."

The coppers chuckled and Britney smiled, and then everyone collected their gear, careful to touch the Oracle's picture for luck before leaving the roll call room.

Jetsam was particularly eager to get started, but Sergeant Hawthorne kept him and Flotsam in the office of the Hollywood vice unit until nightfall, going over the plan ad infinitum. Finally, Jetsam said, "Sarge, can we just land this plane? I mean, what can go wrong?"

The vice sergeant said in earnest, "I haven't had one of my officers get hurt since I've been here, so that's part of it. But it's not only that. It's that we might get just this one chance at the collector, Hector Cozzo, and I don't want us to lose it. He'll be the one who can lead us up the food chain."

Four vice cops, their cover and security teams, breezed in and out of the office while the three men talked. All were dressed for the streets: jeans, T-shirts or other cotton shirts hanging out over their pistols and handcuffs, along with the inevitable tennis shoes for sneaking and peeking. There were mustaches, beards, shaved heads, earrings worn without piercing, openly displayed tats they'd acquired in military service before becoming cops—anything that would make it easier for them to pass easily among the denizens of Hollywood.

"Don't you got anything at all you can bust this guy for right now?" Flotsam asked. "To put a twist on him?"

"Nothing," Sergeant Hawthorne said. "Sure, we know he collects and arranges for immigrant girls to be housed and fed and paid, but so what? The massage parlors and nightclubs are businesses open to the public, and the girls can make any housing accommodation they choose, with anyone they want as a middleman. There's no law against it. Of course, we'd love to prove that they've paid to get into this country illegally, and that they're being virtually enslaved here by never being able to pay back what they owe, but we don't have hard evidence on any of that. Not yet."

"Okay, so when do we get started?" Jetsam said. "All this mission talk is making me so unchill I'll need a massage for real just to get my neck muscles relaxed."

The vice sergeant said, "The last reason that this operation is making me so cautious is because you're not wired. I've only sent an operator into a risky massage parlor operation once since I've been here, and we had a wire in his clothes, so that when he stripped down and carefully laid his clothes over a chair, we could still hear almost everything."

Leering, Flotsam said, "Sweet! That means my partner can break bad and go all sexy and nobody's gonna know."

Sergeant Hawthorne managed a tolerant half-smile. "Once again, this is an intelligence-gathering mission. We're not after prostitution or lewd-conduct violations, so don't go there. Just get your massage, convey the information we've agreed upon, pay the fee, and leave."

Jetsam turned to his partner and said, "Bro, you got lots of massages when you were in the navy. Do you think I should ask for lotion or powder?"

Flotsam said, "Dude, I am definitely a lotion man, and I'll explain. When a deep-muscle massage goes looking for new territory, you want, like, way slick and slippery little fingers doing the exploration. And I'll tell you why . . ."

Sergeant Hawthorne looked at his watch and at the two surfer cops, and wondered if his personal ambition was not leading him into career jeopardy.

The sun was setting over the Pacific, throwing burgundy and indigo light over Hollywood Boulevard, perhaps one of the few places on earth where the ubiquitous smog actually made the sunset more beautiful.

And then, in just a few short minutes, night had fallen on the boulevard and lights were turning on everywhere.

Even though the cops of Hollywood Station were cracking down on the costumed Street Characters who hustled tourists in front of Grauman's Chinese Theatre, the superheroes were out in force on this Saturday night. Some of the tired older ones, like Superman, Batman, and Darth Vader, were being replaced by newer superheroes, like Space Ghost, Mr. Fantastic, and Iron Man, who was the object of intense jealousy.

What aroused the ire and envy of the other Street Characters posing for photos and accepting gratuities for their work was that Robert Downey Jr. had made the Iron Man so sexy on film that his hustling doppelgänger on the boulevard was getting all the play and all the tips. There was a queue of tourists waiting for a shot with him while other superheroes, like Spider-Man, just stood back and brooded. And then the web thrower decided he'd had enough of this shit.

Spider-Man stepped in front of the next pair of tourists and said, "Come on, folks, get your picture with a *real* superhero, not some pile of rusty nuts and bolts."

"Hey, Sticky Foot," Iron Man said, "no poaching."

Spider-Man replied, "Chill, Tin Man, or you might get your fenders dented."

Iron Man, who had seen his namesake's movie fourteen times and was feeling invincible, said, "Crawl back in your web, you fucking insect, or you might get my iron upside the head!"

And with that, he whacked Spider-Man across the skull with an iron gauntlet, except that the "iron" was really molded plastic. Spider-Man responded by kicking Iron Man in the groin, sending him crashing to the pavement on top of Judy Garland's handprints, preserved forever in the forecourt cement.

Spider-Man, standing over the fallen superhero, said, "Better borrow a monkey wrench to loosen *those* nuts, Iron Man!"

The Wolf-Man asked Spider-Man, "How would you like it if someone did that to you?"

Spider-Man flexed and replied, "What's your problem, Fido? Either butt out or bring it on!"

The Green Hornet, who was probably the sweetest and gentlest of the costumed panhandlers and was certainly the gayest, came to Iron Man's aid and scolded Spider-Man, saying, "That was unkind, cruel, and totally unnecessary!"

Spider-Man said, "Buzz off, Hornet, or you'll get swatted next."

That sent the Green Hornet scurrying, and Marilyn Monroe—aka Regis the plumber in another life—let out a scream at the sight of Iron Man lying there writhing in pain. Captain America was the first to draw a mobile phone from his costume pocket and call 911.

It was not the first time a PSR had some fun with this kind of broadcast. The businesslike LAPD radio voice said, "All units in the vicinity and Six-X-Forty-six, a four-fifteen fight in the forecourt of Grauman's Chinese Theatre, between Spider-Man and Iron Man. Person reporting is . . . Captain America. Six-X-Forty-six, handle code two."

"How exciting," Fran Famosa said in disgust after rogering the call. "A Street Character bitch-slapping."

Chester Toles just raised his pale eyebrows a notch, adjusted his aviator eyeglasses, and scratched his rubbery bald scalp before turning north on Highland, but didn't increase his speed by even one mile per hour. "Maybe if we give the young hotshots a chance to jump the call, we won't have to handle it," he said. "They might think a TV crew's gonna roll on this one and they'll end up on the news at ten."

Usually, Fran Famosa would utter an objection to Chester's goldbricking, but when it came to a Street Character donnybrook she was in Chester's corner. Superhero rumbles usually did bring out a TV news team, and when that happened the mob of tourists with cameras seemed to replicate itself, since everybody in Hollywood wanted to be on the big or small screen. The vehicular traffic on the boulevard would slow to a stop so motorists could rubberneck, and the cops would have a mess on their hands.

"Yeah, take your time, Chester," she said. "I'm not up for dealing with freak show panhandlers."

When, four minutes later, they arrived, Chester said to her, "No worries, mate. The situation is well in hand."

There were already two units from Watch 3 at the scene, both radio cars manned by eager young coppers who would love to handle a superhero squabble in front of an audience of hundreds, especially if a news team showed and the audience grew to potentially hundreds of thousands on the nightly news. Chester and Fran stopped in the red zone and made the obligatory gesture of officially handing off the call to the cops of Watch 3, who hadn't handcuffed anyone and were still mulling over the culpability of Spider-Man for the injurious groin kick, after witnesses had concurred that Iron Man had struck the first blow.

In fact, Chester and Fran had just gotten back to their shop when a tourist in an L.A. Dodgers cap suddenly yelled, "Hey, that guy just grabbed my wife's purse!"

The thief was a slope-shouldered guy in a long-sleeved black hoodie that hid his face. He wore dirty jeans and running shoes and he was *fast*. He zigzagged across Hollywood Boulevard, causing several cars to brake and blow their horns at him. He was nearly out of sight before Chester had time to start the engine, with Fran Famosa ready to bail out and give chase on foot. That is, if her fat partner could get the fucking car moving!

"Come on, Chester!" she said. "The dirtbag's getting away!"

"Okay, Fran, don't get your knickers in a knot," Chester said, pulling into traffic with his light bar on, tapping his horn to cut into the lanes of westbound traffic and across the oncoming eastbound traffic.

Fran put out the broadcast that they were chasing a four eighty-four purse snatcher westbound on Hollywood Boulevard from Grauman's, and in a moment the PSR relayed the information to all units in the vicinity. While this was going on, Chester had to blast the siren in order to squeeze through the eastbound number one lane of cars, whose confused and panicked drivers didn't understand what the driver of the black-and-white wanted them to do.

The purse snatcher turned south at the first corner, and by the time they got across Hollywood Boulevard, he'd vanished.

"Maybe he ran into the parking structure," Chester said. "He could hide behind a car and we'd never find him without a K-9."

"There he is!" Fran said.

He'd been momentarily hidden from view by the darkness and a dozen young people walking north toward Hollywood Boulevard for an evening of fun and frolic. The runner turned, saw the black-and-white coming his way, and ran even faster.

"Damn, the dude has an extra gear. He can really move!" Fran said, broadcasting their location for all units.

Chester meant business now, and with his headlights on high beam and his light bar flashing and his siren yelping, he mashed down on the accelerator. When the purse snatcher was all the way to Sunset Boulevard and turning the corner eastbound in front of Hollywood High School, he tripped on the uneven pavement. He did a tumble and roll across the sidewalk, and the purse went flying. By the time he got up, 6-X-46 was stopped at the curb on the wrong side of Sunset, facing oncoming traffic, which had slammed to a stop at the sight of the black-and-white bearing down with its red and blue lights winking and its siren howling.

There was an instant traffic snarl on Sunset Boulevard when Fran Famosa and Chester Toles, who was moving faster than Fran thought possible, got out and took off after the limping thief, who wasn't going to go peacefully. He turned and threw a roundhouse punch at Fran, who ducked and grabbed him around the middle as Chester got him in an LAPD-nonapproved, but usually effective, choke hold. It took the thief to the pavement with both cops on top of him. His hoodie slipped back and his long black hair fell across a scowling face, brown as saddle leather. Fran saw that he was wearing aviator glasses like Chester's, and they went soaring when he broke free of Chester's choke hold.

He was older than they'd originally thought, maybe mid-thirties, and he was strong, far stronger than Chester. He got to his knees, taking

Fran up with him, and he stomped hard on Chester's hand and kicked the baton away just as Chester was getting ready to unload with an LAPD-nonapproved head strike. Then the thief whirled and flung Fran Famosa off him, and he started to run again as they heard a welcome siren headed their way.

Fran had a Taser in her hand, but Chester was between her and the thief with handcuffs in his left hand, and she saw the guy grab for Chester's Beretta. Both men lurched into her, and she lost the Taser. Chester didn't even realize it when his pistol clattered to the sidewalk along with his handcuffs. That's when Fran delivered a nonapproved kick to the face of the thief and followed it with a blast of pepper spray, which caught him in the back of the head instead of the face, and then he was up again and trying to run, with Chester Toles hanging on to his left ankle.

Fran Famosa picked up Chester's lost baton and struck the thief once, twice, across the right knee, to no avail. Saying, "Fuck this!" she tried a nonapproved head strike, but he threw his arm up and took the blow across the wrist.

It sounded like the muffled pop of a firecracker, and he yelled in pain, then said, "I'll kill you, you cunt!" That's when she saw the knife.

And that's when Chester yelled in desperation, "Shoot him, Fran!"

Fran Famosa was trying to do just that, drawing her Glock .40, retreating a few paces, then taking a combat stance.

But she heard a familiar voice yell, "Drop that knife!"

Hollywood Nate, followed by Britney Small, both with their pistols drawn, were running at the thief, who threw down the knife and raised both hands to the top of his head. She'd been so into the adrenaline-charged moment—sound had ceased and all motion had slowed way down—and so close to killing the thief, that she had never heard 6-X-66 squeal to the curb in a brake-locking slide, its high beams lighting up the life-and-death struggle. And she never really registered Hollywood Nate and Britney Small's arrival until Nate was handcuffing the purse snatcher's hands behind his back.

Britney said quietly, "Holster your weapon, Fran. We've got him controlled."

"Ooooh, my frigging back!" Chester Toles said, struggling to his feet with one hand pressed against the small of his back, looking for his glasses, his baton, his OC spray, and his dignity. Everything was strewn around the sidewalk, including the victim's purse and its contents: wallet, keys, lipstick, compact, tissues, and coupons for Pizza Hut.

Then Chester said, "I'm too old for this shit!"

Just then, 6-X-76 rolled up and Mel Yarashi jumped out with Always Talking Tony Doakes, and A.T. started jawing.

"This is some cluster fuck," he told Nate when Fran and Britney were out of earshot, walking the thief to Fran's shop. "This is what happens when you put a chick with a fat old slacker like Chester. They're lucky they didn't get scalped."

Only then did Nate notice that the purse snatcher appeared to be an American Indian. A.T. picked up the knife by the tip of the blade and said, "Uh-huh, a trophy taker. Wonder how many hanks of hair he's got hanging from the lodge pole in his tepee? They should always put someone like me with someone like Chester. 'I'll catch 'em, you clean 'em,' that's my motto. I woulda run that red man's dick into the dirt."

Mel Yarashi, who was accustomed to A.T.'s garrulous ways, said, "Hey, partner, let's police up the sidewalk here. There's property scattered everywhere."

A.T. nodded but, still wanting to chatter, strolled over to the black-and-white where the purse snatcher was strapped into the backseat with the door open and said, "Dude, you are one lucky Injun. The LAPD's head-shot record with a handgun is sixty-three yards. If I'd been the closer here, I woulda just let you get sixty-four yards in front of me and broke that record."

"Go fuck yourself," the exhausted Indian said.

"Are you talking to me?" A.T. responded. "And when exactly did you *have* your lobotomy?"

"I'm not an Injun. I'm a Native American."

"Really?" A.T. said. "Which casino?"

"I want my glasses," the prisoner said.

A.T. said, "I was gonna look for them, but now I have *reservations.*"

He looked around to see if anybody appreciated his Indian humor, but they were all busy talking on radios or cell phones, gathering scattered evidence, and waving off more arriving black-and-whites by holding up four fingers, meaning code 4, no further help needed. There were already too many coppers milling around the fight scene, but more kept coming.

"I need my glasses, goddamnit!" the prisoner said.

"What's your name?" A.T. asked. "And lemme guess. You're a parolee, right?"

The prisoner did not deny his parole status but said, "My name's Clayton Lone Bear. Now go get my glasses, you mud-shark nigger, or bring one of the white cops over here."

"Now you just played the stupid card and made a mortal enemy of this noble buffalo soldier!" Always Talking Tony said, thumping his own chest with a fist. "You want a white cop, try smoke signals." Then he turned and said, "Hey, Mel, come over here and babysit Mr. Lame Bear for a minute. I gotta go talk to Chester and Fran. If he tries to go all Little Bighorn on you, gimme a holler."

Mel Yarashi trotted over to Fran and Chester's shop to guard the prisoner, and A.T. walked toward the searchers, who were sweeping the sidewalk with their narrow flashlight beams.

"Isn't it great to be saddled with safe little baby flashlights," Chester Toles said to Fran Famosa. "In the old days I coulda lit up the whole freaking scene all by myself with my five-cell monster." Chester was squinting nearsightedly when he spotted a dark object and said, "Hey, the guy had a gun!" Then he moved closer and squatted down, saying, "Wait a minute! This looks like *my* gun!"

With the adrenaline overload of the fearful street fight, Chester Toles had been unable to obey the street cop's first commandment: Watch their hands! He hadn't realized that the thief had jerked his Beretta from its holster before losing it.

Chester picked it up, holstered it, and said to Fran with a shiver, "We came close to a bagpiper on the hill." Meaning an LAPD funeral complete with a lone bagpiper playing a dirge, an LAPD custom since the 1963 funeral of Officer Ian Campbell, himself a piper, who was kidnapped from the streets of Hollywood and murdered in an onion field north of Los Angeles.

A.T. strode up to them and said, "Hey, Chester, no big surprise, but I think this PLMF is a parolee-at-large. Way to go, cowboy."

Everyone knew that PLMF meant "parolee-looking motherfucker," but Chester Toles was too old and too sore right then to give a shit.

While A.T. was walking back along the curb to his shop, something glinted in his flashlight beam, and he recognized the prisoner's glasses lying in the gutter beside the curb. He glanced around and saw that everyone was occupied with his or her own tasks, so he turned off his flashlight and strolled over to the gutter in the darkness. And he surreptitiously stepped on them, crunching and grinding the glass and metal into the asphalt.

Mel Yarashi was waving the traffic past the scene when Sergeant Murillo pulled up, parking behind Nate and Britney's shop to take over supervision and make notification to Force Investigation Division about a "categorical use of force."

That was when A.T. saw Chester Toles approach the prisoner and hand a pair of glasses to Fran, saying, "Here, put these on his face. I don't know where the hell *my* glasses are."

"Yo, partner!" A.T. suddenly yelled to Mel Yarashi. "Code four. We're not needed here. Let's bounce."

SIX

AT LAST, NEARLY an hour after darkness had settled on the boulevards and the Saturday night revelry had begun, the vice sergeant decided it was time to head for the massage parlor in east Hollywood. As Sergeant Hawthorne was driving Flotsam and Jetsam there in a plain-wrapper vice car, which happened to be a ten-year-old white Volvo, he said, "One of the biggest massage parlors L.A. ever had was a Russian operation. Of course, the girls could never work off the trafficking debt because the expenses kept rising, but those beautiful girls kept trying. It took a long time to shut it down."

Flotsam was wearing an aloha shirt hanging out over his faded jeans, along with boat shoes, no socks. Jetsam was better dressed, in a Banana Republic long-sleeved paisley shirt, white chinos, and Adidas suede sneakers, but with socks to cover his prosthesis.

Flotsam said, "I guess the recession don't hurt those operations too much."

"The Russian operation never noticed the recession," the vice sergeant said. "Not with an eighty-thousand-dollar-a-month advertising budget. They were really taking in the cash. You know, before we can work a massage parlor like we're doing here, I have to get what they call 'strip authority' from West Bureau. It's only good for a month. The bureau brass does not like officers taking their pants down."

"That must make it an adventure to drop a steamer," Flotsam said.

Sergeant Hawthorne was learning to ignore Flotsam's ceaseless wisecracks. He said to Jetsam, "I figure we'll only need the strip authority for a couple of weeks. I'll send you in two or three times, and if there aren't any nibbles we'll shut down the mission and call it a swing and a miss."

"Nibbles," Flotsam said with a wink to his partner.

By then, Sergeant Hawthorne was sorry that he had brought the tall cop along, but his presence was the thing that had finally persuaded his partner to take this assignment. The vice sergeant said to Jetsam, "If we don't get the information we need, at least you'll get a couple of massages, compliments of the city of Los Angeles."

"Ain't there no way I could get one?" Flotsam asked. "I mean for next time, if the deal goes sideways tonight and we end up with nothing?"

"Sorry," the vice sergeant said, repressing his growing exasperation. "I don't think the bureau would approve of using taxpayer money on just-for-fun massages."

"I'm just sayin'," Flotsam grumbled, "if you, like, wanted to settle for a prostitution bust."

"Okay, let's get back to rehearsal," Sergeant Hawthorne said. "If you do get to talk about your occupation, where're the game machines made?"

Both Flotsam and Jetsam said, "Arizona."

"Just him," the vice sergeant told Flotsam. "And how many machines're needed to take in twenty grand a week?"

"Five," Jetsam said.

"Always be conservative," Sergeant Hawthorne said. "Never overplay your hand."

"Ten," Jetsam said. "But that's in four days, Thursday through Sunday."

"Right," Sergeant Hawthorne said. "Who does your machine deliveries?"

"A couple of Middle Eastern guys. One's an Israeli."

"Good," Sergeant Hawthorne said. "Speak in generalities, but always throw in a specific, like 'an Israeli.' It adds to believability. Are they all electronic machines?"

"No, some're push machines. Depends on what the customer wants."

"Perfect," the vice sergeant said. "Who does the payouts?"

"Usually, bartenders. We been putting our machines mostly in the right kind of bars. And we think they could work really good in residential casinos."

"Do you have a residential casino that you could send Hector Cozzo to for a look-see, in case he should ask?"

"Naw, we almost had one ready to go in Echo Park, but the operator got greedy and we told him to fuck off."

"You're ready," Sergeant Hawthorne said. "Your partner will stay with me, and the cover team will be right outside but you won't see them."

Flotsam said, "The stage is yours, dude."

"Bro," Jetsam said. "All of a sudden I feel like I can't carry a tune and all the judges are Simon Cowell ringers."

"Opening night jitters is all," Flotsam said. "Get your Oscar on, dude. You're Jack fucking Nicholson tonight. Break a leg!"

Jetsam nodded, took a deep breath, and handed his badge and gun to his partner, saying, "Showtime!"

When Jetsam was standing at the intersection, waiting for the traffic light to change, Sergeant Hawthorne said to Flotsam, "You'd never know he has a prosthetic foot. He doesn't limp at all."

"When he's hurting he never lets you know," Flotsam said. "He can still ride more barrels than anybody at Malibu. My little pard's straight-up game. Dead game."

"Please don't use words like *dead* tonight," Sergeant Hawthorne said.

There were three other men in the minimalist waiting room of Shanghai Massage. The plasterboard walls were painted a subtle peach, and the floor was covered in gleaming ebony tiles. Several chairs of vinyl and chrome were set along the walls, and a glass coffee table was covered with magazines. The other customers were forty-something, well-dressed white men, each with a magazine. They looked uneasily at Jetsam when he stepped to the counter, and then they averted their eyes and went back to the magazines.

The woman behind the counter, with pink-framed reading glasses hanging from a chain, was not, as Jetsam had expected, Chinese. She was white—a dyed blonde, of course, in Hollywood's Lady Gaga era. She wore a tight white tee with pink shorts, and her bobbed hair was cut in severe bangs that just cleared her upper eyelids. But she was attractive in spite of a face full of Botox and a bad boob job that had sent each large nipple pointing away from her breastbone.

"Good evening," she chirped. "May I help you?"

Jetsam said, "I got a bad cramp in my leg and I want a deep-muscle massage."

"As you can see, we have gentlemen waiting," she said. "I take it you didn't call for a reservation?"

"No, I was driving by and saw your sign." Then he remembered his earlier briefing and added, "I also read your ad in . . . I think it was a free newspaper at the car wash."

"So you've never been here before?"

"Nope," Jetsam said with what he hoped was a disarming smile.

She looked him over carefully. A very fit guy in his mid-thirties? She could easily picture him in LAPD blue. Her Botoxed expression was unreadable as she said, "Well, it might be better if you came back some other night, after you've made a reservation. We only got so many girls here."

Jetsam played his trump card then, by reaching down and raising the trouser leg of his chinos, revealing his prosthetic foot with supportive bracing. He said, "Living with this causes pain in my upper thigh some-times. Tonight it's, like, way bad. I don't mind waiting till one of the girls gets free."

Her demeanor changed immediately—she would've wrinkled her Botoxed brow if she could. This was no cop! She was genuinely sympathetic when she said, "Oh, I'm sorry. Sure, if you'll have a seat, I think we can take care of you in a half hour or less. My name's Gretchen."

"Fine by me, Gretchen," Jetsam said, and he took a seat, surprised that the reading material was not a bunch of fuck magazines.

There was *Esquire, GQ, Sports Illustrated, Car and Driver,* and even an *Architectural Digest.* This was not what he'd expected at all. In fact, he was hoping that the hundred and fifty dollars the sergeant had given him would cover it. They'd figured that, without sex involved, a thirty-minute legit massage in this upmarket establishment could cost no more than $125, tip included. He only had some thirty dollars of his own money in his wallet.

Two guys emerged from the doorway that led to the massage rooms, one a white guy, one an Asian, obviously regular customers. Both headed straight for the street door and barely acknowledged Gretchen, who said, "Thank you, gentlemen, see you next time!"

The other waiting clients were ushered through the door to the massage rooms within twenty minutes, and yet another customer entered the massage parlor from the street. This one wore a Hugo Boss pin-striped suit and said, in an Eastern European accent, "Good even-ink, my darling" to Gretchen, who replied, "Right on time for your appointment. Go right in. Belinda is waiting for you."

Jetsam had been there exactly thirty-seven minutes when Gretchen said to him, "This way, sir. Your masseuse will be Ivana. She's very well trained, and I'm sure she can help you."

Jetsam followed Gretchen along a narrow hallway with closed doors on each side, obviously the massage rooms. When they got to the last room on the left, Gretchen tapped on the door twice and an eye-catching brunette opened it. She was about Jetsam's age and at least as tall, and she was wearing a powder-blue, gossamer-thin tee and very brief navy-blue shorts, with her hair tied back in a ponytail. Her breasts were larger than Gretchen's, but they were real, and they bounced when she took a few steps toward him, hand extended.

"I am Ivana," she said with a heavy accent. "And I shall help you."

She shook hands with an impressive grip. Though she was carrying a few more pounds than suited his taste, he thought she was very hot in a farmer's daughter sort of way.

"I hear that you need some massage of the thigh. Am I correct?"

"Yeah," Jetsam said. "My goddamn leg's acting up. Where should I put my clothes?"

She opened a small closet and took out two wooden coat hangers, saying, "Here, dah-link, let me help you."

After he unbuttoned his shirt, she pulled it off, noting, "You have very fine muscle tone, yes?"

"I try to stay in shape by surfing, fake foot and all," he said. "So, like, how much will this cost?"

"Is depending what you want and for how long," Ivana answered, with only a trace of impishness in her smile.

"I just want you to, like, work on my thigh and make the cramp go away. And maybe a little up on top by my shoulders. When my stump makes this happen, I get tension around my shoulders and neck."

"Yes, I understand, dah-link," Ivana said. "Can you please remove the shoes and trousers now."

Jetsam sat on the little straight-backed chair next to a table holding the lotions, powders, and towels she used in her work.

Ivana watched carefully when his supportive braces came off, and she looked interested in the prosthesis itself. It seemed evident that she was starting to believe that he only wanted a legitimate massage.

She said, "I think that I can help you in maybe thirty-minute, deep-muscle massage. One fifty is the fee. Okay?"

That stopped him for a moment. A hundred and fifty without the tip? "Okay," he said, figuring he could tip her with his own meager funds and get it reimbursed by the vice sergeant later.

He stripped down to his red briefs and said, "I guess I can leave these on?"

She smiled bigger. "Of course, dah-link. On, off. What gives you comfort is what we wish for. But first you must pay Ivana for her work. Sometimes people who are not honest get the massage and do not pay."

"Of course," he said, taking the front money he'd been given and counting it out on the little table.

"Very good, dah-link." She picked up the money and slipped it into her purse, on the top shelf of the closet.

With his prosthesis and braces on the chair, Jetsam hopped over to the massage table and, before lying down, took a close look at the large white towel covering it. The towel looked freshly laundered, with no disgusting evidence of DNA that he could see. He climbed onto the table and stretched out, facedown.

"What is your name, dah-link?" she asked.

"Call me Kelly," he said, in honor of the surfing champion Kelly Slater.

She placed a pillow under his head and said, "Kelly, you may turn the face this way or the other way, as you wish."

"Okay," he said. "The pain is mostly on the inside of my thigh."

"I shall find it and make it go away, dah-link," Ivana said, and she started.

"This is, like, way nerve-racking and boring at the same time," Flotsam told Sergeant Hawthorne as they sat in the vice car half a block from the front entrance of Shanghai Massage. Flotsam had the sergeant's binoculars in his lap and would look through them every two minutes or so, but there'd been no sign of his partner.

"It's a very busy business," Sergeant Hawthorne said. "He probably had to wait quite a while."

"I don't think I could go for this job," Flotsam said. "Cooling my jets all the time, waiting for something to happen. I was never a fisherman for the same reason. I ain't patient. I like to go out and make things happen."

"Then working patrol here in Hollywood is the job for you," the sergeant said.

"Yeah," Flotsam agreed. "Hollywood's the kinda place where the world's loony tunes gather, but that keeps it from getting boring. I mean, like, the fruit loops can only stand around so long at Ralphs market talking to the radishes before they gotta hit the streets and act out. Know what I mean?"

"I do." Sergeant Hawthorne closed his eyes and leaned his head back on the Volvo's headrest, wishing Flotsam would shut up.

"I'm sure if my li'l pard got in trouble in there, he'd throw a fucking chair through that plate-glass window, wouldn't he?"

"That's what I told him to do," Sergeant Hawthorne said drowsily. "You heard me say it."

"Yeah, I gotta throttle back," Flotsam said. "My li'l pard's probably just enjoying the shit outta his body rub."

"Ow! Goddamn, you're killing me!" Jetsam cried, and Ivana, who had finished working on his thigh and was digging into his neck and shoulders, said, "Do not be baby, dah-link. What I do is good for whole body."

She was for sure the strongest woman Jetsam had ever encountered at close range. "You ever considered pro wrestling?" he asked.

"I was discus thrower back in Ukraine," she said. "Not good enough for Olympics, but not so bad, maybe."

When she was finished she slapped him on the ass and said, "So, dah-link, how you feel now?"

"I hope I can get up," he said.

"Do not worry about it. I shall help you." Then she added, "How you lost the foot?"

He thought of Hollywood Nate then and wished he had Nate's acting chops. He decided to follow Sergeant Hawthorne's advice to stay mostly evasive and noncommittal until there was the right time to be specific and provocative, and to let the questioner pull the information out of him.

Then he heard himself fuck it up completely by saying, "I got the amputation in Tijuana." And he thought, Aw shit! I blew it.

She said, "I have curiousness about how you hurt the foot, Kelly." The Tijuana reference had apparently caused no spark of recognition.

Jetsam swung his legs over the side of the table and sat there for a moment while she washed her hands in a little sink. He thought, Be evasive! "I, uh, well, uh, sorta had an accident with a chain saw. I was, like, pruning a tree and I dropped the saw and I fell on it and somehow the motor kept going and it almost cut my foot clean off, and well . . ."

After drying her hands, Ivana looked at him and said, "You was cutting a tree in Mexico?"

"Well, not exactly," Jetsam said, "I was . . . well, I got such poor work done on me at an ER in Burbank that I had to have the amputation a week later."

Now she was looking him in the eyes. "But why in Tijuana?"

"Cheaper," he said quickly.

"Very strange," she said. "You did not fear the work down there?"

"No, look at it," he said. "Beautiful work, right? I got a recommendation from a doctor here in L.A. He used to, like, work in a clinic there. In fact, he drove down to T.J. and did the job on me."

Now there was no doubt that Ivana was interested. She said, "May I take photo of it?"

"What for?"

"I know a client who has much interest in such things. What do they call the clinic you go to?"

"Clínica Maravilla," Jetsam said.

"And who is the doctor that do the work?"

"Dr. Maurice Montaigne," Jetsam said. "I found him through a guy I worked with."

"What kind of work you do, Kelly?" she asked casually.

"This and that," he said, trying a mysterious smile.

"You are interesting person, Kelly," she said. "Is okay if I take photo or two?"

"My stump only. Not my face."

"Why? You are wanted man? You are, how you say, fugitive?" She asked with a grin.

"Not exactly." He smiled back at her. "Okay, snap away. Are these for your scrapbook? Your first massage of a guy with one foot?"

"Is not for *my* scrapbook, dah-link," she said, opening the small closet again and taking down her cell phone.

She took photos of Jetsam's stump. When she was finished, she smiled mischievously and said, "You like to take a photo of me sometime?"

"Can I pose you the way I want to?" he said.

"Absolutely," she said. "I give you massage and you can do more than take photo if you wish."

"For the same price?"

She laughed and said, "Oh, no, dah-link. Now we talk about very special massage from Ivana. No, no, not same price."

"Do we do the special massage here?" he asked.

"Sure, here," she said. "Or in hotel. Or in your house if your wife do not mind. Maybe she like my massage too?"

"I ain't married," he said. "Not anymore. Anyways, can I have your phone number? I might be ready for this a lot sooner than you think."

"Wonderful, dah-link!" She went back to the closet to get a business card from her purse.

It was cheaply done, with no embossing. It said, "Massage by Ivana." She wrote a phone number on it.

"Would you like a shower?" she asked.

He saw exactly how his clothes were hung and thought about taking a shower to see if she would go through his wallet, but then he figured that this group of players might be savvy enough to pull credit card and DMV information and somehow trace him back to the LAPD, so he said, "Naw, that lotion ain't the greasy kind."

She watched with interest as he attached the supportive braces and the prosthesis, and when he was finished and had pulled on his chinos, she said, "You feel good now, yes?"

"Very good," he said. "But tell me, Ivana, why the photo op of my stump? Are you interested in specialty surgeries, or what?"

"I am not," she said, "but I got special client. He is very much interested. Maybe he is knowing the same doctor that you know."

"Maybe," Jetsam said. "I hear the doc did a lotta work around Hollywood, but I don't think he's in practice these days."

She did not look surprised. "No? Why not?"

"I hear he's zombied out most of the time."

"What is this meaning?"

"All smoked out. A crackhead."

"Oh, yes," she said. "The drugs. Yes."

Jetsam knew he was taking a big risk that might scare her, but he couldn't stop himself from asking, "Is your special client looking for a doctor like that? Or is he an amputee too?"

"He is just special client that sometime need outcall massage, like maybe I shall also do for you very soon. So, do you like what I do today? It was okay?"

He figured that was his cue for a tip, so he pulled out his wallet and gave her his thirty dollars, which left him with exactly two dollars of his own money. He tried a devil-may-care grin and said, "Have a burger on me, babe."

Her smile told him that she was satisfied with the fee and the tip. In fact, she said coyly, "Maybe next time *you* shall become my little hamburger. Maybe Ivana shall eat you up!"

"Yum yum," Jetsam said.

Before he was quite out the door, Ivana startled Jetsam by asking, "May I have your phone number too, dah-link?"

"Why would you want my phone number?" He stalled, trying to remember the vice unit's cold phone number Sergeant Hawthorne had given him. "What if my girlfriend answers?"

"Then I say I got wrong number," Ivana said

He was pretty sure he had the number right before he gave it to her, saying, "I can't imagine why you need it."

Ivana flashed her sexiest smile and said, "Maybe we offer summer special that you must hear about. Maybe we give coupons, dah-link!"

Flotsam was visibly relieved to see his partner leave the massage parlor and cross the boulevard at the intersection. Sergeant Hawthorne got on the tac frequency and told the cover team to stand by.

When Jetsam got to the vice car, parked north of the boulevard, he climbed into the backseat, and both Flotsam and Sergeant Hawthorne turned and waited in anticipation.

Jetsam enjoyed creating suspense, but finally he said, "I got my foot in the door."

"Fuck the jokes, dude!" Flotsam said. "Come on, give it up!"

"Can't I enjoy a Zen moment?" Jetsam asked.

By then, Sergeant Hawthorne just wanted to see the last of the surfer cops forever, and he was half-hoping that nothing of value had come from the massage parlor and he could jettison his whole experiment.

Then Jetsam said excitedly, "This Ukrainian chick has these big over-zealous casabas. Bro, her mammaries are mammoth. And she got these paws that could turn your muscles into risotto. She's fucking brutal!"

The young vice sergeant sighed audibly. "I'm glad you had a good time, but what the hell happened, if anything?"

"Well, first thing was, the chick at the counter looked at me like I was a turd on a stick, till I showed her my foot," Jetsam said. "And by the way, you didn't give me enough bank, Sarge. The massage cost me the Franklin and the Grant. And then I tipped her thirty bucks of my own. I ain't got enough left for a refried bean burrito at Taco Bell."

"Why did you have to tip her, dude?" Flotsam asked, and there was that leer again.

Sergeant Hawthorne was getting very close to telling these two dip-shits that this was a goddamn police mission and not a rager on the beach at Malibu.

But before he had a chance to pull rank, Jetsam finally said, "I think it worked! She took a picture of my stump. Four pictures, in fact. And she claims she got a client that's interested in special surgeries. And she got her game face on when I mentioned that I got mine done in T.J. And I, like, sorta hinted that I know the quack doctor who's a crackhead now, and I got her phone number if you wanna design my next move." Jetsam took a breath and added, "I done good in there."

Neither Sergeant Hawthorne nor Flotsam spoke for a long moment. Then the vice sergeant said, with renewed respect, "Let me get the cover team in on this, and then start from the very beginning and tell me every single word that was spoken in there."

"And not the Reader's Digest version," Flotsam said. "I gotta hear it all."

"I'm hungry," Jetsam said. "I either need my thirty bucks or you gotta feed me, Sarge."

"I'm very happy to buy," Sergeant Hawthorne said sincerely. "Will IHOP do?"

"Why not?" Jetsam said. "I love savory dishes that can clog your arteries so your heart only beats about three times all day. And one more thing: the chick wanted my phone number. I gave her your setup number, so you might get a call for Kelly. That's the name I gave her. Whadda you suppose it's all about?"

"I don't know for sure," Sergeant Hawthorne said. "Just when I was thinking this was the dumbest idea I've ever had, it's starting to look promising. If she does call for Kelly, I may need your UC services ASAP, so I'll need to know where you are, on duty and off duty, for the next few weeks. I'll keep both your watch commander and Sergeant Murillo informed."

After the cover team drove up and parked behind them, the vice sergeant got out of the car to tell them that they'd meet at the vice office in one hour for a debriefing, after he fed his surfer cops.

Alone in the car with his partner, Flotsam said, "So the masseuse was a real gamer, huh, dude? The kind that could make you flame out and crash after an hour of frolic and horseplay?"

Jetsam said, "Bro, remember that time you and me were off duty in that pricey club on the Strip? The one where the decibel level could curdle breast milk?"

"Yeah," Flotsam said. "What about it?"

"Remember the waitress you called Miss Elegantly Elevated Eyebrows? The one with the fiendish smile that scared you?"

"Yeah," Flotsam said. "That babe put me in a devilish state of mind."

"Well, bro," Jetsam said, "compared to Ivana, that scallywag on the Strip was Little Miss Sunshine. I think my spooky masseuse must spend her days watching cage fights."

"I'm falling in love!" Flotsam said. "Are Ukrainian chicks like Russians? Can you mail-order them too?"

SEVEN

THE NEWS ON the following Friday morning was horrific. Dinko Babich hadn't gotten much sleep after smoking some middling grow that he'd bought the night before from a fellow longshoreman he'd spotted on Beacon Street. His grandfather had loved to talk about the days when that was the toughest street in Los Angeles. Legend had it that once upon a time, seamen had actually been shanghaied from saloons there. Now there were no bars on Beacon Street, and nearby Sixth Street was showing signs of urban renewal. There was a modern courthouse, and lofts were being refurbished—the ubiquitous symbol of a comeback.

The grow hadn't been the powerhouse pot Dinko was looking for, and it had left him with some twitch and jitters. When he had managed to fall asleep, it had been a fitful sleep. He was aware that he'd dreamed of Lita Medina, but he wasn't sure what the dreams were about. At 10:00 A.M., when he got out of bed with a blinding headache, he cursed the weed, and the murky dreams, and himself for giving a second thought to what happened to some Mexican whore.

His mother had also slept late, and she was still in her robe, frying ham and eggs, when he entered the kitchen. Brigita Babich looked at her only child and shook her head sadly. She hoped it was a booze hangover and not from marijuana, which had gotten him suspended at work and caused her so much worry.

His mother was large-boned, and tall like Dinko, not fat like her cousin Tina. Whenever she dressed up for church or bingo, she still teased her hair the way she had back in high school in the '60s. Today her auburn hair was tousled, and the roots had grown out very gray. Dinko thought that the attractive young woman who'd won his father's heart was mostly gone. After her husband's death, Brigita Babich had aged very quickly.

"Eggs, honey?" she asked, and Dinko shook his head and poured a mug of coffee before sitting at the kitchen table and looking at the *Los Angeles Times*.

Dinko thought how almost every Croatian in Pedro, and probably every Italian, complained about how they missed the *San Pedro News-Pilot*, but in these hard times, with San Pedro turning Hispanic and seedy, the local newspaper could not survive. He wondered if any part of the insular, unchanging Fish Town of yore could possibly survive.

Since it was only local news, meaning San Pedro news, that ever interested his mother, he asked her, "Anything happen worth reading about?"

She turned away from the stove and said, "My God, yes! Wait till you read about what they found yesterday in the container yard on Pacific Highway. I saw it on the TV news last night before I went to bed. It's awful. Just awful."

Dinko opened the newspaper to the terrible story of security guards finding a container containing thirteen dead Asians, all young women except for one older man. They had been dead for several days, and the odor of decomposing bodies inside the ovenlike steel container was what had alerted the security guards.

A spokesman at the container yard speculated that they had died from carbon monoxide poisoning. In the container they found small chemical toilets and five-gallon buckets full of human waste, as well as bags of clothing and blankets alongside the corpses. Ventilation holes had been drilled through the bottom of the container, along with a small trapdoor, but the container had been stacked in such a way that the trapdoor was blocked and the air holes were partially closed off. Still, someone had made the stupid decision to light a camping stove, and that had proved fatal.

It was estimated that the journey across the Pacific from a likely port of embarkation used by human traffickers would've taken about four-teen days. The number on the container did not square with the numbers on the manifest of the cargo ship that had delivered the container, but the ship was now back out at sea, in international waters. Of course, a spokesperson from Immigration and Customs Enforcement ended his terse statement with the inevitable but hardly reassuring promise: "An investigation is ongoing."

After he'd finished reading the story, fleeting images passed through the mind of Dinko Babich, such as last week's sighting of someone he thought was Hector Cozzo with a well-dressed Asian. And he recalled Hector's search for "new talent," and remembered Hector's stupid story about involvement with a street gang that robbed containers full of goods from storage yards. Were they lies or only half lies? Had a container holding very special "goods" worried Hector and his Asian friend?

All of this passed fleetingly. He felt a sudden stab of anxiety and didn't hear his mother say, "Two eggs or three?"

Hector Cozzo was surprised when he awakened to find two cell-phone messages, one from an Asian masseuse at Shanghai Massage. He listened to the singsong voice he had come to hate, even though he wasn't sure which buckethead bitch it was. He lit a cigarette and saw there were also three calls from Mr. Kim, the hulking Korean who was a kind of assistant to the big boss, Mr. Markov. He was always calling to yap about some-thing that Hector had nothing to do with. He'd check in with Kim later in the day and tell him his cell had died and he'd forgotten to recharge it.

He looked at the clock on the lamp table beside his bed and saw that it was only 9:45. That pissed him off. He hadn't gotten to bed until 4:00 A.M., and he liked to sleep at least seven hours.

When he returned the call to Shanghai Massage, the Asian masseuse called Suki said, "Hector, Ivana need to talk with you."

The phone was given to the Ukrainian masseuse and he heard Ivana say, "Hector, I got to see you. I am here at work because we got the cleanup to do for good clients. They are booking three rooms for all afternoon."

"Yeah, that's fine," Hector said sleepily. "I'm glad business is booming, but why do I gotta hear about it now?"

Ivana said, "I think you got to know about trouble with a girl."

"What trouble?" he said. "Which girl?"

"Not something for the telephone talking, Hector," Ivana said. "Can you come in one hour?"

"Shit!" he said, taking a closer look at the clock. "Make it two hours."

"Okay," Ivana said. "Two hours. Big trouble, Hector."

Always trouble, he thought. Bitches were nothing but trouble. He didn't mind the risk involved in collecting from the massage parlor and from Club Samara, money that would never be reported to the IRS. But he also had to check and recheck the massage parlor's records to make sure that the bogus set of documents prepared for the IRS was okay and that the set of records for Mr. Kim was accurate to the dollar.

He didn't even mind the risk of pissing off some thugs from nearby Little Armenia who thought that the massage parlor would be better served by local "handlers" than by some "little guinea," which is what they called him to his face. These were foreign-born Armenians and their sons who'd come to Los Angeles after the breakup of the Soviet Union. Many families had headed to the suburb of Glendale, others to Little Armenia, so close to Hollywood. The older ones were veterans of terrible times under the Soviets that had hardened them, and their offspring were just as ruthless. The "AP" graffiti tagged on the sides of buildings in Little Armenia warned all whose turf this was. This territory belonged to Armenian Power.

Hector often wondered if it was karma or Carmine that had sent him to Mr. Markov. The Mambellis owned significant property in San Pedro and, of course, lived "up on the hill" west of Gaffey where other wealthy Italians lived, and not down in the flatlands among the growing population of Latinos. Carmine Mambelli's grandfather had part ownership in a Pedro bank, and everyone knew he'd been involved in bookmaking back when bookmaking was big business, before the 1980s, when betting went electronic.

It was Carmine who had found his former schoolmate sitting on the patio outside Utro's Cafe, beneath the awning that boldly proclaimed, "Home of the Proudest People on the Coast."

Carmine had looked at Hector that day and said, "This is a long-shoremen's hangout, dude. Are you looking for waterfront work? Will wonders never cease?"

At first, Hector had bristled, but nothing he'd been doing had brought him much bank and he really was between jobs, so he told his old schoolmate the truth: "Yeah, I need a job, Carmine. And they ain't easy to come by."

Carmine, wearing Italian shoes that were worth more than Hector's entire wardrobe, studied him and said, "I got a little job for you if you wanna do it. There's a guy in Hollywood that used to make transactions at the bank when my grandfather was still running it. I think him and my grandpa did some outside deals together. I'd like you to run a package up to him today. It's paperwork from the bank that he needs this afternoon. You still got a car?"

"Of course I got a car." Hector did not tell Carmine that it was a ten-year-old Hyundai with dented fenders and a body rusted through from being parked in the driveway of the Cozzo home during San Pedro's winter dampness.

Carmine said, "You can save me a drive to Hollywood. Here, take your mom and dad to Sorrento's for a pizza tonight." He gave Hector two hundred-dollar bills. Hector then walked with Carmine to his 7 Series Beemer and was handed a large cardboard box sealed with masking tape.

"Give this to Mr. Markov personally," Carmine instructed, giving Hector a note bearing the address of an east Hollywood bar called Rasputin's Retreat.

"Your grandpa musta did business with Russians," Hector said after looking at the name of the bar.

"He did business with everybody that needed a banker." Carmine passed Hector a business card that simply said, "Carmine Mambelli" with his cell number. He added, "Remember, only to Mr. Markov. You got a problem, you phone me, okay?"

The rush-hour traffic was even more miserable than usual that day, and it took Hector nearly two hours to get to east Sunset Boulevard. Rasputin's Retreat was one of those tricked-up ethnic bars Hector hated. The main barroom was dark, and the walls were decorated with garish frames containing small lighted prints of charging Cossacks on horseback, the onion domes of St. Basil's, matryoshka nesting dolls, and Fabergé eggs. A samovar took up too much space at the end of the service bar, and the sound system played balalaika music. It looked to Hector like a place where the old Russians might come to drink, but he couldn't imagine the younger ones falling for the kitsch. It was such a small joint that he didn't see how it could pay the rent even on this eastern section of Sunset Boulevard.

Hector had left the box in the car and entered Rasputin's Retreat empty-handed; now he asked the bartender if Mr. Markov was around. The bartender nodded toward the corridor leading to the small kitchen and the restrooms. Hector walked back there and found a door marked "Office" and knocked.

A male voice said in slightly accented English, "Come in. The door is unlocked."

Hector entered, and for the first time encountered Mr. Markov. He was in his seventies and sturdily built for his age, but with remarkably feminine hands and manicured nails, making Hector think the old dude had a bit of swish in his tail. His comical Young Elvis hairstyle was dyed black, and that day he was wearing an ivory blazer over a violet sport shirt open at the throat. His face looked spit-shined from a fresh chemical peel, and he wore O.J. shoes, but Hector figured them for Bruno Magli knockoffs. He thought that Markov's English was better than any he'd heard in Pedro from the immigrant Italian friends of his grandfather's.

Markov looked warily at Hector and said, "You do not have something for me from Carmine?"

"Yes, Mr. Markov," Hector said. "I thought I should leave it in my car till I made sure you were here."

Markov smiled. "That is good thinking. Very good. Please go to your car and retrieve it for me."

When Hector returned with the heavy carton, he assumed he'd be thanked and dismissed, but Markov said, "Carmine tells me that you are between jobs and could use employment. He said that he has known you all his life."

Hector nodded. "We went to Catholic school together. Clear through high school almost."

Markov said, "I might be able to offer you some temporary employment and see how you do. Are you interested?"

"Yes, sir!" Hector said.

"I do not hire hoodlums," Markov said. "Do you have a police record?"

"Well, I had an arrest for having somebody else's credit card," Hector said, "and I got busted when I made a mistake and wrote a NSF check, and then there was some trouble for possession of coke, but it was jist a few grams. Because I was driving and had a minor wreck, I done sixty days on that one, but it's the only time I ever served. I'm thirty-two years old now. I outgrew all that childish crap."

Markov smiled slightly and asked, "Why are you being truthful? Do I look like the kind of man who would verify what you tell me? The kind of man who would demand honesty in any dealings I have with my employees?"

"You sure do, Mr. Markov," Hector said.

Sometimes he thought that fate had led him to Markov, and other times he wondered how much juice his old friend Carmine had with his new employer. But whether it was karma or Carmine, within a few months he had a great job and a sweetheart deal, paying very modest rent on a three-bedroom house in Encino subleased to him by Markov.

He'd always doubted that Markov was the man's true name, and he'd never known where Markov lived or with whom. He did not believe that Markov was really Russian, because he'd heard him pause and stammer with uncertainty when he spoke the language briefly to the bartender that first day. Based on his childhood experience with a few Serbian families in Pedro, Hector guessed that Mr. Markov might be a Serb. He often thought that if he only had to do collections and report to Markov, it would've been a dream job.

But it was not a dream job, because mostly he had to collect for, and report to, the big scary Korean who wore those Valentino and Hugo Boss tailored suits. He called himself Mr. William Kim, but Hector knew that half the goddamn population of Koreatown called themselves Kim. When Hector had complained to Kim about the nasty little conversation he'd had with two Armenian thugs who'd waited for him outside the rear door of Shanghai Massage—a conversation about who should be doing the collections at any massage parlor in Little Armenia—Kim had just dismissed it with a wide grin that revealed a gold tooth in his grille.

Kim said, "If we got to, we *deal* with Armenians, no problem."

Hector had decided to take the good with the bad and cope with all of it, because he was making almost six grand a month, tax-free, even on bad months. And there was the little house in Encino, the only caveat being that sometimes, if Markov phoned and said there was a need to entertain an important client, he'd have to clear out for the evening. Then Hector would have to pick up a masseuse or a dancer from Club Samara and drive her to his house to do whatever the special client wanted her to do. Hector would stay in a motel on those nights, and the next day he'd either send his bedding to the laundry or throw it away, depending on how it looked.

On only one occasion had he been asked to stay home during the private party. Markov had sent him a Russian client to handle, and Hector knew that this one was a real Russian because he'd had to pick him up at LAX when he got off a flight from Moscow, and deliver him straight to his suite at the Four Seasons Hotel. He called himself Basil and, after that night, he drank all the vodka Hector had in his house, and he fucked one of the Asian masseuses, who Hector had had to summon on short notice. It was a night that Hector would never forget, because Basil, who Markov spoke of with great deference and respect, was without a doubt the weirdest son of a bitch Hector Cozzo had ever met in his thirty-two years on earth.

Markov had warned that Basil had very peculiar tastes and told Hector to be enthusiastic about anything that titillated this man, who was about to become a primary investor in a Los Angeles business deal being brokered by Markov. After the massage and sex was over that evening, and after Basil got good and drunk and the masseuse was alone in the bedroom getting high on Hector's cocaine, he found out exactly what else it was that titillated the Russian.

Hector would never forget that moment when Basil took him into the living room and showed him a photo album he carried in his briefcase. He had dozens of photos of amputated limbs! Arms, hands, legs, feet. Hector was half-expecting to find a beheaded corpse, but he never saw that. He was shocked, but he had to pretend that the sickening pictures fascinated him as well.

Basil's English was poor, but he made Hector understand that he would love to have a girl sometime who was an amputee. He made it known by whacking at his left arm and leg with a karate chop. And then he emitted a drunken cackle that gave Hector an electric shiver from his neck to his tailbone.

Hector's brief education in apotemnophilia came when, for the first time, he delivered the massage parlor's collections directly to Markov at

Club Samara. They met in the back office that afternoon, and Markov thanked him profusely for showing Basil a good time and for making him feel welcome in Hector's Encino home.

Hector had been employed by Markov for only a few weeks at that point, and he wanted very much to make an impression on his employer. Markov slowly and methodically explained to Hector what the amputation paraphilia was all about and, sadly, how Basil was afflicted with it. He smiled a lot as he explained it and said that Hector had nothing to fear from Basil.

His employer said that Basil was the only son of a Moscow billionaire and that Basil had acquaintances in Moscow and Berlin and Amsterdam who shared his affliction. He told Hector that one of them had undergone an amputation of a healthy arm nearly to the elbow, and that the person, whose gender was not disclosed, had become a kind of legend to the others.

Markov paused when he saw Hector turn a bit pale. "Do not be too shocked," he said. "This is of little concern to us."

And then Markov explained that because of his need of the Russian's money, he had investigated and found a Dr. Maurice Montaigne, who lived in Hollywood and who had done all sorts of underground surgeries in Tijuana before and after his medical license was taken away. Markov had had a long consultation with Dr. Maurice, who, he'd learned, was a crack cocaine addict, and the doctor had promised Markov that if he ever did another "elective amputation" in Tijuana, he would arrange for Mr. Markov's Russian associate to talk to the patient before and after the event.

Hector repeated the phrase to Markov: "An *elective* amputation?"

"Yes, Hector, very much elective," Markov answered with his straight-razor smile. "We have to overlook certain peculiarities in the world of business. And we must keep Basil happy or he will take his father's investment elsewhere."

Before Hector left his employer that afternoon, Markov said, "If ever you encounter anyone, male or female, who may have undergone an *unusual* amputation, please inform me. I have learned that this kind of person enjoys displaying the surgery, and a massage parlor is a place they frequent. I mention this because Basil shall be coming to Los Angeles once a month for the next year or so, and I must keep him as entertained as possible."

Hector felt woozy and feverish. He asked Markov, "How would I know if an amputation was unusual, sir?"

Markov replied, "If it occurred at a Tijuana clinic, especially if it was performed by a Dr. Maurice Montaigne, we can assume that it was . . . unusual."

There were things in Hector Cozzo's life that he'd compartmentalized, and memories that he'd repressed, and that had been one of them. Still, recalling his employer's instructions, he had mentioned to a key masseuse at each of the massage parlors in and around Hollywood that if any of the girls ever got a client who happened to be an amputee, they should ask where the surgery was performed. He promised a reward for such information. He hadn't bothered to mention the name Maurice Montaigne to anyone, because he thought it highly unlikely that he'd ever have to deal with this nightmarish crap again. And Basil's later encounters at Hector's home with various masseuses and dancers had not ended with required peeks at Basil's photo album.

When Hector had once asked Basil if he would prefer to have the girls brought to his suite at the Four Seasons when he came to Los Angeles, Basil had become irritated and said, using mangled English idioms, "I am lonesome wolf who do not make shit where I am sleeping. I shall not fuck wolfess at my hotel."

"Got it, Basil," Hector had replied. "*Mi casa es su casa.* That means I'll bring all the wolfesses you can handle to my crib and you can shit on my bed and even on the wolfess if you want to. No problem."

Now, remembering that first encounter with Basil at his house, and the languorous Asian masseuse he'd supplied for the Russian, he was distressed that even a flash of recall about that night could creep him out. He hated and feared everything about the man, from his purported vast wealth to the white streak that blazed across his hair from the widow's peak to the crown. And he especially despised the way the drunken Russian freak had cackled while showing his horrible photos. Hector was sure that Basil was insane.

Hector Cozzo did remember the last troubling question he'd asked his employer that day. He'd said, "Mr. Markov, Basil would never, you know, want to . . . do something like that to someone, would he? Like, make an amputation really . . . *happen?*"

Markov had chuckled and said, "Basil is a very rich man with a very unfortunate condition, Hector, but he is not Jack the Ripper."

The phone call came after Dinko's breakfast, which consisted of one slice of toast and a half-eaten fried egg with two cups of coffee.

"I only hope you were not smoking marijuana," Brigita Babich said to her only child when he got up from the breakfast table and put his dish and coffee cup into the dishwasher. "I hope it was just booze that makes you look like hell this morning."

"I don't smoke that crap anymore, I told you," Dinko said. "Jesus! You think getting a thirty-day suspension from work didn't teach me something?"

"There's been way too much methamphetamine use on the docks, Dinko," she said. "So of course I'm gonna worry about you. After the trouble you had with your car . . ."

"Not that again," Dinko said. "Can't you let it go?"

"If there'd been anyone in the parked car you hit, you could be in prison now," she said.

"I spent the night in jail. I totaled my car. I paid a fine that almost coulda bought me a new car. I got my insurance dropped. I did my probation. Damn, why not crucify me in Point Fermin Park after Mass next Sunday?"

"It was the marijuana, Dinko," she said. "Drinking and driving is bad enough. Smoking dope and driving is suicidal behavior. I just hope—"

"I'm going back to bed," he said. "I got a headache and you're making it worse."

"Take a shower and you'll feel better," she said.

Back in his bedroom, he heard the cell phone on the nightstand chiming. Later, upon remembering this call, he realized that if his mother had kept ragging on him about smoking weed, he would've missed the call. It turned out to be a very impulsive call, and maybe she would not have left a message. And she might never have called again. He had always believed utterly in coincidence and fate.

"Hello." There was silence on the line for several seconds and he repeated, "Hello?"

A soft voice said, "It is Lita."

"Lita!" he said. "I never thought I'd . . . what happened? Is something wrong?"

"I have hope that you can come to me for little while? I am feeling very much like I wish to talk with you."

"About what?"

"Your friend."

"Hector Cozzo?"

"That is right."

"Is someone there so you can't say what it's about?"

"That is right."

"I can be there in maybe an hour or a little longer."

"Thank you," she said, with a quiver in her voice. "Please come at eleven o'clock."

"Yeah, sure," he said, opening the nightstand drawer, where he kept a pen. "Go ahead, gimme the address where you're at."

She gave him the address of a liquor store on Hollywood Boulevard east of Western Avenue, where Thai Town and Little Armenia overlapped. She said she would be standing in front of the store, and before hanging up, she added, "I am sorry for this. I do not have nobody else."

He was surprised how fast his heart was beating, and he was stunned to hear his own voice say, "I'm *glad* you called, Lita. Very glad."

Dinko took a shower, shaved, and put on clean cargo pants and the newest polo shirt he owned, the yellow one that the salesgirl had assured him would somehow also complement his blue eyes and make his light chestnut hair appear a bit golden. He'd always been such a doofus when it came to cute salesgirls. He slipped into his new deck shoes and told his mother that he might be home late.

"Where're you going?"

"To town," he said.

"Where to town?"

"Hollywood," he said.

"Why in the hell would anyone be going to Hollywood in the morning?" she asked, but he was already out the door.

Shanghai Massage looked far more depressing in the daylight hours, Hector thought, after parking in the limited space at the rear of the business. He used his key to enter through the back door and could hear the sound of a vacuum cleaner, and voices jabbering in some gook language. One thing about Kim: he got his money's worth. He made the girls he'd smuggled into this country do the work of masseuses, whores, janitors, and any other job he could find for them.

Ivana was mopping the floor in one of the massage rooms with her hair tied back under a bandanna when she saw Hector head for the lobby. She followed him and closed the door that led to the corridor.

He lit a cigarette and looked in vain for an ashtray under the counter, but she said, "Is okay. We got to sweep and mop anyways."

"So what's the big problem that I had to come running over here?" he asked. "Something about a girl? What, somebody thinks they can jist quit and not pay off their obligation?"

"Is the thing down at the harbor!" Ivana said, turning involuntarily to make sure the door was still shut.

"What thing at the harbor?"

"The people. All the ones that perish from the cargo ship? You do not know? The big container box is at the storage place when they find bodies inside."

"I got a little bit loaded last night. I ain't heard nothing," Hector said.

"Twelve girls and one man. They die from breathing gas, and the police they find bodies yesterday. And one of dead girls is the sister of Daisy. She was coming on the cargo ship, and now she knows the sister is dead!"

"How does she know her sister was among the dead?"

Ivana said, "She is knowing the smuggler and the ship he uses, and when it arrives. And she wait all week for Mr. Kim to get the girls from outside the container box. It is them, no question."

"I don't know Daisy, do I?"

"Is the new name she chooses. Tall Korean girl who dances at Club Samara? She is home today with grief."

"Oh, yeah," Hector said. "The tall Asian dancer. I remember using her on a couple of parties for somebody."

"You mean Mr. Kim? He calls here today and asks if we seen you. He is showing anger."

"Oh, shit," Hector said. "My voice mail."

"You must talk with Suki," Ivana said. "I get her."

While Ivana was gone he checked his phone and saw another message from Kim. The big slope was gonna break his neck! Hector lit another cigarette with the butt from the first.

Hector couldn't remember which one Suki was. After a while, the names, the faces—they all ran together in Hector's mind. He just had to make sure that somebody semihonest would report exactly how many massages each girl had done and what kind of massage they had given, and that job had gone to Ivana. They got to keep half their tips and 5 percent of the massage fees, but the rest went to Hector Cozzo, and from him to Kim, and on very rare occasions to Markov himself. With Kim's approval, because of Ivana's job as manager and snitch, Hector had forgiven some of her debt for her passage to America and her current living expenses.

"Tell to Mr. Hector what you hear from that new Mexican girl that is living with Daisy and Violet," Ivana ordered the frightened girl she led into the lobby.

Suki turned out to be short and cute, half Cambodian and half Thai, much younger than Ivana, with surgically enhanced breasts. She passed herself off as Japanese to her round-eyed customers because they seemed to prefer the idea of Japanese masseuses, and she sometimes claimed to have been a geisha in Tokyo. Suki was a relatively new girl and would be working off her expenses for a long time. She said, "Violet say to me that Daisy runs away from the apartment when she hears about baby sister dying with other peoples. Daisy tell to Violet and Lita that all the peoples owe for travel to Mr. Kim."

"Running away to where?" Hector asked.

Suki hesitated. Ivana poked her and said, "Tell it all!"

"To police," Suki said, while looking at her sandals.

"What?" Hector yelled it so loud, both women flinched. "And what is she gonna tell the police?"

Suki looked up fearfully and said, "About how Mr. Kim help many to get to America, and how me and Daisy got to work for him very long time and pay to him money for . . . for all things he tell us to do with customers, and . . ."

"Yeah, what else?"

Suki's chin was quivering when she said, "And she say she also going to tell about Mr. Hector, who collect the money for Mr. Kim."

"Son of a bitch!" Hector said. "The cunt is gonna put us in the joint! Where is she?"

Suki said, "Daisy runs away from the apartment this morning crying tears."

"And what the fuck's the other roommates gonna do about it?" He posed the question to both women. "Violet's the Vietnamese girl, right? And Lita's the Mexican."

Ivana said, "Violet told to me that her and Lita keeps shut and says nothing to nobody about what Daisy is saying, but I think you must find Daisy and talk with her before Mr. Kim discover about this and . . ." Her voice trailed off.

"Kee-rist!" Hector said, hearing his ringtone. He didn't have to look. He knew who it was.

Ivana told Suki, "Okay, go back to work now."

When she and Hector were alone, she said, "I got good news, too."

"I could use some," Hector said. "What is it?"

"You remember how you ask me to say if I ever get customer with leg or arm cut off? And to learn if the operation was in Tijuana, Mexico?"

"Yeah," Hector said, almost having forgotten about Basil and his special needs.

"Is missing foot okay?" Ivana asked.

She was wearing cutoff shorts, a tank top with a cotton shirt over it, and tennis shoes. It made her look more than ever like a kid, he thought. A fragile kind of kid. Dinko pulled to the curb in front of the liquor store on Hollywood Boulevard and tooted the horn once. She ran to his car, opened the door, and got in. She seemed different from the last time they'd met. He shut off the engine and looked at her.

"What happened, Lita?" he asked before she could speak.

"I am so full of fear, Dinko," she said.

"Is it your boss? What'd he do to you?"

"No," she said. "I have not done nothing for the boss. He is Russian man who is bartender. I am learning the lap dance from other girls, and I am serving drinks, and one time I do the dance onstage, but the boss he says I am bad dancer, like you say also. I only make little bit of money from tips so far. But yesterday something bad happens down there where you come from. Down by the harbor. Many people die."

"Yeah, the Asians that were found dead in a can at a storage yard. I read about it. What's that got to do with you?"

"I am living with two girls in our apartment. One is call Daisy. They find out on the television about the people dead in the, how you say, container?"

"Yeah, a can. A container. So what happened with Daisy?"

"She got crazy with sadness last night. She scream, she cry. She say a dead one down there is the baby sister. And she say she is running to police. Violet say, 'No, Daisy. You must not run to police. Is great danger to you.' That is what she say to her."

"What? Daisy was gonna rat out the smuggling operation?"

"Sorry, I don't . . ."

"To tell about the people who brought them all to this country?"

"To tell, but the man who pay for them to come to America is our boss. He is the Korean man, call Mr. Kim. Hector sees me dancing in the place where you first meet me and calls Mr. Kim, who is boss over Hector. He is the man all girls must pay money to for our job, even girls like me that come to this country without his help. I still got to pay him for the job and to live in the apartment and for the food and clothing I must wear in my work. And Mr. Hector is the one who collects the money for Mr. Kim."

Dinko thought it over, the consequences if the police learned that Kim and Hector Cozzo were involved in the smuggling caper that had gone way sideways. "I hope you're not worrying about Hector," Dinko said. "He's always been just a second-rate hustler, but if he wants to work for gangsters, then he deserves to go to jail with them. If I know Hector, he'll end up ratting out his boss. Is that what you're worrying about, my old friend Hector getting arrested?"

"No, Dinko, I am in fear for me!" she said. "When Daisy runs away I try to call her back. She is the best girl of all I meet here. I go out of our apartment and run after her. When I arrive to the corner, I see the big car come by. The big black car with shiny wheels. Daisy stops at the corner and the driver of the black car tells something to her and he opens up the door. Daisy looks at him. She yells loud at him in the Korea language. Then she looks very afraid. Then she says something more in the language. But then she has a look of fear and she gets into the car. I run up to see who is the driver of the big black car."

"Let me guess: it was the Korean."

"I cannot say because I only see some of his head, but I *think* it is Mr. Kim."

"I get it. So you're scared that because she didn't come home last night, he did something bad to her. Is that it?"

"That is it."

"So you're scared for Daisy?"

"And for me also," she said. "When I get back to my apartment I am so full of fear I say to Violet that I see Daisy talking to some man in a black car, but I do not say he look like Mr. Kim."

Dinko was stopped cold by that bit of information. Then he said, "This is not my problem."

"No," she said. "Is not."

"I got nothing to do with these Hollywood players."

"No," Lita said.

"Just because I gave you a ride, that don't make me responsible for you."

"No," she said.

"Goddamnit," he said. "Why did you call *me*?"

"You was good to me," she said. "I do not know nobody but the girls I am working with. They cannot help me. They cannot help nobody."

"Goddamnit," he said. "You expect a lot from a stranger."

"I am sorry. I am sorry I call you. Please forgive."

She started to get out of the car. He said, "Wait a minute. Sit down. Lemme think."

Then he said, "Maybe Kim just had a chat with Daisy and talked her outta snitching him off to the police. Maybe she's staying overnight with Kim for a kiss and a cuddle. I think pimps are good at that kind of thing. She's probably fine."

Lita said, "But if Daisy is not fine, Violet can tell Mr. Kim what I say to her. About how Daisy went away in a black car with shiny wheels."

"Are you sure you did not tell Violet you thought it was Mr. Kim in the car?"

"No, I had too much fear to say the man look like Mr. Kim. Then I know I got to run away from those persons."

"Did you tell her that Daisy was speaking Korean to the guy in the car?"

Lita thought about it and said, "Maybe I tell that to Violet."

"Christ," Dinko said. "Tell you what, can you come home with me tonight? I'll take you to my house, and tomorrow you can call and see if she came back. If Kim talked her outta going to the cops and she's back to normal, I'll drive you back here to Hollywood. But I wish you'd stay in Pedro or Wilmington or maybe Long Beach and get an ordinary job."

"I cannot earn enough money cleaning the houses, Dinko."

"Yeah, yeah, you said. Your mother and brothers back in Mexico. Anyways, run back to your apartment now and get a few overnight things."

"People like me do not got things for one night," she said. "All I got is in one big *maleta*."

"Okay, go get the big *maleta*," Dinko said. "Let's get going."

He waited twenty minutes, until she came struggling back along the street, now wearing a jersey-knit wrap dress that he figured she'd maybe bought on Alvarado Street for about twenty bucks. She was carrying a heavy piece of worn leather luggage with both hands.

He got out of the car and took it from her and loaded it in the open hatchback of the Jeep. When he got back in the car and looked at the girl beside him, he thought, What the fuck am I doing? Why am I taking on this kind of crazy responsibility? I'm not her daddy. She's just a Mexican whore!

His frustration rising, he told her, "I'm only thirty-one years old and somehow you make me feel like an old man with these responsibilities I didn't choose."

"I do not understand," she said.

"Neither do I," he said.

He started up the car and headed east, toward the Harbor Freeway. When he was driving south on the freeway he said, "I bet you think I'm bringing you home to have sex with you, right?"

She continued looking straight ahead at the road, as though she was expecting exactly that from him, and she said, "I am no child, Dinko."

"Yeah, you keep saying that," he said. "But I got a news flash. Sex's got nothing to do with why I'm being such a stupid bozo. If it did, it might make a little sense. If it did, I wouldn't be taking you home to my mother's house. There's no sex, drugs, or rock 'n' roll under *her* roof, I can tell you. So I don't know why the hell I'm doing this."

Another silence, until she said quietly, "I think I am understanding why you help me, Dinko."

"Yeah?" he said. "Wanna clue me in?"

"We got words in Spanish." She turned her face toward his. "You have the *compasión*. This mean, I know with my heart, you are very kind man, Dinko."

EIGHT

T HE ROLL CALL that afternoon was boring, as usual. Sergeant Murillo told his officers to report any complaints regarding illegal Somali wire transfers to the detectives. He also alerted them that Vietnamese drug dealers were removing the guts from ordinary battery packs and stuffing them with eight balls of dope for ingenious distribution by Hispanic street vendors.

Chester Toles, who was alert for once, said, "Are there any Americans left in Hollywood? Besides *some* of the people at this roll call?"

Sergeant Murillo looked at the assembly of a dozen coppers and said, "You all look sleepier than Chester tonight. Would it perk you up if we could hand out some awards tomorrow? How about if I buy a super-size pizza with the works for the car that wins the Hollywood Love Story Award tonight? We don't have a Hollywood moon, but there should still be enough domestic violence calls to choose from. But no repeats. The last winner was for the guy that shot his wife, claiming he thought she was a home invader when she came home from the market with an armload of groceries. And now she drives the neighbors crazy by blowing on a whistle every time she sticks her key in the lock. He might shoot her again, but I've already awarded a pizza for that one."

Hollywood Nate said, "What if a pissed-off neighbor shoots her this time?"

Sergeant Murillo thought it over. "Okay, that would qualify if a neighbor shoots her."

Flotsam and Jetsam were back from their brief vice assignment and Flotsam asked, "How about popping for a second pizza for a Quiet Desperation Award?"

Everyone knew that the QDA was an award initiated by the Oracle for the most bizarre or memorable event of the evening involving citizens living lives of quiet desperation. In Hollywood, there were always a lot of entries in that category.

Sergeant Murillo said, "Wait a minute." He looked in his wallet, then said, "Yeah, I can just about cover two if I can persuade the Cambodian at the pizzeria that my twenty percent off coupon should be doubled when I buy two super-size pizzas in a single order. He can't seem to work that out."

"I thought Asians're supposed to be good at math," Chester Toles said.

"Racial stereotype!" Mel Yarashi cried.

Jetsam said, "The guy's name is Benny, and he's a juicehead. Order them after midnight and I guarantee he'll be so toasted you can talk him into paying *you* for the pizzas."

The chance to win a super-size pizza perked up the coppers noticeably, and Sergeant Murillo affected the somber expression he normally showed before a joke, saying, "One last word of warning about citizen complaints. I took a phone call from an indignant gentleman last night who complained that a uniformed officer talked smack to him near Hollywood and Highland at twenty-thirty hours, after the citizen saw four uniformed coppers jacking up some young African-American men near the subway entrance."

"Who happened to be fun-loving Piru Bloods, no doubt," said Mel Yarashi. "Up from south L.A. for some giggles, crime, and violence."

"Regardless," Sergeant Murillo continued, "one of the male officers at the scene was approached by the citizen, who asked him, quote, 'Why is the LAPD always harassing minorities?' The officer affected an

Eastern European accent and described himself to the citizen as a police officer from Moscow Five-Oh on an exchange program with the LAPD. And he replied to the citizen, quote, 'A more relevant question is, Why are your missiles pointed at my country?' I managed to talk the citizen out of making me write a one twenty-eight, but I promised that I would have some harsh words for the officer in question and straighten him out. Now, my question to you is, Does anyone have any idea who that jokester might've been?"

Of course, nobody said a word, but every eyeball in the room shifted in the direction of Marius Tatarescu. After a moment Sergeant Murillo said, "No idea? Okay, must've been some copper from Watch Three. Let's go to work."

The Hollywood Love Story Award was won hands down by 6-X-72 on their second call, and it occurred almost two hours before the sun went down. Marius Tatarescu and Sophie Branson got a call to perhaps the most disgusting hotel in Hollywood Division. It was one of those fleabag weekly rentals where the stairwell reeked of urine and vomit. One of those places where dark wallpaper could move when someone shined a flashlight on it, and you'd suddenly become aware that the wallpaper was a solid mass of cockroaches.

Of course, it was a domestic violence call, and they spotted the person reporting standing in the hotel parking lot in his bare feet, wearing only lime-green sequined shorts that matched one of the streaks in his rainbow Mohawk. Both sides of his shaved head bore tats of various zodiac signs, and he had lip, nose, and eyebrow piercings, a face full of rings and studs. He was a white man in his mid-forties with the malnourished, spidery look of a long-term tweaker, and the front of his bony chest was running bright red from clotting blood. And he was clearly spun out, no doubt from smoking crystal. He waved when he saw the black-and-white, and Sophie Branson pulled into the lot.

"Damn," she said to her partner, "looks like a run to Hollywood Pres," meaning Hollywood Presbyterian Medical Center.

Marius said, "Better now than later, when the ER is filling up. He has maybe been stabbed."

When they got out of the car, the man said, "My old lady is the one that called, but I wanna talk to you first, though, so you can get the true story. My name is Willard Higgins, but my professional name is Ace Fingers. I'm a musician."

The big Romanian cop asked, "And where is this person you call your old lady?"

"Up in our room. Our room for *now*. We're getting evicted tomorrow, and it's her fault. Always yelling and bitching."

Sophie Branson looked closely at his bloody hollow chest but could not detect a wound. "What happened to you?" she asked. "And what does your female companion look like?"

"Look like? With the lights on, she's uglier than a basket of maggots. With the lights out and her clothes off, she's skinny and rough as an old wooden clothespin, so I guess she looks better in the dark. She's tweaked out even though I try to tell her life is about moderation."

Sophie said, "Yeah, I can see that all your face metal makes a very moderate fashion statement."

"It's self-expression," Ace said. "It's who I am."

"You're the Valley Boulevard Junk Yard?" Sophie said.

Marius said, "When my partner is asking what your wife is looking like, she means is your wife all lumped up like you?"

"Sorta," he said. "Follow me and you can see for yourself."

"What kind of weapons were involved in this situation?" Sophie asked.

"No weapons," Ace said. "Our love play went sideways and it pissed her off. There ain't been no crimes committed here. You'll see what I'm getting at when you meet her."

Sophie took a deep breath of smoggy air before entering the hotel behind the man, with Marius trailing behind her.

While climbing the greasy, reeking staircase, Sophie said, "I suppose you'll get around to telling us something about the love play that went sideways."

"It's sorta embarrassing to tell it to a woman," Ace said, "but I can tell it to your partner. I'd rather wait and see what kinda lie she tells first, if you don't mind."

Their room was on the second floor. When they entered, Sophie couldn't tell which smelled worse, the stairwell or this room. The bed was a double that sagged in the middle, making Sophie wonder if one of them would roll down on top of the other after they both fell asleep. It had a bedsheet on it that hadn't been changed since Mick Jagger was a virgin, and a large patch of darkening blood was soaked into it. There was a beat-up chest of drawers, a lamp on a mismatched wooden stand, and a tiny bathroom with the door shut that Sophie hoped she would not have to enter. They heard the toilet flush, so they knew that the woman was still alive in there.

When the bathroom door opened, Ace said to the cops, "May I present my little love truffle? This is Ms. Sadie Higgins."

"Don't call me Higgins, you son of a bitch," she said. "We ain't married and we ain't never getting married. Not after what you done to me." Then she looked at Sophie and said, "And don't ask if this is the maid's day off. I ain't into cop humor."

She might have been about Ace's age, but it was hard to say. She had full-sleeve tats on one arm; the other displayed ink that ran the length of her forearm and said, "Sexy Bee-yitch." Her brittle persimmon frizz was falling out in patches, and it looked like something was moving on her scalp. A spider? Sophie wondered. She had rosacea blooming on both cheeks, and her pale eyes were red and watery. It looked like rats had snacked on her legs. Sophie estimated that the five-foot-eight-inch woman weighed less than ninety pounds. She was wearing a red satin robe that covered most of her, but Sophie could see the dried blood on her bare feet. She was as tweaked out as he, and toothless except for a few upper molars and one rotting tooth in her lower grille.

"We understand that you are the one who called for us," Marius said to her.

"Sure, I called," she said. "The sick bastard raped me!"

"I think it's time to separate and talk privately," Sophie said.

"I can talk in front of him," the woman said. "He raped me and I want you to arrest him, and I want to prosecute his ass in a court of law and send the bastard to the joint, where he can find out what it's like to get choked and raped."

"He *choked* you?" Marius looked at Ace, who grimaced and shook his head slowly, to indicate it was all a terrible lie.

She sat down on the side of the bed, causing an explosion of dust motes, and said, "Excuse me, but I'm a little bit weak from his vicious assault."

"How long have you two been together?" Sophie asked.

"Two weeks," she said. "We met at a rock concert. He claims to be a musician, but his so-called silky guitar riffs sound like a baboon fucking a ukelele."

"Two months," Ace said. "Maybe more. We're as good as husband and wife, and we had lotsa sex before this. So how can sex with me all of a sudden be called rape?"

Neither cop was sure if there was going to be an advisement of Miranda rights here, but before Marius could tell Ace to wait outside with him the musician said, "Furthermore, I got a permission slip from her."

Sophie said, "A permission slip? For what?"

"It's in the top drawer in my wallet," Ace said to Marius. Then, to Sadie: "By the way, did you steal the twenty bucks while I was downstairs waiting for them?"

"I don't want nothing from you," she said, "except to hear you whimper like a sick dog when they lead you down the steps in handcuffs."

"Please, Officers, will one of you get the permission slip?" Ace said.

Marius opened the top drawer of the chest but jumped back, cursing in Romanian, when a Captain America cockroach shot across the drawer with a spectacular leap and landed on his hand.

"I gotta give that cockroach a perfect ten," Sophie said while Marius cursed some more and brushed the roach onto the bed, where several of its cousins skittered away.

Marius pulled on a latex glove and gingerly retrieved the wallet with a thumb and forefinger, handing it to Ace, who opened it and extracted a folded piece of yellow lined paper.

"Would you please read that to your partner?" Ace asked, casting a triumphant look at his woman, who was in a hands-on-hips snit, shooting mean looks at him.

Marius handed the note to Sophie, who read aloud: "'I hereby give you permission to do whatever you want with me. I am your kinky whore. You are my master of seduction. You can choke me while you fuck me with a jackass dildo.' It's signed 'Sadie Higgins.'"

"See, that ain't a valid permission slip!" Sadie cried in triumph. "We're not married. My name is Sadie Sloane, so it ain't legit. Now handcuff the bastard and get him outta here!"

"Is that what he did to you," Sophie asked Sadie. "What it says on the note?"

"Exactly," Ace answered. "That's what she wanted. The trouble is, she started bleeding real bad and I had to stop. I took her in the bathroom and tried to clean her off, but she wouldn't let me. She got real mad. Like it was my fault or something."

Marius Tatarescu, looking a bit queasy, asked Ace, "Is that how you got blood on you?"

"No," Ace said. "The sick bitch got so mad at me, she took the washrag she was mopping up her love rug with and threw it at me. Smacked me right in the chest with it. It's on the floor in the bathroom if you wanna see it."

"I shoulda threw a kitchen knife at you," Sadie said.

"I am taking your word that it is on the floor in there," Marius said. Then he looked beseechingly at his senior partner to deal with this one.

Sophie told the warring couple, "Stay put for a minute. We gotta talk." She motioned for Marius to follow her out into the hallway, leaving the door open in case combat might resume inside.

In the hallway she said sotto to Marius, "Partner, I've been on the Job twenty years, and as a matter of professional pride I almost *never* call a supervisor to a scene, but this one needs someone above our pay grade to sign off. If we just leave them, they might smoke some crank and turn violent. She might start hemorrhaging again and go into shock and die."

Marius said, "I got a good idea. Let us call for a detective. I think Charlie Gilford is not going to say we got to deal with these people. He will get us out of here."

"Excellent idea," Sophie said. "He can always find a way out of doing *any* kind of work. Let him decide if we've got a bookable offense here and if we need to transport Sadie to the ER."

Sophie Branson drew her rover from her Sam Browne and keyed the mike.

"Compassionate Charlie" Gilford was a D2 who had been on the Job long enough to retire, and he was probably even lazier than Chester Toles. He was the sole night-watch detective on duty, and he spent most of his time watching a little TV he kept in his desk or trying to figure out how to get a free burrito plate from a gourmet taco truck, or maybe something tasty from a Chinese dim sum joint where they gave him a "police discount" that he had previously negotiated.

Fortunately for 6-X-72, Charlie happened to be out and about, checking on new eateries, and was not far from the dirtbag hotel in question. They only had to wait ten minutes before the rangy, unkempt detective, who always wore sport coats and skinny pants that spoke of the 1970s at its worst—and the most outrageously ugly neckties on the entire LAPD—sauntered in, sucking his teeth as usual, ready to offer an expert opinion on just about anything. Sophie thought the color and pattern on this particular tie reminded her of decaying meat crawling with blowflies.

Sophie led Charlie inside the little hotel room and said to Ace and Sadie, "I want you to tell Detective Gilford exactly what you've told us. He's gonna decide what we should do about this."

Charlie remained with the couple, and Sophie went back out into the hallway, where she said to Marius, "Partner, somehow I don't think a bouquet's gonna be enough to settle this one. And I'll just hate it something awful if Charlie fails us here and we gotta take Sadie for medical treatment, and then haul Ace to jail for choking her out. I don't wanna occupy the same car space with either of them. They say everyone finally gets the face they deserve, and these two prove it. Which reminds me, did you see Barbra Streisand before her recent lift?"

"When it come to, how we say, the kiss-off artist, there is nobody better than Charlie Gilford," the Romanian said reassuringly. "Keep up the faith, Sophie."

Ten minutes passed, but they could still hear muffled conversation inside the room, with Sadie's voice only briefly rising in anger. Then the door opened and Charlie Gilford sauntered out with the couple still inside. The cops could see that the formerly warring tweakers now had an arm around each other's waist and were cooing softly.

Charlie sucked his teeth a couple of times and asked Marius and Sophie, "Do you know why they don't do regular sex?"

Sophie answered sotto, "Yeah, because they're a couple of degenerate skanks and her bug rug is probably crawling with crabs."

"See," Charlie said, shaking his head sadly, "that's why you bluesuits need a detective at the scene when a situation calls for subtle diplomacy as well as super sleuthing. For your information, the reason they don't do regular sex is because he recently got himself a Prince Albert."

"What is a Prince Albert?" Marius asked.

Charlie said, "Don't they teach you people nothing these days? Man, this is fucking Hollywood! A Prince Albert is a bolt through the pecker. He showed it to me. Wanna see it?"

"I think I can live without that part of a more complete Hollywood education," Sophie Branson said. "I'll pass."

"I shall pass also," Marius Tatarescu said, looking even queasier.

Just then, Ace and Sadie came to the open doorway. They still had an arm around each other, and her head was on his shoulder.

"Remember what I told you," Compassionate Charlie Gilford said to the cuddling couple. "When the going gets tough, you gotta step back and recall the songs of your youth. You're a musician, Ace. It should be easy for you."

Ace nodded, turned his face to Sadie, and sang in a raspy tenor, "'They say we're young and we don't know, we won't find out until we grow!'"

She sang back at him in a quivery soprano, "'Well, I don't know if all that's true, 'cause you got me and, baby, I got youuuuu!'"

And then they sang together, "'Babe! I got you, babe! I got you, babe!'" With Sadie grinning toothlessly at the man she loved for now.

Charlie Gilford turned to Sophie and Marius and said, "No medical treatment needed. She's all right. And there's been no crime here. It's all code four. You can go back out and clear."

As a farewell to Ace and Sadie, Charlie extended his arms, palms up, in a theatrical gesture and said to them, "You live in the land of dreams. This is Hollywood. Don't ever let the music stop playing."

"Bye-bye, Detective Gilford!" Ace called, beaming. Then he whispered to Sadie and they sang to him in unison, "'And the beat goes on! The beat goes onnnnn!'"

"Sonny and Cher would be proud!" Compassionate Charlie Gilford responded with a flourish, before descending the reeking staircase.

When Sophie and Marius were back in their shop and had cleared for calls, Sophie said, "Marius, are you in the mood for pizza?"

"I am always in the mood," he said. "Why do you ask?"

"Because I think we just iced the Hollywood Love Story Award. We caught one that *nobody's* gonna beat."

Dinko Babich had decided to take Lita Medina for a late lunch in San Pedro before the dreaded meeting at his mother's house. First he wanted to sit with her and talk more, and look at her, and try to think what he was going to do to help her. What *could* he do? Then he thought he could do what Croatians always do with a guest. He could feed her, that's what. He bought some sandwiches and a bottle of screw-top wine from the Italian deli and drove to Point Fermin Park.

They sat on the grass for two hours, she talking about her life in Mexico, glossing over the last few years spent working at the awful cantina in Guanajuato.

When it came to those years she said, "I do not wish to say to you how I live when I work at that place. It was very bad."

"You don't have to talk about that," Dinko said. "Not to me. Not ever." He wondered at his choice of the word "ever." Wasn't this the last time he'd ever see her?

"I am ashame," she said.

"Don't talk about it, don't think about it," he said. "You done what you had to do in the crummy world you were born into."

She said, "We wait one year for my father to come home, but he never come. He went with the coyotes to cross the border for work and we never hear nothing more."

"What month was it when he made the crossing?"

"*Agosto.*"

"That's a dangerous time," Dinko said. "A lotta migrants die of heat stroke."

"Me, I cross at Easter time," she said. "There was rain, but was okay. I pray to Santa María. The coyote is not a bad man, but I have to pay to him much of my money I save from the cantina."

"And you ended up dancing where I found you."

"Jes," she said, and he smiled at her pronunciation.

"It's not *jes,*" he said. "It's *yes.* Y-y-yes."

"Y-y-yes," she said, and they both laughed.

When it was his turn, he talked about working on the docks and living in Pedro all his life, so close to the big ocean.

Then Lita heard what she thought was a woman shrieking in terror. "What is that?" she cried.

Dinko laughed and said, "It's just a South Shores peacock. They're protected and feral. Nobody owns them. They'll walk up to your car and look at their reflection on the side of it and start pecking the hell out of your paint job. One musta wandered down here to the cliffs."

Lita turned and watched the colorful bird strutting across the lawn in the direction of the sidewalk, where a child had thrown cracker crumbs on the grass.

She laughed and said to him, "San Pedro is a beautiful place to live, Dinko."

"You think so?"

"Jes—I mean, yes. Very beautiful."

He peered out at the ocean. "Maybe you're right. When I see it through someone else's eyes." Then he looked at her and said, "Somebody else's lovely eyes."

She lowered her gaze and said, "You are lucky man to be in this place. I wish I do not have to go away to Hollywood. But I must. Is only way for me."

Time had never passed faster for Dinko Babich than it did that afternoon, as they looked out at the calm Pacific and at Catalina Island, which always seemed so deceptively close when the weather was clear. It felt as though Santa Catalina were a haven, a prize, something out there virtually within reach, but so far beyond them. They sat silently, content to gaze at the horizon with youthful daydreams, forgetting the threats from the real world around them.

When Dinko realized it was time to leave, he came to an inescapable understanding of his dilemma. He had a young girl with him who was a virtual stranger, with all she owned in the world in the back of his Jeep. And he was suspended from his job as a longshoreman with his checking account running dry, and his Croatian mother was going to crap a crucifix when he walked into the house with Lita. And yet . . . every time he looked into her upward-tilted, heavily lashed amber eyes, his heart started dancing and he couldn't focus on the hazardous burden he'd voluntarily shouldered. If he could be logical for a few minutes, he could think again that she was just a Mexican whore. And yet he could not be logical, not when looking directly at her, and listening to the soft lilt of her accented English.

As the end of their second hour together grew near he said, "Lita, we gotta go and face my mother."

* * *

Brigita Babich seemed confused, more than anything else, when Dinko entered the house at twilight and said, "Mom, this is Lita Medina. She's a friend who needs a place to stay tonight. I told her we'd help her."

The three-bedroom, three-and-a-half-bathroom home on the hill west of Gaffey was comfortable and solid, as befitting a crane operator like Jan Babich, who'd made a handsome living during his thirty-five years on the docks prior to his untimely death at the age of fifty-nine. The house had a red tile roof and white stucco walls, and had been worth nearly a hundred thousand more during the housing boom than it was now. There was a large family room where Dinko and his late father had played pool and video games. Although the living room's overstuffed furniture was getting old, it had been costly in its day and was still comfortable and solid, like the house itself.

Every veteran crane operator in San Pedro might've had a house as substantial as the Babich home, but to Lita Medina it was a grand mansion, easily the finest house she had ever entered in her life.

Lita said to Brigita Babich, "I am very honor to meet with you, señora. I am sorry to be a problem."

"Yes, nice to meet you, too," Brigita Babich said, without offering her hand. Then: "Sit down for a moment and relax while I have a private chat with my son."

Lita Medina waited uncomfortably in the living room while Brigita led her only child into the master bedroom, where she closed the door and said, "Dinko, what the hell is this all about?"

"She's a girl I met through Hector Cozzo, and she has nowhere to go tonight."

"Hector Cozzo?" she said. "That boy was no good when *times* were good. He's a bum who always got in trouble. What were you doing with Hector?"

"He was never bad," Dinko said. "He was just a little hustler and still is. I ran into him and did him a favor. He's kind of an . . . agent. Still so lame he calls himself Hector the selector, and he saw this girl and got her a job in Hollywood. But it's not working out so good."

"A job doing what?"

"She's a dancer."

"A dancer? What kind of dancer?"

"In a nightclub. And she's also a cocktail waitress."

"Boy, are you crazy?" his mother said. "What's got into you?"

"She's basically a good girl," Dinko said. "A lost girl. She's trying to make enough money to send to her sick mother and little brothers in Mexico."

"Dinko, that's what they all say, the kind of girls that dance in Hollywood nightclubs."

"You don't know nothing about Hollywood nightclubs," Dinko said.

"I know about the kind of young girls who would work in them," Brigita said. "And how old is she, sixteen?"

"She's nineteen plus."

"So she says. She looks like a child."

"She's nineteen years and four months old. She's an adult."

"And you're thirty-one going on seventeen. Behaving like you're still in high school! Are you having sex with her?"

"No! I barely know her. This is the second time I've ever even been with her. Why can't she sleep in the spare bedroom? It hadn't been used in . . . I don't know how long, till Tina and Goran used it."

"I haven't changed the sheets yet."

"She won't care. She's desperate and in trouble."

Brigita Babich took her son by the shoulders and said, "What kinda trouble? And you better tell me the truth."

Dinko said, "She got a job at this nightclub, thanks to Hector. And a girl that dances there has disappeared, and . . . well, she may be okay, but maybe not. The trouble is, Lita saw the guy who took her away. And the guy's sort of a . . . bad guy."

Brigita Babich retreated two steps in disbelief and then came back to just inches away from Dinko and said, "That's perfect. So you bring her here, where we can all get murdered in our sleep?"

"It's not like that," he said. "We'll probably find out tomorrow that the girl's fine, and I'll drive Lita back to her place in Hollywood."

"No!" Brigita said. "I don't like this. I won't have it. And aren't you the one that's always complaining about Mexicans taking over Pedro? You change your tune when it comes to a beautiful young one like her, don't you?"

It was then that he played his trump card. He used the only word that could possibly move his mother to relent. He said, "Mom, she's a good Catholic girl in trouble. What could I do?"

Brigita paused and looked away, bobbing her head angrily because he'd stooped to using her religion to persuade her. She said, "If she's afraid of gangsters, she should call the police."

Dinko said, "She's not exactly in this country legally. And she just needs a place to stay for one night. What would Jesus do?"

"Don't you Jesus me, Dinko Babich!" his mother said. "You, who never go to Mass on holy days and only go on Sunday when I drag you. Don't you talk Jesus to me!"

"I go to the Saturday vigil Mass lots of times that you don't know about."

"You lie too easy," she said.

Dinko lied again: "Lita asked me if we have a church near here. She wants to go to Mary Star of the Sea tomorrow and light a candle for the missing dancer and pray for her safe return. That's the kind of girl Lita is."

After a long pause, Brigita Babich said, "You have *always* been a con man! So all right, strip the sheets from the spare room and put them in the washer. Nobody's gonna sleep on soiled sheets in *my* house." Then she opened the door and walked down the hallway to the living room.

Lita Medina jumped to her feet, but Brigita Babich said, "Sit down, sweetheart. Rest yourself. Are you hungry? I have some *mostaccioli* I can warm up for you. And we have sauerkraut, made the Croatian way, with tomato sauce."

* * *

Hector Cozza finally bit the bullet, and it was a hard bite. After he'd read the entire *Los Angeles Times* story about the disaster at the container yard in Wilmington, his call to Kim resulted in his having to hold the cell phone away to save an eardrum.

"Hector!" the Korean shouted. "I call you six times yesterday and today! Where you were?"

Hector had never known the Korean to be this angry. He said, "My cell phone died on me and I didn't even know it. I was kinda sick, too. Musta ate something that didn't agree with me."

"You meet with me in one hour. The Russian bar. You be there, Hector. You listening to me?"

"Yeah, I'll be there," Hector said. "Rasputin's Retreat in one hour."

When he clicked off, he thought, Christ! Not that miserable place. He figured maybe he should get there early and have the surly commie bartender pour him a few ounces of vodka. He was going to need it before facing Kim. He understood vaguely that part of the calamity in the container storage yard was somehow going to blow back on him so that Kim could evade responsibility for it with Markov, or whoever the fuck was Kim's partner on that deal.

That was the thing about working with these people: Hector never quite knew who was totally in charge. By now, Hector was sure that neither Markov nor Kim were bucks-up businessmen. The more he nosed around and checked licenses at the establishments, the more he came to conclude that everything was leased: the property, the cars, even some of the kitchen equipment and restaurant furnishings. He'd seen a bill from a restaurant supplier that proved as much.

He wished he could find out where they both lived. He suspected that Markov lived up on Mount Olympus, in the Hollywood Hills, because Kim had said something about coming *down* from the boss's house, near where "other Russians lived." Hector knew that there were a number of Middle Eastern and Eastern European home owners up there, some of them with holdings but some of them living on fast talk and flash money. As to Kim, well, he just figured that the big slope probably lived in Koreatown with the rest of the pig-guts-and-kimchi crowd. Kim had probably invested plenty in the latest human-trafficking venture that went very sideways, so Hector guessed he was low on bank.

All this made him remember that the horrible Russian pervert Basil was back in town, and Hector had the phone number Ivana had given him of a dude with one foot who might turn out to be a soul brother to the Muscovite freak. If he was to lose points with Kim, maybe he could get some back with Markov. That is, if he could make Basil happy by organizing a little drinks party with the peg-leg guy and fulfill the Russian's fantasies. He could get Ivana to be there too, or one of the other bitches that would fuck anything if the price was right, even freaks that got off on amputation.

Well before it turned dark, 6-X-66 had started getting routine calls in east Hollywood. There was a burglary report to be taken at an old bungalow owned by a Hispanic legal secretary who worked in Century City. And a van had been stolen on Western Avenue near Fountain while a pest control specialist whose van was lettered with "Virgil the Vermin Slayer" was away from it, treating a house for dry rot.

The exterminator's first words to Hollywood Nate and Britney Small were "I only wish I could poison the fucking vermin that stole my truck!"

The reports were Nate's to write, since Britney was the driver, and afterward she drove to the station to get them signed by a supervisor.

While they were sitting in the report room, Nate said to her, "A sure sign of aging is when a cop would rather write reports than drive. If you notice, the young hotdogs always wanna drive. None of them wanna ride shotgun and keep books."

"I guess I must be aging," Britney said. "I don't mind writing reports at all. In fact, I kinda like it. I always got A's in English."

Nate smiled at his young partner. "Sure, Britney, you're aging. In about five years you might actually be able to walk into a club on the

Sunset Strip and buy a drink without getting carded. How old're you, twenty-two?"

"Twenty-four," she said. Then she grinned and added, "I'm getting to be an OG, too."

None of the Old Guys ever complained about being assigned with petite Britney Small, by virtue of her proven bravery and the street cred she'd earned in last year's gunfight. In the two years she'd been at Hollywood Division, she'd made a name for herself as a calm and reliable partner with a quiet sense of humor who always had your back.

Nate said, "Please tell me that you don't see a thirty-nine-year-old hunk like me as an OG. I'm an actor, and the aging process makes actors irrelevant. Tell me you're kidding or I'll kill myself in the parking lot before my fortieth birthday."

"Okay, I'm kidding," Britney said. "You'll *never* be an OG. And you really *are* a hunk. All the women in the locker room talk about Hollywood Nate and how you're so ripped from all the working out, and how they'd die to have your gorgeous wavy hair—"

"Which is getting very gray on the sides, if you'll notice."

"Which only makes you sexier. And I think that one of these days you're gonna get a call from your agent—"

"I fired the worthless bastard."

"Or a call from somebody in show business about a big movie where they need a handsome copper type, and it'll be you that gets the gig."

Nate took a five-dollar bill from his wallet and said, "Young Britney, you just earned yourself a soda. Get us both one, and make mine diet."

It was 9:15 P.M. by the time Hector Cozzo got to Rasputin's Retreat. The small parking lot was jammed, so he parked his red Mercedes SL on the boulevard, making sure there was plenty of room fore and aft of his bumpers, since those fucking old Russkie drunk drivers would be coming and going all evening. When he got inside he couldn't find a place to sit except at the end of the bar.

It took several minutes for the burly Russian bartender to saunter down to him and raise his chin an inch or two by way of recognition.

"Has Mr. Kim come in yet?" Hector asked.

"No," the bartender said.

"Gimme a vodka," Hector said. "Better make it a double."

"Russian or shit vodka?" the bartender mumbled.

"Russian, of course," Hector said, with a smarmy smile that brought a scowl from the bartender. Hector thought he'd better watch the big asshole to make sure he didn't spit in the glass.

Hector finished that one and was about to order another when he saw Kim enter. Hector watched the Korean go straight to the back office and he knew that the slope had a key to every door in every building Markov leased. As Hector was walking through the dark and increasingly noisy barroom, he saw two men in Members Only jackets sitting at a small table near the door. One of them looked to him like the Armenian who'd stopped him outside Shanghai Massage to inform him that only Armenians should be operating massage parlors in or near Little Armenia.

Hector got to the office door, tapped three times, and opened it. When he entered, Kim stepped from behind the door and, grabbing him by the back of the neck, threw him across the room, where he banged his right hip into the corner of the desk and yelped in pain. Then Kim strode forward and, with a leg sweep, kicked Hector's pins out from under him. He hit the Oriental rug hard on his back, his head bouncing off the floor.

Hector yelled, "What the fuck?"

"You shut up your mouth or I kill you!" Kim said.

"Okay, I won't say nothing!" Hector promised, cringing. "I won't even *think* nothing!"

The Korean was about fifty years old and only a little over six feet tall, but he was very wide, large-boned, and heavily muscled. Kim had hands like goalie mitts and the lantern jaw of André the Giant, and while Hector was on his back looking up, he felt that he *was* looking at the

Giant's buckethead cousin. The Korean's eyes were lifeless, and his big yellow teeth were bared, as if he wanted to take a bite out of the small man cowering at his feet.

"Mr. Kim," Hector said, averting his eyes. "Can I jist ask why I'm being treated like this?"

The Korean sat on the edge of the desk and stared down at Hector Cozzo, who didn't dare get up. All Hector could hear over the buzzing in his ears was Kim breathing. It sounded rheumy, like the wheezing of Hector's asthmatic younger brother, which he'd listened to for years.

"You promise me the container will get stolen and brought to me," Kim said.

"No, Mr. Kim!" Hector said. "I'm sorry to disagree, but you got it wrong. I said I would *try* to make that happen for you. I only promised I would talk to a cruiser I know with the Harbor City Crips. I said that if you were sure of the exact location and the number on the can, his posse *might* be able to go in with guns and a stolen truck and do the job. That's what I promised, because it's been done before. But the stupid nigger got busted, and there was a parole hold on him and the plan fell apart!"

"You know how much money I lose?" Kim said.

Hector spotted a relaxing of Kim's neck muscles and felt he might be able to cross this hazardous stream without disturbing the dead-eyed croc eyeing him on the bank.

"Mr. Kim," he said, "please let me remind you I was jist suggesting a stopgap service when your deal fell apart. I mean, I didn't ask you no questions, but I know it musta cost you plenty to bribe somebody, maybe a security guard at the container yard? But it was really the trucker that screwed you big-time when he went south with the retainer money you musta paid him. Am I right? If your trucker had picked up the container as planned, none of this woulda happened."

Kim held up a hand to silence Hector's babbling. He said, "You say you will help me get the container."

Kim's lip was still curled in menace, causing Hector to hang on to his cringe and reply, "Not exactly, Mr. Kim. Because I'm an old San

Pedro guy, I jist said I *might* be able to help you, but I never asked you for no front money, did I? How could anybody have predicted that the"—he almost said "stupid bucketheads" but stopped himself in time—"that the migrants in there would light a stove or a heater or whatever the fuck they lit after the escape door got blocked? Was that my fault, too?"

Hector could literally see the Korean mulling it over, his jaws clenching and unclenching, his brows knitting, relaxing, then knitting again as the thug reconsidered.

Finally Kim said, "Stand up on your feet."

Hector got up painfully, saying, "My hip feels broke."

Kim said, "I lose money. Mr. Markov, he lose money. Now *you* will lose money, too. You will pay me a fine of twenty thousand dollars. You pay to me five thousand a month. You don't pay, the interest adds on. You understand me, Hector?"

"Mr. Kim, you don't see tits on me, do you?" Hector whined. "Why do you treat me like a bitch for trying to help you?"

"I am make it very easy on you, Hector," Kim said. "You do not got no idea how much we lose on this deal."

Until then Hector had thought that Kim was acting as an independent contractor without Markov on Asian smuggling operations. "I did my best for you," he said. "And for Mr. Markov."

"Next time you try more hard," Kim said. "Now go. If Mr. Markov is very mad and wish to fire you, I will still want my twenty thousand dollars. You understand?"

Before he opened the door, Hector said, "Mr. Kim, jist to avoid more trouble here, do you have any idea what happened to Daisy?"

Kim's eyes narrowed again, and he stood up from the edge of the desk abruptly. In a guttural voice he said, "Why do you talk about Daisy?"

Hector said, "I was told by a girl at Shanghai Massage that Daisy's sister was one of the dead girls and that Daisy was threatening to go to the cops. The second I walked in I was gonna tell you that, but you didn't give me a chance."

Kim said, "I know nothing about the sister and nothing about Daisy. Where is Daisy at?"

"Nobody knows," Hector said. "She ran away."

"Let her go," Kim said. "We do not need her. We got other employees who do better work. Tell those girls they better forget Daisy. You understand me?"

"I understand." Kim had moved so close to Hector he could see long scratches along the Korean's jawline on one side of his face.

"I want you to know something I learn from a Filipino," Kim said. "He learn it from the drug smugglers. Seven-Up keeps the fizzy longer than Coke or Pepsi."

"I don't get it," Hector said.

"For shooting up the nose when you sit in a chair with hands tied behind you. The pain feels like your head blows up. I always keep plenty of Seven-Up, Hector. You remember that."

Hector opened the door and shuffled back out through the crowded barroom, grimacing from the pain in his hip and from Kim's terrifying talk of torture. He noticed that the two men were not at the table by the door. That was when he remembered that he was going to tell Kim he thought he'd seen the Armenian who'd fronted him off, but he wasn't going back in that office now. Not for anything.

When he got to his car he was relieved to see that nobody was even close to either bumper, even though the street was jammed with parked cars and the night traffic was as relentless as usual.

He was about to use his keyless entry when he spotted it. Scratched across the hood of his beautiful red Mercedes SL, in eight-inch letters, was "AP."

Hector stood beside his car and yelled, "Motherfuckers!"

He heard brakes screech, and a male voice beside him said, "Is everything okay?" He looked around and saw that a black-and-white police car had stopped in the traffic lane with its light bar turned on.

"No, things ain't okay!" he yelled to the passenger cop. "Look at my car!"

Hollywood Nate Weiss got out, shined his light on the scarred hood, and said, "AP stands for Armenian Power."

"No shit!" Hector barked. "Some Armo cocksucker keyed my new Benz!"

"Probably a local vandal," Nate offered.

He was joined by Britney Small, who also shined her light on the scarred hood and said, "That's a shame. A beautiful car like that."

"Aw, fuck!" Hector said. "I may as well make a police report for the insurance company as long as you're here. My name's Hector Cozzo. Here's my address."

He took out his driver's license, but Nate said, "Sir, we're very short-handed and our superiors want us out here on patrol. That's the kind of report you need to make at the front desk of Hollywood Station. It's at One three five eight North Wilcox."

Hector said, "You mean my car gets keyed by some Armo son of a bitch and I can't even make a police report at my convenience?"

"You can, sir," Britney said. "Whenever it's convenient, drop by Hollywood Station and—"

Hector sneered, "This is the kind of police service us taxpayers get, huh? Well, forget about it. I'm calling my councilman." He turned to Nate and said, "So thanks a lot, Officer . . ." He looked at Hollywood Nate's nameplate and said, "I shoulda known." Then he got into his car, started it up, and drove away.

After they got back in their shop, Britney said, "What'd he mean when he said, 'I shoulda known'?"

Hollywood Nate Weiss said, "He means that he shoulda known that I'm a Jew."

Britney was incensed. "What a rude dirtbag!" she said. After she was driving for a few minutes she asked, "*Are* you?"

"Am I what?" Nate said.

"Jewish."

"I used to be," Nate said, "a long time ago."

"What're you now?"

Hollywood Nate thought it over and said, "A fair to middling copper and a failed actor."

Britney Small shook her head slowly and drove for a while before saying, "Nate, even it that were true, which it certainly isn't, it would still be better than the other way around. Can you see that?"

Hollywood Nate looked at his earnest young partner in surprise. Then he smiled ironically. "Britney, I think you're absolutely right. Which means you've just succeeded in wrecking a lot of the enjoyment I get from self-pity. I owe you another soda for that. No, make it a burger with the works. You're a little too lean from spending too much time in the weight room."

NINE

LATE THE NEXT morning Dinko Babich was doing something he thought he'd never do in his lifetime. Lita Medina had him strolling with her along Pacific Avenue in San Pedro, exploring various low-end stores and examining goods sold on the street by vendors as she chattered in Spanish to practically everyone she encountered, especially young Hispanic mothers with babies riding on their hips. And the most astonishing thing was, he was actually enjoying himself!

Lita was wearing faded jeans, a tank top, and tennis shoes, and Dinko thought she looked sensational. And so did just about everyone else on the avenue, as he could tell by the appreciative glances she received.

At one point he said to her, "You really rock those jeans."

She said, "'Rock'?"

"Never mind," he said. "Everyone around here thinks I'm one lucky gringo."

She shrugged and said, "You think I talk funny? I think *you* talk funny."

"I'd buy us a taquito or something," he told her, "but I'm stuffed from breakfast."

"Your *mamá*," Lita said, "she make for us the most food I ever see on a morning table. I cannot eat nothing until tomorrow maybe."

"She's trying to make a Croatian outta you," Dinko said. "But I like you just the way you are."

Lita smiled at the compliment and said, "And you? How can you stay so . . . how you say . . . ?"

"Tall and handsome?"

She laughed and said, "No. I mean, jes, you are tall and handsome, but . . ."

"Y-y-yes," he said.

"Y-y-yes," she said, laughing again. "But what is the word for not fat?"

"Skinny," he said, "*Flaco*. That's me. But super handsome."

She gave him a light poke for his banter and said, "I am very happy today. I am never so happy since I come to this country. You are very lucky man, Dinko. This San Pedro is place of magic, I think."

Dinko Babich looked around and wished he could see his Pedro world through the eyes of this girl. And suddenly it occurred to him that he, too, was very happy today. He hadn't been so happy since he was a kid going out fishing with his father and other Croatian men and their sons. Back when his life was full of possibilities and Pedro was the only world he wanted.

"Dinko, look!" she said, grabbing his hand and rushing him toward a man selling knockoffs of famous clothing brands from a display on the sidewalk. The man wore a black beret and a Zapata mustache and had a large green parrot on his shoulder. He was feeding the parrot nuts to make it talk to customers.

When Lita stood in front of the parrot, her eyes shining with excitement, the man said to the parrot, "*¿Qué piensas, mi hijo?*"

And the parrot looked at Lita and said, "*Muy hermosa.*"

Lita clapped her hands like a child and Dinko gave the parrot man a few dollars, saying, "That bird's got good taste."

A few minutes later they were strolling again, not talking, just looking at the street and the sky and feeling the breeze from the Pacific blowing through their hair. She took his hand once more and they walked, with Dinko Babich imagining she could hear his heart thrumming a powerful pulse into his throat.

This girl! he thought. What was happening to him? The tiny world in which he lived was shape-shifting. Nothing seemed the same when he looked around now. Was he truly seeing everything through *her* eyes? Was that good or bad for him? She was so . . . *alive.*

She held his hand firmly and he raised her hand up and looked at it. "You have beautiful hands," he said. "*Muy hermosa.*"

Lita smiled self-consciously and pointed to a flower vendor, saying, "I wish to buy flowers for your *mamá.*"

He watched her carefully checking how much she had in the pocket of her jeans, and he realized that whatever she had there and in her purse back at the house was *all* she had. She peeled ten dollars from a small fold of bills and said, "What you think, Dinko?" She pointed to a yellow rose. "She likes the yellow *rosas?*"

Her pronunciation of "yellow" came out as "jellow."

"Jell-O is something we eat for dessert," Dinko said, "particularly when we're counting calories."

"*¿Cómo?*"

"I'll explain it later. You pronounce the color 'yellow.' Y-y-yellow."

"Y-y-yellow," she said. "You think I ever learn?"

"I'll teach you with the greatest of pleasure," he said, "no matter *how* long it takes."

She stopped smiling and studied him for a moment, then shifted her gaze back to the flowers, pointed, and said, "*Lila.*"

"We call it 'lilac,'" Dinko said. "It figures. Your mother's maiden name means 'flowers' in English."

"I do not understand," she said.

"Lita Medina Flores," he said. "You're a child of the flowers."

"My funny boy," she said, squeezing his hand.

She paid for a small bouquet of lilacs and Dinko pulled a sprig from the bunch and held it up beside her face. "Yes, that's your flower," he said. "No doubt about it. Shall we go home and give my mom your *lila?*"

Brigita Babich was leaning against the kitchen counter and talking on a wall phone that had been there for thirty years. When she heard them come in the front door, she finished her conversation with one of the women from church who was planning a huge wedding at Croatian Hall.

Brigita entered the living room and found Lita standing shyly next to Dinko with a bouquet of lilacs, which she held out, saying, "Señora, I thank you with my heart for the kindness I have receive from you here."

"For me?" Brigita said. "You bought lilacs for me?"

"She did," Dinko said.

"Oh, sweetheart!" Brigita said, taking the lilacs and wrapping a sturdy arm around the willowy girl.

Dinko looked solemn when he pulled the cell phone from his pocket and said, "Lita, take this into the bedroom and call your apartment. Find out if Daisy has returned."

Her mouth turned down at the corners with this sudden intrusion from her other world and she said, "Yes, I must call. Is time for me to go back."

After Lita was in the bedroom and out of earshot, Dinko looked his mother in the eye and told her, "If that girl Daisy is still missing with only the clothes on her back, I'm not gonna let Lita go back there today."

Brigita Babich said, "Son, she's not a stray puppy you can find and just keep. She has her own life to live."

"That's a dangerous life."

"Then take her to the police."

"There's nothing that can be proved at this point. A Korean roommate left suddenly in a car with a Korean they work for. That's according to Lita. But what if the guy denies it and Daisy doesn't come back? What is that guy gonna do if Lita drags him into a very suspicious missing persons case with her suggestion that he knows what happened to Daisy?"

They stopped talking when Lita rejoined them in the kitchen, holding Dinko's cell phone in her hand.

She said gravely, "Violet says that Daisy is not there. She is not phoning nobody. Violet says she made a phone call to Mr. Kim but he says he don't know nothing about Daisy. He says he is not seeing Daisy for a week. Mr. Kim is saying a lie!"

"Lita," Dinko said, "this is very important. Did Violet let Mr. Kim know that you saw Daisy with somebody in a black car outside their apartment?"

"She says no, she does not tell him that."

"Do you believe her?"

Lita thought it over and said, "Violet is not such a good girl like Daisy. I think maybe she tells him if he pays her money for telling."

"Does Violet know that you left that place with my son?" Brigita asked with urgency.

"No," Lita said. "I never tell nothing about Dinko. I tell to Violet that I go to my old job because I no longer wish to work at Club Samara."

Both Dinko and Brigita Babich could clearly see the fear on the girl's face, and it was Dinko's mother who spoke first. She said, "Please stay with us for a few days, sweetie. We'll need a little more time to figure this thing out."

Hector was still in bed at 2:00 P.M. He had drunk nearly half a bottle of vodka the night before, and he'd swallowed a couple of zannies with it. For the past two hours he'd been lying there thinking of how to escape the trouble he was in. There had to be a way to avoid the twenty-grand obligation to Kim, but no matter how he figured it, the only answer was to go over Kim's head to Markov.

Then again, the way things were falling apart, he wasn't even sure if Markov was the main man in the human-trafficking operation. Christ, maybe there was somebody making them *both* dance? Kim had flat-out claimed that Markov had lost money in that calamity too, so how eager would Markov be to answer a plea for intercession from Hector Cozzo?

Hector tried to convince himself that Kim was all bluff, that he was basically a pimp and a smuggler but not a killer. That pitiful attempt at solace sustained him for about sixty seconds, and then the fear resumed. Hector was positive that Kim could kill him and that it wouldn't be a merciful death. And death made him think of the missing Daisy, who'd threatened to go to the cops and report all of them, including Hector the collector.

He had never before tried the cell number Markov had given him, along with orders to use it only in an emergency. Well, if there was ever a fucking emergency, this was it. He dialed, hesitated, then pressed the send button.

Markov answered so fast it startled him: "Yes?"

"Sir," Hector said, "I'm sorry to be calling you like this, but it's an emergency."

"What is it?"

"Can I talk on the phone?"

"From this end, yes. I hope your end is secure. Be discreet in what you say."

Hector said, "Sir, I paid a visit to Mr. K., and he's very unhappy with me and he's being very unfair. He thinks some of what happened to his . . . recent overseas shipment is my fault. He thinks I promised to rescue the situation, but I never promised that. I only said I'd try to help. It turns out I couldn't, and now he's punishing me in a very severe way. I need you to get him off me. Would you like to know what he's done to me so far?"

"No," Markov said. "I will talk to him and get back to you. Is that all?"

"No, sir," Hector said. "Another thing is, one of our employees went missing the other day after making very serious threats. I thought you should know."

There was quiet on the line, and then Markov said, "Why have I not been told of this before now?"

"You gotta ask Mr. K. about that," Hector said. "I'm jist trying to be loyal to you."

"Is that all?"

"Not quite," Hector said. "You remember the thing you asked me to inform certain employees about? Regarding the kind of person that Mr. B.

from Moscow would be interested in? Well, I think I have someone who Mr. B. will be excited to meet."

"A woman?"

"No, that's the only drawback. But he got the work done down in T.J., so I think this meeting is gonna work for Mr. B. Maybe I could pick up one of the girls and invite this guy to a party that'd make Mr. B. so thrilled he'd be begging to do business with you. But if something don't work out, please don't put all the blame on me the way Mr. K. does."

"All right," Markov said. "Set it up the way you usually do at the usual place. If the investment comes in from Mr. B., I will make sure that Mr. K. never troubles you again."

"Thank you, sir," Hector said.

"But before you hang up," Markov said, "I want you to find out all you can about the missing employee. I am very surprised and very disappointed that I have not heard about all this from Mr. K."

"I'll do that right away," Hector said. "And thank you again, sir."

Hector Cozzo immediately dialed the number Ivana had given to him for her peg-leg customer named Kelly.

The cold phone at the Hollywood vice unit was answered by Sergeant Hawthorne, who simply said, "Hello."

Hector said, "Can I speak to Kelly?"

Sergeant Hawthorne had given up on his wild idea and could hardly believe this. "He's not here at present. May I take a message?"

"When's he coming back?"

"Hard to say, but can I have your number?"

"Never mind," Hector said. He was about to terminate the call, but Sergeant Hawthorne said, "Wait! I can get a message to him. Can you call back in an hour?"

"Okay," Hector said, and clicked off.

"I can't believe it!" Sergeant Hawthorne told one of his bearded vice cops working at a computer. "It worked!"

"What worked?"

"My apotemnophilia idea!"

"I can't even say the word," the vice cop said, "but I'm glad it worked."

Sergeant Hawthorne looked at the clock. The surfer cops were on Watch 5, and their roll call started at 5:00 P.M., two hours from now. He dialed Jetsam's home number. No answer. Then he dialed Flotsam's home number, with the same result. Then he said to the vice cop, "Those surf monsters couldn't still be at the beach this late in the afternoon, could they?"

It turned out that they could. Both of the surfer cops' cell phones rang, but the phones were wrapped in a large towel on the warm white sand of Malibu Beach. Jetsam was doing his famous (by now) barrel ride after he'd caught a juicy, and two surf bunnies were on the shoreline cheering on the brave surfer with a carbon-and-polyurethane prosthesis attached to his stump.

Flotsam was in a black wet suit, floating on his board nearby and watching the action, ready to move in when Jetsam came ashore and personally invite the bunnies to a rager they had planned. He felt thirsty and decided to walk back to their beach towels to get a soda he'd packed in an insulated beverage container.

That was when he checked his cell phone and saw the message. Three minutes later he was running through the surf, yelling to Jetsam, who was waiting for the next wave: "Hey, pard, we gotta go to work *pronto*!"

Flotsam was speeding to Hollywood Station in his Ford pickup with his partner beside him when the call was forwarded to Jetsam's cell number from the cold phone in the vice office.

Jetsam said, "Hello?"

Hector Cozzo said, "Is this Kelly?"

"Yeah," Jetsam said. "Who's this?"

"I do some work for the Shanghai Massage parlor," Hector said. "I got your number from Ivana the masseuse."

"Yeah?" Jetsam said.

"She wants you to come to a party at my house in Encino either tonight or tomorrow night."

"That's pretty short notice, ain't it?" Jetsam said.

"Yeah, it is," said Hector, "but another very important client of hers is calling the shots. I'll know in an hour or so if the party's gonna be tonight. I can phone you as soon as I know."

"Why am I being invited?" Jetsam said. "I only got a massage from her one time."

Hector said, "She says you had your foot amputated at a clinic in T.J., and our other important client is really interested in that."

"Interested how?" Jetsam said.

"He . . . he might wanna think about getting his . . . his hand amputated," Hector said, not knowing how else to deal with these deranged bastards other than to mention things that might excite them.

Jetsam was excited all right, nodding his head furiously to Flotsam as he asked, "Is there something wrong with his hand, or what?"

"I think that's the kinda thing he'd like to discuss with you. Ivana's gonna be there, and maybe another masseuse if you want, and we'll have some good booze and anything else you might like. This is a party for the special client, but you might have a really good time, too. Ivana asked me to remind you of what she promised you by way of a massage."

"Call me when you know if it's on," Jetsam said. "I had a date tonight, but I'll cancel."

He closed the cell and said, "We hooked them, pard! But now what?"

Jetsam called the Hollywood vice unit and said, "We're almost there. I'll need to shower and change, but if he calls again, send somebody up to the locker room and I'll get over to your office as fast as my mismatched feet will carry me."

At roll call, Sergeant Murillo said, "We've got one car missing from the lineup. Six-X-Thirty-two is working a special detail with the vice unit. Once again, if you see either of the surfers out there, do not acknowledge them in any way."

"This is getting curiouser," Always Talking Tony said. "When're we gonna find out what Flotsam and Jetsam are up to?"

"I don't even think the watch commander knows for sure what they're up to," Sergeant Murillo said. "But in the meantime, I'm happy to announce that Six-X-Seventy-two won the Hollywood Love Story Award and got the super-size pizza with the works."

Everyone but the winners, Marius and Sophie, began some jealous booing, and Chester Toles said, "How about the Quiet Desperation Award? Did anybody win it?"

"Nope," Sergeant Murillo said. "Nothing happened last night that would qualify as a legitimate submission. Would you like me to reinstate the award tonight?"

Everybody applauded and whistled, so he said, "Okay, it's reinstated. Bring me a Hollywood story of someone living a life of quiet desperation, and a super-size pizza will be yours to savor."

Two important calls in the business world of Hector Cozzo came in just after 6:00 P.M., when he was thinking about a shower and shave before his nightly visits to the establishments he serviced. The first call was from Markov.

Hector answered on the second ring, after seeing who was on the line, and Markov said, "We are in luck. Our Moscow friend is prepared to take us up on our generous offer of a meeting tonight at your house. He does not need transportation and will arrive by limousine at ten o'clock. Buy some fresh canapés and plenty of vodka. Make sure the entertainer is of high quality and, above all, make sure that the new guest with the unusual condition is there. Without him, our Moscow friend would be highly disappointed, and we cannot permit that, especially since our recent business setback with Mr. K. New investment is *urgently* needed in light of all that has transpired."

"I understand, sir," Hector said. "Everything will be ready by ten. Don't worry."

Hector lit a cigarette and scrolled through his phone's file for Ivana's number and the number of the peg-leg freak. But before he could call either of them, his cell rang. The number was from an apartment where some of the employees lived.

"Mr. Hector," the voice said, "this is Violet. There is a problem!"

Jesus! He'd thought he wouldn't have to deal with another bucket-head problem for a few days. He took a drag off the cigarette and said, "Yeah, Violet, what is it?"

"You know Daisy ran away?"

"Yeah, I know."

"Well, Lita is running, too."

"She moved out?"

"Yes, she is gone," Violet said. "And Mr. Kim is very mad."

"I can't make an independent dancer stay if she don't like the job. Why is Kim mad?"

She hesitated for several moments.

He said, "Are you there, Violet?"

"I am here," she said. Then: "Mr. Hector, you say you will take care of me if I always call when there is trouble. Call to you, not to Mr. Kim. Correct?"

"Yeah, I said that. Why?"

"Mr. Kim was here this afternoon and says because Daisy is running away, I can keep her clothes and have her bedroom. Is bigger than mine. Then he asks where is the Mexican girl, and I tell him she runs away too. And I do not want to say no more. I want to call you, but he don't give me no chance."

Remembering his own battering by Kim, Hector asked, "Did he hurt you?"

"He grab me by my arm and make me tell why the Mexican girl runs away too."

"Why did she run away too?" Hector asked, but a picture was forming and he didn't like any part of it.

"Is because after Daisy tells us she is going to talk to cops, the Mexican girl follows her out to the street and she sees something."

"Jesus Christ, get to the fucking point!" Hector said. "What'd she see? What happened?"

Violet stammered, "She sees Daisy shout to a man in a car. And . . . and now, Daisy has not come home. And the Mexican girl gets scared and she is gone too!"

Violet started crying then, and Hector stubbed out the cigarette and let her sob. Then he said, "Get hold of yourself, Violet. Daisy coulda jist been yelling at some dude that was trying to pick her up. She's a hot-looking chick." He added, "You say Mr. Kim came to see you this afternoon?"

"Yes, maybe three, four hours ago. I want to call you first, but Mr. Kim, he scares me bad. I have to tell him what Lita tells me about the man in the car."

"Did Lita say where she was going?"

"She says maybe back to her old apartment somewheres . . . I forget."

"Wilmington," Hector said.

"Yes. I think that is it. She says maybe she comes back if Daisy comes back."

"How did Lita go? Did she call a cab or bus, or what?"

"I do not know. She packs her suitcase and she just goes."

"And you told all this to Mr. Kim?"

"Yes. I got no choice. He was very scaring."

"Okay, okay," Hector said. "I'm not mad at you. But don't talk to nobody else. Not about Daisy and not about the Mexican girl. Okay?"

"Okay, Mr. Hector," Violet said.

Then a last question occurred to him. He said, "By any chance, did Mr. Kim ask you if Lita said what language Daisy was speaking when she yelled at the man in the car?"

"Yes," Violet said. "He was very concern to know if she shouts in English? I tell him that the Mexican girl does not tell me that. But maybe he do not believe me."

"How many languages does Daisy speak?" Hector asked.

"Just Korean and little bit of English." After a beat she stammered, "The Mexican girl says to me that Daisy shouts at the man in Korean language."

"I'll give you a bonus when I see you next time," Hector said. "Now forget everything you told me, understand?"

"Thank you, Mr. Hector," Violet said. "I think maybe I must take a vacation to see my brother in Hong Kong."

"That might be a good idea," he said. "I appreciate this call."

Hector's fear was growing exponentially. Daisy was gone. Lita was gone. If that lunatic gook really drove Daisy away on her last ride, was he now going to do the same to Lita? And where the hell *was* Lita? Did she really go back to Wilmington? She had to keep her mouth shut in case the Korean really did snuff Daisy. If Lita went to the cops and they started connecting the dots, it would eventually get all the way back to Hector Cozzo! He wanted to crawl under the covers and stay there until tomorrow, but he had to throw a "party" in a few hours.

He called Ivana's cell and said, "Take a taxi and be to my house in Encino by ten o'clock sharp."

She protested, saying, "I got three special clients coming: nine o'clock, ten o'clock, and eleven!"

"Give them to the other girls or cancel them. You'll be paid for missing the appointments, and the guy you'll do tonight is very rich. He'll tip you out big-time."

She said, "The one that like the cut-off body parts?"

"Yeah, and your footless friend Kelly will be there. I need you on this one, Ivana. Don't let me down if you wanna keep your job."

"Okay," she said glumly.

Hector looked at his cell and called the number Ivana had given him for Kelly. It rang at the cold phone in the Hollywood vice unit, and Jetsam picked it up, saying, "Hello, this is Kelly speaking."

Hector said, "The party's on for ten tonight. My crib's in Encino. Got a pencil?"

Before taking down Hector's address, Jetsam said, "By the way, my brother's in town. Any chance I could bring him with me?"

"Sorry," Hector said. "This is a private party. The other special guest don't want outsiders, if you know what I mean. He figures you and him will understand each other."

Jetsam looked at Sergeant Hawthorne, who was listening, and the vice sergeant gave him a "don't push it" signal.

Jetsam said, "Okay, I got a pencil. What's the address?"

Brigita Babich was preparing an early dinner because she had a bingo night planned. Lita tried to help in the kitchen, but Brigita wouldn't let a guest work. But she'd call Lita in from the back patio every so often to taste what she called her "Croatian creations."

Dinko and Lita spent most of the afternoon sitting on chaise longues drinking iced tea and playing with Ollie, the family cat, who pretty much did what he pleased around the Babich house.

It was during a moment when Ollie was frolicking with a toy on the grass, and Lita was laughing out loud, that Dinko said to her, "You're welcome to stay here with my mother and me for a while, Lita. I hope you know that. She likes you a lot, and she doesn't usually warm up to strangers right away."

"She is very kind woman," Lita said.

Dinko said, "She's got a gleam in her eye that says, 'I wonder what it'd be like to have a daughter.'"

Lita looked embarrassed. "Dinko, please do not make jokes on your mother."

"I'm not joking," he said. "I think she sees that you're good for me."

"Good? How?"

"Well, for one thing, you're a very mature girl for your age. Me, I'm a very immature guy for my age. A typical only child. So even though I'm twelve years older than you, we're about the same age in the ways that count."

Lita picked up Ollie and stroked the cat until he purred noisily; then she said, "I cannot be here a long time in the house of your mother, Dinko. It is, I forget the English word, imp-imp something."

"Imposing."

"Yes, that is the word."

"It's a blessing," Dinko said. "I haven't been so happy in a very long time."

"Why, Dinko?"

"I don't know for sure, but I'm starting to *think* I know."

"Dinko," she said, "you say I am very mature girl, no?"

"Yes, you certainly are."

She said, "I am older because the life has make me this way. Not a nice life. Not a life for your *mamá* to know about. I do lots of things in Guanajuato, and I shall do things in Club Samara. To make the money, I shall do lots of things."

"I told you to forget all that! It happened in another life!" Dinko said. Then, realizing that his voice had risen, he quieted himself, saying, "Look, a new life for you began yesterday. I got some money in the bank, and I got a very good job. I think you'd be surprised at how much a longshoreman can make if he really wants to log some hours in the book. I've always been a lazy bastard and spoiled rotten by my mom, but I feel different now. I feel like working hard to help you get some money to send home to your family. Call it a loan from me until you get on your feet."

"Dinko, how you can be talking like this?" Lita said. "It is not good sense!"

He quickly added, "And you can get some kinda work here in Pedro. My mother knows lots of old Croatian families who still own businesses. We'll find you some work you can do. Some decent work."

He thought she looked heartbreakingly sad when she said, "You are right. You are more younger than me, I think. You do not know nothing about me. I am no child."

Dinko said, "I *know* you're not a child, and I wish you'd stop saying that. You lost your childhood prematurely while I kept hanging on to mine way too long."

"Come on, you two! Supper's ready!" Brigita Babich called from the kitchen.

Dinko and Lita stayed where they were for a moment, looking at each other, but Ollie bolted for the kitchen door and the tuna treats that awaited him every day at this hour.

TEN

I T DID NOT qualify for the Quiet Desperation Award, but just before sundown an event happened that was the talk of Hollywood Station for a day or so, and it involved most of Watch 5.

Shop 6-X-76, manned by Mel Yarashi and Always Talking Tony Doakes, was southbound on Gower, passing the Hollywood Forever Cemetery, where stars of yore are buried. The radio car turned east on Melrose Avenue and was driving past the famous gates of Paramount Studios when a stolen Toyota 4Runner traveling eastbound well in front of them blew the stoplight at Western Avenue.

Mel, who was driving, said, "Ticket time. You're up." And he switched on the light bar and hit the siren just long enough to get across Western Avenue.

The siren alerted the driver of the 4Runner, who stomped on it.

A.T. picked up the mike, requested a clear frequency, and announced, "Six-X-Seventy-six is in pursuit of white Toyota 4Runner eastbound on Melrose from Western!"

The chase was on, but it was short-lived. The 4Runner made a screeching, sliding right turn onto Serrano but skidded and crashed broadside into a slow-moving northbound Chevrolet pickup. The driver of the pickup stopped and jumped out, screaming at the 4Runner's driver, a short, thickset white guy in a T-shirt whose head was shaved and whose face was inked up with Aryan Brotherhood tats.

The driver of the 4Runner hollered, "Fuck you," leaped out of the disabled vehicle, and took off southbound.

The two crashed vehicles, as well as the cars parked along both curbs, made it impossible for 6-X-76 to continue for the moment, but other units, hearing that the suspect was running south on foot, raced eastbound on Beverly Boulevard, hoping to intercept him.

Their quarry turned a corner, and then he was gone. Just like that. Six patrol units from Watch 5 and Watch 3 searched the residential streets for twenty minutes.

By the time Mel Yarashi and A.T. arrived at the search area, Chester Toles and Fran Famosa, along with Marius Tatarescu and Sophie Branson, were knocking on doors along the street to ask occupants if they could search their rear yards and garages.

Mel Yarashi got out of the radio car and shouted to all the cops at the immediate scene, "The Toyota license comes back to a Ralph Monroe Rasmussen, but not at this address. We ran the name and got one with the right description who happens to be another freaking parolee-at-large. No doubt it's him, so heads up!"

Surprisingly, it was Chester Toles who spotted a faint blood trail on the sidewalk leading toward the side door of a nearby gray bungalow with peeling paint and a sagging roof. Within moments, Chester and Fran were at the front door, with Marius and Sophie watching the side door.

Chester and Fran had their weapons drawn and were holding them down by their legs, standing on either side of the front door, when Fran knocked loudly and said, "Police! Open up!"

They heard a radio playing inside, so Fran knocked again and repeated the command. It took a full two minutes before anything happened. An overweight redhead in her late twenties, wearing a turquoise tank, red shorts, and lots of eye shadow, opened the door and said, "Yes? Is there a problem?"

Fran said, "Do you know a Ralph Monroe Rasmussen?"

There was just a slight hesitation before the woman said, "No. He don't live here."

Fran said, "Did anyone enter this house in the last twenty minutes or so?"

"No," the woman said, looking at the Glock .40 Fran was holding alongside her right thigh. "Nobody's here but me. My name's Gloria Clampett."

Chester Toles said, "There's a fresh blood trail leading along the sidewalk, onto your driveway, and up to your side door. Can you explain it?"

"I didn't cut myself or nothing," she said. "I don't know what you mean."

"Would you like to see it?" Fran asked.

"No, I take your word for it."

"Well then, maybe somebody slipped in your side door without you knowing about it," Fran said. "Maybe we should come in and look around."

The woman fiddled nervously with her desiccated, overly dyed hair, and said, "I been told I should ask if you got a search warrant before I let cops in my house."

"Why, are you hiding something?" Chester said.

"I should think you'd want us to have a look around for your protection," Fran said.

"Okay," Gloria Clampett sighed. "Come in and satisfy yourself."

Fran and Chester entered, followed by a team from Watch 3, and with four cops cautiously entering the small cottage, the woman sat in the living room, her cell phone in her hand, texting.

When Fran looked at Gloria Clampett, she lied and said, "I'm texting my lawyer, just in case."

"You have a lawyer?" Chester asked. "Why, have you been arrested in the past?"

"The lawyer's my cousin," she said. "He gives me a special family rate."

Chester opened the side door for Marius and Sophie, but as Marius was about to enter he spotted something shiny lying in the ice plant, where its owner had apparently lost it in his haste to get inside the house. He bent down and picked up a cell phone.

The bungalow search took only a few minutes. There was a bedroom with a small closet, a bathroom, a tiny kitchen, a living room, and that was it.

The team from Watch 3 was already out the door and Fran was about to offer an apology for the intrusion when Marius came in and said, "Everybody is lazy these days. No imaginations."

Sophie looked at the big Romanian quizzically. "What're you talking about?"

Marius said, "I was guessing that the code is one, two, three, four, and I am correct. Look."

Sophie squinted and read the text message aloud: "'Stay up there until I tell you the assholes are gone.'"

Marius grinned at the woman on the couch and said, in his heavy accent, "This clumsy asshole cop you see standing in front of your eyes is on exchange program from Russian KGB, where we learn cold war code breaking. Watch!"

He hit the send button, and when the cell phone in her hand rang, Gloria Clampett dropped it and said, "Oh, shit."

Chester Toles and Fran Famosa immediately ran back into the bedroom closet and saw the attic trapdoor, behind a pile of clothes that Gloria Clampett had hastily thrown up on the shelf to hide it.

Fran yelled, "Open that trapdoor and climb down or we'll put a K-9 with big teeth up there to keep you company!"

They heard some scraping and shuffling, and then a pair of legs in baggy khaki shorts showed through the trapdoor, followed by the rest of the man, his nose and lips bloodied by the traffic collision.

When the career burglar, drug addict, and parole violator was handcuffed and led out, Fran Famosa said, "I'll be taking your cell phone, Gloria."

She said, "I need my cell phone."

"You can use a jail phone to call your cousin the lawyer. You're under arrest as an accessory. Now stand up."

It looked as though all was going to end well for Marius Tatarescu and Sophie Branson until A.T. ran in again, his rover in hand, and said to Sophie and Marius, "Hey, you guys, did you know that this dude left a pet in the Toyota?"

"That's Lenny," Ralph Monroe Rasmussen said. "Don't let the Animal Control people take him. They'll put him down. He's friendly and loves people. Take him to my mother's house. She lives over on Willowbrook and Vermont. His leash is in the Toyota, on the passenger seat."

Sophie Branson, ever the animal advocate, said, "What is Lenny, your White Power pit bull mascot?"

The prisoner said, "I outgrew that Aryan Brotherhood shit, but I'm stuck with these fucking jailhouse tats. Anyways, Lenny is sweet and lovable. I can kiss him on the mouth. Have a heart and save him!"

Marius, who could see that his partner was ready to rescue another creature, said, "What is Lenny, a sweet and lovable rottweiler with the jaws of death?"

The question was answered by Always Talking Tony, who grinned large and said, "Not exactly."

The pursuit unit was in charge of booking the parolee-at-large and his girlfriend, but, predictably, 6-X-72 agreed to take care of the "pet" that had been left in the crashed Toyota 4Runner before the vehicle got impounded. After A.T. described the pet, Sophie Branson was beside herself with excitement as Marius drove them to the crash scene.

"I've seen documentaries about the Argentine black-and-white tegu!" she said. "Do you know it's the most intelligent of all lizards? It makes a great pet!"

"Are you knowing how big it is, Sophia?" he asked, worried. He always called her by the proper Eastern European version of her given name when she had him frustrated or irritated. And he was feeling both emotions now.

She said, "I'm not sure, but pretty big for a lizard, I think."

The Romanian said, "Maybe we should call Animal Control. They got the dog poles they can use to take Lenny into custody. What if I got to shoot Lenny? What does it do to my career if I shoot a goddamn lizard? I don't like none of this, Sophia!"

"For chrissake, stop worrying," Sophie said. "Think of this as an adventure."

"Sophia," Marius said, "you are not the female version of Saint Francis of Assisi. You are just a cop like me. It is not our job to be lizard ropers. This is not a good thing."

"He's harmless," she said. "Didn't the dude say he could kiss Lenny on the lips?"

"That is what he says. But I wish to say to you that the tegu lizard is not the cute little gecko. This is the *giant* gecko with the dark side. You do not see this one on the TV commercials selling goddamn insurance! Are you understanding me, Sophia?"

Their black-and-white arrived back at the crash scene just after dark, and by then, flares were already diverting traffic. Two tow trucks were hooking up both damaged vehicles, and one truck driver was peering doubtfully through the rear window of the 4Runner.

Marius was the first out of their shop. He ran to the Toyota and shined his light onto the backseat before saying, "Sophia, you can kiss him on the lips if you want, but I think I am passing."

Lenny was four feet long, and Sophie thought he was gorgeous. She loved his stripes and his beaded skin. The lizard was understandably upset with what had happened and kept flicking his tongue out at them and hissing. Without hesitation, Sophie Branson opened the front passenger door, picked up the dog leash, and opened the back door, talking soothingly to the reptile.

"There there, Lenny," she cooed. "Pretty baby. What a pretty baby."

She didn't try to put the dog leash around his neck right away but sat on the backseat for a few minutes, until the hissing diminished and Lenny crept forward, his snout only inches from her hand. "That's the good boy," she said. "We'll take care of you, honey. Don't worry." And ever so slowly she slipped the noose around Lenny's neck and said, "Wanna go see Grandma?"

On the way to the house of the parolee's mother, Sophie stayed in the backseat next to Lenny, who kept nervously snapping his tail against the metal screen dividing the front seat from the back.

Marius Tatarescu said, "Sophia, Lenny is giving me most outrageous discomfort. Can you please make him stop doing hokey-pokey dance and smacking the cage behind my head?"

"Did you see how docile he got once I had his leash on him?" she said. "He's just a love."

"Yes, Sophia," Marius said, "and I am sure he is more nice than any man you ever been married with, and all the boyfriends in your lifetime, but I am getting all nervous-wrecked by him."

Marius parked in front of the address given by the arrestee, went to the door of the modest east Hollywood home, and rang. An older woman in a pink floor-length bathrobe, with her hair in old-fashioned curlers, answered. She bore a resemblance to her son, and she was not surprised to hear what had happened.

"I've been living with this kind of thing for a very long time, Officer," she said. "Sometimes I think he's better off when he's safely back in prison. Thank you for telling me. I'll deal with his car at the impound garage. It was a car I bought him, of course."

"And we got something out in our car for you," Marius said. "Please say you can take him, or my partner will make me work the rest of the night with Lenny as extra partner."

The woman said, "Lenny? I thought he was with my son's girlfriend! Oh, bring him in, please!"

Marius signaled to Sophie, who walked the lizard on the leash to the front porch. The reptile tugged hard against the lead, trying to run inside, to a person and place he knew.

The woman took the leash from Sophie, saying, "Thank you ever so much, Officers. Lenny loves to play in my backyard. This is his real home, and he gives me more pleasure and contentment than my son *ever* did."

"I understand perfectly," Sophie said. "He'll be a faithful companion for many years."

While walking to their shop, Marius said, "That guy was living okay with a girlfriend that was giving food to him and his lizard. And I am betting she paid for gasoline for him and Lenny to drive around. And then he makes one little mistake and runs through a red light. It is proof of what they say about best-laid plans of mice and rats."

"Men," she said.

"What?"

"On second thought, what's the difference," Sophie said.

When they were back patrolling their beat, Marius said, "Sophie, I am thinking that until now Lenny was living the life of quiet desperation with his master and the chubby girlfriend. I am thinking we must submit this one to Sergeant Murillo and maybe win *another* super-size pizza. That would make me happy as a mussel."

"Clam," she said.

Flotsam kept up a running commentary in the vice sergeant's office the whole time Jetsam was being rigged with a wire by a tech from the Scientific Investigation Division.

"Dude, when you get inside that house, be sure to keep in mind where the doors are at," he told his partner. "I mean, you might, like, be all disoriented if you get to doing martinis with Ivana. You never know when a quick exit might be in order, so every minute you gotta know where you're at. Feel me?"

"I feel ya, bro," Jetsam sighed. "Stop fretting."

He was wearing a long-sleeved navy shirt with utility pockets, which he figured would provide more room to hide the transmitter. He'd also chosen relaxed-fit chinos so he could more easily pull up the trouser leg to show the pervert his prosthesis. Flotsam was wearing a long-sleeved, white baseball T-shirt and stone-washed jeans. They both had on tennis shoes and socks in case some running might be in order.

"I still think you should be packing a hideout gun in an ankle rig," Flotsam said. "I ain't so sure it's a good idea to be in there unarmed, wire or no wire."

"Bro, there's gonna be a security team half a block away, listening to everything that happens in there. I'll be partying with my huckleberry Ivana, along with that little punk Hector Cozzo and some rich Russian. How dangerous can it be, for chrissake?"

"A *weird* rich Russian," Flotsam reminded him.

"Bro, look where we work. This is fucking Hollywood," Jetsam pointed out. "Everybody's weird."

"I'm just saying, like, I don't wanna see a copper not packing heat no matter what kinda mission he's on," Flotsam said. "When things *can* go sideways, they usually do."

"Bro, we got some time before we gotta head up to Encino," Jetsam said. "Maybe we should take you out to IHOP or somewheres and load you up on some death-wish cholesterol. It might slow down your pulse rate."

When the wire was rigged and the SID tech had gone out to do a radio check from the van, Sergeant Hawthorne came in. "This is something I thought only had a very remote chance of panning out," he said.

"Yeah, I hope it's a career maker for you, Sarge," Flotsam said, "but I still wish you'd let me be out on foot and on tac frequency in the yard next door."

"There will be seven of us out there, all close enough for any eventuality," Sergeant Hawthorne said. "We have them outnumbered. Don't worry."

"That's what I keep telling him," Jetsam said. "But he goes all Woody Allen mopey in orchestrated situations. Like, nothing in life is gonna go the way you think. He's been that way ever since a Malibu rager where his week-long plan for a midnight swim ended when his surf bunny went, like, *Jaws* hysterical on him."

"My God!" Sergeant Hawthorne said to Flotsam. "You were at-tacked by a shark?"

"I think it was a dolphin that bumped us," Flotsam said, "but you can't tell that to a chick that's screaming like the shower scene in either version of *Psycho*. I didn't get laid by her that night, and no other guy will neither, not if there's so much as a gurgling swimming pool around when he makes his move."

"So my pard threw away his playbook," Jetsam explained. "He just thinks you should go all playground and take the ball and slam it, what-ever situation you're in."

"Can I buy you both a bite to eat before we go to Encino?" Sergeant Hawthorne asked, suddenly fearing that Flotsam might be right.

"Thanks, Sarge," Jetsam said. "How about IHOP?"

Hollywood Nate Weiss had been working with Britney Small for three deployment periods and figured he knew the young woman pretty well. She was reticent by nature and he always kept his show business con-versations to films or TV shows that she was likely to have seen, but with she being twenty-four years old and he being thirty-nine, that wasn't so easy. He was caught off guard that evening when, unbidden, she brought up a troubling issue right after he'd finished discussing an Oscar-nominated movie where at least a hundred people got shot or killed in a dream sequence.

Britney said, "Nate, I've got a personal question I'd like to ask."

"You're my partner," he said.

"It's about when you shot the guy that killed your partner."

Nate grew solemn. "Dana Vaughn was her name."

"Yes, Dana," Britney said. "I wish I'd known her."

"She was a good cop," Nate said. "Way better than me."

"Well," Britney said, "when you shot the guy, did you hear the rounds you fired and the rounds he fired?"

Hollywood Nate looked over at her. After a moment he said, "I'm not sure. I think I heard his, but I'm not sure. Why do you ask?"

"Because I dream about the young guy I killed last year," Britney said. "They're recurring dreams, and in the dreams the rounds I fired at him echo like cannon fire."

"Yes?" Nate said. "What do you take from that?"

"I don't know," she said, "because it wasn't like that when it happened. I'd never believed in auditory exclusion until then, but, well, I never heard a single round I fired. I saw my muzzle flashes, but I didn't hear the gunfire. And I didn't hear other coppers yelling, and I didn't hear the guy scream out when I was killing him. He was only my age, you know."

Hollywood Nate looked over again at his young partner. Slowing the black-and-white, he said, "The guy had a gun and was trying to shoot you, Britney."

"I know," she said. "That part doesn't bother me the way it used to, when all the OGs started treating me with respect for the first time, instead of like a little-girl probationer they used to laugh at. I killed a guy, so I was a gunfighter to them, and I got their respect, but that isn't how I wanted to earn it, and I didn't like it."

"Did you ever go talk to a BSS shrink about this?" Nate asked.

"Only when I was ordered to," she said. "Right after the shooting went down. But I didn't tell her about the dreams, because they hadn't started yet."

"Wouldn't hurt to make an appointment and talk to one of the psychologists," Nate said. "It's confidential, you know."

"Did you talk to one after you killed the guy who killed Dana?"

"I did because I was ordered to," Nate said. "I wouldn't admit it at the time, but it might've helped me to stop feeling like I'd let Dana down somehow."

"I hope you don't get mad at me for asking, but do you dream about that night?"

"Not the way you do," Nate said. "But I dream about *her* all the time. She had a chuckle that sounded like wind chimes."

"I hope it's okay that I asked these questions," Britney said.

"I'm your partner, Britney," Nate said. "I've got your back in every way you might need me. And by the way, you and me might be the only two on Watch Five that've been in officer-involved fatal shootings. So who else would you talk to about things like this?"

They were interrupted by a message on the MDC computer. It was assigned as an "unknown trouble" call, but the PSR had partly figured it out and added, "possible DB," meaning there might be a dead body at the scene.

The condo was on Stanley Avenue north of Fountain, in a very well tended and moderately pricey two-story building. The old woman who answered the door was petite and immaculately groomed. Her silver hair had recently been permed, and she wore a straight linen dress with a floral pattern and black shoes with a low heel.

"Come in, Officers," she said, with what Britney thought was the sweetest smile she'd seen lately.

They smelled the food the moment they entered, and Nate guessed it was a robust stew, like the kind his mother had made at least once a week when he was a child. The condo was nicely decorated in prints and pale shades, but the decor was dated. It looked as though the occupants had been living there for many years.

She said, "I'm Sybil Greene. My husband is Howard Greene, and he's lying in bed and won't get up. I'm afraid he's sick or maybe he's hurt. He's fallen down several times lately, so I'm worried."

"Where's the bedroom, ma'am?" Britney asked.

The old woman led them to a tidy bedroom, where a hairless old man lay on his back, eyes open slightly, mouth agape, covers pulled to his throat. Rigor had already begun.

"I've called him ever so many times," she said. "And I'm making one of his favorite dinners, but he won't get up."

"Let's go in the living room and sit down," Nate said.

When he was sitting beside her on the living room sofa, he said, "I'm afraid your husband has passed away, Mrs. Greene."

She looked at Nate in astonishment and then at Britney, waiting for her to refute him. Then she said, "Oh, no. He'll get up soon. He always takes an afternoon nap. It's just a longer nap this time."

"I'm sorry, dear," Nate said, taking her hand in his. "Mr. Greene is dead."

The back of the old woman's hands looked like a network of sparrow bones clearly visible under the papery skin. Britney kept her eyes on those hands and not on the old woman's face.

Then Britney spoke for the first time: "Do you have someone we can call for you? Do you have children or grandchildren we can call?"

The old woman looked up at Britney and said, "Our daughter, Margie, died in nineteen ninety-nine from breast cancer. We have three grandchildren and two great-grandchildren."

"How old are you, Mrs. Greene?" Britney asked.

"I'm ninety-one," she said, "and my husband's ninety-three. You'll like Howard. He's very funny. We should wake him now."

Britney said, "Do you have a phone file somewhere? With important personal phone numbers and names in it?"

"Yes," Mrs. Greene said. "It's in the kitchen drawer. I have to write down everything that my husband tells me to write down because my memory isn't so good anymore."

Britney went into the kitchen, where she could hear Mrs. Greene say to Nate, "My husband and I have to go to the market tomorrow. Tomorrow is Sunday, isn't it?"

Britney tried the name and local phone number at the top of the list, written in a shaky scrawl. It was answered by a woman, and Britney said to her, "This is Officer Small of the Los Angeles Police Department. I'm at the home of Mrs. Sybil Greene and I'm sorry to inform you . . ."

In the meantime, Nate was being shown a photo album, and Mrs. Greene was pointing out vacation photos she and her husband had taken at the Grand Canyon decades earlier.

She said, "Of course we're too old for that kind of vacation now, but we haven't ruled out another trip to San Francisco. We loved riding the cable cars."

Britney walked back into the living room and nodded at Nate, saying, "Her granddaughter is on the way from Pacific Palisades."

"Why is my granddaughter coming?" the old woman asked Britney.

"To take care of you, Mrs. Greene," Nate said.

"But Howard takes care of me," she said.

"He's dead, Mrs. Greene," Nate said, "and we're so very sorry."

"I think you must be wrong," she said. "May I see him?"

Nate nodded to Britney, who took the old woman's arm and led her to the bedroom, where she stood looking down at the lifeless face of her husband. She touched his cheek for a moment and then turned away, and Britney led her back to the living room, where she sat down on a wingback chair.

"But who's going to take me to the market tomorrow?" she asked. "And who'll pick out the best produce? I'm not very good at that." And then she broke down and started to weep.

The old woman's granddaughter and her husband arrived promptly and said they had already placed a call to the Greenes' primary care physician, who would sign the death certificate, and had contacted the local mortuary, which was sending someone. The officers of 6-X-66 were thanked for being thoughtful and kind.

When they were walking to their car, Nate said to Britney, "I'm always relieved when there's a doctor involved and we don't have to call in the body snatchers. That's too much like calling Animal Control to haul away a dead dog. You know, this story might win the Quiet Desperation Award, but somehow I don't feel like sharing it with anybody."

Britney didn't respond, and when they were back sitting in their shop, she turned on her flashlight to make the log notations before Nate started up the car.

He said to her, "As you get older, you'll find that it gets hard to deal with stuff like that. It's because you've started to face your *own* mortality."

Britney still didn't reply, and Nate looked over to see two wet droplets on the log sheet, and in the moonlight streaming through the windshield shiny rivulets were running down both her cheeks.

"It's not any too easy when you're young, either," she said, hastily wiping her cheeks with the heel of one hand. "I suppose you're gonna tell me that big girls don't cry and I should man up and leave this stuff back there. Right?"

Hollywood Nate said, "No, I was only gonna tell you that even gunfighters have to cry sometimes."

After a quiet moment, Britney Small managed a sheepish smile and said, "Nate, if I put myself up for adoption, will you please become my mom and dad?"

Brigita Babich had been at bingo for less than an hour when Lita and Dinko finished tidying up the supper dishes. It hadn't been easy to convince Brigita that their guest should be allowed to do a little bit of work around the house. As for Dinko, Brigita had told Lita in Dinko's presence that he hadn't washed a dish or even tidied up his room in his entire life. That is, before Lita had arrived as their houseguest.

"I guess Lita's a good influence on me," he'd said to his mother.

That made Brigita study Lita for a moment and then say to her son, "I suppose she might be, at that." Then she was off to bingo night at Croatian Hall.

When they were alone, sitting on the sofa and watching the local news, Dinko said, "Would you like me to take you to a movie or something?"

"How do they play the bingo game?" Lita asked.

"Is that what you want?" he asked. "To go play bingo?"

"No," she said. "I am just thinking if bingo is a very hard game."

"It's an easy game," he said. "Next week we can go to bingo with my mom. It'll be fun, even though I can hardly believe I'm saying this. Me, playing bingo?"

Lita looked wistfully at Ollie, who was sleeping on the sofa, and then ran her gaze around the Babich house and said, "I cannot be going to play the games with you and your mother. I must leave this place and go to work. I shall call tomorrow to Violet. If Daisy is not with her, I am going to where you first see me dance. The pay is not too good but is enough until I maybe get another job in Hollywood."

"You can't!" Dinko said. "You can't go back there, and you can't go anywhere near Hollywood or those thugs might find you. I won't permit it. You're staying here, Lita, where you're safe."

"You are doing crazy talk again," Lita said.

"It's not crazy!" Dinko said. "Look at this big house. Since my father died the two of us rattle around in here."

Lita tried to tone down his intensity by saying, with a smile, "Three of you. There is Ollie."

"We have plenty of room for you," he said. "How about my idea of you finding a decent job and living here for a while? Just to see if you like it?"

"I cannot pay the rent in such a grand—"

"Stop it, Lita," Dinko said. "We're not rich, but we're very comfortable. My dad had an insurance policy and my mom's gonna be collecting Social Security, and like I said, I'm gonna start stacking up the hours. You wouldn't believe how much money a longshoreman can make, even during this recession. You won't have to pay anything. Just be our guest for a few months, okay? Let's see how it goes."

"That would bring shame," she said. "I am not someone for . . . I cannot think of the word for poor peoples who must accept money for nothing."

"Charity," he said. "You're too proud to accept charity. But I'm not offering charity. I'm offering . . . I'm offering . . . Christ! I think I'm offering a . . . a lifetime commitment!"

"I do not understand what is that," she said.

He said, "I told you I could lend you some money to send to your family, but you don't want that. Well, what if it was *your* money? What if half of everything I got is yours? I can't think of you leaving here and going back to hell on earth. I just can't!" He paused and suddenly said, "What if I married you?"

That stopped everything. She sat quietly for a moment, then stood up and walked into the spare bedroom and closed the door softly. When she opened it a moment later, she called out, "Please come, Dinko."

He got up and walked slowly to the bedroom. When he got inside, he saw her standing beside the bed, naked. Now the hammering of his heart actually startled him. Finally, he said, "You're breathtaking."

"This," she said, "this is all I got. This is all men want from me. Take it. You do not have to lend to me nothing. Take it. Is yours for free. Then you shall see me with eyes more clear."

"Please, Lita," Dinko said weakly, but she rushed forward and threw her arms around his neck and kissed him. It was tongue and teeth and velvety lips, and he wanted to resist and show her she was wrong about him, that he was not like those other men, but her long fingers were on him, sliding over his body. And with a shudder that started in his throat and ran to his loins, he kept thinking that this was not merely lust. This was something *more*.

The lovemaking was the same and not the same. It was familiar and not familiar. Afterward, misty and spent, he didn't know if he'd been lying supine for ten minutes or sixty. Time had become irrelevant. Vaguely, he realized that his mother would be home soon if her favorite cronies didn't happen to be at bingo night, but he didn't even care about that. He didn't care about anything in the world, except convincing this girl not to leave him. But at that moment he couldn't even speak of it. She spoke first.

"Now, Dinko," she said, "you got all. There is no more. Now do you see me with eyes more clear?"

"Yes," he said. "I'm seeing you with eyes more clear. And there is *so* much more. I see you in here." He touched her temple. "I see you in here." And he touched her chest. You are *very* clear to me. And I'm asking you . . . no, I'm begging you. Please stay with me, Lita. Please become my wife."

She instantly sat up and said, "You wish to marry with me? Foolish talk! We shall see tomorrow how you are thinking. Now we must get dressed before your *mamá* is returning. And we must not talk to her about this."

"I've gotta do whatever it takes to keep you," he said. "I'm so crazy for you I might jump off the freaking Point Fermin cliffs if you leave me."

"This kind of talk is not for joking," she said. "If anyone do that thing, they burn in hell for all time."

"Then I'll burn in hell. Better than thinking of you back in that slime pit. Better than stumbling through life like I always have, screwing up every chance I get. Never loving somebody till now."

With that, she put her hand to his face, saying, "You are *really* loving me, Dinko? Are you for sure? You are loving *me*?"

"You are loved," he said. "Believe me, you are loved."

ELEVEN

"ARE YOU NERVOUS, dude?" Flotsam said nervously.

"No, I ain't nervous," Jetsam said. Then, to their driver, Sergeant Hawthorne, who was wearing the same UCLA sweatshirt as when they'd first met with him, minus the ketchup stains: "But I gotta warn you, Sarge, if the dude gets a man crush and tries playing hump the stump, I might get all goosey and cry like a molested girl. Right before I go all street and tear his fucking head off and throw it in the punch bowl or whatever they're serving at this ghoul gathering!"

"Don't think like that," Sergeant Hawthorne said soothingly. "The worst you'll have to do is look at his photo album and humor him about your supposed shared fascination, and tell him about the great time you had in T.J. at the hands of Dr. Maurice."

"Whatever can go wrong . . ." Flotsam said.

"Will you please stop saying that!" Sergeant Hawthorne said. "You're starting to make me jumpy. We're just trying to shut down a prostitution ring. These aren't serial killers, for God's sake."

During the vice unit's ride north to Encino there was another drive taking place that also involved Hector Cozzo, but this one came south, to Los Angeles Harbor. A black Mercedes four-door S-Class with chrome wheels, purchased from the same dealer who had leased Hector's car to him, arrived in Wilmington and parked half a block from the strip joint where Lita Medina had worked. The driver got out and entered, ignoring the smile he got from the overweight dancer writhing on the stage.

"Where is the boss?" the Korean said to the Latino bartender.

"He comes in at about nine-thirty."

"I will wait."

The Korean threw a ten-dollar bill on the bar and said, "Tomato juice."

He stood at the bar, ignoring the empty stool next to him, and didn't touch the juice. The bartender flicked a glance at the big Korean a few times, but turned away when those cold black eyes looked back at him. The bartender was relieved when the boss arrived early.

The Korean recognized him waddling through the entry door, and he left his drink, stopping the boss before he'd reached the first tables. The boss's comb-over looked like it had been painted on by a brush that was missing half its bristles. He was about the same age as the Korean but flabby, and he smelled sour from sweat and wine. He might have been Latino, but it was hard to tell.

"You remember me?" the Korean said.

The boss looked at the Korean's face, and at the double-breasted oyster-colored Armani suit, and said, "Sure, you're the guy that came in here about Lita. Couldn't dance, but a great-looking chick. Hector came and offered me some green and I let her go to a Hollywood club. I sorta felt like he worked for you. Like maybe it was your club or something?"

"I got a new job for her," the Korean said. "She is not in the Hollywood club no more."

"No? Well, she didn't come back here," the boss said. "There's the other strip bar down the street. Did you check with them?"

The Korean said, "I will check her home. Where she use to live when she was working here. Give me the address."

The boss got cagey, eyeing the Korean conspiratorially, and said, "We ain't accustomed to handing out the addresses of employees or former employees, not even to the cops. I don't think I can do that."

"You can do that," the Korean said.

The boss peered into those glaring black eyes, and when the big Korean bared his yellowing teeth in what was supposed to be a smile, the boss said, "Well . . . I suppose . . ."

The Korean produced a fifty-dollar bill, and the boss grabbed it and went to his office, returning in a few minutes with a piece of notepaper.

He said, "I think she lived at this address with two or three other girls. It's right here in Wilmington. You don't speak Spanish, do you?"

"Everybody understand money," the Korean said.

He followed the directions the strip club boss had written down and found a boardinghouse catering to minimum-wage workers. He eyed a group of teenage Latinos slouching on the porch steps next door, drinking beer out of cans. He entered the building and saw plastic numbers tacked to each of the apartment doors. He knocked at number four.

A Latina in her early twenties opened it and looked quizzically at the Korean, saying, "No English. Sorry."

Kim said, "Lita. Where?" Then he tried to remember the Spanish word for "where," but he couldn't.

The young woman shrugged and said, "No *aquí*. Hollywood. Lita in Hollywood." Then she pointed vaguely in a northerly direction.

The Korean dialed Hector Cozzo even before he got back to his Mercedes, glad to see that none of the Latino teens had bothered his shiny new car.

Hector didn't think there was any more he could've done. He'd spent three hundred dollars on food and booze, as ordered by Mr. Markov, and he'd laid everything out as best he could. The bruschetta was beside the baked artichokes and Brie. There were three kinds of crostini, and he'd gone all out and bought a large plate of smoked salmon and red caviar, along with truffle canapés. And, of course, there was the ubiquitous plate of assorted sushi with wasabi, ginger, and soy sauce. He had a bottle of Vivid vodka on ice for himself and two bottles of Stolichnaya for the Russian, and he'd washed and carefully wiped all of his glasses until they gleamed.

Hector said, "This ain't prom night" when Ivana showed up in a coral side-slit dress with spaghetti straps, along with four-inch heels. Her naturally dark hair had been recently dyed a honey blond, and he wasn't wild about it. He thought if she was going to go blond, then the blonder the better when it came to back rubs and blow jobs. And why the fuck didn't she just wear her tee and shorts from Shanghai Massage? These bitches. Go figure.

Ivana had brought her lotions, powder, and towels, arranging them on a small folding table she'd carried in and placed beside Hector's bed.

She looked at her watch and said, "Maybe they are not coming, Hector."

"Don't sound so hopeful," he said. "Do you know how much you're gonna make tonight? That fucking Russian tips like Frank Sinatra, back in the day."

"I admit I am a bit in fear, Hector," Ivana said, sipping a cold martini. "I know he is generous. Lotus told me that when she was still with us. But this crazy shit about the cut-off arms and legs and feets and hands? It makes me feel like snakes crawl on my back."

"Okay, so he's got some kinks," Hector said. "Who don't? But he ain't one of those guys that asks you to do really spooky stuff with handcuffs and weird objects. Tell him your G-spot's where only your dentist can see it. Then control your gag reflex during the face rape and you'll walk outta here with enough green to buy out Victoria's Secret."

His cell rang, and he looked at it and said, "Fuck! This is all I need." Then he opened it and said, "Yes, Mr. Kim."

The Korean said, "Hector, I am down by the harbor looking for Lita. Do you know she run away too? Like Daisy."

"So what?" Hector said, but he felt a wave of fear, remembering what Violet had told him about Lita seeing the black car drive off with Daisy. "Why do you need Lita? We got better dancers. If she don't come back, who cares?"

"I want to offer to her more money," Kim said. "You will find her for me tomorrow. You look, you find."

"Goddamn!" Hector said. "I'm doing a party tonight. A party ordered by Mr. M. I don't know when the fuck it'll end. I gotta get some sleep. I'm being run ragged by everybody!"

"Tomorrow," Kim said. "You will find Lita. She don't know nobody in Hollywood. I think she is back down near the harbor."

"Aw, crap!" Hector said. "I guess I can check that strip joint in Wilmington where you sent me to reel her in."

"I already check there," Kim said. "She did not go back there."

"Okay, then I'll get the address where she was staying down there and—"

"I check that too," Kim interrupted. "The girl there tells me that Lita is in Hollywood. So she don't know nothing neither."

"Well, how am I gonna find her?" Hector said. "I can't start asking all over the goddamn Spanish-speaking community down there. I don't even talk the language except for a few words!"

"You go down there. That is where she is. Somewhere down by the harbor. I am offering her money to come back and be happy at Club Samara."

"Okay, I'll try," Hector said. "But if it don't work, I hope you don't show your disappointment the way you did last time. My fucking hip is still killing me."

When he closed his cell, he felt it again. The fear. Kim wasn't going through all this just to hire her back. Hector was suddenly out of his depth, with the growing panic of a drowning man.

The doorbell startled him.

"I get it," Ivana said.

Hector watched her sashay across the room in those sky-highs, thinking, Why couldn't the fucking Russian just want a girl like Ivana to stomp on mice and gerbils in those four-inch heels, or walk up and down his back until he bled? Something more Hollywood normal, for chrissake! Why did it have to be severed arms and legs that stiffened his sausage?

Hector was surprised to see a buff, healthy-looking, thirty-something dude walk in. Christ, he looked like he just came from a tanning salon, but Hector could tell the difference. This guy's tan was real. And he could not detect any limp. Why in the fuck would a guy like this go to T.J. and pay some quack to—

"Dah-link!" Ivana said, kissing Jetsam on the cheek. "I am full of delight that you have come. We are going to have a special evening."

"I'm Kelly," Jetsam said, offering his hand to the host. "You must be Hector."

They shook hands, and Hector said, "Is Kelly a first name or a last name?"

"Does it matter?" Jetsam said.

"Not at all," Hector said. "Not around here. Vodka? Scotch? A martini?"

"I could pound a brew or two," Jetsam said.

"Sure, I got beer." Hector went into the small kitchen and took a bottle of Corona from the fridge. He brought it back, asking, "Need a glass?"

"This'll do," Jetsam said, thinking the dipshit really did wear his hair in a mullet. The top and sides were cropped short, and the back of his black hair hung over his collar. And his silky, green-tomato shirt was open halfway down his skinny chest. And those snakeskin knockoffs on his feet? Must be his lame idea of what an up-to-the-minute Hollywood pimp should look like.

Hector said, "Whadda you do, Kelly?"

Jetsam thought, What the hell. With Sergeant Hawthorne listening, he might as well take his performance straight to the top and deliver the rehearsal lines. He said, "Right now, I'm all into buying video poker machines in Arizona and selling them to residential casinos around L.A. If you're, like, ever in the market, get in touch with me. You can easy take in a couple grand a week on one machine. There's way big potential, bro."

"Yeah, well, that's not really my line," Hector said.

They started grazing at the canapé table, and Ivana sidled up to Jetsam and ran her hand over his ass, saying, "You are having a good week in business, dah-link? You are very tense from all the customer problems? Maybe I got to give you the Ivana supreme massage tonight?"

"That'll do till Mr. B. gets here," Hector said. "Let's keep things at room temperature for now."

Ivana scowled for being chastised in front of a potentially big tipper, and went into the kitchen to pout and pour another martini.

They heard her say in a loud voice, "James Bond is full of shit! Stirred is only way to make fucking martini!"

Hector shook his head at Jetsam and held his palm up, saying, "Hypersensitive bitches. What can I do?"

"So whadda you do to pay the rent, Hector?" Jetsam asked, stuffing a cracker loaded with something he thought might be spicy crab into his mouth and washing it down with the brew.

"I do a little of this and that," Hector said, lighting a cigarette.

Jetsam finished the beer and said, "Okay, man, but I told you what I do."

Hector knew he couldn't afford to offend this freak, so he said, "I'm kind of a selector. Like an agent. I find new talent to work at Shanghai Massage and at a few other businesses around Hollywood."

"Yeah?" Jetsam said. "Nice job. What're the other businesses? Massage joints?"

Hector checked the time on his fake Rolex again and said, "Not jist massage parlors. I find talent for nightclubs, too. You know Club Samara?"

"Club Samara?" Jetsam said. "I don't think so. I mostly hang at the happening clubs on the Sunset Strip, with all the wretched-excess chicks."

Hector wondered if this fucking pervert was putting him down. He said, "Club Samara is better than any of them short-pour nightclubs that cater to the pimple-and-zit crowd looking for Paris and Lindsay. Club Samara is for grown-up people, like the Russian gentleman who's coming here tonight to meet you."

"The dude must be bucks up, huh?" Jetsam said, moving casually to the ice buckets and checking out the vodka. "To rate all this attention."

Hector was starting to get annoyed by so many questions. He said, "All I know is, the guy has a . . . passion for the work that our former doctor done in Tia-juana."

"Your former doctor?" Jetsam said. "You mean *my* Dr. Maurice?"

"Dr. Maurice took care of us girls real good," Ivana volunteered, rejoining the party, and Hector could see that she'd had more than one martini in the kitchen. "You can't sleep, you go to Dr. Maurice," Ivana went on. "You get too much sleep, Dr. Maurice give you the energy shots. You got something wrong with the . . ."

"Okay, we get the idea," Hector said. "He was a regular Dr. Schweitzer. Shoulda been doing missionary in the Congo or somewheres."

"Why you are talking smack to me, Hector?" Ivana said, slurring her words. "I am getting another martini, and I ain't staying here all night waiting for no Mr. B." Then she stalked into the kitchen to pour another drink.

Jetsam was getting excited. Ivana had not so much as blinked when he'd mentioned Dr. Maurice during his visit to Shanghai Massage, as though the name meant nothing to her. This *was* starting to look like a full-scale criminal conspiracy, maybe even involving human trafficking, and complete with a drug-dealing quack to keep the hookers happy!

"I lost contact with Dr. Maurice after my operation," Jetsam told Hector.

"I think he retired," Hector said. Then he checked his watch again and said, "Where the fuck is Mr. B.? Ivana gets to be a problem when she's juiced. Goddamnit!"

"I could deep-throat another Corona," Jetsam said.

"Help yourself," Hector said. "Drink till you hit the wall. If our other honored guest ever shows up, the house belongs to the three of you till tomorrow morning. I'll be outta here soon as I make the introductions."

Jetsam grabbed a brew and then poured himself a double shot of vodka, while Hector crossed the room, sat down on the sofa, and lit another smoke. Just as his cell rang.

"Oh, shit," he said, figuring it was the Korean with something else to bitch about. He was stunned to see that it was Markov.

"Yes?" Hector said diffidently.

"Has Mr. B. arrived yet?"

"No, sir," Hector said. "Have you heard from him?"

"He had an early dinner meeting at his hotel. It must have gone on longer than he anticipated."

"We'll wait a couple more hours," Hector said, lowering his voice, "but you know, I got this other guest here. I don't know how long I can hold him."

"Let your girl work on him if you have to," Markov said. "Everything depends on Mr. B.'s investment now. Things are going badly for all of us."

"Yeah, I'm getting that idea," Hector said. "Our friend Mr. K. is leaning on me heavy. He wants me to find the Mexican girl that quit. In fact, he insists. I don't understand where he's coming from, and I don't like any of this."

"It will work out if you do as you are told," Markov said, his tone changing abruptly.

"Told by you or Mr. K.?" Hector asked, surprised by his own boldness.

"We speak as one on this issue," Markov said. "I have had a disturbing meeting with Mr. K. in which he revealed all of the mistakes he has been making of late. The mistakes have been costly and dangerous for business. Mr. B's investment can save everything. I have gone all out to please him tonight. That is why I am calling. I have arranged for a surprise guest to arrive. At least, I hope I have it arranged. If he does show up, he will ask for a fee for his presence there. Pay him what he asks. All of the moneys you spend tonight will be reimbursed next week."

"A surprise guest?" Hector said.

"It is Dr. M.," Markov said.

"Damn!" Hector said. "How'd you find him?"

"Anything can be done if we are willing to pay for it," Markov said. "Keep him happy, too, before you leave them alone. Make sure there is taxi fare for all who need it."

"Is he . . . okay?" Hector asked, meaning, Is the degenerate crackhead able to communicate on the level of a functioning primate?

"I did not see him," Markov said, "but I spoke to him on the phone and he sounded rational, though I am sure he is in need of funds. That is why I think he will keep his word and not disappoint us."

"Well, yeah," Hector said. "He's probably sucked the price of three Rolls-Royces into his lungs since last year."

"We are talking on the phone," Markov reminded him.

"Sorry," Hector said. "Okay, I'll take care of everything. I always do, lately."

When he closed his cell and put it back in his pocket, he sat back and stared at the ceiling until he was aware that the peg-leg guy was standing next to him, like he was trying to eavesdrop. Ivana was pretty much confining herself to the television room, where she was watching a movie, except when she went to the kitchen for a martini refill.

"Everything okay?" Jetsam asked, indicating the phone call.

"Yeah," Hector said, feeling really tired of this guy and his questions.

"Was that our Russian guest?"

"No," Hector said. "Why don't you pour yourself a drink?"

"I just did," Jetsam said.

"Then have some of that chickpea crostini. It's really good."

"What's it take to get into your agenting business?" Jetsam asked, and Hector could see that the guy was getting a buzz from the booze.

"Gotta be in the right place at exactly the right time."

"Maybe you could use a helper," Jetsam said. "I got some time on my hands."

"I thought you were busy selling video poker machines," Hector reminded him. "What's up with that?"

"I am," Jetsam said, "but still. Pink and green? Pussy and money? I could work for free till I learn the business. With me helping out, you could cut your work hours in half. Keep it in mind."

Hector was thinking that the only thing on his mind was getting the fuck away from this den of debauchery when the doorbell chimed.

Ivana stumbled in from the TV room, and Hector thought, Yeah, she's wrecked already. He went to the door and opened it.

"Hector!" the guest of honor said, spreading his arms for a bear hug.

The Russian kissed Hector on both cheeks, and Hector said, "So good to see you, Basil!"

The Russian had left his suit coat and tie in the limo waiting in front of the house. His white dress shirt was open at the throat, tufts of furry salt-and-pepper chest hair springing out. Jetsam saw that Basil was middle-aged and beefy, with the most amazing head of hair: black except for a streak of white that began at the widow's peak and swept back to the crown. He was carrying a small photo album in one of his big, hairy hands.

"You look younger than ever, Basil!" Hector said, slapping the Russian on the back a few times.

"I am young! Full of blood like a Siberian tiger!" the Russian responded with a booming laugh.

During the noisy greetings, Jetsam, standing by the canapé table, turned his back and whispered, "I guess you know that skunkhead is here" into the wired mike strapped to his chest.

Ivana walked uncertainly to the doorway with her most seductive smile, but she didn't make physical contact until Basil held out his arms and grinned. Then she staggered forward and kissed him on the mouth and said something sotto in Russian.

"And this is the young man I am hear-ink about," Basil said. His eyes went immediately to Jetsam's shoes, obviously trying to determine which held the prosthesis.

Jetsam stepped forward with an uneasy smile and said, "Nice to know you, sir."

"We are friends!" the Russian thundered. "You shall call me Basil. We have much to talk about. Many thing to share. I must hear all, but first I must have vodka!"

Ivana had already poured half a crystal tumbler full of cold vodka, no ice. She smiled saucily when she handed it to him and led him over to the hors d'oeuvres table, and he winked back at her and swallowed half of it down in one gulp.

Hector felt relieved. He wanted desperately to leave and head to the moderately priced local motel he always used on nights like this. In fact, he'd forgotten about the possible appearance of Dr. Maurice until the doorbell chimed again. Then he remembered.

He was shocked to see the former physician. Dr. Maurice was sepulchral, his belly receding to his backbone. In the past year the former physician must have aged ten or more. He had a face full of scraggly hair that he never bothered trimming. The hair on his head was colorless and sparse, drooping over extra-large ears, and a stray nose hair hung down nearly to his upper lip. The lines in his cheeks and brow had turned into deep crevices, but the saturnine eyes told it all. They were filmy and red, darkly rimmed, and had sunk into hollow shadows. The blue of the irises was washed out and ran to a grayish hue, like the rest of him. He was a fading-to-nothing gray man with tiny, jagged, darkened teeth.

He coughed and sniffled for a good twenty seconds before he nodded almost imperceptibly, by way of greeting.

"Dr. Maurice, I presume," Hector said, trying a little levity to mitigate the shock he knew must be registering on his face, and thinking, Welcome to the wonderful world of chemistry.

Dr. Maurice said, "I want five hundred dollars before I step foot in there."

"Sure, Doc," Hector said, reaching into his pocket and peeling five Franklins from the roll that had been allocated to pay for the party. He'd set aside two thousand, and now hoped it would be enough to get him through this night of the iguanas.

The former physician tucked the money into the inside pocket of the threadbare sport coat he wore over a black T-shirt. Then he entered.

Hector led him into the living room where the Russian was stuffing his face with smoked salmon and caviar, and the host announced, "Basil, I have a surprise. This is Dr. Maurice Montaigne, who is known to other guests in this room!"

Basil lumbered forward with a little bow, as though he were meeting the patriarch of Moscow. Ivana staggered toward Dr. Maurice, so drunk she'd made up her mind to get him alone and ask him to look at a suspicious sore on the lip of her vagina. Jetsam froze in place, standing by the canapé table, a crostini halfway to his mouth.

Basil's thunderous voice was quieted a bit by the august presence of the infamous surgeon, and he said respectfully, "Dear Doctor, I am waiting three years to meet with you. I am full of eagerness to learn about your work."

Jetsam used that greeting as a chance to turn his back and whisper into the mike, "Maybe I can bluff my way through this. Or maybe not."

Now Jetsam remembered Flotsam's admonition to know where the exits were, and to be ready to use anything at hand as a weapon. He saw Dr. Maurice staring at him but saying nothing.

Hector and Basil were looking from the doctor to his putative former patient and back again. Only Ivana was oblivious to the doctor's reluctance to greet the man whose foot he'd purportedly amputated.

Then Dr. Maurice simply said, "I have never seen you before in my life."

"Come on, Doc," Jetsam said, feeling the heat in his face and the chill in his gut. "A year ago. Clínica Maravilla, in T.J. Remember?"

Dr. Maurice looked at Hector and at Basil and said, "I have never seen this man before now."

"What is happen-ink here?" Basil demanded. "Hector, I do not like this! What is go-ink on here?"

Jetsam tried an affable smile. "Doc, you look like you might be doing a little too much of that crack you smoked down there at the clinic. Remember when we talked about how the T.J. crack was better than—"

"I have never seen this man," Dr. Maurice interrupted. "And now I'm leaving here and driving home with my fee. Don't try to stop me."

"Hector!" Basil bellowed again. "What is this about?"

"He's confused. Look at him," Jetsam said to Hector, who stood frozen, a cigarette dangling from his lips, his eyes moving from one man to the other in utter bewilderment.

Dr. Maurice grew white around the corners of his mouth, and spittle formed on his lips. His sunken eyes opened wide when he glared at Jetsam and shouted, "Confused? Confused? I'm not confused! I know who you are, Judas!" Then he turned to Hector and said, "I know who this is!"

"Who?" Hector said.

Dr. Maurice said, "He's a treacherous, sneaky paid informant for the California Medical Board!" He turned again to Jetsam and said, "Haven't you people persecuted me enough? I have no license to practice, and I can't make a living! Isn't that enough? What do you want from me, a pound of flesh?" He picked up a knife from the canapé table and said, "Here, take it! Take my flesh, but leave me alone! All I want is to live out my life without you people hounding me! *Hounding* me!"

Ivana screamed when Dr. Maurice raised the knife overhead, but Hector grabbed the frail upraised arm, taking the knife away and saying, "Calm yourself, Doc! Calm yourself!"

"All I've ever tried to do is help people by giving them what they want from me!" Dr. Maurice cried out. Then he screamed at Jetsam, "Judas!" And began weeping.

"Are you trying to run a game on me?" Hector said to Jetsam. "Something's sideways here!"

"Well, yeah, bro," Jetsam said. "The doc's all sketched out from smoking crack. He's totally thrashed and in, like, the final stage of addiction. He don't know his ass from the sushi pile over there. *He's* the thing that's sideways."

"But I know *you,* Judas!" Dr. Maurice sobbed as Hector led him to the door.

Then Hector turned to Jetsam and said, "You stay right here till we find out what's going on!"

Hector Cozzo wasn't aware that the moment Dr. Maurice had parked his rusted junkyard Pontiac and shuffled up to the entryway, Sergeant Hawthorne of the Hollywood vice unit had realized who this new guest was. And he'd set in motion an emergency escape plan for Jetsam by using the tactical frequency to request a patrol unit from West Valley Division, code 2.

After having ordered his peg-leg guest to remain where he was until he could get to the bottom of things, Hector took Dr. Maurice out to the front porch to calm him down. It was there that he encountered pandemonium.

"Stop!" a voice yelled, scaring the living crap out of both Hector and Dr. Maurice. "Stop, or we'll shoot!"

Hector was about to throw up his hands and plead for his life when he saw a tall man with a suntan like the peg-leg guy's running along the sidewalk, where he was overtaken right in front of Hector's house by a uniformed police officer with a flashlight in one hand and a gun in the other.

The cop yelled, "Down! Get down on your knees, hands on your head, or I'll blow you away!"

That did it. Basil bellowed something in Russian and came running outside, followed by Ivana, who grabbed her purse but didn't bother with her massage accoutrements. They both raced toward Basil's limo, where the dozing driver had been jarred out of his snooze by all the commotion.

The uniformed cop's partner ran onto the scene in front of the house and handcuffed the tall blond guy. Then he turned to Hector and Dr. Maurice and said, "Did you see him throw a gun anywhere?"

"No!" Hector said. "We jist heard you guys and came out to see what's what, is all. We didn't see nothing."

"I want to go home!" Dr. Maurice wailed to Hector Cozzo.

"Where's the gun?" the cop demanded of his handcuffed "prisoner," now proned out on his belly.

But the prisoner responded, "I want my mouthpiece, copper!"

The doorway was filled again. Jetsam pushed past Hector and Dr. Maurice, saying, "I'm outta here, bro. This fucking party sucked!"

He fled from the residence in all the confusion just as everyone else had done, even though Hector yelled weakly, "Hey, man, you stay here, goddamnit! We gotta talk! Who the fuck *are* you?"

"I told you who he is!" Dr. Maurice screamed in Hector's face, his breath smelling like a dead rat. "He's a paid informer sent by the California Medical Board to torment me! They won't be satisfied until I hang myself, just like my former colleague Dr. Cepeda!" And then, without realizing it, he actually got part of it right when he said, "You fool! Can't you see? This is a sting! It's been set up by the medical board to entrap me into revealing damaging information so they can send me to federal prison! You fool! You fool!"

The limo carrying Basil and Ivana was driving away into the night, and Dr. Maurice's putative patient had run across the street and disappeared into the darkness. Hector Cozzo was left alone on the porch with a psychotic crack addict who was quaking in terror from the noisy police drama taking place on the street in front of them. Hector stood helplessly, trying to figure out what had just happened to him, and how the fuck he could ever explain this Bedlam meets Encino to Markov?

When the handcuffed man was being led away by the police, Hector heard him yell, "If I hadn't dropped my roscoe, you never woulda taken me alive, copper!"

"I want to go home!" Dr. Maurice wailed again.

Hector found it all incomprehensible. He kept wondering how he had come to this, finally deciding it was Hollywood. The insanity of Hollywood will eventually overwhelm you, he thought, and you'll submit to nutty schemes like the one with Basil and this quack.

Hector gave the former doctor a shove in the direction of the street and said, "Get the fuck outta my sight, termite teeth."

Sergeant Hawthorne drove silently back to Hollywood Station, contemplating how he would cover this aborted mission in his report to the captain, but it was hard to think with his passengers babbling excitedly about the evening adventure.

"Dude!" Flotsam said, "When we saw that zombie heading for the front door, we knew he had to be either an extra from *Walking Dead* or Dr. Maurice. And the sarge here, he comes up with an idea to turn it all into a fire drill to get you outta there with no hassle."

"The guy had a nose hair seven inches long and a mouth full of licorice bites!" Jetsam said. "I was fascinated."

The vice sergeant felt exhausted, demoralized, wiped out. He said listlessly to Jetsam, "Actually, I already had that escape option cleared with the West Valley watch commander, if needed. I didn't want Hector Cozzo to find out you're a cop, in case there might be future possibilities with this operation." He added, "But there won't be. My big idea has turned into—"

"I don't know, Sarge," Jetsam offered by way of consolation. "I think I convinced Cozzo and Ivana that the doc's brain has liquefied. And I made that offer to work with Hector for free as an assistant, didn't I? Maybe he'll call me."

Sergeant Hawthorne said dejectedly, "Pimps don't have interns. Hector Cozzo will hire you as an assistant when Ivana joins the Little Sisters of the Poor."

"I stuck to the script," Jetsam pointed out, fishing for compliments. "Considering I found myself in a degenerate version of Circus Maximus, with a real heavy freak-and-mutant act on the program."

"You were slammin', dude!" Flotsam said. "Hollywood Nate, with his SAG card and all, couldn't have done no better. We got in the van, and listened. I loved the way you go, 'He's confused, look at him' when Frankenstein's stepdad is all acting out and screaming like Saturday night in the drunk tank."

179

"Did you hear the way I delivered my lines?" Jetsam said. "I tried to stay way George Clooney cool."

"You were totally cool, dude," Flotsam assured him. "Red carpet all the way!"

Jetsam was all smiles from Flotsam's accolades and from the 80 proof vodka he'd sampled, and he said to his partner, "You ain't no slouch neither, bro. I could hear you from inside the house when you yelled out stuff to the West Valley coppers. Where'd you come up with that retro dialogue about your mouthpiece and your roscoe? Was that, like, method acting or something?"

Flotsam said, "Hollywood Nate got me watching Turner Classic Movies. Those lines came from Edward G. Robinson. Or was it James Cagney? You know, bro, the next time we do this, we should demand an A-list Winnebago for our dressing room."

Sergeant Hawthorne felt a fierce headache coming on, coupled with an incipient death wish for his two jabbering companions. In a feeble effort to momentarily escape, he tried blocking out the inane chatter by tripping down memory lane, back to his life's best days at UCLA. Back when his biggest worry was getting tickets to football and basketball games, and trying to date a busty classmate. Back in those halcyon days when he used to argue with his acerbic and cynical older sister about his impractical academic choices, using retorts like "There're *plenty* of things I can do to improve my life from the study of Philosophical Analysis of Contemporary Moral Issues!"

What would she say if she could see him right now? Feeling like an utter burnout at age twenty-eight, after his half-baked scheme involving apotemnophilia had blown up like a Taliban IED. A scheme that the Watch 5 sergeant had told him to his face was bizarre and harebrained and would never work. At last, here he was, exhausted, with two surfer goons he hoped he'd never see again.

He could almost hear his sister say to him, "So, our brainstorm du jour blew up in our face, did it? Thad, honey, you've always had the intensity and drive of a Vincent van Gogh. But I'm afraid your life's self-portrait will look like it was painted by Cheeta the chimp."

TWELVE

Dɪɴᴋᴏ ᴀᴡᴏᴋᴇ ᴇᴀʀʟʏ the next morning. He showered and shaved and dressed up better than he ever had when he was accompanying his mother to Mass. Lita wore her best dress, a creamy white one with long sleeves and an empire waist, and flats, her only shoes, besides sneakers, that weren't for use on a stage while straddling a pole. Even Brigita Babich went a little dressier than usual in a summer pastel, cut just below the knee but allowing room for an expanding middle.

"My, don't you look beautiful, Lita!" Brigita said. "And look at my handsome son, all spruced up for a change."

"Thanks, Mom," Dinko said. "You look very beautiful, too."

"Now you've gone too far," Brigita said. "Let's go to Mass."

She had found Dinko and Lita watching television when she'd returned from bingo the night before, but there'd been something different about them, a certain look when their eyes met. She correctly suspected that this new friendship had turned into something more for them while she'd been trying to catch bingo numbers on all four corners of her card.

They attended the 9:00 Mass in English at Mary Star of the Sea, a church with a diverse parish that also offered Sunday Masses in Croatian, Italian, and Spanish. Brigita was interested to see if Lita and Dinko would go to Holy Communion. She wondered if they felt they were in a state of grace or not. She assumed that Dinko would go to Communion

181

regardless, because despite her most strenuous efforts, he'd never been a devout Catholic like she and his father had been. She figured that Dinko would take Communion just for show even if he'd committed every mortal sin up to murder, without even bothering about confession and absolution.

When it was time for Communion, Brigita got up and walked down the aisle toward the altar, but both Dinko and Lita remained in the pew. Brigita thought that was evidence that they'd been intimate, and that Lita needed to confess to a priest before accepting Holy Communion. Brigita liked that. It meant that the girl respected the rules of the Church even if she'd broken a law of God.

That made Brigita wonder how many times this child had broken other laws of God, coming from who knew what kind of life in Mexico, and then as a dancer in a Hollywood nightclub. Still, Lita hadn't been disrespectful and taken Holy Communion while not in a state of grace, and that had to be counted in her favor. Brigita was already fond of this girl and liked the positive effect she was having on Dinko, but where would it lead? He'd known her for only a few *days*. It was very worrisome.

Upon returning home, Brigita said, "You two can change and feed Ollie while I squeeze some orange juice and get brunch started."

Lita said, "Please can I help? My mother, she like to cook also. She can make very good chipotle roasting beef, when she got the money for the beef. And she like to make *arroz con leche* for finish. You know the one?"

"I do," Brigita said. "Rice and condensed milk, either warm or cold, with cinnamon on top. We used to order that when we'd go for Mexican food at Ports O' Call. Remember, Dinko?"

"I remember," he said, but really he didn't. He found himself not wanting to remember anything that had happened before the last few days. Before Lita, that was another life, all of it. He was beginning anew.

"I'll buy some chipotle chilies next time I go to the market," Brigita said. Then: "When was the last time you saw your mother, Lita?"

"When I have to come here," she said. "It is three months when I leave Guanajuato, and I ride the bus to Tijuana for one week and meet the coyote, and then I cross with ten other people."

"With that big suitcase?" Dinko asked.

"Yes," she said. "A man help me. I pay him, and after we cross, we see cars that wait and they drive me to the bus station in San Diego. And I take the bus to Los Angeles."

"Have you phoned your mother in the past four months?" Brigita asked.

"She do not have the telephone," Lita said. "But I make the calls to the lady who is living in the rooms above my mother and brothers. She always runs to get my mother for us to talk. I do not wish to trouble the lady, so I only call maybe one time each week. My mother says she is okay and my brothers go to school and they are okay. But my mother has the diabetes and the weak heart, so I must send money when I can. That is why I come here. To make more money than I make in Guanajuato."

"Lita," Brigita said, "how did you earn money in Mexico?"

The young woman lowered her eyes and said, "I dance in the club. Same like the one in Wilmington."

Dinko thought the interrogation had gone far enough, and so did Brigita. When Dinko asked, "Are we ever gonna get brunch?" Brigita said, "We certainly are. Lita, how about squeezing those oranges?"

"Yes!" Lita said with enthusiasm. "I am very good making the orange juice."

Early that Sunday evening, at about the same time that Lita Medina and Dinko Babich were being stuffed with the third meal of the day, a homeless octogenarian derelict known as Trombone Teddy was sound asleep in a dumpster just off Hollywood Boulevard near Vine Street. He'd had a successful Sunday morning panhandling on the boulevard and had managed to get himself so lubricated in the early afternoon that he needed a nap in his favorite summer snoozing spot. Trombone Teddy was having one of those heavenly dreams of the days when he was a good sideman playing in several West Coast jazz spots, including at legendary drummer Shelly Manne's famous nightclub, Shelly's Manne-Hole, on Cahuenga Boulevard. As far as Trombone Teddy was concerned, those were the days when real music ruled, and he knew they would never return.

Teddy, who was known to many of the cops at Hollywood Station, was an extremely sound sleeper, especially after so much afternoon imbibing, and while he slept, a Honduran janitor working an overtime job at a nearby commercial building carried a trash can loaded with office detritus to the building's seldom-used dumpster. He heard the buzz of circling flies, and when he opened the lid immediately leaped backward, dropping the trash can, but not before getting a good scare from the grizzled countenance of Trombone Teddy, who looked and smelled very dead indeed. As the lid slammed down, the janitor ran back to the job site to phone the police.

The midwatch had just cleared from roll call, and at 5:45 P.M., 6-X-76 got the call. The janitor, who spoke English well enough to explain what he'd found, led Mel Yarashi and Always Talking Tony to the last resting place of Trombone Teddy, who was not known by either cop.

When they were still fifty feet away from the dumpster, Mel Yarashi turned to his younger partner and said, "Whoa! We got a stinker, all right. The dude's deader than a lawyer's conscience."

Except that when they raised the lid, Teddy snorted and tried to roll over on the trash pile for a more comfortable repose.

Mel Yarashi told the janitor, "This is either Lazarus or the old bum ain't dead."

"Dead drunk, maybe," A.T. said.

Then the older cop said, "Jesus, the smell!"

That's when Teddy's sleeping partner revealed herself. Teddy's rolling movement had put his face on top of her extended hand, her flesh the palest of gray, and supple, rigor having come and gone.

"Goddamn!" Mel Yarashi cried, and he shoveled away some crumpled newspapers and cardboard boxes, seeing that the hand was attached to the clothed body of a woman. "Call for a homicide team!" he told A.T. "And notify the watch commander!" Then he shook Teddy, yelling, "Get the fuck up!"

Teddy threw up his hand to shield his eyes from the low-angled solar rays, and blinked uncomprehendingly at the Asian cop staring slack-jawed at him while a black cop talked excitedly into a hand-held radio.

"Good day, Officer," Teddy said. "Am I preventing access to the dumpster this afternoon? If so, I'll be glad to move to—"

"Get outta there!" Mel Yarashi sputtered, and he grabbed Teddy by the front of his greasy coat, lifting the scrawny derelict out onto the asphalt.

Still stunned, the cop blurted, "What'd you do to her?" Then he calmed himself, drew his handcuffs, and said, "You're under arrest. You have the right to remain silent. You—"

Teddy interrupted the Miranda warning by saying, "But this dump-ster is almost never used, Officer! They pick it up once a week, and it's never more than half full. I woulda picked another one if I knew the people in the office building cared this much. They often wave to me and give me doughnuts sometimes. I'm sorry, Officer. If I'm trespassing, I won't sleep in this one no more."

Mel Yarashi ceased Mirandizing. He looked at Teddy's watery blue eyes and childlike expression, and then at the extended arm of the dead woman in the dumpster, whose smell made him want to retch. He put his handcuffs back on his Sam Browne and said, "Tell me something. Did you know you went to bed with a corpse?"

Trombone Teddy blinked again, scratched his belly, and asked, per-plexed, "Are you talking about that time last year when the guy next to me at the homeless shelter croaked during the night?"

The moment the crime scene criminalists had finished their preliminary work, and the coroner's body snatchers had lifted the dead woman from the dumpster and placed her on their corpse cart, she was identified by her nickname and place of employment. The strip club dancer was wearing a Club Samara silver anklet, engraved with her professional name, "Daisy"—a gift that each of the dancers had been given with their holiday bonus in December. The second team of detectives at the scene drove to the nightclub, closed on Sunday, and got the head bartender's phone number from one of the Latino busboys doing a cleanup prior to the Monday lunch opening.

Leonid Alekseev, the Russian bartender, was called. He drove to the club, where he met the team of detectives and quickly identified their death photo of the Korean dancer known as Daisy. He provided her employment name, Soo Jeong, and her Social Security number and driver's license information, along with the address of her apartment in east Hollywood. Violet, aka Li Pham, Daisy's roommate, was interviewed, but she could provide no information other than that Daisy had gone missing for unexplained reasons earlier in the week, and Violet claimed to be unsure of the exact day. She implied in broken English that such was the topsy-turvy world of exotic dancers, who did not always sleep at home.

By early evening, a sixty-two-year-old Georgian immigrant and retired pawnbroker, Bakhva Ramishvili, whose name appeared on the liquor license and the building lease, was sitting inside an interview room at Hollywood Station, perspiring noticeably. He assured a woman homicide detective that he was a minor investor in Club Samara but that the nightclub's management was the responsibility of the Russian bartender, Leonid Alekseev. When pressed as to who else was an investor in the club, the Georgian gave the name Pavel Markov and an address on Mount Olympus.

After dark, a very weary Hollywood Division D2, Albino Villaseñor, drove alone up Mount Olympus, where local realtors claimed there were more Italian cypress trees per acre than anywhere else on earth. Bino Villaseñor was very familiar with Mount Olympus, a section of the Hollywood Hills preferred by well-to-do foreign nationals. There were plenty of residents from Israel, Iran, Russia, Armenia, and many Arab countries. The number of Bentleys and Rolls-Royces attested to that.

The detective had been hoping to spend Sunday evening watching a video of his granddaughter trying her hand at lacrosse. Instead, he'd been called from his home thirty minutes after Trombone Teddy had been found alive and well, but with a dumpster partner who was not. And Bino had been hard at work ever since.

He'd received another call that evening, from Sergeant Hawthorne of the Hollywood vice unit, who'd told him that the Club Samara dancers were being "serviced" by a dirtbag named Hector Cozzo, who was an unofficial facilitator for this nightclub and for a massage parlor that was an upscale brothel. The vice sergeant said there might also be a Korean named Mr. Kim who was connected to the nightclub as a provider of entertainment. Then Bino had been given a short version of the extraordinary undercover operation that had gone awry at Hector Cozzo's Encino home.

After parking in front of the Mount Olympus address he'd been given by the license holder and part owner of Club Samara, the detective studied the house from the street. It wasn't particularly impressive, not like some of the view homes near the top, and the detective was fairly certain that the house would turn out to be leased rather than owned by the resident. That, too, was common around these parts.

Bino Villaseñor examined his wardrobe after he got out of the car—an automatic response, he believed, to being in Hollywood Hills neighborhoods where his Mexican immigrant grandfather had actually worked as a gardener back when Bino was a child. His three-year-old brown gabardine suit was good at hiding coffee spills but was looking pretty sad of late, and he made a mental note to call tomorrow and see if they had any sales going on at Men's Wearhouse. He adjusted the knot on his salsa-stained maroon necktie before ringing the bell.

The door was opened by a rather flamboyant-looking older man with a black Elvis hairdo, obviously dyed, wearing a pearly jumpsuit that had gone out of style in the 1980s or earlier. The resident looked with some disappointment at a bald, rumpled Latino with a bushy white mustache who was holding a large notepad in his hand. It seemed as though Markov might've been expecting someone more impressive and formidable.

Bino pulled his coat back to reveal the LAPD shield on his belt and said, "I'm Detective Villaseñor, the one who phoned you. If you're Mr. Pavel Markov."

Markov said, "That's a name I use in business, Detective. My correct name is Pedrag Marcovic. It seems more profitable in Hollywood these days to be from Russia rather than my homeland of Serbia, so for business reasons I have adopted a name that implies I am an ethnic Russian, even though my poor grasp of the Russian language usually gives me away. Please come in."

Bino entered the foyer and sized up the house in a glance, thinking, Leased for sure, with rented furniture. The guy was not wealthy, but was trying to be a player among those who were.

"What business are you in, sir?" Bino asked.

"Mostly real estate investment and entertainment," Markov said. "Why don't we have a seat in the living room? Can I get you some iced tea?"

Bino shook his head, saying, "No, thanks, I'm fine," and followed Markov into the living room, thinking, Yeah, rented furniture. He'd seen identical sofa and love-seat combos in other homes in the Hollywood Hills. Bino Villaseñor figured that if he had an Andrew Jackson for every Hollywood player who claimed to be in real estate investment or entertainment, he could afford to retire to that little condo he and the wife dreamed about, down in Seal Beach, only two blocks from the ocean, where he could forget murder and teach the grandkids to build sand castles.

The detective said, "I understand you're a part owner of Club Samara?"

"I am an investor," Markov answered reluctantly, never wanting any of his nightclub or massage parlor connections to be publicly known. "I want you to know that I seldom go to the club except on certain occasions when I have to approve a new act, and I have never, to my knowledge, seen the unfortunate dancer you have come about."

"Her name is Soo Jeong, as far as we know, but around the club she was known as Daisy," Bino said. "Does that nickname ring a bell?"

Markov shook his head. "I do not think that I have visited that particular investment in nearly two months. I do not know any of the entertainers by name."

"So, for the record, I guess you wouldn't know who might've killed her and thrown her body in a dumpster?"

"Of course not. Was she perhaps killed by someone who ambushed and raped her?"

"I have no idea," Bino said. "We'll wait for the postmortem before learning that sort of thing."

"I imagine that in the nightclub business the dancers meet a certain element, who seduce them into compromising situations with money offers. And then, who knows what can happen? Am I correct in thinking that?"

Markov used his expressive hands when he spoke, and Bino thought they were graceful, like a dancer's hands.

The detective said, "You're the one in the nightclub business, so you tell me."

That dropped Markov's hands quietly to his lap and made the Serb remind himself not to talk too much, and only in response. He said, "I guess I watch too much television. I think I am trying to be a detective."

"Do you know a man named Hector Cozzo?" Bino asked, looking down at the legal pad on which he was making notes. "I believe he works for that particular investment of yours?"

Markov hesitated for just an instant, then decided not to be too clever, saying, "Well, yes, of course. Hector Cozzo is a kind of handyman who runs errands, takes the dancers for fittings, that sort of thing. I am not sure exactly what he does with each of the two business investments I have in Hollywood. I am also invested in Shanghai Massage, but you may have already discovered that."

"Is Hector Cozzo on your payroll?"

"Heavens, no," Markov said. "He is the type of person who enjoys to be in the company of beautiful girls. Leonid Alekseev is the manager of Club Samara, and I believe he repays Hector by giving him free meals, or rewards him with an occasional cash payment. Nothing significant, just what you might call a tip for service. I can assure you that if Hector were on the nightclub payroll, he would be given a W-2 and we would report his earnings to the IRS. I am a grateful immigrant to this country and have no wish to cheat my Uncle Sam out of taxes." He smiled when he said that, as though the detective should be amused.

"Did you know that Leonid Alekseev has a police record?"

"Yes, but a minor one," Markov said. "He used to manage another nightclub owned by one of his countrymen, and he had to get physical with unruly customers on a few occasions."

Bino said, "My understanding is that the last time he got physical, the customer ended up in the hospital with two broken arms."

"Leonid was a lumberman back in Russia," Markov said, "and does not know his own strength. But he is a splendid maker of drinks. He loves working behind the bar and never flaunts his authority as manager of the club. He makes sure that things run smoothly and that moneys are properly reported to my accountant. That sort of thing."

"And is there a Korean who does managing duties?"

The hesitation lasted a bit longer before Markov said, "No, we have no Korean employees. There used to be a Mr. William Kim, who was kind of a talent agent. He would bring girls to the club for auditions. I am not sure if he does that anymore. I have not seen him in over a year, but maybe Leonid still deals with him from time to time. I am not certain."

Bino said, "Did you pay Mr. Kim for his services?"

"No," Markov said. "We never had to pay him for his service. I believe he received a percentage of his client's pay, like any talent agent. I believe that Leonid can verify that. Once again, I would not try to escape paying my taxes for any moneys earned at Club Samara or Shanghai Massage."

"Do you have Mr. Kim's address and phone number?"

"No, I do not. I doubt that Leonid does, either. These self-styled talent agents who deal with exotic dancers just come and go."

Bino looked Markov in the eye and said, "What do you know about the Encino house that Hector Cozzo lives in?"

Markov said, "Ah, yes, I neglected to mention that as a further reward for his services as an errand boy and handyman, Hector subleases the Encino property from me at a favorable monthly amount."

"So you don't own it?"

"No, I lease it from a gentleman named Garo Seropian, who owns a real estate company in Little Armenia."

"Do you own this house?"

"No, I lease it. Why do you ask?"

The detective surprised Markov when he said, "You lease your businesses from property owners, as well as this house and Hector Cozzo's house. You lease everything and own nothing. Is that how it's done these days? I'm just a midlevel civil servant with little understanding of current business practices."

"I think the Great Recession has taught us that leasing is the wave of the future," Markov answered affably. "Easy in, easy out. My cars are also leased. The only thing that I own and can actually sell is the goodwill generated by my customers. I am a kind of modern-day Gypsy traveler."

"Which means you fold your tents and jump on the caravan and are gone by morning, huh?" Bino said.

Markov tried to chuckle, but it didn't work. He said, "Have you spoken to Hector Cozzo about this terrible incident?"

"Your Russian manager gave us his home address in Encino and a cell number, but the number's no longer in service. I told Leonid Alekseev to inform Hector Cozzo that I need to speak with him, but if he doesn't call soon I'm going to have to drop by his house in Encino. Or should I say *your* house in Encino?"

"In point of fact," Markov said, trying another chuckle, "the house of Garo Seropian."

"Yeah, I almost forgot," Bino said. "You own nothing but goodwill."

"I see how peculiar our way of doing business must seem to you," Markov said. "I think it is because we immigrants have trouble adjusting to the meticulous American ways. We come from places where record keeping is . . . slapdash, if that is the correct English word."

Bino said, "Hector Cozzo is not an immigrant. If he doesn't contact me soon, I'm going to start wondering about his slapdash ways. And speaking of slapdash, the other investor, Mr. Ramishvili, whose name is on the building's lease and the liquor license, doesn't know any more about the managing of the club than I do. So now I'm wondering how handy your handyman Hector Cozzo really is, and exactly what he does to help Leonid Alekseev. You have a lot of people between you and your investments, don't you?"

Markov again attempted a chuckle; and it came out even worse than last time. He said, "Are you sure I cannot get you something to drink?"

Bino shook his head and said, "About Hector Cozzo: did you know he has a criminal record?

Markov looked up, as though trying to remember. "I may have heard that he had minor skirmishes with the law when he was younger. But I think everyone deserves a second chance, don't you?"

"Like Charles Manson?" Bino asked.

It was hard to see if the detective was smiling under the bushy white mustache, so Markov opted for ignorance and said, "I am afraid I do not know that person."

"Doesn't matter," Bino said. "We'll be talking to Mr. Cozzo and maybe Mr. Kim if we can, to see what they can tell us about Daisy. But in the meantime, if either of them should call you, give them my number." Bino dropped a business card on the coffee table and stood up.

Markov hesitated before saying, "Detective, I am very sad about the poor girl, Daisy. If there is anything I can do for her family . . . well, do they live locally?"

Bino answered, "As far as we know, all of her family is in South Korea. We think she was smuggled into this country."

"I see," Markov said. "Well, please be assured that I would never have anything to do with an investment if I knew it involved illegal immigrants. As a young man I waited for a long time before I received a visa to come to America, and I have always tried to be grateful for the privilege."

"I'm sure you're a real credit to your heritage and to this country," Bino said, and Markov was frustrated because again he couldn't see if the detective was grinning at him under that bushy white mustache. And those penetrating brown eyes revealed nothing.

THIRTEEN

Sᴜɴᴅᴀʏ ꜰᴏʀ Lɪᴛᴀ Medina at the Babich house had meant food, followed by a stroll through the shops at Ports O' Call with Dinko, where a mariachi band was playing on a restaurant patio. Then more food, and another stroll with Dinko along the cliffs at Point Fermin Park. Then an evening in front of the television watching *60 Minutes.*

This was the first day that Dinko had not pressed Lita about the possibility of a future together. It had been a peaceful day with lots of hand-holding and nuzzling and, a few times, a serious kiss. One of those had taken place on the Point Fermin cliffs with the offshore summer breeze blowing her hair around her face. Dinko had to gently sweep the hair back to find her lips.

After they'd kissed, all he could think of to say was a reprise of what he'd said to her before: "You are loved."

She'd said nothing in reply but had put her head on his shoulder as they walked across the grass to the car. They saw the feral peacock fan its tail feathers and squawk when a child approached too close.

Both Dinko and Lita had groaned and laughed when Brigita Babich said she was retiring early and wanted to know if they'd like her to make a snack for them while they continued watching TV. She'd glanced at them and knew they were going to make love after she went to bed. And though in past years she'd told Dinko, "Not under my roof," requiring that Dinko's occasional overnight girlfriends sleep alone in the guest room, this time Brigita knew things were different. Lita Medina was different. Her son had become astonishingly different since meeting this girl. She could say nothing about where they slept or what they did under her roof.

Brigita Babich had spent the day searching her heart for answers to her deep misgivings. She was ashamed to think it could be because the girl was Mexican. Her husband had always hoped that Dinko would marry a Croatian girl, or at least an all-American hybrid who could produce babies that would look Croatian. What would he say to *this* potential match? That made her shame deepen, and she thought, No, it's not that the girl is Mexican. It's her past. A dancer from a strip club in Wilmington? The girl was virtually a prostitute. What had she done in Mexico to make a living? What was she doing in Los Angeles now?

Brigita knew her only child better than he knew himself. She'd been the one who'd spoiled him, especially after her husband died. She knew he was lazy and immature and had never taken advantage of the good job on the docks that nepotism had provided him. Nevertheless, he had a big heart, even as a child, always taking care of stray cats and dogs and, on one occasion, an injured seagull that had lived with them for a month before being set free. She'd wanted a strong woman to take him in hand and make him grow up and be responsible.

And that was the troubling thing about this child, Lita. By virtue of who she was, Lita *was* making Dinko seem more mature, more responsible. This change was in his eyes, in every word he said, in every gesture since he'd met this girl. He'd spoken in front of Lita about taking more shifts on the docks and earning the kind of money a longshoreman should make, the kind of money his father had made. The kind of money that had built their house, which was owned free and clear. In a few short days, this girl had somehow transformed Dinko in the very way Brigita had always hoped a good woman might do it in a few *years*.

But then she thought, No! Not a nineteen-year-old girl from a strip club. Not an illegal immigrant whose story about an ailing mother and younger brothers in Mexico did not ring true. All of that made Brigita Babich fear Lita Medina, for the sake of her son. And yet . . . when Brigita looked into the unsettling amber eyes of this child, she saw goodness there, regardless of the kind of life she'd lived or the doubtful history she'd recounted. Brigita saw an uncomplaining hard worker and a strong, intelligent girl who could make Dinko happy and turn him into a real man, like his father. And Brigita could see a helpful, beautiful daughter who she could grow to love very easily, and who would surely provide Brigita with pretty grandchildren.

All of this soul searching left Brigita Babich bone weary when she retired for the night, leaving Dinko and Lita blissfully alone in the living room with Ollie the cat. Brigita fell sound asleep before 9:00.

When Dinko was sure that his mother was asleep, he kissed Lita and whispered, "Let's go to my room. I wanna tell you about the house I'm gonna buy for you and how I'm gonna help your family. I'm gonna keep bugging you till you say y-y-yes just to shut me up!"

By midnight, most of the preliminary work was finished at the taped-off crime scene near Hollywood and Vine, and it had drawn a television crew that had slipped Teddy twenty bucks for a ten-word interview, which had made the local news at eleven. Trombone Teddy had also been given ten more by Flotsam and Jetsam, who were back on patrol after their undercover adventure, and who'd stopped by the crime scene to see what was going on. The surfers had known Teddy for a few years and, like the other coppers on Watch 5, were amused by the quickly circulating story of him sleeping with a dead body.

And then, much to Teddy's delight, Hollywood Nate and Britney Small cruised by out of curiosity, and Nate, also an old acquaintance of Trombone Teddy's, gave him another ten dollars just for having been through such a grueling ordeal earlier in the evening. A few more black-and-whites drove by to look at him and chuckle.

Teddy couldn't figure out what the fuss was about and why he was being rewarded. He hadn't seen the dead girl at all and hadn't even smelled her; nor had he been able to smell much else in the past ten years. But with forty bucks in his kick, he did the sensible thing as soon as the detectives let him go. He went straight to the nearest liquor store and bought all the 80 proof gin the largesse could buy, and drank much of it before he could begin heading to his favorite doorway, where he kept an old blanket for serious sleeping.

The problem was, he'd gotten hammered in a hurry. He hadn't guzzled a bottle of gin like that in he didn't know how long. Teddy was lurching from one side of the sidewalk to the other as he staggered along Hollywood Boulevard. Then he slouched off to a side street and didn't know where the hell he was.

Both Chester Toles and Marius Tatarescu were off that night, so Sergeant Murillo had teamed up their partners in 6-X-46. At Selma and Las Palmas, Fran Famosa and Sophie Branson had jammed up four young cruisers from a Compton Crips gang, who'd come up on the subway wearing gang colors for a night of hustling and strong-arming the gay men who frequented those streets. They'd already begun harassing gay pedestrians when 6-X-46 spotted them.

Sophie was finishing up field interrogation cards on all four and had run them for wants and warrants with negative results. Their shop was parked fifty feet away on Selma Avenue, with the parking lights on. Fran had left the passenger door hanging open in case she had to run back for assistance.

Sophie finished up the four FIs and said, "Okay, why don't you head for the subway now and go home. Your Hollywood evening is over."

The four Crips grinned and whispered to each other, and blew kisses at Fran Famosa while sauntering away singing the theme from the *Cops* television show, changing the "boys" to "girls."

"Bad girls, bad girls, whatcha gonna do? Whatcha gonna do when they come for you?"

"Assholes!" Sophie said, but Fran had to laugh.

Sophie headed back to the radio car while Fran stayed put to make sure the Crips kept moving. Sophie opened the driver's door and sat down, but then she felt peculiar, only she didn't know why. It was one of those moments where she literally felt the hairs rising on the back of her neck. She turned around and, through the dividing screen, saw a man sitting behind her.

Sophie screamed and leaped from the car, pulling her pistol and yelling, "Get out! Get the fuck outta the car!"

But, of course, he did not have that option, not from the backseat, where prisoners sit. He could get in, but not out. Fran Famosa came running up and jerked open the back door, and Trombone Teddy stared at both of them, thoroughly confused. He staggered out and looked at the car, suddenly aware that it was painted black and white.

Fran said to Sophie, "This is the guy from the dumpster. This is Trombone Teddy!"

"What in the hell are you doing in our car?" Sophie yelled.

"I got lost," Teddy said. "The other officers made me leave my dumpster and I can't find my favorite doorway and I saw the car with the door open and I wanted to lay down for a while. I'm sorry."

"We'll give you a place to sleep!" Sophie said, still steaming, her heartbeat barely beginning to slow.

"I understand," Teddy said. "This has not been my day."

But Fran Famosa said, "Partner, I saw Hollywood Nate handing him money. It's partly Nate's fault that Teddy got wrecked like this. And he's kind of a celebrity tonight. Maybe we can help him find his doorway?"

"It's on Cherokee," Teddy said, "right off Hollywood Boulevard. I'm slightly lost at this moment."

"That's right around the corner," Fran said to Sophie.

Sophie Branson reluctantly told Teddy, "Okay, get back in the car and we'll take you to your doorway."

A few minutes later, Trombone Teddy was overjoyed to spot his doorway with his blanket folded up where he'd left it.

"That's it!" he said. "That's my doorway!"

He got out of the car and said guilelessly to Sophie, "I'm real sorry, Officer, but if I may say, it was charming to hear you scream like a little girl. We sometimes forget that police officers are human beings."

"Get your ass to bed!" Sophie said as the radio car roared away from the curb.

FOURTEEN

THE DISCOVERY OF the body of a strip club dancer was covered by the *Los Angeles Times* the next morning. The story said that an unidentified source at the club indicated that the dancer may have been an undocumented Asian immigrant, and that her name and identification might be fictitious. It wasn't a big story, but it was big enough for Brigita Babich to notice and read with her coffee, before Dinko and Lita had showered and dressed.

Dinko, entering the kitchen ahead of Lita, saw at once the grim set of his mother's mouth.

"What's wrong?" he asked.

"Look at this," she said, showing him the newspaper story.

"My God," Dinko said, and crossed himself involuntarily.

"Now are you ready to take her to the police?"

"Yes," he said. "Now I'm ready."

Lita entered the kitchen wearing her jeans and her only tee that was clean, and asked, "Is okay if I wash my clothes today?"

"Sit down, Lita," Brigita said. "Let me read this to you."

As Brigita read, Lita's eyes widened and the corners of her mouth turned down. After Brigita was finished, she put the newspaper down and, without a word, poured a glass of orange juice for Lita.

Dinko said, "We gotta call the police today, Lita. There's no choice now. You gotta tell them you saw someone resembling Kim driving Daisy away. Understand?"

Lita nodded, her eyes glistening. "I have much fear," she said.

"You don't have to fear the police," Brigita said. "They'll treat you very well because you're an important witness. They won't be worrying about your immigration status."

Lita said, "No, I have fear that Mr. Kim will find me!"

D2 Albino Villaseñor drove straight from his home in Montebello to San Pedro in the city car that he got to take home by virtue of his job as an on-call homicide detective. His detective partner would be attending the postmortem, scheduled to begin at 11:00 A.M., where they'd be told officially what they already knew: she'd died from strangulation, probably on the day she'd disappeared. The contusions on her neck suggested that she'd been garroted.

Bino Villaseñor remembered back thirty-one years to when he was a young cop and the OGs used to refer to Harbor Division as "San Pedro PD," as though, by virtue of its remote location, it was not part of the LAPD. He'd been told by coppers who'd worked Harbor Division that you were on your own down there if you needed an airship. By the time a police helicopter could get to a San Pedro incident, chances were good that the crisis would've been resolved in some other way. And the nearest LAPD division that could help you was housed at Seventy-seventh Street Station, a long way from Pedro, especially in heavy traffic. The Port Police was the closest agency they could depend on for faster emergency assistance.

In many ways, Harbor Division was sort of a police department unto itself. When Bino was a young cop, he'd always wondered what it would've been like to work way down there, back in the day when the Porthole Saloon on Sixth Street used to stay open until 4:00 A.M. to illegally accommodate the Fish Town coppers. Now the Porthole was gone.

He found the Babich house easily enough, arriving just as Brigita was preparing a brunch of *cevapcici*, a kind of Croatian hamburger made of spicy pork, with a side of *blitva*, Swiss chard with potatoes and garlic and lots of special olive oil, and bread from an Italian bakery. Of course, she insisted that Bino Villaseñor have something to eat before his interview with Lita Medina, but the detective asked courteously if he might speak to Ms. Medina privately and then join them for the Croatian brunch.

Bino and Lita spoke outside on the patio, each with a glass of iced tea. The entire interview was in Spanish, and Bino was careful not to alarm the young woman with any hint that she might be in danger. He made it seem no more urgent than if she were making a routine police report on an annoying neighbor who was disturbing the peace with loud parties.

But he asked her twice in Spanish if she was sure that Daisy had yelled angry things in her mother tongue at the driver of the big black car with the shiny wheels.

And Lita answered, "*Sí, señor.*"

Then he asked her twice if she was absolutely sure that the driver of the car had said something to Daisy and that Daisy had looked fearful when she got into the car.

And Lita answered, "*Sí, señor.*"

Then he asked her if she'd seen enough of the driver's profile to positively say that it was Mr. Kim. She hesitated and shook her head, indicating that the glimpse she'd gotten was of a big man with black hair who looked similar to Mr. Kim, but she could not swear that it was him.

Bino took down the address of Lita's mother and brothers, and the telephone number of the neighbor in Guanajuato who could be relied upon to fetch Lita's mother to the phone. This was just in case Lita Medina decided to escape the duty of testifying in a murder case and opted instead to return home to Mexico.

After they were finished, and Bino was satisfied that he had all that might help build a case against the elusive Mr. Kim, Bino and Lita joined Dinko and Brigita Babich in the kitchen.

Bino Villaseñor sat at the table, tucked a corner of a cloth napkin inside his shirt collar, and said, "This looks like the kind of midday meal my mother used to make on Sundays."

Dinko said, "And this is Monday. You shoulda seen what she made yesterday."

The detective was talkative, and told funny stories about police work in Hollywood. When it was time to leave, he thanked Brigita Babich. And he thanked Lita Medina, saying he would be in touch with her at the Babiches' phone number. Then, with a subtle movement of his head, he indicated that Dinko should walk him to his car.

As soon as they were out of earshot of the women in the house, Bino told Dinko, "I don't think you have anything to worry about. We'll find William Kim if he's still in L.A., but it might take some time. Half the population of Koreatown is named Kim and the other half is Lee, but his name doesn't appear on any of the documents or records at Club Samara. Personally, I think that after hearing we found the dancer's body, he might've already booked a flight to points west."

"How would he know that Lita saw him with Daisy?"

"Ms. Medina made the mistake of telling too much of what she saw to the other roommate, Violet," Bino said. "Like the fact that Daisy spoke Korean to the driver of the black car. I'm guessing that Violet coughed that up to Kim the second he gave her the bad eye or a couple hundred bucks. So we gotta figure that Kim believes that Lita can positively identify him as the guy who took Daisy on her last ride that day. Even though she can't."

"If he thinks that, it's not good," Dinko said.

Bino said, "But Kim might feel confident that an undocumented Mexican girl would be too scared to call the police. He might be lying low for a while to see what shakes out. What you have to understand about these organized crime foreign nationals from former Eastern bloc countries, and I'll lump the Koreans in there with them, is that they don't do business like our OC types. They're basically cold war hoodlums. No matter what kind of show they put on with big cars, and tailor-made suits, and houses on Mount Olympus, they're still thugs. Which makes them unpredictable. And that means that Kim could be very dangerous if he's still around L.A. And if he's guilty of the murder."

"Can Lita get police protection?" Dinko asked.

Bino shook his head. "We can't begin to prove yet that Kim's the one who killed Daisy. He's just another person of interest as of now. But if we can link him to her murder, this case will likely be taken away from me. It'll involve federal crimes and human trafficking that caused the deaths of thirteen people in the container yard."

Dinko said, "Is there *anything* you can do for us right now?"

Bino said, "I'll personally contact the watch commander at Harbor Station and request that cars make frequent drive-bys at this address around the clock, even though from what you've told me, there's no way Kim could know that Ms. Medina is staying here at your house. Still, be alert until we make contact with him or until we're sure he's fled the country." He added, "And if our investigation clears him, I'll let you know right away."

"I don't think you believe in that possibility," Dinko said, but Bino only smiled and replied, "If it walks like a duck . . ."

Dinko said, "If he *is* the killer, will you find other evidence that'll tie him to Daisy's murder so that Lita's testimony is not so important?"

"We're hoping," Bino said. "When they're finished posting the body today, we might get some idea if there's a chance for DNA evidence. If there is, it'll take a while to get results, given the backlog and the process itself. On *CSI* they get DNA hits in about thirty minutes, but it doesn't work that way in real life."

"I really appreciate the way you've handled this with Lita," Dinko said, shaking hands vigorously with Bino Villaseñor. "You were gentle."

By way of a good-bye, the detective simply looked at Dinko and said, "She's a very fine girl, son." And then he was in his car and heading north from Fish Town.

It was a day that Hector Cozzo would never forget. He wasn't sure if his life had begun to unravel at the off-the-hook Saturday night fiasco at his home, or if this was the day it happened. Hector had slept late after doing too much cocaine and vodka the night before, and he hadn't read the morning newspaper, nor heard any news on TV. It was late afternoon when he decided to drive to the Mercedes dealer to show the service manager what some Armenian asshole had done to his car and to set up an appointment for bodywork. But when he got there he was told to first make a police report, which was required by the dealership's insurance company.

He grumbled to no avail, but after stopping at a bar for a quick drink he drove to Hollywood Station on Wilcox to make the written report, precisely as he'd been advised to do outside Club Samara by the snarky Jewish cop and his little female sidekick. Hector parked on the street in front and walked across the marble-and-brass stars bearing the names of Hollywood Station cops killed in the line of duty. He entered, seeing two cops manning the desk in the lobby.

One of them was Asian and one was Latino, and Hector thought, Jesus! Isn't there one fucking white Christian left in all of Hollywood?

The Latino cop said, "Can I help you?"

"Yeah," Hector said. "Some Armo shithead keyed the hood of my Benz with some Armenian Power bullshit, and the dealer where I leased it says I gotta get a police report with a certain number on it before they'll do anything."

"Did the car dealer ask for a DR number?"

"Yeah, that's it, I think."

"It's just an LAPD crime report number," the desk officer said. "I'll be glad to take care of you."

Hector made his report, signed it, and left the lobby, thinking his luck just had to change somehow. And it did, instantly. For the worse.

The midwatch roll call had just ended and the six cars were pulling out of the parking lot, with the partners in 6-X-32 deciding to head north on Wilcox and maybe grab something at Starbucks to get their engines revved with an instant buzz from an *americano*. Hollywood Nate had always told them that a few shots of bitter espresso could wake up Sleeping Beauty and Rip van Winkle, but maybe not the Unicorn.

Flotsam was driving and Jetsam was keeping the books and filling out the spaces on the log when they drove past Hector Cozzo as he was getting into his car. They didn't notice him, not with the setting sun glaring into the driver's side window and careening off their windshield. But he noticed them.

Hector Cozzo clearly saw Kelly, the degenerate peg-leg guy, now wearing a police uniform. There was no doubt about it! And the other cop driving looked like the suntanned, trash-talking hoodlum that'd been chased down and put in handcuffs!

Hector Cozzo's legs went weak. He had to sit down in his car and try to process what he'd just seen, and wonder in amazement how the cops could've known about Basil's perverse fascination with amputees. And how in the hell could they even have a peg-leg cop working at Hollywood Station to sell the sting? And what were they after if not Markov's entire cash business of selling upscale pussy, and that included the participation of Hector Cozzo? And now he was grateful that the crazy quack had shown up at his house on Saturday night and prevented any illegal activity from taking place in front of the fucking peg-leg cop!

It just became too much to fathom, and Hector cried out, "THIS AIN'T FAIR!" which scared away a hungry crow that was hopping around Hollywood Station's Walk of Fame while pecking at a half-eaten taco lying on a brass-and-marble tribute to a long-dead cop.

Hector started up his Mercedes, but he was so shaken that he almost rammed another radio car exiting the Hollywood Station parking lot, and he had to slam on the brakes.

The passenger in that radio car, known to all at Hollywood Station as the Unicorn, looked out the open window of his shop and growled, "Pay attention, buddy."

Hector muttered, "Yeah, okay." Then, under his breath: "I hope you buy it tonight, you fat asshole!"

The defenders and colleagues of Officer Chester Toles—who knew nothing of Hector Cozzo's curse—would later maintain that it was the case on trial in Los Angeles Superior Court on that very Monday that effectively ended Chester's police career. They said that if he'd not been needlessly subpoenaed, and if he'd not sat through hours of terrible testimony that day, what occurred later that night on Watch 5 might never have happened the way that it did.

The preliminary hearing in superior court earlier that day had concerned the kidnapping and rape of an eight-year-old girl who'd been ambushed two months earlier while walking home from school with an older neighbor girl. Both girls were the children of Thai immigrants who were restaurant workers, and both lived in rented houses they shared with other Thai families in similar straits. The kidnapper had jumped out of his borrowed car and grabbed the girl, pulling her right out of her shoes.

Just prior to the kidnapping, the defendant, a parolee named Earl Jesse Newhouse, had been involved in a violent daytime encounter with a streetwalking drag queen on Santa Monica Boulevard, called "Sodom Monica" by the cops at Hollywood Station. The dragon, whose true name was Morton Allan Griffin, had demanded seventy-five dollars for the kind of service Earl Jesse Newhouse had requested, and an argument over price had led to Morton Allan Griffin being punched so hard that three teeth were dislodged and later found on the curb by officers responding to a call from a passing motorist.

It was after that act of violence that Earl Jesse Newhouse had smoked a bud and drank a forty, then gone cruising for the kind of action he'd enjoyed while serving seven years in Corcoran for strong-arm robbery. And that's when he'd grabbed the little Thai girl, whom he'd raped and sodomized and, three hours later, pushed out of his car in Griffith Park, where she'd been found by a horrified family on a picnic. Chester Toles and his partner had received the radio call and, after seeing the condition the child was in, had called the ambulance that transported her to Cedars-Sinai Medical Center.

Chester Toles heard much testimony that Monday concerning those three terrible hours the child had endured. The testimony came from the report of the physician who'd treated the little girl at Cedars for her brutal injuries, and from an evidence tech who'd received the DNA swabs. But the testimony of one of the detectives who did the follow-up investigation that eventually led to the arrest was what disturbed him most.

The D2 was a woman who testified to having served twenty-nine years with the LAPD, eighteen of them as a detective. She described how the child had remembered the name of the street where the assault had taken place in an underground parking lot. The girl remembered an elevator there, and that when the door opened and people got out, the kidnapper had pushed her to the floor of his car, but not before she got a glimpse of the elevator carpet, which was gray. Despite the horrific trauma she had suffered, the child still remembered the last three digits of his license number as he drove away after dumping her in Griffith Park.

At the conclusion of the detective's testimony, when she was asked by the deputy DA if the victim had been of help to the investigation, the detective's voice cracked just for an instant and she said, "The child was just *great*." And those five words, more than anything else, were the most unbearable for Chester Toles.

The evidence was overwhelming, and the lackluster questions asked by defense counsel hired by an uncle of the defendant made Chester think that all this was nothing more than a way for the lawyers to wring more money out of the old man and to set up a plea bargain, rather than going to trial with this loser of a case.

After being in court from early morning to late afternoon, Chester had finally approached the prosecutor and said, "What the hell am I doing here? You don't need me."

He was excused then, and he drove straight to Hollywood Station in time for the 5:00 P.M. roll call, furious and resentful that he'd been forced to sit all day and revisit that awful case again. Even after nearly thirty-five years on the Job—or maybe *because* he had nearly thirty-five years on the Job—his skin had grown thinner and sometimes bled easier, and this kind of crime involving a child he'd met could torment him.

Chester Toles, the lazy, normally phlegmatic Unicorn, was in a foul mood as Fran Famosa drove them from the Hollywood Station parking lot just after 5:30 on that Monday evening, which was when Chester saw some little maggot in a red Mercedes SL with his head up his ass almost take them out broadside.

And Chester Toles growled at him, "Pay attention, buddy."

It was very hard for Hector to get his mind around the sighting of the two men, now in police uniforms, that he'd seen at his house on Saturday night. He didn't know what to do or who to tell. Or should he tell anybody? That whole freak-o-rama with the amputation shit had been a police sting! And the foot chase and "capture" of the tall cop had been just a way to get the peg-leg guy out of the house with no question-and-answer session, so they could come back at him another day.

Well, there wasn't going to be another day! The cops were after *him*. And they no doubt had designs on rolling up Markov and Kim. And thinking of the Korean made Hector remember that he hadn't bothered trying to find the Mexican dancer, because he hadn't the faintest idea where to start looking. Who the fuck did the buckethead think he was—Hector Cozzo, private eye? All of that made him check his e-mail messages for the first time that day, and he saw the new cell number Markov was using that month. It made him think that he should dump his own go-phone and buy another one. But right then he didn't have time. He figured his pay-as-you-go phone would be okay for a little while longer.

He might ignore Kim's phone calls, but he couldn't do that to Markov, not if he wanted to keep his job. Then Hector thought that maybe he *didn't* want to keep his job, now that the cops were after him. It was all so confusing. Was it only for running some hookers in a few skin joints? Or could it have to do with the dead gooks in the cargo container down at the harbor? But that was Kim's deal, not his, Hector reasoned. That had nothing to do with *him*. That thought made him stop at a liquor store and buy a *Los Angeles Times*.

He sat in his car outside the liquor store and looked for it and there it was, the thing he'd feared. Daisy's body had been found in a dumpster next to some sleeping bum. Hector Cozzo now realized that he was up to his armpits in murder. He was terrified. He felt a powerful urge to drive home and do some blow and drink a little vodka and try to figure it out later. His cell phone rang, and he saw that it was Markov again. He was afraid to answer and afraid not to answer. He answered it.

Markov's voice was quivering with rage when he said, "Come to my house in one hour." And for the first time he gave Hector his address on Mount Olympus, then hung up before Hector could reply.

Hector sat in his red Mercedes SL and considered his options. First, he could just blow off Markov, move his things out of the house he subleased from his boss, and take the leased car back to the dealer. Then he could go home to his parents' house in Pedro and lie low until all of this, whatever it was, cooled down.

Thinking of that almost made him nauseous. He could hear his mother's yammering about his failure to settle down with a real job. Or maybe she might try to hook him up with one of their Italian relatives who worked at a small cannery on Terminal Island, by the U.S. Coast Guard station, where they turned bonita into cat food. That job might be just *slightly* better than a jail cell to Hector Cozzo.

His second option would be to drive straight back to Hollywood Station and ask to see a detective, then make a deal to testify against Markov and Kim, and even give them what little he knew about their smuggling of the thirteen dead gooks, as well as what Violet had reported about the Mexican dancer witnessing the slopehead driving off with Daisy. He might have to get booked for pimping or pandering or something, and maybe take another hit for federal income tax evasion, but if he gave up the murderers, surely he wouldn't do any significant time. And then he thought of himself in jail, even as a protected witness, and he imagined climbing into his bunk with the fear that one of Kim's paid assassins might wake him with a blade slicing through his throat.

His third option would be to go to Markov and tell him about the undercover cop that came to the freak show on Saturday night, and make the old bastard see that he had to dime Kim for his own sake and for Hector's, and to save the whole business enterprise. Kim had to go down, and he had to take that ride alone.

The third option made him decide to drive to Mount Olympus and present the situation to Markov with all of the logic he could muster.

FIFTEEN

Officer Chester Toles's long police career essentially ended within an hour after encountering Hector Cozzo in front of Hollywood Station. The cops in 6-X-46 received a radio call that took them to Thai Town, and just going to that location made Chester think of the little Thai girl and the horrible day he'd spent in court.

In fact, on their way to the call, Fran Famosa asked him, "What's wrong, Chester? You look like you're ready to go a few more rounds with the Indian that broke your glasses."

"Had a bad day in court," he mumbled.

"Yeah? What kinda case?"

"The kind you don't talk to your civilian friends about," he said.

"I'm not a civilian," Fran said, and for once, she was truly worried about the old slacker. He looked *angry*.

"Not worth talking about," he said.

The rented house was in Thai Town, but the residents were not Thai. They were a white family of six people plus a boyfriend, and a rescue ambulance had arrived there ahead of the cops.

The rusty screen door was torn open, and the small living room was thick with cigarette smoke. The officers of 6-X-46 found Mom and Grandma sitting in front of a blaring television, and three children under the age of seven were perched on a greasy sofa, looking scared.

A pair of male paramedics, one white, one African-American, looked as though they were eager to get out of there the moment the cops entered. The white paramedic pointed to a tiny bedroom off the kitchen, and the cops went inside. They saw a two-year-old boy lying on the bed. He wore a vomit-soaked jersey and shorts, and his strawberry-blond hair was damp and plastered down.

The black paramedic closed the bedroom door behind himself for privacy and said, "That baby's been dead for a while. Rigor is already setting in the jaw and legs. When I asked the momma why they didn't call sooner, she said the child always takes long naps." He pointed to the wall beside the bed and said, "That's vomit. This child did a whole lot of vomiting. There's serious bruising at the base of his skull and on his body under the jersey. I've seen this kind of battering before, where the skull's fractured and ribs're broken. And I'll bet his liver is lacerated." With that, he headed for the door, saying, "It's all yours now."

Fran went out to the car to request detectives and crime scene criminalists as well as a team from Children and Family Services, while Chester stayed inside and turned off the TV.

"Would you like to tell me what happened here?" he asked the mother in a very quiet voice.

She looked to be about thirty years old and had strawberry-blond hair like her dead son. She wore a tank and cutoff denim shorts, and was a younger version of her fifty-something mother, who sat smoking and sipping from a can of beer without saying a word.

Trying to sound sober, the mother said, "He got into some cleaning product and started vomiting."

Chester looked around the filthy house and said, "I don't see any evidence of cleaning around here."

The mother said, "Well, that's what happened, and then he fell down."

"Where?" Chester said.

"Off the porch," she said. "I think he hurt his head."

Then the grandmother spoke for the first time. She said, "Can I walk down to the 7-Eleven and get some cigs?"

Her hairline was so high he suspected that the dirty blond hair was a wig. She had protuberant eyes, and those eyes stared at him unhappily. Chester didn't answer her, but instead advised both women of their Miranda rights, receiving dull responses of understanding.

The oldest of the children started sobbing then. At first they were quiet sobs, and then he was wailing.

His mother said, "Hush, Terry!"

But Chester walked over to the sofa, lifted the six-year-old up until he was standing on the sofa cushions, and said, "What is it, son?"

Terry sniffled and said, "I killed my brother."

"Oh, for chrissake!" the mother said. "Terry, go wash your face!"

Chester gave the woman a look that silenced her, then asked the boy, "Why do you say that?"

Terry said, "I took too long to find a phone!"

"Where did you look for a phone?" Chester asked.

"The houses on the street," Terry said. "I went to three houses but nobody was home or they didn't speak English, and then the lady in the fourth house let me in and phoned for me. If I hadn't took so long, my baby brother would be alive!"

"Come outside, son," Chester said, taking the boy out to the front porch. He told Fran, who had finished the notifications, "Go inside with Mom and Grandma while I have a chat with Terry."

Fran nodded, but she didn't like the look in Chester's eyes. His pupils behind the aviator glasses almost looked dilated, and he spoke in such a quiet voice it was unnerving.

Then he said sotto to the boy, "Terry, you didn't have anything to do with your baby brother's death. He was already dead when you went for help. Did somebody hit your baby brother?"

The boy began sobbing again and nodded his head.

"Did your mother hit him?" Chester asked.

The boy nodded again.

"Anybody else?"

"Buster," the boy said.

"Who's Buster?"

"Mommy's friend."

"Does Buster live here?"

The boy nodded.

"Where is Buster now?"

"He left when I went looking for a telephone," the boy said.

"In a car?"

The boy shook his head and said, "The car's broke. That's it." He pointed to a wreck of an old Pinto up on blocks in the side yard.

"Then he left on foot?" Chester said.

The boy nodded again.

"What was he wearing?"

The boy said, "A Dodgers shirt."

"Which way did he walk?"

Terry pointed north and Chester nodded slightly, because there was a neighborhood tavern at the end of the block.

Unit 6-X-72 cruised slowly down the street and stopped. Sophie Branson held four fingers up to ask if everything was code 4, or if further assistance was needed.

Chester Toles called out, "Can you come in for a few minutes."

The boy and Chester walked back inside the house, and Chester said to his partner, "Fran, let me have the shop keys for a minute. I'll be right back."

Fran took the keys from the belt of her Sam Browne and handed them to Chester, asking, "What? Something in the trunk we need?"

"Be right back," Chester said a bit too casually, and he shuffled out the door and down the narrow, oil-stained driveway to the radio car.

Minutes later, he'd parked the black-and-white in an alley behind the bar at the end of the street. It was frequented by a number of Asian patrons, but there was also a sprinkling of old men from nearby Little Armenia, and there were some Latino customers as well. It was the end of the Monday workday and the bar was crowded, with only a few women sitting at the tables.

Several customers looked surprised to see the bald, overweight fifty-eight-year-old uniformed cop standing inside the doorway, scanning the crowd.

Then he walked up to a husky, thirty-something white guy in an L.A. Dodgers T-shirt. His neck was acne-pocked, and there were serious sweat rings on the shirt.

Chester said, "Step outside with me, Buster. We need to talk."

Twenty minutes later, two detectives had arrived at the crime scene, and 6-X-72 was still at the house, assisting. Fran Famosa looked at her watch and went outside to peer up and down the street for her partner. She figured he'd had to take an urgent dump and had probably driven to the nearest gas station to get it done. That's when she saw their shop driving back toward the house.

She stood, hand on hips, ready to needle him with an admonition that his urgent bowel movement was a good reason to eat Cuban black beans, like her mother used to make, instead of the lard-laden refried frijoles at his favorite Mexican taco shop. But when he got out of the car, Fran didn't say anything. She put her hands to her face and uttered a little cry of alarm. Blood ran from a laceration over Chester's right eye, and his hands looked like he'd experienced stigmata.

Fran ran to him, saying, "Chester! What the hell happened to you?"

He pointed toward the backseat of the radio car, where she saw a handcuffed man whose face was a mask of blood. He was trying with great effort to breathe through a mouth full of broken teeth, and both eyes were swelling shut. He was whimpering, attempting to say something to Fran Famosa, but he seemed to be drifting in and out of consciousness and couldn't manage it.

Chester said, "We better notify the watch commander and get Buster to Hollywood Pres. He resisted arrest in the alley behind the bar. I had to fight."

Fran Famosa didn't say much to her partner on the code 3 run to Hollywood Presbyterian Medical Center, where the injuries to the prisoner were deemed severe enough that he had to be transported by ambulance to the thirteenth floor of L.A. County–USC Medical Center, where the jail ward was located.

Later, in a Hollywood Station interview room, a member of Force Investigation Division gave Chester Toles the same Miranda warning Chester had given the mother and grandmother of the dead child.

After affirming his understanding, Chester pointed to the six white service stripes on the left sleeve of his blue uniform shirt and said to his interrogator, "Count 'em. Five years for each hash mark, for a total of thirty-four years and six months. So don't talk to me like I'm a boot right outta the academy. I could demand to have a rep from the Protective League here right now, but I'm gonna cooperate as long as you show respect."

The FID investigator, an up-and-comer on the lieutenant's list with only nine years on the Job, who looked to Chester like the guy on *American Idol*, said, "Okay, no bullshit then. Let's cut to the quick. Why would you go to that bar all alone if not to give some payback to a baby killer? Maybe you were very upset by what you'd seen and weren't behaving like you normally would?"

Chester replied, "I thought you said no bullshit."

The FID man smiled mirthlessly. "All right then, you tell me what was on your mind."

Chester said, "After talking to the little boy Terry about the direction Buster took, I wanted to see if I could spot him anywheres. I saw the bar on the corner and decided to have a look inside. If I saw a guy in a Dodger shirt, I was gonna go outside and call for backup."

"Then why didn't you do that?"

"He spotted me in the bar and looked like he was gonna rabbit, so I asked him to step outside with me. I think the bartender mighta seen that and can verify what I'm saying."

"Then what happened?"

"We went outside and I asked him to step to my car in the alley and produce some ID. That's when I was getting ready to call for backup."

"Did he ask you what it was about?"

"No."

"Did he give you his ID?"

"No," Chester said, pointing to the taped bandage across his fore-head. "He gave me this. The minute we were alone in the alley, he head-butted me. I got six stitches here."

"Then what happened?"

"Whadda you think happened? The fight was on. Nonstop and desperate."

"Why didn't you call for help?"

"I couldn't. He was all over me."

"Give me a blow-by-blow."

"He's a strong young guy and I'm a flabby old man, fifty-eight years old. I used the force needed to overcome his attack and to effect the ar-rest. And I'm lucky I was able to do it."

"The no-bullshit pledge cuts both ways," the FID man said. "The ar-restee suffered a concussion, a broken nose, a jaw fracture, four broken ribs, and he lost a few teeth. At least two dozen stitches were needed to close lacerations over and under both eyes. Were you a professional fighter before you came on the Job?"

"I was a U.S. Army Ranger before I came on the Job," Chester said. "Long before you ever took your first swig of mother's milk."

With an unchanging expression, the FID man said, "Your uniform is barely disheveled and your glasses weren't even broken. And except for that cut on your forehead and your chewed-up fists, you came out of the fight unscathed."

"I fought sober, he fought drunk," Chester said. "I had the edge. And yeah, I tried to break his nose. The blood goes down their throat and they feel like they can't breathe. Ever tried clocking a guy like that?"

Chester paused, but the FID man said, "I'm still listening."

Chester said, "As for my glasses, I took them off the second we got to the alley, just as a precaution. I got my last pair smashed by an Indian purse snatcher in a fight last week. And by the way, the Indian brave was a stand-up guy. He never made any whiny complaints about excessive force. But you probably know all that already. So how does the baby killer say it went down?"

The FID man thought it over for a moment and said, "He claims he cooperated, but the minute you handcuffed his hands behind his back, you started pummeling him with punches and kicks."

"I suppose you wanna test my boots for blood evidence?" Chester said. "Want me to take 'em off?"

The interrogator said, "I'd rather just hear the truth of what happened out there."

"Got any witnesses that claim it was a total beatdown?"

"I can't say at this time."

"You'd say if you had any."

"The truth would help everyone."

"How about the head-butt?" Chester said. "What's he have to say about that?"

"He thinks it may have happened by accident while he was struggling to escape the beating."

"He's a liar," Chester said calmly. "Isn't this a lotta fuss for a baby killer? Especially one who's a *white* guy?"

The interrogator said, "Everyone has a breaking point. Maybe you reached yours today. Maybe seeing that dead baby triggered rage you couldn't control."

Chester scoffed, "You mean, you think just because I was arresting a guy that raped a child and beat a baby to death, I somehow went off my rocker? Is that what you're saying here?"

The FID man cocked his head quizzically. "Who said anything about him raping a child?"

Chester Toles did not reply to that question. His blue eyes behind the smudged eyeglasses opened a bit wider, and he stared at the interrogator as though he didn't quite understand the question, or even his own answer.

The FID man repeated it, saying, "Who said anything about him raping a child? What're you talking about?"

Chester Toles finally replied, "I'll do any further talking through a lawyer. I think it's time to retire on my vested pension and go fishing. And if you think you can get the DA to issue on me for tuning up that guy, send your nastygram message to the office of my future congressman in Idaho."

Chester Toles removed the LAPD badge from his uniform shirt, saying, "I'll give this to the boss on the way out." With that, he made his exit, leaving his interrogator sitting alone in the interview room.

Fran Famosa and others on Watch 5 expressed the opinion to Sergeant Murillo that Chester's court experience earlier that day, and the feelings it had evoked in him, had played some part in whatever happened in the Thai Town alley, involving a cop who, for fifteen minutes in his long career, was not the same apathetic, indifferent slacker they'd known for years.

As to the surprising feeling of sadness they all felt at losing the Unicorn from their ranks forever, Hollywood Nate spoke for many on Watch 5 that day when he said, "Why the hell couldn't the lazy old bastard have been as hard to find as usual, when they assigned him that goddamn call to Thai Town?"

SIXTEEN

A LITTLE OVER AN hour had elapsed before Hector Cozzo arrived at the surprisingly unimpressive house of Mr. Markov on Mount Olympus. Then Hector thought it over and decided that he shouldn't have been surprised. Everything he'd learned about his boss so far had indicated that Markov was just another player, perched only a few rungs above Hector on the Hollywood hustlers' totem. And with that thought in mind, he felt emboldened when he went to the front door and rang the bell.

Markov was dressed in a collarless white jersey with black stripes, white linen trousers, and Gucci loafers with no socks. His Elvis do had been recently dyed, and Hector thought he looked Eurotrash faggy.

"You are late," Markov said with the slight accent that Hector had come to hate.

"There was traffic," Hector replied, without groveling.

"Come in and sit down." Markov led Hector into an unremarkable living room that didn't even have a view.

Hector sat and showed as much attitude as he dared by asking, "Got something to drink?"

Markov looked as though his lowly employee had just slapped him, but he managed to say, with only a hint of a sneer, "The market has not delivered this week's liquor order."

"Never mind," Hector said. "You probably only drink Russian vodka anyways. I'm sick of that potato juice."

Now there was no doubt about it. Markov could see that Hector Cozzo was being deliberately insolent. But he checked his growing anger and said, "Things are going very badly for us."

Hector recalled seeing the peg-leg guy and his partner in police uniforms. "You don't know the half of it."

"What do you mean?"

"You first," Hector said. "This is your meeting. I guess you're really pissed off at the way things got off the hook on Saturday night with Basil and Dr. Maurice."

"You are once again tardy in reporting events to me," Markov said. "Ivana has already telephoned me with the details of that disastrous evening. Which, by the way, has no doubt cost me the investment from Basil that we need so much."

"It wasn't my fault," Hector said.

"It was partly mine," Markov admitted. "I should never have sent Dr. Maurice there in an attempt to please Basil. Do you suppose he really did operate on that man Kelly, or did he not? I do not fully understand it all."

Hector said, "The doctor's a badly bent and drugged-out lunatic. You can't go with anything he says."

Markov said, "Well, the entire debacle is water under the bridge. I did not bring you here to chastise you for that. Surely you know that the police have found the body of our missing dancer?"

"Who doesn't by now?" Hector said.

"When was the last time you saw Mr. Kim?"

"I heard from him a couple days ago," Hector said. "He's got lethal anger-management issues. The guy could kill, jist because."

"What did he want?"

"He wanted me to find a certain Mexican dancer for him."

"Why?"

"You'll have to ask him."

Markov clenched his jaws. Then his eyes grew darker and, with an ice-pick smile, he said, "Do not toy with me, young man. You will be making a big mistake to do so."

Hector's insolence faded and he lost his nerve, remembering that these people had survived in places far removed from his Pedro salad days. He became more conciliatory, saying, "Mr. Markov, I don't think I oughta get involved with whatever Mr. Kim wants, and I'm not even sure if I oughta keep my job with you."

Somewhat mollified by the new deference in Hector's tone, Markov said, "The business down at the Los Angeles Harbor began originally with Mr. Kim freelancing. I did not know about it at first, not until he needed money from me to complete the arrangement. I invested money without fully understanding the nature of my investment. Had I known from the beginning that he was smuggling human beings from Asian countries, I would not have become involved at all."

Hector no longer believed anything Markov was telling him, but he shrugged and said, "Okay, if you say so."

"But now you see what has happened, do you not? Mr. Kim has admitted to me that Daisy made certain threats, the kind of threats that would bring the local police and the federal authorities to our doorstep. She made accusations that might bring very serious charges against me and perhaps even against you."

"Why against me? I didn't do anything."

"You talked with Mr. Kim about a street gang, and about having the container robbed from the storage yard, did you not?"

"I jist spitballed with him about the Crips doing a takeover of the security office!" Hector said. "I didn't actually take any steps. The stupid silverback I was supposed to meet got himself busted, and the whole plan went away."

"If the authorities find out about those meetings, they might consider it part of a larger criminal conspiracy," Markov said. "Thirteen people dead? Kim could drag us both into it."

"Maybe I'm not big enough to play with you people," Hector said, a bit of a whine creeping into his voice. "Maybe I should jist give you back the keys to the house and go home to Pedro."

"It is a bit late for that," Markov said. "How many people are aware that Daisy made certain accusations about Mr. Kim before she disappeared?"

"How do you know about that?"

"Mr. Kim knows," Markov said. "So why would I not know?"

Now Hector was sure. Markov and Kim were not employer and employee. They'd been partners in everything from the get-go, including the human trafficking that had gone awry.

"Okay, I don't know who all mighta heard by now," Hector said. "Every one of them bitches have mouths that never shut. For sure, Violet and the Mexican heard Daisy ranting. After that, Suki and Ivana also heard about it secondhand. And in another couple days they'll probably be talking about it on the *Today* show, and maybe Whoopi Goldberg and the rest of them other bitches at that morning hen party will be clucking about it by Friday."

"There is a difference, though," Markov said. "With the others it is either hearsay or nothing but the ravings of a grief-stricken girl. A girl who is now dead and cannot prove any of her accusations. But the Mexican dancer knows something more than the others. I believe her name is Lita Medina, is it not? The Mexican dancer can provide what the lawyers call direct evidence. She *saw* something."

Hector was stunned. "Why do you say that? How do you know what she saw?"

"Because after Mr. Kim learned that Lita had also disappeared the very next day after Daisy did, he persuaded Violet to tell him why Lita ran away."

Hector's throat constricted. "Why did she run?"

Markov said, "Because she saw Daisy go away from her apartment with somebody on that day she disappeared. Lita did not identify the somebody to Violet."

"Who do you think it was?" Hector croaked.

"Do not insult my intelligence," Markov said.

"Mr. Kim?"

"That would be a reasonable guess," Markov said. "Now, what I would like to know is, did the roommate Violet also share the same information with *you*?"

Hector took a breath and decided he had to lie. "No, this is the first I heard that Lita saw somebody with Daisy that day."

Markov looked hard at Hector. "I would hate to think that you keep secrets from me."

"I tell you, this is the first I heard of it!" Hector lied again. "And I wish I hadn't. Now I really think I oughta go home to Pedro and leave Hollywood and all its problems to smarter people like you."

"Do not talk like an idiot," Markov said.

"Look, Mr. Markov," Hector said. "If Mr. Kim is . . . somehow *involved* in the disappearance of Daisy, then the cops're probably gonna find it out sooner or later. Can't you distance yourself from him? Like, get him the fuck outta all your investments?"

In a rare moment, Markov spoke with what, Hector figured, was something approaching honesty: "Mr. Kim and I have a business relationship that cannot be severed. We must protect each other for mutual economic survival."

Markov's ferocious stare was making Hector's hands sweat. He said querulously, "I don't know what more I can do for you."

Markov said, "If Kim were gone, I believe you and I could proceed with business as usual. Except that there would be more for me in your regular collections, and I would share a percentage of it with you. However, Mr. Kim does not intend to leave."

"You got the wrong guy if you want something like *that* set up! *That* goes way beyond my job description!"

"What are you talking about?"

"About Mr. Kim leaving for good!" Hector said.

"I meant leaving the country," Markov said. "Not leaving the world."

Bullshit, Hector thought. I know what you meant. He impulsively lit a cigarette, even though there was no ashtray in the room. Markov got up and went to the kitchen, returning in a moment with a saucer for the cigarette ashes.

He said, "Then we have no alternative other than to protect Kim from arrest, because I greatly fear whatever he might feel compelled to say in order to make a deal with prosecutors. And that would be very bad for me, and I could make it very bad for you by making a plea bargain of my own if I were to be arrested."

"Are you saying you'd rat me out?" Hector asked. "The cops don't want a grifter like me! I'm a flunky! I jist take care of a bunch of bitches for you!"

"You conspired with Kim when there were thirteen people alive in that storage container," Markov said. "Living human beings that you knew about. You did not inform the authorities about those trapped people."

"They were already dead!"

Markov said, "How do you know exactly when they died? They could have been alive when you first learned about them. They could have been rescued if you had even bothered to call the authorities with an *anonymous* tip. But you did nothing to help them. That is what a federal prosecutor would say. We are all in trouble because of Kim's stupidity, and that includes you."

"Well, I'm not hooking up with some Crip to do a job on Kim! I don't get down with that kind of shit," Hector said. "It'd be real nice if Kim went to his reward with Buddha, but I can't make it happen. I got an inner coward that tells me what I can do and what I can't. And he's speaking to me right this minute and telling me to get the fuck outta Dodge!"

"Calm yourself, Hector," Markov said. "You have the ability to protect Kim from arrest, at least for the time being. At least until this search for Daisy's killer hits a dead end."

"How do I do that?"

"Find the Mexican dancer, Lita Medina. And give her location to Kim. He won't be so clumsy and violent next time. If she is no longer a threat to him, then he can be dealt with at some later date. But right now there is no time to waste."

"You're telling me to set the girl up for—"

"No, of course not," Markov interrupted. "I am asking you to do nothing more than find her and tell Kim how to find her. He will pay the girl to forget what she saw. Perhaps he will give her enough money to go back to Mexico and thrive. Then everyone will be happy."

"But maybe he'll decide to save the money and jist deal with her like he dealt with Daisy!"

"Hector, we are all facing arrest and trial, and you are talking like a fool," Markov said. "You found the girl dancing in a strip bar down in the harbor area. You told Kim about her, and he went there and gave his approval to hire her. You picked her up and brought her to Hollywood. You know that much about her, therefore it cannot be hard for you to locate her acquaintances down there and offer them money to tell you where she might be. You are a San Pedro boy, are you not? Just find her and let Kim handle her with money. Are you not being overly concerned? What is she to you but just a Mexican stripper?"

"Gimme a minute to think," Hector said, smoke sliding from his lips. "I'm starting to lose my shit here."

"Let me see if I can find you a drink," Markov said. "Is chardonnay all right?"

"Yeah, anything," Hector said, and Markov went to the kitchen.

Hector Cozzo was having trouble processing all this information. It was way too much. Now he thought of a dizzying array of things— about the scratches on Kim's face, for instance. He figured you didn't have to watch every episode of *CSI* to know that fingernail scrapings might reveal enough DNA material to identify an assailant. And sooner or later, Violet was going to tell somebody *else* what Lita had told her about seeing somebody pick up Daisy in a car. Or maybe Violet would go to the cops herself if there was a reward posted. And that would make the cops go balls out to find Lita Medina, a very important eyewitness. And the Mexican dancer would lead them to the Korean. So Kim looked like he was cooked one way or the other, unless Lita Medina went away and stayed away.

Then he recalled something else Markov had just said: "You picked her up and brought her to Hollywood." But he hadn't! Dinko Babich did that job, Hector thought, but Markov doesn't know about Dinko, and neither does Kim. Hector remembered how Dinko couldn't take his eyes off Lita Medina even though she danced like an organ grinder's monkey. Dinko took her to Hollywood, and he might've taken her *away* from Hollywood!

And then there was the little matter of the peg-leg guy and his tall sidekick, who happened to be fucking cops. But at this moment there was no way he was going to reveal that bit of information to Markov. Hector figured it meant that their whole enterprise was under police scrutiny and Markov was going to be put out of business soon, no matter what.

He decided that the best course of action was to walk away from this shitstorm ASAP and return to Pedro to hide out for a while and hope for the best. That's exactly what he'd resolved to do, until Markov reentered the living room with his drink, as well as an offer that changed everything.

"It is a decent chardonnay," Markov said, "not like the so-called *drinkable* bilge we sell at Club Samara."

Hector took a sip. "It's okay."

And then Markov said, "How would you like forty thousand dollars?"

Hector almost spilled his wine before muttering, "I'm not plotting with nobody to ice Mr. Kim! I already said."

"Of course not. Forty thousand with an additional ten-thousand-dollar bonus if you find Lita Medina in the next three days *and* if the dangerous situation is successfully concluded by Mr. Kim. I think you are right that the police will soon be looking for him. And by the way, I do not even know where he is right now. Probably with a lady friend of his in Koreatown, I should think."

"Fifty thousand dollars jist for the location of the Mexican dancer?" Hector said, needing to hear it again.

"Only if you can do it in within three days *and* if Kim concludes the matter satisfactorily," Markov said. "Time is of the essence. If you do not succeed, I am afraid that I may be liquidating all of my investments for fifty cents on the dollar and leaving Hollywood quickly and forever. They say that Costa Rica is very pleasant and not expensive."

Hector figured that his mentioning Costa Rica meant that it would be the last place he'd go. Then he thought about fifty large. A stake until he got back on his feet. Enough to buy time to find a new hustle. Actually, when the undercover peg-leg cop had been trying to do his sting, he'd brought up something that Hector had already heard good things about: the illegal video poker machines. Hector wondered if fifty grand could get him started in that currently thriving enterprise.

Hector said, "If I find her in three days and give her up to you, you'll order Mr. Kim to pay her off, right?"

"Fair enough," Markov said. "Then do we have a deal?"

"I'm down," Hector said. "But we gotta work out how and when the money is paid to me, and you gotta guarantee the girl won't be getting the Daisy treatment."

"She will not," Markov said. "And in any case, what happened to Daisy could have been an accident. That kind of unintended thing can occur in the heat of the moment when passion overtakes reason."

Hector lit a cigarette while driving back down from Mount Olympus, past all the cypress trees that had been used to beautify and sell the development. And he thought, They really are just hoodlums. Markov and Kim had seemed so powerful and impressive to him before all this. He'd been in awe of Markov in particular, with his nightclub and massage parlor. But now that the squeeze was on, they reminded him of the catch on the Pedro fishing boats. Those glorified pimps, Markov and Kim, were thrashing around like the mackerel trapped by the gill nets.

SEVENTEEN

Most of the next day was spent cleaning the house. Lita Medina had been in the Babich home long enough to be a bit assertive when she saw Brigita Babich breaking out the cleaning equipment early in the morning, and Brigita reluctantly allowed her guest to pitch in. Even before Dinko was out of bed, he could hear the vacuum going in the living room and his mother and Lita laughing at Ollie the cat, who was attacking the dustcloth Brigita was using to polish the walnut coffee table.

Dinko came sleepily into the living room barefoot and shirtless, wearing only faded jeans, and saw the tornado of dust motes swirling against the glare of the rising summer sun, which was pouring through the picture window.

"Why don't you just roll up that cat hair and take it to the homeless shelter," Dinko said. "They could stuff their lumpy mattresses with it."

"Why don't you just help us work?" his mother replied wryly.

To her astonishment, Dinko said, "The windows could use a once-over. I'll get some paper towels."

She'd been joking with a son who had never so much as picked up his clothes from the floor of his bedroom, and who had to be nagged to simply haul the trash receptacles to the street for pickup. But in a few minutes he was outside on the front porch spraying the picture window, and doing a pretty good job of polishing the glass without smears.

"This is a miracle," Brigita said to Lita.

"Sorry," Lita said, indicating she did not understand.

Brigita remembered the Spanish word. She said, "We must offer a prayer of thanks to Our Lady of Guadalupe for *el milagro*. Dinko is actually working!"

Lita understood that, and they both laughed while Dinko made comical faces at them through the window.

The three of them worked hard for an hour, and then with apologies to Lita for a late breakfast, Brigita entered the kitchen to prepare the first huge meal of the day. Lita followed her and squeezed fresh orange juice.

Lita and Dinko were sitting at the kitchen table, drinking coffee, and Brigita was frying eggs when Dinko said to Lita, "With those wheels you should wear cutoffs all the time."

"Wheels?" Lita said.

"He's complimenting your pretty legs," Brigita said, "in his uncouth way."

"I got bags full of couth," Dinko said. "I'm a Pedro pirate."

Lita looked quizzically to Brigita to translate, and she said, "The pirate is the mascot at San Pedro High School." She added, "Which was where he ended up after spending three years at Catholic school."

"Got tired of those holy Joes and Janes pushing us around," Dinko said. "Besides, I didn't figure I needed a Catholic school diploma to work on the docks. I liked saying I belonged to a crew of pirates. I had a pirate on my T-shirt and my baseball cap."

Lita said, "Do you like the job on the docks, Dinko?"

"In a weird way, I really do," he answered. "My father was a longshoreman, and his father, too. It's different now, though."

"How?" Lita asked, refilling Dinko's coffee cup.

"It's about sixty percent . . ." He hesitated, trying to decide whether to say "Hispanic" or "Latino," but finally just said, "Mexican."

"Is true?" she said. "Men from Mexico?"

"No," he said. "We call everybody Mexican if their ancestors came from there. Or somewhere near there."

"But they are Americans, no?" Lita said.

"Yes, honey, they are," Brigita interjected. "He should've said that the union is about sixty percent Hispanic nowadays."

"Is a problem, yes?" Lita said to Dinko. "Too many people there that look like me?"

"Nobody looks like you," Dinko said. "Almost every woman in L.A. County would kill to look like you."

Brigita said, "People like Dinko feel . . . not so comfortable when they work around too many people not like themselves."

"I understand," Lita said.

"Don't get me wrong," Dinko explained. "I got lotsa union buddies that're Mexican-American, but we don't have many that're *real* Mexicans." Then he thought about it and asked, "What do real Mexicans like you call our Mexican-Americans anyways?"

Lita shrugged and said artlessly, "We call them gringos, same like you."

Brigita and Dinko exploded in laughter, and Lita flashed a good-natured smile but really didn't understand the humor in what she'd said.

"You're priceless, Lita," Brigita said, wiping tears from her eyes.

"What means 'priceless'?" Lita asked.

"It means that you're worth everything in the world to us," Dinko said, taking her hand in his. "And that's the truth."

Brigita put the eggs on a platter with the ham slices, and felt the worry growing in her heart. This was all happening too quickly. It was *much* too soon. Yes, she was an adorable girl, but they hardly knew each other!

Hector had had another very bad night. With all the worry he was experiencing, mingled with the excitement of earning fifty grand, he needed extra zannies to sleep, and he felt like shit when he woke up at noon. He attempted to read the morning paper but couldn't focus. No matter how many times he tried to revisit recent events to determine what he'd done wrong, he could not come up with much.

The night with Basil and the crazy quack had been foisted on him. He hadn't asked for it. And that had brought him into direct contact with undercover cops. So now his name was in a written report, or on a bulletin board, or in a police computer, or however the fuck the cops did it these days.

And as for the so-called conspiracy to help Kim get his smuggled slopes out of the storage yard, he hadn't done anything but talk to a Crip and set up a meeting that never worked out. How was that so wrong? Despite what Markov claimed, he didn't believe he could ever be convicted of anything involving the deaths of those people, but he still might get busted for it along with Kim and Markov. And he might get indicted on a RICO statute or on a state charge of conspiracy, involving the massage parlor and Club Samara, where they were running whores and evading income tax. That much might happen to him. He could still end up in state or federal prison for a few years.

It made his stomach burn and gave him a headache. He had an overpowering urge to "get back to town," which was what all the old-timers like his parents and uncles and aunts called returning to Pedro. He truly wanted to get out of Hollywood and get back to town, and stay there for a while. And he would too, if that old pimp hadn't put fifty grand on the table. Now what choice did he have?

There were two reasons to be sad at roll call that day. Of course, the first was that Chester Toles had unceremoniously retired. Regardless of how often they'd bitched about him kissing off calls, along with anything that might require tedious paperwork, now that he was gone forever, it almost felt like a death in the ranks.

The thumping of the baby killer was the talk of the station, and it triggered much speculation as to which version was closest to the truth, the arrestee's or Chester's. Most of the experienced coppers on Watch 5 figured that there was some truth in both versions. What everyone really liked, and what made them proud of the old Unicorn, was the way he'd told the FID investigator to stuff it and had walked out of the interview room and into the civilian world to enjoy the pension he'd earned.

Sergeant Murillo suggested at roll call that Watch 5 should wait a couple of months until the FID investigation had chilled, and then organize a retirement party for Chester Toles. Like most street cops, something in their natures made them admire Chester for doing what they'd all fantasized about doing at various times in their careers, for lesser reasons than Chester had that day. The Unicorn's partner and frequent critic, Fran Famosa, said she'd take the responsibility of organizing the party as soon as Sergeant Murillo thought the time was right.

And then came the second part of the sad roll call. Velma Longstreet, a former Watch 5 copper who'd transferred downtown to Burglary Special Section after being appointed as a detective, had shot herself at a Venice Beach condo she shared with her fiancé, a detective from Major Crimes Division. There was nothing like a cop suicide to silence a raucous roll call or make an already somber roll call more grave. And, of course, there was the inevitable message from West Bureau about suicide signs that should be watched for, and encouragement for all to schedule a confidential appointment with a Department psychologist at Behavioral Science Services at the first sign of unusual depression, either in themselves or in a partner.

It wasn't just that a cop suicide brought forth sadness; it also instilled fear, because every man and woman in the room knew that the national police officer suicide rate was sometimes five times the rate of police officers being killed on duty. That many more murdered themselves than were murdered by others. Cops referred to the impulse toward self-destruction as "the Coppers' Disease." And for a moment at least, members of the midwatch looked at each other and wondered, Could anything ever make me do that? Could it ever happen to *me*?

Sergeant Murillo didn't have any jokes or stories for them to take to the streets, not on that evening. The only thing he said was that if anyone got a call or saw any unusual activity in east Hollywood at Shanghai Massage or Club Samara, they should report it to Detective Villaseñor.

And then descriptions of Hector Cozzo and his red Mercedes SL were given to the watch, along with the caveat that he was not a suspect in the murder of the strip club dancer Soo Jeong but was a person of interest. Especially if he was accompanied by a big, middle-aged Korean whose name might be William Kim.

"That last name narrows it down to half the Koreatown phone book," Flotsam said. "In fact, the description fits one of the FID people that came out here to jack up Chester Toles. Maybe it's him."

Mel Yarashi said to Flotsam, "The FID guy's not Korean. He's a Buddhahead like me, from Little Tokyo. His family's owned a restaurant in J-Town for fifty years."

Flotsam said wearily, "Koreatown, Thai Town, J-Town, and Chinatown, which happens to be full of Vietnamese these days. What's the difference, dude?"

"Sergeant, I demand that you cut a face sheet on this round-eyed surfer scum for racial insensitivity!" Mel Yarashi cried out to Sergeant Murillo. "And I'll go on a hunger strike if you refuse! Except for Bessie's burritos. I gotta have them."

"Let's go to work," Sergeant Murillo said, at least able to send them to the streets with a semblance of a smile. They all touched the Oracle's picture before leaving the room.

That day of housecleaning turned into a very late spring cleaning, with every window in the house being washed inside and out, floors waxed, bathrooms scrubbed top to bottom, and even the organizing of pantry and refrigerator items.

Dinko was exhausted by late afternoon, and so was his mother. Lita Medina, being only nineteen years and four months old, fared better, but she, too, was tired.

Brigita said, "I'm too pooped to cook."

Dinko said, "I'm too tired to eat at the moment. Maybe after a shower I'll revive."

"I can cook!" Lita volunteered. "Please?"

"It's okay with me, dear," Brigita said.

Dinko said, "What a day. I actually worked at cleaning the house, and my mother says she doesn't wanna cook a meal. Something strange is happening around here. I think we're bewitched." And he looked at Lita Medina in such a way that his mother thought he might be right.

"I'm gonna take a very long bath," Brigita said.

While she was soaking in the tub, Brigita Babich thought of a local Croatian girl who'd joined the LAPD several years earlier. When other Croatians would see her on the streets, they'd run right up to her and pinch her cheeks or touch her uniform and sing her praises. They were all that proud of her. Brigita used to have a fantasy that Dinko might someday marry a girl like that.

Hector Cozzo always felt a slight tug of nostalgia that embarrassed him when he drove south on the Harbor Freeway, heading "back to town." The remote, incestuous nature of Pedro was something all the old residents forever talked about, especially the Croats and Italians. It was still a small town where the white people knew one another. They all liked to say, "Pedro is full of inbreeding, which is why we're so weird."

Hector understood that their working-class seaside "town" was not like any other on the California coast. The inhabitants were blue-collar right down to the soles of their sensible shoes. And though they bemoaned the changes that had brought a hundred halfway houses and sober living homes—more than anywhere else in Los Angeles—Pedro was still special to them. Even though now he knew he might see more Latinos than Anglos, still there was something that made members of the younger generation, like thirty-two-year-old Hector Cozzo, experience an occasional yearning to come home.

As he reached the freeway's end that afternoon, under a summer sky that was clear and dry over the harbor, he saw the countless containers stacked high on Front Street, near the train tracks that boxed everyone in during peak traffic hours. There was no beauty to any of that, but it spoke to him of hardworking people who'd stayed when the fishing business had faded and the big canneries had closed.

He felt again the bittersweet pang of nostalgia, and an impulse to drive straight to his parents' house and grovel sufficiently. He could ask them to let him move home for a few months, and let the cops deal with Markov and Kim. But by his very nature, he knew he was unable to reject the offer of so much money. When it came to big bank, he was in. All in. After he had the money, he could consider going home to lie low and endure the ear pounding he would get from his family about what a failure he was. They might sing a different tune if his pockets were full of dead presidents.

When he got to the heart of San Pedro, he stopped by a popular waterfront restaurant to use the outdoor restroom beneath the eatery. Recreational fishermen parked their cars in the lot next door, and a sign inside the restroom said, in both English and Spanish, "Please don't clean fish in the bathroom sink." Someone had penciled next to it, "Where should we clean them, the toilet?"

Uh-huh, Hector thought, I'm back home in Pedro. And for no other reason than a wish to assuage the nostalgia, he toured the area in his Mercedes SL, hoping to see someone from the old neighborhood, and to be remembered and admired.

There was nobody out in front of the Italian American Club. No old men gassing about the good old days. Ditto for the Croatian Hall, but at least there was still the "God Bless Croatia" sign, which nobody had tagged as yet. There'd been weddings there, he recalled, where six hundred guests had attended. He remembered the time when some incompetent Serbs had tried to set off a puny bomb there, but it had detonated while still in their car.

Hector had always liked hearing stories from his father about how, in the old days, the longshoremen's unwritten law said that if a container broke open, the dockworkers could help themselves to the contents. The containers full of toys somehow always managed to break open during

JOSEPH WAMBAUGH

the Christmas holidays. There was a reason why most longshoremen drove pickups back in the day.

Pedro had been like a European town then, but just before he was born, it stopped being a white workingman's paradise. By the time he was in his junior year of high school, masses of Latinos and blacks walked east after school, and white kids like Hector Cozzo walked west to the hills. Pacific Avenue was the dividing line.

Hector cruised his Mercedes past the old YMCA by Harbor View Park. Now it housed four floors of resident patients, many of who wore a key hanging from a shoestring around their neck. He recalled one of the loons that everyone called "General MacArthur," who would march about the nearby streets wearing an army surplus uniform, chewing on an unlit corncob pipe, debating an imaginary President Truman, and periodically shouting, "Old soldiers never die!"

Another of the crazies was called "the mayor of San Pedro." One day he'd wear a gray suit and carry a briefcase. The next day it'd be a brown suit, but he'd be shoeless. The next day he'd wear a suit and necktie, but no shirt under the tie.

The fruit loop Hector remembered most clearly was the one they called Julius Caesar, who wore a red cape with a Burger King crown. He'd parade up and down the promenade beside Ports O' Call on his way to and from the Cruise Terminal, telling all to beware the ides of March. People using the Red Car line would give him pocket change, and kids riding by on the bike path would try to steal his crown.

Hector's best boyhood memories were of Sunken City, at the southern tip of San Pedro, a strange and eerie place where in 1929, for inexplicable reasons, the oceanfront residential properties and the land beneath them started to slip into the sea at the incredible rate of almost one foot per day. Soon the houses were gone and the land was a litter of uprooted trees and broken sidewalks, with streets that went nowhere—a mayhem of junk and debris.

Over the course of Hector's life, graffiti artists had taken over Sunken City and painted almost everything they found down there. Despite the

238

"No Trespassing" signs and the dangerous footing, young daredevils like Hector Cozzo would squeeze through holes in the fence with their girlfriends. Sunken City turned out to be a perfect place to drink and smoke dope and to look around at a vanished neighborhood and realize that nothing is forever, and you can't fuck with Mother Nature, who is one scary bitch that can sweep you away with the tides. It was there that a girl two years older than Hector, from one of the most established Italian families, had popped his cherry. He wondered whatever happened to her. How he wished she could see him now, cruising Pedro in his red SL.

Hector looked at his watch and decided it was late enough to do what he'd come down there to do. He drove to the family home of Dinko Babich, the big, comfortable house he'd envied as a child, where only three people had lived. He recalled that he was never in the house for long before Mrs. Babich would give him something to eat and ask why she never saw him at Mass.

He parked a block away, between two other houses on the hill where he didn't think anyone would get nosy and question why he was parked there. After all, he wasn't some "onionhead," which was what he always called Latinos with shaved heads. And how many burglars drove cars like his?

He rolled the windows down and lit a cigarette and waited for Dinko's car to either leave the garage or return home. He remembered that Dinko was on suspension, and he felt certain that they would be at home in the late afternoon. He also thought that if they were at home, they might leave to go to the market or maybe to get some takeout food. Or maybe Dinko and the girl would head out to a motel so they could do what Hector knew they could not do in the traditional home of Mrs. Babich. And what else could Dinko want from a Mexican whore anyway?

He tried not to consider that he could be wrong about where she was. Lita Medina could've taken a taxi or a bus to Union Station, in downtown L.A., and by now be on her way to anywhere in the country. Or maybe she could've met some bucks-up player in the few days she'd worked at Club Samara, some guy she was lap-dancing. She was certainly hot-looking enough to have affected some rich guy the way she'd affected Dinko Babich, so maybe she was ensconced in some six-million-dollar crib in the Hollywood Hills without a thought in her head about Daisy's murder. He had to admit that he *could* be wrong, but he did not think he was. He believed that Lita Medina was in that house, and if he was patient and didn't spook anybody, she'd be worth fifty thousand to him.

He passed the time by thinking that he'd make Markov pay all of it upon receipt of the street address. Hector once again tried to assure himself that Kim would simply give her a few grand and that she'd be glad to get out of town with more money than she'd ever seen in her short but miserable life of poverty and whoring.

The housecleaning and the long bath had made Brigita Babich very sleepy, and she decided to take a twenty-minute nap, which ended up lasting two hours. She had vague and mixed-up dreams of her youth, about hula hoops and lava lamps and sock hops. When she awoke, she could almost remember dancing slow and sexy to "Donna," not with the man she'd eventually married but with an Italian boy named Tommy DeFranco, who'd been the dreamiest boy in their class. It occurred to her that she wore her hair in the same style at age sixty-three that she had at age fifteen, in short layers with curling-iron waves and teased up tall. The difference was that now it had to be dyed.

Then she smelled the aroma from the kitchen, and it didn't smell like anything she was used to cooking. She threw on a sweatshirt, loose-fitting long pants, and bedroom slippers. After running a comb through her hair, she went out to the kitchen.

Dinko, who was only a fair cook but could eat huge portions despite his lanky build, was watching Lita at the stovetop sautéing chicken cutlets.

When Brigita appeared in the doorway, Dinko said to his mother, "Lita's making something she says is a chipotle chicken sandwich from whatever she found in our fridge and the cupboard. I offered to go out and buy some tortillas or whatever she was used to cooking with, but she said she'd work with what we have."

"It smells divine," Brigita said. "What's in it?"

Lita smiled. "Oh, is hard for me to say in English. I learn from a family in Guanajuato where I work, but they are Greek people who love Mexican cooking. I do not have the Greek bread, so I am making with the bread you have here. Is Italian bread, no?"

"French," Dinko said, "from a local bakery." To his mother he said, "I can tell you, some of the ingredients are chipotle peppers, but I don't know how you happened to have those, and yogurt and peanut butter. Yes, peanut butter! And oregano and garlic powder. Then she shredded lettuce and grated cheddar cheese, and sautéed onion and red peppers, and now she's sautéing the chicken. It's all gonna be stuffed into the French baguettes, and I'm salivating and dying to bite into one of her chipotle sandwiches."

Brigita took a bottle of California pinot grigio from her small wine fridge and poured three glasses for the table. Then she sat and said, "Okay, I'm game for anything."

And it turned out that she loved their supper almost as much as Dinko did. Lita dropped her gaze every time they praised her culinary talents, which they did often during the meal, and finally she said to Dinko, "Is nothing like what your *mamá* can do. I wish to learn much from your *mamá*."

Perhaps it was her growing admiration for this young girl from God knows where, or perhaps it was the bolstering that her courage got from a tasty meal and a second glass of wine; in any case, Brigita said to them, "All right, you two. I think you're pretty serious about each other, aren't you?"

"As tumors and taxes," Dinko said.

"But so *soon*!" Brigita said.

Lita said nothing and only stared at the glass of wine on the table in front of her.

"What do you wanna do about it?" Brigita asked.

"What you would expect two people who love each other to do," her son said. "We wanna get married."

"Is that true, Lita?" Brigita asked. "Do you wish to marry my son?"

Lita Medina looked up at Brigita Babich and then at Dinko and said, "I do love him very much. He is very kind."

"I'm gonna be a different longshoreman when I go back to the job," Dinko promised his mother. "I'm gonna work all the hours I can and do what you've wanted me to do for years. I'm gonna grow up." He looked at Lita. "This girl did it to me. Don't ask me to explain it, because I can't."

"Lita," Brigita said, "you came to America to earn money for your sick mother and brothers in Mexico. Has that plan changed?"

Lita looked at Dinko, who answered for her: "I'm gonna turn into one of the hungrys of the Dispatch Hall. I can easily earn enough to send a few thousand a month to her mother. That's a lotta money in Mexico, and it should help. I'm gonna work enough to earn a hundred grand a year."

Lita said apologetically to Brigita, "I tell Dinko my family is not his . . . what is the word, Dinko?"

"Responsibility."

"Correct," Lita said. "Is not his responsibility. Is for me to take care of my family. Is not for Dinko."

"I can help, though," Dinko said. "I wanna do it, and I will."

"That's fine, son," Brigita said, "but wouldn't you like to continue to learn more about each other first? My old family ways are not ironclad. I know I've gotta change with the times. If you and Lita wanna live here like . . . well, like husband and wife, that's okay with me. We can get rid of the double bed in your room and buy a king-size, if it would be more comfortable for the two of you. Maybe in a few months you'll both know better whether or not you're ready to commit to each other for life." She looked at Lita. "What do you say about all this, sweetheart?"

Lita said, "If you wish for me to go away, is okay. I understand."

"No, I'm not saying that!" Brigita said. "I don't want you to leave here. I worry that everything is happening too soon, that's all."

"Nothing's gonna change for me, Mom," Dinko said, "because I'm just like you in many ways." He paused before adding, "I always loved hearing the story of how you first met Dad at Croatian Hall when he asked you to dance with him. During that very first dance you somehow knew in your heart that the young longshoreman was gonna be the love of your life. Remember?"

Brigita said nothing for a long moment. She started to take a sip of wine but changed her mind and put down the glass. Then she said, "All right, let's go see the priest tomorrow and get things started."

Dinko took Lita's hand with a huge smile of relief.

It had been a tiring and emotional day for all concerned. Brigita turned in early, and Dinko and Lita sat watching television for an hour, then went to bed and made the most tender and fulfilling love Dinko had ever experienced. Before falling asleep, Lita said, for the first time, "I wish to be with you for all my life, Dinko."

"You will be, I promise you, Lita," he said. "When you're beside me I feel so . . . *alive.*"

Then she said to him, "Please tell to me again what you always say. I like to hear how you say it."

Dinko tenderly brushed a strand of hair from her cheek and said, "You are loved."

Hector Cozzo passed the time while watching the Babich house by thinking about all the crime spawned by the incredible wealth that passed through the Port of Los Angeles every day. Like how this crew of a dozen thieves had followed a container truck from the port to Vernon, not far from downtown L.A., where the cans were loaded onto train cars fitted for containers. After dark, when the train was on its way, one of the thieves jumped aboard and opened up the can they were after. Most of the others followed the train in SUVs through the Inland Empire, out to the desert near the Palm Springs cutoff, where one of their point men had disabled a stolen car by flattening its tires, after first parking it on the tracks.

The train operators needed considerable time to get the car hauled away, and during that time the posse climbed onto the train car and rolled off the big-screen TVs, laying them flat on the desert floor. After the train was long gone, a rented box truck appeared and the crew retrieved all of the TVs, returning them to L.A., not far from where they had begun their short train journey. That's the kind of crime that Hector felt could be profitable for him if he could only rely on gangs like Rancho San Pedro or the Dodge City Crips to follow orders and work for a white man of superior intelligence.

But there were even less complicated capers he felt were more feasible, like the recent big theft at the distribution warehouse in Pedro on the west side of the Harbor Freeway. An onionhead working in the warehouse simply made a routine call to the waste management company to replace a forty-foot dumpster that the homie had purposely damaged *after* he'd loaded it with stolen electronic goods.

His brother-in-law drove the trash truck that dropped a new dumpster and picked up the damaged one, transporting it to a housing project, where he left it while he went off to have lunch. Of course, when he got back, the dumpster was empty, and he picked it up and returned it to his company for repair. Hector figured that only half a dozen greasers were used in that operation, but one of them couldn't keep his mouth shut after getting busted with a box full of "shaved" keys he kept for stealing Hondas and selling them to chop shops.

The more Hector considered those moneymaking schemes, the more he figured it'd always end the same way if he chose to deal with beaners and coons. There were other options for a smart white man around the harbor if he took the time to check things out. The Armenians from Hollywood had made a bundle when they'd shipped in imported vodka in fifty-five-gallon drums labeled "window-washing fluid." They knew that the LAPD didn't investigate international smuggling, and that at worst it would be a tariff violation that nobody else would really bother with. If necessary, he could hook up on some deals with the Hollywood Armos, and then maybe he'd never get his ride keyed again.

He dozed off just after 10:00 P.M. and awoke thirty minutes later, startled to see a black-and-white police car cruising slowly past the Babich house, which was still dimly lit. He started up the Mercedes and began the tiring drive north. When he was on the Harbor Freeway, heading to the city, he looked at the beacon lights on the east side of the highway, thousands of lamps on the tops of tall poles glowing burnt orange, announcing that this was the Port of Los Angeles. There was money to be made out there for an angle man like Hector Cozzo. He was sure of it.

He was acutely aware that he'd used one day of the three he'd been allotted, but the better part of him was strangely content with that. Part of him even wanted to fail. Part of him wanted to be free of his overwhelming lust for money. Yet as far back as he could remember, he'd always been Hector the hustler. It had *always* been about money, and he was willing to take risks for it.

Then, for a reason he could not explain, he began thinking about how many people came to Pedro to die. He recalled an Asian woman and her daughter who'd tied themselves together and jumped from the Vincent Thomas Bridge, reaching terminal velocity before missing the water but hitting the parking lot. And another buckethead who'd thrown her kids off the docks at berth 22 and dove in after slashing her own throat.

And there was always someone doing a swan dive off the Point Fermin cliffs. He remembered reading about two young white chicks that were all into Goth, misery and depression. They held hands on the top of the cliffs reciting doggerel that they considered intensely poetic. When they were spotted and surrounded by emergency responders, the girls had two last words for all of them: "Life sucks."

A cop asked them, "How old are you two?"

One of them answered, "Thirteen."

It was reported that someone tried gallows humor, telling them, "Hang in a while. It gets worse."

But they didn't care to wait and they jumped, ending up among the litter from a car at the foot of the cliffs, which two months earlier had sped from the Hollywood Bowl all the way down Western Avenue in a police pursuit that had lasted forty minutes. The pursuit ended when the driver of the car, who'd smoked a shit pipe full of high-quality ice and didn't know there were cliffs there, did a Thelma and Louise into space, perhaps seeing a few Catalina Island lights twinkling in the distance on his way down.

A lot of people came to Pedro to die. That concept made Hector think of Lita Medina, and he did not like what he was thinking. He was getting a headache and had a craving for some zannies and booze. It made him drive faster in his leased car back to his leased house in Encino.

EIGHTEEN

Both 6-X-32 and 6-X-76 received calls to phone the station at just about the time that Hector Cozzo arrived at his house with a stress headache so severe he was almost in tears. Sergeant Murillo had told the midwatch cops that there were reports of very excessive panhandling going on at Hollywood and Highland, and not involving the Street Characters in superhero garb. In fact, it was Darth Vader who'd made the cell call to the Hollywood Station desk to alert the cops that a quartet of Gypsy women and a clutch of homeless male transients were wrecking the business for everyone else by harassing the tourists.

Shop 6-X-76 arrived first at Grauman's Chinese Theatre, and as soon as the group of Gypsies spotted the black-and-white, they decided it was time to stop working the crowd and get the hell out of there. One of them dug into the enormous swag purse she was carrying, found her cell, and made a call for a fast pickup. In less than two minutes, a fifteen-year-old Dodge station wagon that had been circling the block swiftly pulled in at the curb in front of the famous Hollywood landmark to pick up the four women. As they pulled out, the radio car fell in behind them with its blue and red lights winking and honked them over before they'd gone half a block.

Mel Yarashi was driving, with Always Talking Tony riding shotgun. The last citation had been written by Mel, so he said to A.T., "You're up."

All four Gypsy women were in their forties and appeared slightly rotund. That was because they all wore very full skirts and baggy cotton tops hanging out over their hips in case someone got lucky and grabbed a purse, a wallet, or a camera and needed a place other than an obvious booster purse in which to stash the loot if the cops were called. There were no golden hoop earrings or other Gypsy clichés to mark them. An observer might've taken them for some recently arrived immigrants in slumdog couture.

Mel Yarashi approached on the passenger side of the station wagon, shining his flashlight beam into the car as a safety distraction, and A.T. advanced on the driver and said, "License and registration, please."

The driver, who was perhaps a decade older than the four tourist-hustlers, flashed an obsequious smile and said, "Of course, Officer, anything you say. I hope I didn't break the law?"

"That was a no-stopping zone," A.T. said. "And you parked there."

"But, Officer," the woman said, "it was just long enough to pick up the ladies. I didn't block traffic or anything."

"And your right taillight isn't working," A.T. said, looking at her license and registration, which were okay. "Have you paid all your prior tickets?"

"I only got one in the last two years," the woman said. "And I paid it."

"I'll check on that," he said. "Please wait in your car."

Mel Yarashi stayed put at the right rear of the station wagon while A.T. checked for wants or warrants. Finding none, he got out of the car with his citation book and started writing the ticket.

The Gypsy woman looked in her rearview mirror, saw what was happening, and quickly leaped from the car, leaving her smile behind.

"What're you doing?" she cried.

"Writing you a citation for parking in the no-stopping zone and for having a burned-out taillight."

The Gypsy woman said, "But you told me you were going to check to see if I paid my tickets!"

"I did. You don't have any traffic warrants, and I'm citing you for the violations."

"Wait a goddamn minute!" she said, and the sudden change in tone and volume made him pause.

Mel Yarashi took a few steps in her direction, saying, "You better get back in the car, ma'am."

"I got one of those no-stopping tickets before!" she said, glaring at A.T. "That's an expensive ticket. You can't write me for that. Haven't I been cooperative?"

"Up until now," A.T. said. "Now please wait in the car."

She said, "Why can't you give me a warning?"

A.T. said, "Okay, I'm warning you to go wait in your car or you might get yourself in serious trouble here!"

A.T. saw the Gypsy woman grow silent; then she raised herself up to a more erect stance and almost seemed to levitate. The fawning smile and fleshy chin were replaced by a hardened, wrathful set of the jaw. Wisps of dyed black hair growing out gray at the roots appeared to spring up like the horns of a goat, from the onshore summer wind blowing across Hollywood. As she stared into the face of Always Talking Tony, he went rigid. Mel Yarashi took a slightly defensive posture, as if anticipating a physical attack on his partner.

But the Gypsy woman's weapon was words. She said, "If you write that ticket to me, your first child will be born with a terrible birth defect. And you will contract testicular cancer one year after that, and have both testicles surgically removed."

Mel Yarashi said to the Gypsy, "Okay, you had your say. Now I'm telling you to get back in the car."

The Gypsy ignored the Asian cop and drilled the black cop with her smoldering eyes. Then she moved slowly to the station wagon, opened the door, and got inside. A.T. turned to look toward her, his pen poised in midair.

Mel Yarashi said, "Come on, A.T., let's get the ticket done and bump on outta here."

A.T. glanced at his partner without comment, then walked to the driver's window and said sotto to the Gypsy, "This is no way for a citizen and a police officer to communicate with each other. I know you wanna take back what you said, right?"

"About what?" she said.

"About the baby and my . . . body parts."

"What's done is done," the Gypsy said.

"How about just the part about my . . . cancer surgery?" A.T. whispered. "Take *that* part back."

She stepped out of the car and said quietly to the cop, "Would you take the ticket back?"

"I can't," he said, "I got it half-written. I can't just stop. These things're numbered, and we gotta account for them."

She said, "I see. You are telling me that as far as you are concerned, what's done is done."

"Wait a minute!" A.T. said. "I can just write you for the taillight. You get the taillight fixed and the ticket can get signed off. I won't write you for the red zone, okay?"

"I can accept that," she said.

Always Talking Tony finished the citation and the Gypsy woman signed it and said to him, "The curse is lifted."

Mel Yarashi stood speechless in the street, watching the station wagon drive away. When they were back in their car he said, "I don't believe what I saw. You looked like you thought she was gonna sprout fangs and bite your neck!"

"Don't start!" A.T. said. "I seen shit in Afghanistan. You can't fuck with tribal people. They got special juju, and it don't pay to dis them."

"You musta taken crazy pills today!" Mel Yarashi said. Then, referring to section 5150 of the Welfare and Institutions Code, which describes involuntary commitment for dangerous psychos, he said, "If you ain't fifty-one fifty, you're at least fifty-one forty-nine and a half. You totally bought into a fucking Gypsy curse, is what you just did!"

"So riddle me this," A.T. argued. "The Gypsy mentioned my first-born because she somehow knew I don't already have kids. How could she know that I don't have kids?"

"You're not wearing a wedding ring," Mel said, "and you're young. It was a good guess."

Knowing what gossips coppers are, A.T. said, "Now, before you go spreading this story around the whole midwatch, lemme ask you something. Did you touch the Oracle's picture before we hit the streets tonight?"

"Of course," Mel said.

"Well, then?"

"That's different. It's kind of a prayer when we touch the Oracle's image. She's nothing but a Gypsy grifter."

"Are you gonna touch the Oracle's picture tomorrow?"

"Of course."

"Why? Because you don't wanna get shot or something, right?"

"Yeah, I guess so."

Always Talking Tony said, "That means *you* believe in juju. You don't wanna get shot, and I don't wanna have my balls removed. I rest my case."

It was nearly midnight when 6-X-32 handled the other part of the problem with panhandlers, not half a block from where the Gypsy woman had delivered her aborted curse. Three homeless transients had been working the more obvious tourists, especially the ones with cameras hanging from their necks, who were the easiest touches.

The transients were about a decade younger than Trombone Teddy, but they had the ancient faces and watery eyes of hopeless juiceheads. Their only real difference from Teddy was that they usually slept at homeless shelters rather than in dumpsters. The mild summer nights precluded layered clothing, but even without the layers they still gave the impression of growing their clothes rather than wearing them. Their shirts and trousers were so stained and filthy they'd lost their color and seemed to sprout from them like fungus. Two had splotchy skin with open sores, and there were not twenty teeth among them. As younger transients, they'd covered more territory than Lewis and Clark, but as they got older they'd begun to vaporize into specters that nobody really saw until they spoke. The unholy ghosts of Hollywood Boulevard.

All three were staggering drunk as they sidled among the thinning throngs of tourists, hoping to get enough for a few forties of Olde English, saying, "Any spare change for a hungry man?" Or "Help a disabled veteran?" Or "Some Christian charity for a man down on his luck?"

Flotsam and Jetsam parked their shop in the lot, got out, and corralled all three before they could scatter. The cops took them to the car, and while Jetsam lit them with his flashlight, Flotsam patted them down, wearing latex gloves. Two of the transients had half-pints of cheap whiskey in the pockets of their trousers. Jetsam took down their names, birth dates, and descriptions on FI cards, and got in the radio car to run them for wants and warrants.

It turned out that the oldest of the three, a seventy-five-year-old bearded beanpole named Jerome Darwell, had an outstanding traffic warrant for crossing against a red light. Which likely meant that some cop got pissed off watching these bums run across Hollywood Boulevard during busy nighttime traffic and wrote Jerome Darwell a ticket that he knew very well would never get paid. Then it would go to warrant and eventually land the transient in jail for a couple of days the next time he got checked like this.

Jetsam was happy to get the warrant information because it had been a boring night so far, and now they'd get to play their favorite game.

Flotsam looked equally pleased when Jetsam nodded to him, then said to the three drunks, "Who wants to play Panhandler Jeopardy?"

"What's that?" asked Daniel, the shortest one, who was book-ended by his fellow drunks. As he spoke he lurched into Spencer, causing Spencer to say, "Hey, you stepped on my foot!"

Flotsam told them, "Don't squabble, and pay attention. See, our problem is, we gotta arrest one of you to set an example here. But we don't wanna have to, like, dick around with all three of you, so we'll take the loser of the game, okay? Do you ever watch the *Jeopardy* show on TV?"

The three bums looked blankly at the cops and at one another, so Jetsam said, "It's real easy. We'll pick a category of questions and we'll ask you for answers. But you gotta give the answer in the form of the question."

Jetsam said, "You'll get the hang of it. So, Daniel, Spencer, and Jerome, what'll we choose for our first category?"

More blank looks. Flotsam said, "I got it. Any of you guys been in the navy?"

Spencer said, "Army," but the other two just shook their heads.

Jetsam said, "Okay, so you're all equally ignorant about seagoing vessels. Our category is Name the Ships. First question to you, Daniel. This ancient wooden vessel in the Bible was, like, all crammed full of farting, shitting, stinking animals and birds and fleas."

Daniel looked like he wanted to just lie down in the parking lot and go to sleep, but Jerome said, "I got it!"

"No, not your turn, Jerome," Jetsam said. "How about you, Spencer? Any idea?"

"Noah's ark," Spencer said.

"Okay," Flotsam said, "but you gotta give your answer in the form of a question. You gotta say, 'What is Noah's ark?' Get it?"

"What is Noah's ark," Spencer said, lurching again, this time into Daniel, who yapped at him.

Jetsam said, "Okay, settle down for the next question about a boat or vessel. This ship became the name of a song that a cute little movie star with big dimples used to sing about maybe a hundred years ago, when you guys were in the third grade and probably still sober most of the time."

No answers whatsoever, so Jetsam said, "Okay, I'll give you a hint because you guys are really dumb contestants. The name of the boat in the song is the good ship . . . ? Any guesses?"

Nothing, except that now all three drunks looked like they wanted to lie down in the parking lot, so Jetsam said, "*Lollipop*! Goddamnit, the good ship *Lollipop*! What the fuck's wrong with you guys?"

"We're drunk!" Daniel said.

"Next question," Jetsam said. "There was this big humongous boat that, like, crashed into an iceberg and went all swirly before it nose-dived right down the fucking drain. They made a movie outta the story starring Leonardo DiCaprio and Kate Winslet, who happens to be a babe I, like, *really* get off on every time I lay eyes on her."

"I know it!" Jerome said.

"Not your turn, Jerome," Flotsam said.

"Why not?" Jerome said. "When's it my turn?"

Jetsam said, "Daniel, what's the name of the big boat?"

Daniel didn't have a clue, so Jerome said, "The *Titanic*."

Jetsam shook his head. "You gotta give the answer in the form of a question, so you're disqualified, Jerome." Then he stepped in front of Daniel, who was reeling, and said, "Now you try it."

Daniel pulled himself together just enough to mumble, "The *Titanic*."

"He's disqualified too!" Jerome said.

"Give it in the form of a question!" Jetsam said.

"Give what?" Daniel mumbled.

"This is depressing me," Flotsam said.

"Wait a minute," Jetsam said, grabbing Daniel by the shirtfront because the codger was reeling again. "Here's another one. This ship went to Tahiti and the crew went all, like, titty crazy. And they drank moonshine in their coconut milk, and smoked ganja or something, and, like, danced the hula and boogaloo. And they pulled a big mutiny led by Marlon Brando before he stuffed cotton in his jowls and made people deals they couldn't refuse."

"I know the answer," Jerome said.

"Dummy up, Jerome," Flotsam said.

Jetsam was getting desperate now, so he said, "Maybe we got the wrong category going here, but I'll give this thing one more try." He got in Daniel's face again and said, "Remember the question about the good ship *Lollipop* and the little girl actor with the dimples? In fact, her last name almost rhymes with 'dimple' and 'pimple.' Well, they named a drink after her, and it's a drink you can find to this day anywhere they serve booze. I gotta believe that a guy like you who's lived in saloons will know the answer to a goddamn drink question!"

Daniel said, "A Bloody Mary?"

"That's pretty close," Jetsam answered despondently, "but no cigar."

Flotsam said, "Step off, pard. Lemme break it down to him." The tall cop stood in front of Daniel, whose nose came up to the cop's badge, and looking down at the old drunk, Flotsam said, "Listen, hobbit, they make this kiddie drink by squirting cherry juice or some red shit into it, and they give it to any brats that happen to be in the gin mill while their parents sit at the bar slapping the shit out of each other and regretting the day they ever got married."

Jetsam added, "It's the drink that can be given to sissies of all ages, for chrissake!"

Daniel said, "Oh, you mean the Shirley Temple?"

"Say it like a fucking question!" Flotsam yelled.

"What is a Shirley Temple?" Daniel cried.

"Thank you, Daniel!" Jetsam said, patting the geezer's cheek with his gloved hand.

"That's got nothing to do with boats and ships! Take him to jail!" Jerome said.

"Who the fuck you think sang the song about the good ship *Lollipop* then?" Flotsam said. "There's a direct connection with boats here."

"It's your turn now, Jerome," Jetsam said.

"About time," Jerome said.

Jetsam said, "For a daily double, this Japanese aircraft carrier took more casualties than any Nip ship in the Battle of Midway."

"What kinda question is that?" Jerome demanded. "You asked them about ships like Noah's ark and the *Titanic* and the good ship *Lollipop*!"

"Time's up," Jetsam said. "Your answer shoulda been, 'What is the *Kaga*?' Okay, Jerome, get in the backseat. You other two, shuffle off into the night, and may the force be with you."

"This is a fucking sham!" Jerome protested. "I was the smartest contestant!"

But he was taken to Hollywood Station and booked, not for being drunk in public but on the old arrest warrant for an unpaid traffic ticket that he could not remember ever having received. That was because when he'd gotten the ticket, he'd been, as usual, drunk in public.

Hector Cozzo did not fall asleep until 3:00 A.M., despite the zannies he'd washed down with vodka. He'd received three calls on his cell late in the evening. When he saw that one was from Markov and two from Kim, he knew they wanted a report on his first day of looking for Lita Medina. He did not respond to the calls but, instead, spent the late-night hours devising a plan where he could safely put his demands to them. He was sure that Kim would want to kill him, but they'd pay. They had no choice. Never once, prior to sleep overtaking him, did he doubt that he'd find her the next day at the Babich home in San Pedro.

NINETEEN

Hector Cozzo thought he'd better get out of bed early and head for Pedro before they were finished with breakfast at the Babich house. He was half-asleep when he made the drive south on the Harbor Freeway in terrible traffic that got him to San Pedro by 8:45 A.M.

But by that time, Brigita and Dinko Babich and Lita Medina were already at the Catalina Terminal, preparing to board the *Catalina Jet*, one of four sleek white catamarans in a fleet of eight, this one a three-decker that could transport 450 passengers to Avalon Harbor at thirty-five knots per hour. It happened to be leaving from Pedro that day rather than from Long Beach or Dana Point.

"I have much excitement!" Lita said, squeezing Dinko's hand in both of hers, giddy with the thrill of it.

"Wanna sit up on the open-air deck?" Dinko asked his mother.

"That's for kids like you," Brigita said. "Not for old broads that just spent an hour with a curling iron."

"They advertise a reverse windscreen," Dinko pointed out.

"Sure," Brigita said. "I really wanna see the loose skin on my face blowing forward."

"I don't think that's what it means," Dinko said with a chuckle, over-joyed to see Lita totally lost in the experience, her troubles forgotten, her lovely face beaming in the morning sunlight.

257

"I'll take the inside airline seats, thank you," Brigita said. "Besides, the snack bars're down there. Breakfast was pretty skimpy."

"Whatever you like," Dinko said, glad that he and Lita could then sit topside and snuggle, which they were both uneasy about doing in front of Brigita. "After all, it's your sixty-six fifty."

"That's your price," she said. "It's sixty bucks for seniors, and I'm gonna get my money's worth in comfort. But you're buying the lunch, buster."

"That's a deal," Dinko agreed, and he and Lita climbed to the top deck and found seats.

When the catamaran's engines began to rumble, Lita's eyes widened and he said, "The distance to Catalina is about the same as it is to downtown L.A. Twenty-five miles, more or less. But the trip to downtown L.A. in any kind of traffic takes a lot longer than the one hour we'll need to fly over the waves."

"We shall fly!" Lita said, putting her head on his shoulder and grabbing his arm as though for an anchor.

And it seemed to Lita Medina that they *did* fly. The Pacific was calm, and the boat could easily handle its thirty-five-knot cruising speed. They had to speak loudly to hear each other over the rush of wind and the roar of engines.

While she was gazing out at the approaching island, he kissed her on the cheek and said, "How do you feel? Not seasick, are you?"

She looked at him with a sparkle in her amber eyes that he had not seen before. "I have *very* much excitement, Dinko!"

"You *are* excited," he reminded her.

"I *am* excited," she said.

"You are loved," he said.

"I am loved," she said.

Where the fuck can they be at this hour of the morning? Hector Cozzo wondered. The garage door had been left open, and the car was gone. One of the residents on the hilly street where the Babich family lived was leaving for work, and he gave Hector a glance before getting into his car and driving away. But a brand-new Mercedes SL, even one with ugly scratches across the hood, even one driven by a man with a mullet haircut, was not the kind of thing that would arouse suspicion.

Hector didn't recognize the guy as one of the Italians he'd known on this street when he was a kid. He figured the guy for a Croat, and that was a good thing about being an "ich" or a dago in Pedro. The cops only came in contact with you during landlord-tenant or business disputes. The Croatians and Italians were the landlords, not the tenants, and they were the proprietors of the businesses, not the customers. He supposed that if one of the residents did get suspicious of his car being parked there for hours, he could still come up with enough Italian or Croatian family names to satisfy any cop from Harbor Station.

After two hours of sitting and waiting, he had to take a leak and was dying for a cup of coffee. He started up the Mercedes and drove down the hill and east, toward the harbor, remembering that when commercial vessels would come to the fuel dock back in the day, the dock manager happened to be a crook who turned back the rollers on the tanks and sold the red maritime fuel in ten-gallon "blister bags" very late at night to any of the locals he could trust. He certainly sold to Hector Cozzo, especially after Hector lied and said he was a cousin of the Italian family whose business checked all of the catches of fish coming into the harbor, and had been doing so before Hector's father was born, back when most of the fishermen were Italians.

Passing the Scandinavian Hall, he heard the loudspeakers playing an anthem for one of the Viking countries, and sure enough, he saw the flag of a Danish cargo ship steaming into the harbor. Then he drove straight to Point Fermin and Walker's Café, a bikers' hangout where he knew he could get a good cup of coffee and a bite to eat at a reasonable price.

"You have *got* to be kidding," Brigita Babich told Dinko when he suggested motorboating or kayaking around the Catalina coastline. "Next thing you'll want me to do the zip-line tour and fly around the cliffs clinging to a rope like Tarzan."

"No, you gotta book those in advance," Dinko said. "But how about bike riding?" Then he turned to Lita and asked, "Can you ride a bike?"

"Of course, Dinko," Lita said. "I come from Mexico, not from the moon."

"Don't tell me you can play golf, too?" Dinko said.

Lita said, "No, but I shall learn if you teach me."

"Next week," he said. "You can use Mom's clubs."

"How about if this old lady goes shopping?" Brigita said. "I can stroll around Avalon all day and check out the shops and load up on souvenirs for suckers. You two go ahead and do your bike ride."

Dinko and Lita rented mountain bikes and cruised the streets of the little town and then ventured up into the hills on trails. There they could be alone except for groups of hikers, some with backpacks, and the occasional biker returning to Avalon.

Nature had bestowed scores of endemic plant species on Santa Catalina Island and nowhere else on earth, such as the Catalina ironwood tree, and Saint Catherine's lace, a blossom that begins its life white in color but changes to light brown during the summer. And they saw the island's only succulent, a delicate growth with the vainly optimistic name of Catalina live-forever. A wildfire four years earlier had done damage to much of the flora, but scores of native species could still be seen from the trails.

"They have buffalo on this island," Dinko told Lita when they stopped for a rest on a hillside overlooking Avalon. When she looked puzzled, he got off his bike and did an impression of a lumbering bison walking slowly along the trail.

Still seated astride her mountain bike, she hadn't the faintest idea of what sort of animal he was miming, and she burst into laughter, not stopping until she could hardly catch her breath.

Her infectious laughter made Dinko start, and they held on to each other, laughing like children. They gradually settled down when he wiped her tears away with his hand, and kissed her left cheek and then her right.

"You are very silly, Dinko," Lita said. "You are my silly boy."

Their foreheads touched as a cloud shadow passed over the entire twenty-two-mile length of the island, the solar rays momentarily blocked by the gusting alabaster efflorescence directly overhead. Dinko looked up and then back at her and caught a scent of . . . lilac? Was there lilac growing wild here or was it only his imagination?

"I'm glad the priest couldn't see us till tomorrow," Dinko said. "This is a lot more fun than dealing with God stuff, isn't it?"

"God is here in this place, Dinko," Lita said. "Do you not believe this?"

"You can make me believe anything," Dinko said. "Would you like to come here for our honeymoon? Or should we go to Guanajuato and be with your family?"

"Here, Dinko," she said. "I wish to come to this island with you."

"Sure," he said. "There's plenty of time later to take you home and meet your family."

"*Home.*" Lita said the word as though it was foreign not just in sound but in meaning. With the vast blue ocean stirring from sea winds, and with the throb of blood singing in their ears, she said, "I am home when you are near to me. And I wish to be home with you for always."

At the end of what Lita Medina tried to explain repeatedly to Brigita and Dinko was the most glorious day she'd ever experienced, they decided to stop for a meal before returning to the house. Brigita insisted that she wanted to buy them dinner, so they went to Ante's Restaurant for some *sarma,* minced meat wrapped in cabbage, grape, or chard leaves, and *cevapcici,* more minced meat on a flat bread with onions, sour cream, cottage cheese, and Croatian spices, and the inevitable *mostaccioli.* By the time they got home, nobody wanted to do anything but sleep. They were laughing and joking about bulging tummies when Dinko parked in the garage and they walked to the back door of the house.

None of them saw the man standing across the street, a cigarette cupped in his hand so that the glow did not reveal his presence.

The man clearly heard Lita Medina say to Brigita and Dinko, "This is the most perfect day of all my life."

"In all nineteen years and four months?" Dinko asked, blissfully.

"Soon will be nineteen years and five months," Lita said. And then to both of them: "Thank you, thank you, thank you for this day!"

When they were inside the house, the shadow figure snuffed out the cigarette and walked quickly back to the Mercedes SL parked two blocks away. He never saw the old Italian widower watching him suspiciously from his home across the street from the Babiches. As he started up the car he spotted another black-and-white cruising very slowly by the Babich house, and he thought, Yeah, the cops know all about her seeing Kim with Daisy. The Mexican dancer's already dimed him.

After he got home to Encino, his bladder and bowels almost failed him on the front stoop. In the doorjamb was a business card from Detective Albino Villaseñor of Hollywood homicide, with a message on the back. It said, "Call me ASAP."

TWENTY

Sleeping had become nearly impossible for Hector Cozzo. When he did sleep it was fitful, for only thirty minutes at a time, and he dreamed of dancing. It was strange dancing, the kind he'd never done, like movie dancing. He'd have a female partner without a face and then he'd be alone. He'd dance in toward a line of other dancers of both genders and then he'd dance back, always feeling safer when he retreated, because he didn't really know the dance steps he was supposed to be doing, the way the other faceless dancers did. Each time he awakened the bedsheets were soaked with sweat. In the morning, when he dragged himself out of bed, he was exhausted, and he felt more fear about the plan he'd formulated than he'd ever felt in his life.

He fretted for more than an hour about the business card from the LAPD detective, but he finally persuaded himself that it was only natural that his name would've been dropped by someone at Club Samara, where Daisy had worked. He figured that Markov would also be contacted by the detective. But even if he could convince himself that he was still okay, he was positive that the detective would know about the peg-leg cop's investigation of him as an employee in a massage parlor brothel. He didn't want to talk to *any* cop just yet.

At 11:00 A.M. he returned the call from Markov that he'd been avoiding thinking about. His employer answered on the second ring.

"Yes?"

"It's me," Hector said. "Sorry I didn't get a chance to call sooner."

"I will not be ignored," Markov said.

"Sorry, sir." Hector always avoided names during phone calls, per Markov's orders.

"I wanted a report," Markov said.

"That's why I didn't get a chance to call," Hector said. "I was working for you."

"And?"

"I found what you wanted me to find."

"Good!" Markov said. "When can I receive your report? I want it delivered in person."

"Today," Hector said. "I made your deadline, so I'll expect you to keep your part of the agreement."

"If you will recall, that will take place only when the third party deals with the matter."

"No, that's been changed," Hector said. "This has been too hard and too risky, so I'll need you to keep your part of the deal today, when I give you my report. That means I want *all* of it."

The silence lasted so long that Hector thought Markov had hung up, until he said, "You are making a mistake if you think you can give orders to me."

Hector mustered all the courage he had left. "No, you're the one making the mistake. I'm moving outta the house today, and you ain't gonna be seeing me no more. So if you wanna wait till all the shit in the sky comes down, that's up to you. I can tell you this much: the person in question ain't gonna stay quiet for long, not if she gets a visit from Five-Oh and . . ."

"You have said enough!" Markov interrupted.

"Call me when you're ready to keep your part of the deal," Hector said, and closed his cell phone.

He took a shower and shaved, then packed his car with all his clothes and personal items, which were the only things in the furnished house that belonged to him. He had to make frequent nerve visits to the bathroom, and his hands remained clammy. He decided not to wait around long enough for Kim to drive to Encino from Koreatown, if Markov had alerted him.

He looked at his watch and had just decided it was time to go when he heard the ringtone.

"You called jist in time, sir," he said.

"All right," Markov said. "I can make the arrangements for half of the promised trading material by four o'clock. I will see you at my house. Be on time."

"No, you won't," Hector said. "You will see me at six o'clock on the Hollywood Boulevard Walk of Fame with the *correct* trading material. And I mean *all* of it. Look for Frank Sinatra's TV star. He's got other ones too."

Markov virtually hissed when he said, "Have you gone completely insane?"

"You won't think so when I tell you about some dangerous things that you don't know about."

"This is outrageous!" Markov said.

"I forget the address of the star, but if you Google it, you can find it," Hector said. "When you get there, I'll be close by. And if I was you, I'd buy a new go-phone tomorrow."

Hector could hear Markov's breathing when he said, "Why are you doing this?"

"The star meeting place?" Hector asked. "Because Sinatra was Italian and it's a place where we can be safe. I don't want no surprises from your Korean business associate or any of his friends when we make our trade, like what might happen to me if I went to your house all alone. He showed me what he can do when he's unhappy. So if any Asian approaches me on the Walk of Fame, even if it's the Dalai Lama or Yoko Ono with her dumb hats and goofy shades hanging off her nose, you'll never see me again. And you and your associate can take your chances with what's sure to come down on both of you very soon."

More silence on the line, until Markov finally said, "What do you mean when you say you know dangerous things that I do not know about?"

Hector said, "I have some critical information that I been holding back from you, and when you hear it you'll be ready to liquidate your holdings ASAP and take that trip to Costa Rica. I can buy you a little time to get that done, but only if you show up at Sinatra's star with the correct trading material."

Hector shut his cell phone again, and no further calls came in other than one more from Kim, which he ignored. He wondered what Markov would say when he heard about the investigation already under way by the peg-leg cop and his cohorts at Hollywood Station. He decided to go to the phone store tomorrow and buy another go-phone, but he needed this one until the meeting with Markov. He hoped he wasn't keeping the phone a day too long. If they were already surveilling him and bugging his house, there might be more than Markov waiting for him at Sinatra's star. But at this point, what choice did he have? The money made all risks worth taking.

There was one more essential call he had to make. He speed-dialed her number and, knowing the hours she kept, hoped she'd be awake. She was, but barely.

"Ivana," he said. "It's me. I got an important question. Are you awake?"

"What time is it?" she groaned.

"Listen to me!" he said. "Remember the time a couple months ago when you did a job for our Korean associate and some of his friends? You said you were at his house in Koreatown, right?"

"No." She cleared mucus from her throat. "It was a condo of his friend. A woman he knows even before they come to America. Maybe he lives there with her, but I am not for sure."

"But they were tight, weren't they?" Hector said.

"What?"

"He was fucking her, wasn't he?"

"I do not know!" she said impatiently. "I guess so. He fucks every-body he can fuck. One way or other."

"What's her name?"

Silence on the line and then: "Madame Wang or Tang, something like that. I think it is Tang."

"I want you to take me there," Hector said. "I need the address."

"I do not got to take you," she said. "It is the top-floor condo above the big restaurant with name of Kimchi Heaven."

"Thanks, go back to sleep," Hector said.

Now I got you where I need you, buckethead, Hector thought. You and your woman. Yin and yang, Kim and Tang. I got you on my GPS!

Sergeant Murillo had finished reading the lineup very quickly. There were only five cars on Watch 5 that night, and with Chester Toles gone and no replacement from Watch 2 or Watch 3, he was juggling car as-signments until the new deployment period started.

"Got some roll call training to kill time," he said, and, of course, the announcement brought no enthusiasm from the troops.

"More on racial sensitivity?" Flotsam moaned.

"Is it because of the deaf Samoan?" Jetsam asked. "Did his girlfriend, like, come in and make a complaint on us?"

"Did you have to write up a one twenty-eight?" Flotsam asked.

That made everyone turn toward the surfer cops, so Sergeant Murillo said, "No, but now that you've got everyone's attention, go ahead and enlighten us about what you did with a deaf Samoan last night."

Flotsam said, "The dude was, you know, King Kong tall and weighed only a little less. And he'd just finished smoking dope with a Hispanic guy and a white chick on the corner of Hollywood and Gower. And we pull up and we know what they're doing 'cause we can smell it on them. And the Hispanic guy's a smart-ass, and when I ask them what they're doing he goes, 'Jerking off and smoking dope, but we're done with both now.'"

Jetsam picked up the story: "And the deaf Samoan starts bitching at us and we're supposed to, like, understand sign language, right?"

"Then how did you know he was bitching?" Sergeant Murillo asked.

Flotsam said, "His banana fingers got to flying all over the place, saying he wanted a sergeant."

"How did you know he wanted a sergeant?" Sergeant Murillo asked.

Jetsam said, "He only made these spooky grunting sounds, but he stuck up three big fingers and started pounding them on his bicep. Three fingers for sergeant stripes. We figured it out."

Flotsam said, "That's when the chick stepped in and started mouthing off, but the Hispanic guy, he decided to bounce and was gone in a flash."

"How did this saga end?" Sergeant Murillo asked.

Jetsam said, "We wrote FIs and decided to kick them loose after the chick said they were in love and were gonna get married. Except they had to wait for his divorce 'cause he'd been married six times back in Samoa and had lotsa kids, and the last divorce wasn't final."

"That's what she called to complain about, right?" Flotsam asked. "What came next?"

"You've gone this far," Sergeant Murillo said. "Tell us what came next."

"It was just a little . . . banter, Sarge," Jetsam said. "Me and my partner were talking to each other, and the Samoan couldn't hear us, of course. And she looked too smoked out or shot out to hear a frog fart, but I guess she did, and . . ."

Flotsam said, "I just sorta gave my impression to my partner of a six-time-loser deaf Samoan, standing at the altar with number seven and talking to her in sign language. So I do signs with my fingers and I go, 'Me love you long time. *Not!*' That's all I did."

With the whole watch bursting into cackles and hoots, Sergeant Murillo said, "See, that's just the kind of ethnic banter we've got to avoid these days! Lucky for you, I took the call and told her you guys have never been the same after you both fell from the police airship during a daring rescue and got brain injuries. She said she sympathized and didn't make me cut paper on you. But don't push your luck."

"Roger that, Sarge," Flotsam said.

"Ditto, boss," Jetsam said.

"Now about police business," Sergeant Murillo said. "We've been asked by West Bureau to inform you that there's been a lot of activity at local gas pumps. Skimmers are being put inside selected pumps without so-called parasite devices on the outside that might tip off the station owners. They're manufactured in China, and they dump info onto cell phones nearby. It's an Armenian game, done only in gas stations that can be seen from the freeway. An SUV pulls up to a pump and gets quick access. One key fits certain types of pumps all over the state and, probably, all over the country. It's the same kind of key that opens every motor home. So, it's like having Stephen Hawking in a wheelchair spitting out numbers for them. They get the credit card info and run up purchases as fast as they can. Techs say that a skilled DNA lab can take apart the electronic skimmers to look for sweat droppings."

"What good is that?" Flotsam asked. "DNA from some Chinaman in Shanghai? Don't their DNA all look alike?"

"And any DNA that comes from Little Armenia would be all degraded by onions, garlic, and olive oil," Jetsam added.

"I protest and I accuse!" Mel Yarashi said in an outraged voice. "Sarge, I'm reporting these racially offensive surf Nazis to the inspector general's office as soon as I leave this room."

His partner, Always Talking Tony, said, "Me, I'm turning these here Mel Gibson imitators into the EEO Commission. Those government tools and fools always take the side of us brothers against white trash."

"And here we were gonna invite you both to a rager at Malibu two weeks from Saturday," Flotsam said to Mel and A.T.

"Seven surf bunnies promised to be there in butt-floss bikinis," Jetsam added.

"And we're buying all the beer," Flotsam said.

"I withdraw my complaint, Sarge," Mel Yarashi said.

"I'll give them another chance, too, Sarge," Always Talking Tony concurred.

"Okay, if the Comedy Club is finished for the evening, let's go to work," Sergeant Murillo said, "and remember to check the action around Club Samara and report anything unusual or interesting to Detective Villaseñor. He's still interested in locating a big middle-aged Korean, possibly named William Kim, who drives a black, four-door sedan with chrome wheels. And yes, we are aware that there are thousands of Kims in L.A., so no further ethnic commentary from the surfboard chorus is needed on that subject."

D2 Bino Villaseñor was working late, as he usually did these days. His junior partner, D2 Flo Sanders, was a single mom, twenty years younger than Bino, and had three young children to care for. Bino seldom asked her to work overtime unless he was forced to do so.

The DNA lab had actually acceded to his rush request for once, and he'd received a disappointing telephonic report. The fingernail scrapings taken from Daisy—whose name, as far as he knew at this stage of the investigation, was Soo Jeong, and whose previous known address was in Hong Kong—had not yielded enough material to make a positive identification. All that the LAPD crime lab had come up with were some silk fibers that had been gouged into her throat when she was garroted. It was sad to think of shadow people like Daisy, who'd traveled the waters of the world inside awful steel containers on lonely cargo ships, ending up in a trash dumpster, garroted by a band of silk that had possibly also made its journey to America from her part of the world.

All he had now was the inconclusive witness statement of Lita Medina as a way to link the big middle-aged Korean who Markov had referred to as William Kim, talent agent, to the murdered girl. Neither the criminal databases, nor DMV records, nor Immigration and Customs Enforcement files were of any value with such little information to feed into them. A man named William Kim would be harder to find than a William Smith, because the given name had undoubtedly been chosen to replace a Korean passport name, if indeed Kim even *had* a valid passport. But it was all Bino had to work with, so he was determined to keep at it.

NOCTURNE

*   *   *

The south side of the Hollywood Boulevard Walk of Fame was seldom as crowded as the north side, where Captain America was busy posing with tourists. Hector arrived fifteen minutes early and found throngs of tourists and stargazers milling about. But there weren't so many that they were bumping into each other yet, except for the distracted over-gelled teens outfitted by Tommy Hilfiger and J. Crew, with cell phones glued to their ears. These entitled children wouldn't stop texting and talking while driving Daddy's car if the traffic fine turned into a five-year jolt in San Quentin.

Hector had to endure some smack talk from strolling couples who breathed in his cigarette smoke while passing by. He ignored the comments from guys that were way too young for Social Security and thus might kick his ass if he retorted. But when an elderly couple passed and the old man said, "Those things will kill you, young man," Hector pointed to the old woman and said, "Yeah, then I'll be deader than Gramma's clit."

At a few minutes before 6:00 P.M., with the summer sun still blazing down on Hollywood Boulevard, Hector spotted Markov walking east among a group of tourists with cameras, and he was relieved to see that none of the tourists was Asian. Markov would always look like a for-eigner, with his wraparound shades and dyed Elvis do, especially when wearing a tacky aquamarine shirt with eggshell trousers, and reptilian wingtips that looked like snakeskin knockoffs. It was easy to see he wasn't armed, unless he had a weapon in the tan valise he carried under his right arm, with his left hand gripping the handle.

Hector stood directly on Sinatra's star and said, "Thanks for being on time."

Even behind Markov's sunglasses, Hector could see the dark eyes glaring. "We cannot do our business here," Markov said.

"Let's walk," Hector said.

They were silent as Hector led Markov to Highland Avenue and turned south, all the time looking behind him.

271

"I came alone," Markov said.

"So far, so good," Hector said. "I moved all my stuff outta the house. The key's under the flowerpot on the back porch."

"Fuck the key," Markov said, the first time Hector had ever heard him utter an obscenity. "Why are you playing this cloak-and-dagger game?"

"Because I've come to realize that you and Kim are partners in everything. What's yours is his, and vice versa. And I know he ain't gonna be happy about giving up fifty pictures of Grover Cleveland."

"I am not happy either, especially because I do not know if what you have is worth very much."

"It is," Hector said.

By the time they were approaching Hollywood High School, Markov said, "This has gone far enough, has it not?"

"Do you and Kim keep all your money in safety-deposit boxes or what?" Hector asked. "I mean, you do have fifty grand in that little suitcase, right?"

"Let us sit down," Markov said. "I am too old for this."

There wasn't anything going on at this hour of a summer evening at Hollywood High School, so they walked onto the campus and sat on the concrete steps.

Hector held a scrap of notebook paper in front of Markov with Dinko Babich's address printed on it in block letters.

Markov reached for it, but Hector said, "Don't touch. Jist memorize it."

After a few seconds Markov said, "All right, it is memorized."

"A guy my age named Dinko Babich lives there with his mother, Brigita," Hector said.

"Croats," Markov said, and his lip curled slightly.

Hector grinned. "I always figured you for a Serb. I grew up with Croatians."

Markov said, "Who are these Croats? And why is Lita Medina with them?"

"I went all through school with Dinko," Hector said. "He happened to be in the sleazebag saloon in Wilmington the day I went down there to persuade her to come dance at Club Samara. Dinko almost jerked off on the spot when he first laid eyes on that girl. But right then I got a call from Kim telling me he was on his way down to the harbor to talk about the container with the people in it. Somehow he thought me and the Dodge City Crip could jist bust them outta there like Butch Cassidy and the Sundance Kid."

"What did your Croat friend do with the Mexican dancer?" Markov asked.

"Because I had to go meet Kim right away, I paid Dinko to drive her to Club Samara to see if she met with your approval, and then to drive her back to Wilmington to get ready for her permanent move to Hollywood the next day. Now, she's a very tasty, blue-chip chick, and I thought he might buy a blow job off her or something, but I didn't know he'd make some kinda live-in arrangement with her. She's there at his mother's house. Trust me on that."

"Oh, I am trusting you on that," Markov said, his lips drawn tightly over teeth that the setting sunlight exposed as dentures. "Does anyone else live in the house?"

"Negative," Hector said. "Jist his mom."

"Are you sure?"

"Positive," Hector said.

"How can Mr. Kim get to her without the young man or his mother being there?"

"You mean so he can bribe her into leaving?"

"Exactly."

"I don't know. That's not my problem."

"All right," Markov said. "And the dangerous information you have for me?"

"Let's see my Clevelands," Hector said.

"I brought one-hundred-dollar bills," Markov said. "You will have to settle for President Franklin, not Cleveland."

Markov opened the valise for Hector, who had to catch his breath as he caressed the stacks of hundred-dollar bills. He counted three of the stacks at random and said, "Okay, I trust you."

That made Markov emit a bark of a laugh. "Now the information, please."

Markov held the valise pressed to his chest as Hector said, "The first thing is, the day after Daisy disappeared, Kim roughed me up because I couldn't help him get the people outta the container yard."

"Yes, yes, I know about that," Markov said.

"Well, what you *don't* know is, he got very up close and personal with me that day and I saw scratches on the side of his jaw. Fingernail scratches."

Markov didn't respond to that but just stared at Hector for a moment, and Hector said, "I see you watch *CSI,* too."

Markov said, "It does not mean that they will positively find DNA material from Daisy."

"Do you wanna bet your freedom on it?" Hector said.

"Is that your dangerous information?" Markov asked, hanging on to the valise ever tighter.

"Not even close," Hector said. "Remember our fucked-up evening with Basil?"

"Of course."

"Well, the peg-leg guy who called himself Kelly works here in Holly-wood, and I think you're gonna see more of him and the guys he works with. And maybe a lot sooner than you'd like."

For the second time, Hector heard Markov use an obscenity. "Son of a bitch! Can you just say what you are meaning?"

"He's a cop!" Hector said. "And so is the guy that was supposedly being arrested right in front of the house. That's why they caused so goddamn much commotion that everyone ran home, including Kelly."

Markov's eyebrows lifted. "How do you know this?"

Hector said, "I went to Hollywood Station to make a report about the fucking Armos carving 'AP' on the hood of my new ride. And who do I see there but both those guys! In uniform!"

"And they saw you?" Markov leaned forward in alarm.

"They were driving outta the station parking lot, and I'm positive they didn't see me. So I think you have a little time, but not much."

"A little time?" Markov said.

"You're the guy with brains," Hector said. "Kim don't have any. Maybe you can work it out if I help you. The LAPD sends a peg-leg cop to infiltrate your action at Shanghai Massage because they know about Basil and his weird tastes. So that means they're real interested in shutting you down and throwing you in jail for running a high-end whore operation. And while that's going down, one of your Club Samara girls gets snuffed. And her roommates, Lita and Violet, know it has to do with the thirteen dead people in the storage yard because Daisy *told* them that. And Lita sees what? Kim picking up Daisy on that day, that's what! You think all these dots ain't gonna be connected? You think it ain't gonna all come down on Kim? And after they find him, you think it ain't gonna rain shit on you if Kim makes a deal to avoid being strapped down in the little green room up in San Quentin where they shoot you full of good-bye juice?"

The hard set of Markov's jaw crumbled, and he said weakly, "How do I know you are correct about the man with the amputated foot? Maybe you saw a police officer who only *looked* like the amputee that called himself Kelly."

"I either saw Kelly or his stunt double," Hector said.

"How can I be sure?" Markov said, with a tremble in his voice that Hector loved hearing.

"You're the one higher up the food chain," Hector said. "Use some imagination. Get ahold of Gretchen, the dopey hostess with the bad tit job at Shanghai Massage. Send her to Hollywood Station to tell the desk officer that she works for a charity providing services for war amputees. She can say they heard about the brave officer at Hollywood Station with a prosthetic foot. I guarantee you, the dumb cop on the desk will give you Kelly's real name and probably brag about him. And if that ain't enough, then have Ivana stand on the sidewalk by the parking lot at six o'clock like I did, and watch him drive out in his patrol car."

For just an instant, Hector thought that Markov was going to curse again, but the man sagged and said, "Yes, I think that Costa Rica might be a pleasant place to spend a year or two."

"So are you gonna give Kim the Babich address?"

"Of course," Markov said. "I have paid dearly for it."

"But if you're gonna get outta town, why bother with the Mexican dancer? Jist go."

"Such things cannot be done overnight," Markov said. "I must buy time to liquidate my holdings. And during this time Kim must remain free from arrest."

"She *may* already have called the cops about seeing him with Daisy," Hector said, looking at the valise and thinking that Markov might blow-off the whole deal if he knew there were already cops cruising by the Babich house.

"Perhaps she has already contacted the authorities," Markov said. "But even so, if the Mexican girl is never seen again, it will be much more difficult to build a case against Mr. Kim, and frankly, I doubt if they can do it without her."

"But what if they *do* have his DNA under Daisy's fingernails?" Hector said.

"DNA evidence is often not recoverable," Markov said. "With any luck, Mr. Kim may escape unscathed this time. But it is truly troubling that the local police know enough about our business that they were trying to use Basil to gain intelligence and arrest all of us. I cannot imagine how they learned about Basil and his unfortunate proclivities."

"Then you don't know the bitches that work for you," Hector said. "There ain't one of them that can stop jabbering even with a cock in her mouth."

"I presume you know that I will no longer need your services," Markov said.

"Yeah, and I ain't giving you two weeks' notice neither," Hector said. "I'm leaving Hollywood tonight, and I won't be back."

"If anything you have told me today is a lie, you will be dead very soon," Markov said.

"Don't you think I know that?" Hector said. "It wouldn't be hard for Kim or anybody else to find me. In fact, the Cozzos are in the Pedro phone book."

"Farewell then, Hector," Markov said. "You have done me a good turn today despite the outrageous price I had to pay you."

He handed over the valise, and Hector grabbed it.

"Kim will jist bribe Lita to leave town, right?" Hector said, feeling a sudden shiver in his gut and a need for reassurance. "He'd be afraid to have another dead body connected to him, wouldn't he?"

"Of course," Markov said. "Good-bye."

He stood up painfully, showing his age, and began walking slowly north, toward Hollywood Boulevard. Hector watched him, waiting a moment before heading south to his parked Mercedes, believing that Markov would phone the Babich address to Kim even as he walked to his car. And Hector Cozzo knew in his heart that Kim would try to kill the girl as soon as he could manage it.

The Watch 5 cars that worked near east Hollywood spent some time that evening driving past Club Samara, looking for a late-model black sedan with chrome wheels, but none was spotted.

Mel Yarashi and Always Talking Tony went code 6 at that location and even entered the club, standing near the doorway and making the Russian bouncer uncomfortable while they scanned the crowd. There was no big middle-aged Asian in the nightclub, and it was an uneventful night in Hollywood, California, for the coppers of Watch 5, which was just as well. They needed to store up some energy. Tomorrow was the night of a Hollywood moon, and that meant *anything* could happen.

TWENTY-ONE

THE VISIT WITH the priest to begin plans for the marriage of Dinko Abel Babich and Lita Medina Flores was scheduled for 3:00 P.M. Because this first step toward a new life was such a momentous occasion, they awakened as dawn was beginning to blaze over the harbor of Los Angeles. Brigita Babich was already in the kitchen making coffee by the time they entered and sat at the table.

She smiled at the two of them and said, "I couldn't stay in bed, either."

Lita's luxuriant hair was tied back in a ponytail, and she was wearing a T-shirt, jeans, and tennis shoes. She beamed when she blurted, "I have so much excitement!"

"You *are* excited," Dinko said.

"I *am* excited," Lita said.

"You are loved," Dinko said.

Before Lita could echo their refrain, Brigita said, "Stop it, you two, or I'm gonna start bawling."

"Bawling?" Lita said, turning to Dinko.

"It means crying," he said. "But it's happy crying."

"Is okay then," Lita said. "I must do bawling also."

Brigita put cups of coffee in front of them and told Lita, "You look so young with your hair like that."

"I have nineteen years and four months," she said. Then she added, "Almost five months."

Dinko said, "No, you *are* nineteen years and four months old."

"It is seeming strange, but okay," Lita said. "I am nineteen years and four months old." Then she asked, "Is okay to say I am *age* nineteen years and four months? Is not so strange that way, yes?"

Dinko and Brigita both smiled, and Dinko said, "Yes, that's perfectly okay."

"Even you look younger today," Brigita told Dinko. "Like a boy. My baby boy."

"Better start breakfast, Mom," he said. "Before you start bawling."

That made everyone laugh. It was that kind of day, full of joy and excitement for the members of the Babich family of San Pedro.

"I'm going to Dispatch Hall today to see the hall man," Dinko said. "Gotta get ready for my first day back on the docks. I'm gonna take jobs six days a week and work my way up to crane operator ASAP, just like Dad. This soon-to-be-married San Pedronian has something to prove and something to work for."

"Not *too* soon to be married," Brigita said. "The process takes weeks. This is just the start, where we gotta fill out the Church's prenuptial inquiry forms. I'll have to dig up your baptismal record and your First Communion certificate. And, of course, we'll have to see if Lita's mom has church documents that she can send to us."

Lita said with concern, "Documents?"

"Nothing to worry about," Dinko said. "You were baptized, weren't you?"

"Yes, of course," Lita said.

"And you made your First Communion, didn't you?"

"Yes, but my family in Guanajuato . . . I do not know if they still have the . . . documents."

"Nothing to worry about," Dinko repeated. "The Catholic Church is nothing if not flexible these days. They'll give you dispensation if the paperwork is lost."

"Don't get so caught up in hall business that you're late for the meeting at the rectory," Brigita said.

"Nothing could make me be late for that," Dinko said.

"And how will you pass the time today, Lita," Brigita asked, "until we go see the pastor?"

"I am thinking of doing a bike ride," Lita said. "If Dinko permits me to ride his bike."

"Sure, I'll pump up the tires before I go," Dinko said. "But where will you ride?"

"Not far," she said. "Maybe by the harbor. Maybe to the park."

"You'll be very careful, won't you?" Dinko said. "It can be dangerous riding in traffic."

"You remember our bike ride on Catalina Island?" she asked.

"I'll never forget it," Dinko said with a wistful eye.

"I am a very careful bike rider, no?"

"Yes, you are," he said.

"So do not be worrisome, okay?"

"Worrying," he said.

"Okay, lovebirds," Brigita said, "who wants scrambled and who wants easy over?"

It was late morning by the time Dinko was ready to drive to the Dispatch Hall. Lita waited for him, sitting astride his bike in the driveway, next to the Jeep.

Dinko yelled good-bye to his mother, looked at his watch, and walked to his car, telling Lita, "You should have a bottle of water with you. It's gonna be very hot in the next hour or so."

"Do not be worrisome, Dinko," Lita said.

He looked at her, and she laughed and said, "I know. 'Worrying' is the correct word. I am just joking on you."

Dinko surprised them both by sweeping her into his arms and kissing her with both tenderness and passion. "You are loved," he said, before he jumped into the Jeep and drove away.

Brigita came out to the front porch and waved to Lita as she rode the bike into the street, calling after her, "Don't tire yourself out. And be careful of the cars!"

Lita Medina waved to Brigita Babich and headed down toward Gaffey Street, never seeing the black Mercedes with chrome wheels a block behind her.

Lita pedaled east, to the harbor, and rode along the dock looking at small fishing boats, all that was left of what had once been a formidable fleet. The big commercial boats, docked in Mexico without the expense of crew insurance and workmen's compensation, had ended their good life, but at least there was squid in local waters, and bonita for the cat food cannery, so a few of them still prevailed. Lita saw huge heaps of nets stored on the docks with yellow floats attached, right beside the dinghies that hauled those nets out into the water to surround the fish just before the catch was winched up and put down in the hold, eventually to be fed to household pets.

Two perspiring Latinos were working on the nets when they noticed Lita watching them. She spoke to them in Spanish, commenting on what a fine day it was. They concurred and smiled at each other, delighted to have exchanged pleasantries with such a beautiful Mexican girl. They waved when Lita rode off in the direction of Point Fermin Park, that peaceful place so special to her and Dinko.

There were hundreds of tourists already at the park on this clear summer day when Santa Catalina Island appeared so close. Lita dismounted near the slope leading up to Angels Gate Park and the Korean Bell of Friendship. A dozen children of grammar school age were frolicking around the bell, and she walked her bike up the knoll to the bell pavilion to listen to a docent lecturing the children.

The docent informed her young audience that the seventeen-ton bell, a gift from South Korea to celebrate America's bicentennial, had been cast from several metals for good tone quality. Figures of the Goddess of Liberty were engraved in relief on the bell, along with a dove of peace.

The bell was without a clapper and was struck four times a year from the outside with a wooden log. It rested inside a stone pagoda supported by twelve columns, each representing one of the twelve designs of the Oriental zodiac, and with a carved animal guarding each column's base. The children were told that the pagoda's remarkable roof of blue tiles and the sweeping curves at the four corners had been designed in a style that has been extant for more than four thousand years.

After the children had moved on, several Asian tourists, both men and women, walked to the pavilion and began chattering in their various languages and dialects. One of them was a big middle-aged man wearing a dress shirt and necktie who had his back to Lita. When she saw him, her heart pounded and she felt like running or screaming or both, until he spun around and looked past her. He wore glasses and had a round, cherubic face, which took on a worried expression when he called to a little girl who had disappeared behind the gathering crowd. When the little girl heard him calling, she ran to him and grabbed his hand. It was the first time in several days that Lita had had a fearful thought of Mr. Kim.

Lita walked her bike down to the street and began pedaling for home, feeling a strong urge to thank God for guiding her here to Dinko Babich and the wonderful new world surrounding her. When she got to Eighth Street she rode west, to the church, and looked up at the bell tower, with its ten-foot bronze of the Blessed Virgin standing on top, her arms outstretched to the sea. Lita gazed at the mosaic over the front doors, which also pictured Mary, this time standing on ocean waves. And Lita Medina entered the church hesitantly.

The interior of the church was elaborate and baroque, reflecting the tastes of the Italian, Croatian, and Portuguese working families who had founded and financed it, as well as of the growing number of parishioners from Mexico and Central America. The altar sat upon a level four steps high, and in this place, Christ had to give way to his mother. It was Mary, Star of the Sea, who stood tall, directly over the altar, holding a tuna clipper in one arm, as a mother would hold a baby. Christ crucified was relegated to a smaller and lower position to the right of the altar.

There were only two elderly women in the church, praying in one of the pews near the front, and after a moment they got up and walked down the aisle and left. Lita dipped her fingers in the font of holy water and crossed herself, ending by kissing her thumbnail as a way of symbolically kissing the cross, in the custom of her homeland. She chose a pew near the rear of the church, genuflected, then knelt, crossing herself again and thanking God for never giving up on her, and for providing her with this chance of redemption and love. She thanked the Holy Virgin for guiding her during her long journey, and for bringing her here, to a home at last.

Lita Medina never saw or heard the big Korean who entered the church silently. He removed his silk necktie when he saw her kneeling alone at prayer.

Returning home from the Dispatch Hall, Dinko chose to drive up Eighth Street from Gaffey for no other reason than that he would soon be driving back the same way to go to the rectory for the wedding preliminaries. He was shocked to see several black-and-white police cars, several other official-looking vehicles, and two ominous-looking vans parked in front of the church, where there was yellow tape strung across the entrance.

A uniformed police officer was directing traffic, waving all the curious motorists past. Dinko lowered his window and said, "What happened, Officer?"

The cop didn't answer, only gestured with more urgency, so Dinko continued driving west, but when he looked back at the church's entry, he saw a familiar bicycle lying on its side. He slammed on his brakes in the middle of the street, leaped from the Jeep, and ran panic-stricken to the church doors, where he was physically intercepted and restrained by two detectives and a uniformed officer. Another uniformed officer ran from the black-and-white parked directly in front of the church to assist, and soon all four cops were yelling commands at him.

But Dinko Babich didn't understand a word they were saying. The tears were running into his mouth, and he couldn't do anything but scream, "LITA!"

TWENTY-TWO

Hᴇᴄᴛᴏʀ Cᴏᴢᴢᴏ ʜᴀᴅ not gone to his parents' home the prior night, after he'd left Markov on the streets of Hollywood. Instead of going home, he'd decided he needed solitude, and he'd checked into the DoubleTree Hotel in San Pedro, where he'd swallowed the last of the zannies, washing them down with several ounces of Scotch from a bottle in one of his suitcases. He'd decided that he was going off the vodka now that he'd left behind the Russians of Hollywood and the Serbian Markov.

Hector had spread the packets of money on the bed and opened each stack and counted every hundred-dollar bill. He'd held many of them up to the light and then recounted. Everything checked out correctly, but the exercise had given him no satisfaction. He'd picked up his new go-phone several times to call Dinko Babich and warn him that Kim would be coming to kill Lita Medina. The last time he'd held the phone in his hand, he'd been certain he would do it. He'd dialed the first four digits of Dinko's number before tossing the phone onto the bed.

Hector had finally convinced himself that Kim, brutal and stupid thug though he was, would not try a home invasion to wipe out Dinko and his mother, along with Lita Medina. He wasn't crazy enough for that. He'd find a way to get her alone; Hector was sure of it. The thought of it had sent splinters of fear up his spine, and at one point he'd actually gotten tears in his eyes. Then he'd sniffled and taken another gulp of Scotch, and told himself, She's just a Mexican whore.

He made arrangements for a late checkout, and it was nearly 2:00 P.M. when he went to the front desk. After he left the hotel he drove to his parents' house, and even though neither parent had seen him since his last visit, three months earlier, their greeting was less than lukewarm.

His father said, "How long will you be staying?"

His mother said, "Have you been arrested again?"

Hector was making the third trip from his car with his clothes when his father asked, "Where'd you get the fancy car? I hope it belongs to you."

"I leased it," Hector told him with a sigh. "I'm gonna turn it in tomorrow. I was hoping I could use your car till I can buy a decent used one."

"So does this mean you didn't conquer Hollywood?" his father said.

"Yeah, and it means I'm still jist the same crappy son I always was," Hector said, "but I'll be paying you six hundred a month to put up with me."

Neither parent had a comment about that, and then his mother said, "I guess you heard the terrible news about the murder in the church today?"

Hector's heart fluttered. "What murder?"

"A young woman was strangled right in the pew at Mary Star of the Sea," she said. "Our own church. Can you imagine such a thing?"

"No, I can't," Hector said.

"It's the bad element that's taking over Pedro," his father said. "I'll bet some Mexican did it. Nobody's safe these days."

That was the busiest day in months, at both Harbor Station and Hollywood Station. Bino Villaseñor and his partner, D2 Flo Sanders, headed for San Pedro the moment the call came in from Harbor homicide that the young woman in the house for which Bino Villaseñor had requested extra patrol had been murdered in a Catholic church. By midafternoon, the nature of the crime and its location had brought TV crews and print journalists from all over Los Angeles. There were so many people with cameras and notebooks in their hands, swarming the streets and mingling with the crowd gathering around the church, that the uniformed lieutenant directing the attempts at crowd control was red-faced and sweating, barking orders that the news gatherers mostly ignored.

The Hollywood homicide detectives took a look at the chaos around the church and Bino said, "What say we drive straight to Harbor Station?"

The new station on John S. Gibson Boulevard had everything a modern police facility could wish for. It was huge and well designed, with a heliport and a parking lot adjacent to the building and accessible by a footbridge. There were flat-screen televisions all over the station, and each room was more impressive than the last. The roll call room had seven rows of tables, with eight fixed chairs at each table, and a grease wall, supplied with pencils, was mounted behind the elevated table in front—a vast improvement over the old chalkboards. There was a break room with six indoor tables and two more tables outside, on a terrace. The weight room would be envied by any commercial fitness club.

But the jail was a marvel. There were metal benches outside the holding tanks with handcuffs attached to a steel bar for temporary restraint, and anyone in the tanks could be observed through the shatterproof glass. There were even special holding tanks for juveniles, and the jail design divided the space into a women's side and a men's side. This divisional jail was so large that it could accommodate sixty-eight prisoners, but there were *none* to accommodate. The LAPD—like the city of Los Angeles and the state of California—was nearly bankrupt, and this cavernous jail, recently finished to perfection, went empty and unused.

Bino and Flo Sanders, coming as they did from Hollywood Station, which was so outdated and overcrowded that they had to use interview rooms as storage closets for records and squeeze themselves into tiny cubicles the size of parrot cages, could only gawk at what they saw in the state-of-the-art detective squad room. Flo Sanders nudged Bino with an elbow when they saw the "kiddie room," full of toys, along with another flat-screen TV, for victims of child abuse or neglect.

Bino nodded to Flo and said, "I'm so tired I wish I could go in that kiddie room and watch cartoons with some milk and cookies, before a nice long nap."

The Hollywood detectives met their Harbor Division counterparts, and after the visitors were given cold sodas, all pertinent information on each homicide was shared. That done, Bino was directed to one interview room, where Dinko Babich awaited him, and Flo Sanders went to another interview room, where Brigita Babich had been weeping, sometimes uncontrollably, during a one-hour interview, prior to the arrival of the Hollywood detectives.

Dinko sat in a chair next to a small table. He didn't even look up when Bino sat down and said, "Mr. Babich . . . Dinko . . . I'm so sorry."

Dinko's eyes were raw and swollen, and the young man looked at the detective with a blank stare. Bino said, "I know you've been interviewed already, and I know you're exhausted and would like to go home, but I just have a few questions that I need to ask so we can find the bastard that did this awful thing."

Dinko blinked a few times but did not respond. Bino said, "I have to try to find out how the killer knew where to find Lita. I know you've already been asked that, but the answer you've given was that you don't know. But was there *anything* that Lita ever said to you that might provide a clue for us? Did she ever mention phoning one of the other dancers or any club employee after she was living at your house? For any reason whatsoever?"

Dinko shook his head but did not speak.

"How about the former roommates she had when she worked for the club in Wilmington? Is it possible she could've phoned one of them and told them she was back at the harbor and living at your address in San Pedro?"

Dino shook his head more forcefully, as though that was impossible.

"Okay," Bino said, "then how about Hector Cozzo? Have you seen him anywhere around San Pedro since the day you met Lita and drove her to and from Hollywood?"

This time Dinko said, "No."

"Then did you phone him, or did he phone you at any time after that day?"

Dinko shook his head once more.

The detective said, "Can you think of anyone at all who could connect you in some way with Lita Medina? Anyone who might've given the information to someone in Hollywood, like the Korean?"

"Nobody," he said.

"I'm very sorry to be badgering you like this," Bino said. "I'm determined to talk to Hector Cozzo before I go home tonight, and I was hoping there was some link to William Kim that I could make before I talk to Cozzo. We learned a few hours ago that he's vacated his rented house in Encino, and I'm betting I might find him here in San Pedro, at his family home. I just thought there was a moment in the last few days when he could've spotted Lita with you, maybe in a San Pedro restaurant or something?"

At last Dinko said something significant to the detective: "That first night when I drove Lita to Hollywood, I saw a car exactly like his, parked just off Pacific Highway. There was a big guy in a suit and tie who looked Asian talking to the driver. I couldn't see if it was Hector behind the wheel, but the driver was smoking a cigarette, and I thought at the time it mighta been him."

"Thank you, Dinko. Thank you for remembering that," Bino said.

"But I've known Hector Cozzo all my life," Dinko said, "and I can tell you he's not the type to be involved in murder."

"I'll let you go home now," Bino Villaseñor said. "There's nothing I can say to you and your mom except that we're going to get the guy that did this. Lita was a very special girl."

After Brigita and Dinko Babich left the station to be driven home by Harbor detectives, Bino said to his partner, "Flo, would you ask the patrol watch commander to send a radio car to the Cozzo house to bring Hector Cozzo here?"

"You're *that* sure he's moved back home to Mommy, are you?" she said.

"I'll bet you a taco and raise you an enchilada that he's there," Bino said. Then he addressed a Harbor Division detective: "In case I win this bet, do you have any good Mexican takeout in San Pedro?"

"You gotta be kidding," the detective said, echoing an oft-heard complaint. "Pedro's becoming Tijuana by the sea."

Thirty minutes later, Flo found Bino sitting alone in the kiddie room watching cable news. She told him, "You won the bet."

Hector Cozzo didn't like the look Bino Villaseñor was giving him. In fact, he didn't like anything about the old Mexican cop. And he didn't think the younger lesbo partner was much of an improvement. Hector had never liked big, athletic-looking women in Hillary Clinton pant-suits, and figured most of them for box bumpers. Her pale blue eyes were even colder than the Mexican's nearly black ones, where Hector couldn't tell the pupils from the irises.

After Hector was advised of his Miranda rights, Bino said, "Did you get my card asking you to call me ASAP?"

"No, sir," Hector said. "I was real busy moving outta the house in Encino, and maybe I missed it. Where did you leave it?"

Bino said, "Why did you move back home to San Pedro?"

"Well, sir," Hector said, "I wasn't making a living up there in the city, and I thought I should move back home and rethink my options."

Flo Sanders said, "How did you make your living up there?"

Hector looked at her with a skewed smile. "I sorta hate to admit it in front of a lady, but I kinda did odd jobs around a strip joint."

Neither detective returned his smile, and Flo said, "Describe your job for us."

"At Club Samara?" Hector said. "Well, I sometimes drove to different clubs to look for talent, and then I'd report back to Leonid, the manager. If he gave me the okay, I'd go and meet the dancer and try to sell her on the Club Samara operation. And if any of the girls from the club needed costumes, I'd drive them all over the fucking—pardon my French—I'd drive them all around. And sometimes I'd even have to shop for groceries, because they liked to live in bunches in east Hollywood apartments. And like that."

"So you were an errand boy," Bino said.

"Well, I wouldn't say that," Hector said.

"Were you on salary?" Flo asked.

"No, I'd jist get a little green once in a while. I mostly hung around the club hoping to meet people that might offer me a better job."

"Doing what?" Flo asked.

"This and that," Hector said. "I'm a good salesman. Maybe a sales job."

"How could you afford your car?" Bino asked.

"I don't own it. I lease it. In fact, now that I'm back home, I'm gonna return it to the dealer."

"How were you able to even lease it with a job that paid no salary?" Bino asked.

"There's a new-car manager at this one Mercedes dealer," Hector said. "He hangs around the nightclub, and he kinda excused the normal lease requirements for me."

"What did you do for him?" Flo asked.

"Bought him a drink once in a while." Hector shrugged.

"And provided him with a girl at a discounted price once in a while?" Bino said.

"Wait a minute, Detective!" Hector said. "If those bitches sold their asses to customers, I didn't profit from it. I ain't no pimp."

"Where is Kim?" Bino said.

"Who?"

"William Kim, the Korean talent agent," Flo Sanders said.

"Oh, him," Hector said. "I don't really deal with him real often. Maybe I picked up one of his clients a few times, is about all."

Bino said, "The night that Dinko Babich drove Lita Medina to and from Hollywood for you, he saw you with Kim."

"He said that?" Hector said. "Where did he see me?"

"Parked off the boulevard as he was heading for the Harbor Freeway," Bino said. "Kim was standing by your red Mercedes SL, talking to you."

Hector said, "If Dinko told you that, he's mistaken. I hardly know Kim."

Both detectives heard the faint tremble in Hector's voice and the clicking of his teeth after he said that. Bino continued: "What if we can prove that you tipped off Kim or Markov about Lita Medina living with Dinko and Brigita Babich? That would make you a principal in the commission of a murder, wouldn't it?"

"Wait a minute!" Hector objected, his face hot with fear. "Wait a fucking minute here!"

"Maybe if you'd tell us how to find that Korean who calls himself William Kim, we'd feel that you want to see a killer brought to justice," Bino said.

"So you think he did it, huh?" Hector said, his mouth so dry that his tongue was sticking to the roof of his mouth. "Why would he do such a thing?"

"Where is he, Hector?" Bino said, moving his face a few inches forward.

And that was when Hector's resolve collapsed. He said, "I swear I don't know for sure, but one time a girl from the massage parlor did some kind of party in Koreatown. She said there's a condo above some restaurant called Kimchi Heaven. An old buckethead babe lives there who knew Kim from back in whatever fucking country he lived in before coming here. Her name is Tang. And that's all I know, so help me! I wouldn't tell you this if I was somehow involved with the guy, would I?"

Flo Sanders left the interview room without a word, to make a call that would send arrest teams heading for Koreatown.

Hector said, "Can I go home now, sir? I told you all I know."

"You'll keep yourself available for me, won't you, Hector?" Bino Villaseñor said.

"Absolutely, sir," Hector promised. Then he added, "I hope you catch Kim, if he's the one that did the crime, but I'd like to offer a piece of advice, if you wanna hear it."

"By all means."

Hector said, "Anyone who'd kill a girl in the house of the Lord is beyond dangerous and beyond reasoning with. That kinda guy will no doubt be armed, and I think you should tell your officers to shoot him down on sight, like a mad dog."

"Thank you for that advice, Hector," Bino Villaseñor said, for the first time showing a hint of a smile under the bushy white mustache. "Dead men tell no tales, do they?"

That afternoon, there was something taking place on Eighth Street in San Pedro, across the street from Mary Star of the Sea Catholic Church, that would bring about the conclusion of their investigation more directly than anything the detectives themselves had done. And a resident of Harbor View House was the one who made it happen.

Franklin Abernathy was a senior-citizen resident of the intermediate-care facility, with which none of the Los Angeles news gatherers was familiar. He was always well groomed and well dressed, and nobody noticed the room key Franklin Abernathy wore around his neck on a shoelace. Nor did they know that he often roamed the streets close to the facility with General Douglas MacArthur, and they certainly had no reason to doubt his claim of being a professor emeritus at the University of Southern California. It did not take more than twenty minutes for the word to spread that there was an eyewitness who could identify the killer, after Franklin Abernathy approached the first television news crew with the exciting news that he'd seen a man run from the church at the time of the murder and speed away in a car.

When asked to describe the car the killer drove, the eyewitness simply said that he'd been concentrating so hard on the license number, upon realizing that something was amiss, he'd failed to be aware of the make or model. He said that the sun had been in his eyes, but he thought the car was dark in color. When asked to give the license number during an on-camera interview, he said that he'd written it down, but he wished to have it cleared with the police before the number was given out to the public.

That interview with the seventy-six-year-old resident of Harbor View House would be broadcast on the 5:00 television news before a print journalist and a detective from Harbor Station had the opportunity to interview the "eyewitness." Franklin Abernathy told the print journalist and the detective that the number he'd written on a Taco Bell napkin was the license number of the killer, and he gave the napkin to the cop. The license number he'd written down was "666 Antichrist."

Unlike the reporter, the detective noticed Abernathy's shining eye, and he asked the witness what he'd taught as a professor at USC.

Franklin Abernathy answered, "Microbiology. And I think I've recently discovered a DNA sequence that can be altered to turn bulldogs into mice."

The detective congratulated Franklin Abernathy on his discovery and verified his in-patient residential address. But before anyone bothered to alert the local television channel about its eyewitness, the on-camera interview went on the air. The broadcast news program later apologized for airing the interview, and had to endure much derision and horse laughs from the cable-channel newsies, but the damage had already been done.

One of the residents of Koreatown, whose name and address were on the registration of the black Mercedes with chrome wheels, received an unexpected phone call that afternoon as a result of the information given to Bino Villaseñor by Hector Cozzo. The woman who called herself Madame Jin-Sook Tang was alerted by employees of the downstairs restaurant she owned that half a dozen cars containing police officers were converging on the building. Madame Tang immediately called the cell number of her lover, telling him not to return to her condominium under any circumstances, and suggested that he might be wise to leave Los Angeles as soon as possible, after he dropped her car at the Hollywood Roosevelt Hotel.

When LAPD cops with shotguns arrived in force at the condo of Madame Tang and demanded admittance, she opened the door with the same serenity she showed when she acted as hostess at Kimchi Heaven on weekend nights. She stood back and watched big-footed cops swarming through her immaculately tidy condominium, and expressed what she thought was appropriate shock in hearing that her longtime companion, Joo-Chan Lee, aka William Kim, was a wanted man. She said she was horrified by the news and wished to be fully cooperative and to tell all that she knew of Joo-Chan Lee and his possible whereabouts, and she said she was concerned for her car, which he had borrowed. Madame Tang told the police a great deal that afternoon, almost none of it true.

After receiving that phone call from Madame Tang, Kim had to breathe deeply and exercise great discipline in order to observe the speed limit while driving to the Hollywood Roosevelt Hotel. He parked in front, leaving the car with the valet, and checked in for one night, intending to lie low until he could find out what was happening and how the police could have discovered where he lived.

Kim sat at the bar of the Hollywood Roosevelt Hotel drinking brandy for almost two hours. He was trying to decide if he should risk calling Madame Tang even from a public telephone, but he decided against it. Soon he felt himself getting a bit drunk and thought he should go to his room and lie down, but when he reached for his wallet, which he normally kept in the inside pocket of his suit coat, he realized that the wallet was in the pocket of his trousers. He had forgotten that the inside coat pocket contained the crumpled silk necktie that he'd used to garrote the Mexican dancer. Before going to his room he went to the men's restroom and buried the necktie under paper towels in the trash receptacle, and readjusted the holster of the 9-millimeter pistol attached to his belt in the small of his back.

At 5:00 P.M. he turned on the TV in his room and channel-surfed for the local news to see if the murder in San Pedro would be covered. It was, and, in fact, it was the lead story. Kim heard words like "horror" and "outrage" and "sacrilege" from the lips of the news anchor, and then he watched interviews with San Pedro locals, including "Professor" Franklin Abernathy, who was questioned by a breathless blond reporter with expressive television eyebrows. Kim learned that a license number had been written down by this strange little man, whom Kim had not noticed when he'd fled from the church.

After watching the news coverage, Kim paced the room and pondered. He thought he should wait until dark before he dared drive from the hotel in a car whose license number must be known by now to every cop in Los Angeles. His hands would not stop sweating, and he decided he needed another drink. He had a sudden and irrational urge to buy a new necktie, as though appearing in the hotel bar in a tailored suit and dress shirt but without a necktie would mark him as the church killer. But he did go to the bar, and he did have another brandy, several of them.

The midwatch roll call at 5:00 P.M. was not the jolly morale lifter that Sergeant Murillo always preferred for his personnel before he sent them to the streets. The reason for this became apparent when Detective Bino Villaseñor entered the roll call room for a prearranged visit right after Sergeant Murillo had assigned the cars.

"Detective Villaseñor has some important information for you," Sergeant Murillo said, and Bino stepped up and stood next to the table where the sergeant sat facing the troops.

Bino said, "You all know about the strangled dancer from Club Samara who was recently found in a dumpster, but you may not have heard about a similar murder of another former dancer from the same club that happened in San Pedro this afternoon. We believe both murders were committed by a Korean national who calls himself William Kim or Joo-Chan Lee. He's the guy who drives the black car with chrome wheels that I told you about the other day. Well, now we've received the license number of that black Mercedes from the registered owner, and we think he could be hiding out either in Koreatown or here in Hollywood, the two places where he's lived and worked. The principal owner of Club Samara lives up on Mount Olympus, and I'll give you his name and address just in case you spot the Mercedes anywhere near there."

Everyone in the room listened attentively and jotted down notes as the detective gave them a rundown on the afternoon murder in the Catholic church and a description of the suspect, who had no criminal record under either name. Bino was unusually intense during the briefing, and it was apparent that the murder of the Mexican dancer, as well as where and how she had been killed, had disturbed the usually placid veteran.

Bino concluded by saying, "Watch for the black Mercedes, and please stay on the air as much as possible. At this moment, Kim's longtime squeeze is being interrogated, but she's a real dragon lady and I don't expect we'll get much out of her. If I receive any further information that'll help you locate this guy, I'll get it out to you right away. It goes without saying that a guy like Kim will be armed."

Sergeant Murillo said to his people, "There's a Hollywood moon tonight, so be extra alert. All the crazies will be out there howling and prowling."

A Hollywood moon always made each cop more careful to touch the picture of the Oracle before heading for the streets.

TWENTY-THREE

It was Kim's longest day. He sat in the bar of the Hollywood Roosevelt, not wanting to be alone in his hotel room, and he continued ordering brandies. He couldn't risk driving the Mercedes until after dark, now that the police had the license number. He wondered if they had discovered his criminal record yet. He'd been arrested twice in San Francisco fifteen years earlier, for pimping and pandering under the name Chung-Hee Park. He'd paid a Chinese lawyer plenty, and had gotten only probation both times. But then he thought, What difference does it make if they had verified his criminal record? Regardless of which name he used, he was a wanted man. No matter how he tried to rationalize his choice of action, and no matter how many brandies he drank, he had to run.

Kim had learned as a young man, living in both Macao and Hong Kong, that a wise man always carried a passport with him, and he had his under the name Joo-Chan Lee. But he was concerned that the police might have alerted airline ticket counters and customs agents at LAX, so he decided it would be safest to drive to San Francisco International Airport. He could fly out of the country from there, less noticeable among thousands of other Asians coming and going.

But first he needed more money and a different car, and there was only one place he could think of to get them now. That was from the man who had been his financial partner in everything, from the massage parlor and the nightclub to the ill-fated human trafficking. He could only turn to the man who had provided the information that had led him to the Mexican dancer and to his being a wanted fugitive. They were in everything together, and his partner owed him.

As soon as he figured it was dark enough in the skies over Hollywood, he left the bar and walked unsteadily to the entry doors and outside. There were three taxis waiting for hotel guests to emerge for the evening, and he signaled to the first in line. He looked up and was sorry to see the white glow of a full moon. He felt as though he were standing in a spotlight, like all of those whose names were displayed in brass and marble on the sidewalks around him, many of them already faded, irrelevant, and forgotten.

William Kim was not the only participant in the recent deadly event near the harbor of Los Angeles to have seen the 5:00 news. As soon as the news hour ended, Pedrag Marcovic, aka Pavel Markov, locked all the doors in his house, struggling against a surging panic attack.

He made a phone call to Bakhva Ramishvili, the Georgian whose name was on the liquor license at Club Samara. He asked the retired pawnbroker if he would like to buy the business for half of what it was worth. Before the conversation ended, Markov said he was willing to let the business go for 30 percent of what it was worth, and that he'd throw in Shanghai Massage for an additional fifty thousand dollars, adding that it had been a good little cash cow for the past two years. Markov settled for 20 percent of what he thought the business should fetch, and said that the sale and leasing documents would be handled by his lawyer in the coming week. Markov asked that the Georgian cooperate with the lawyer to forward the money via wire transfer as soon as the documents were signed and he got settled at a new address, which likely would be outside the United States.

After all the terms were agreed upon, Markov had to begin the wrenching job of deciding which items in his extensive wardrobe would have to be left behind, and he wondered if there might be time to set aside some minor objets d'art to be shipped at a later time. He wondered how long William Kim could possibly remain free, and he cursed the fool for the deplorable way in which he had disposed of the Mexican dancer. Kim had promised him that he would be patient and make her death appear to be a result of random violence, even if her Croat boyfriend had to be terminated along with her to make it believable. But to strangle her the same as Daisy! And in a church, of all places! If only the brainless Korean could get himself killed by the police. Then Markov realized that he did not dare do the packing until daybreak. Kim might actually drive here this very night in desperation. He turned out all the lights in the house and sat in the back bedroom, hoping in vain that the darkness might make him sleepy.

Kim asked that the taxi drop him half a block away from Markov's leased home on Mount Olympus. He paid the driver and walked to the house, cursing when he saw that all the lights were out. But when he was standing in front he saw a glimmer flash in the kitchen, where he and Markov had often sat discussing business. It was light from the opened refrigerator door! Markov was home with all the lights out, even though he was a man who stayed up until well after midnight, reading or watching television. This could only mean that he didn't want visitors, especially one as desperate as his partner was this night. Kim reached under his suit coat and touched the pistol for comfort.

The Korean was feeling the full effect of the brandies then, and he knew it. Whatever he was going to do, he'd have to do it quickly. He walked up the driveway to the portico and rang the bell. Then he moved as fast as he dared, in his unsteady condition, around to the back of the house, almost tripping over a wheelbarrow the gardener had left out. He stood by the rear door, which opened onto a well-kept garden, the charmless home's best attribute.

As he'd expected, there was no movement in the house. Markov did not go to the door, wherever he was hiding. Kim could see well by the light of the full moon and used his elbow to break the pane of glass beside the dead-bolt lock. Then he drew his pistol from its holster and reached a meaty hand inside, turning the bolt. He opened the door and entered without stealth, knowing that Markov had probably heard the glass shatter.

The tension was broken and he uttered a braying laugh when Markov called out tremulously, "William, is that you?"

"Is me, my friend!" Kim called back. "Where are you at? Your friend William must have a drink."

"You better get out, William!" Markov said. "The police are looking for you!"

"Yes," Kim said, lurching toward the hallway leading to the sound of Markov's voice. "I must go away from here. You got to help me."

"I cannot help you!" Markov said. "Get out while you can, William!"

When he got to the back bedroom, he turned the knob quietly, but the door was locked, and he heard Markov let out a sound like the muffled wail of a baby.

"Do not make me call the police!" Markov shouted.

That made Kim laugh drunkenly, until he began to cough. When he stopped, he said, "Yes, call police. I talk to them, too. We go to prison and live in same cell. I sleep on bottom bed, okay?"

Then Kim let out a maniacal cackle that made Markov expel a dozen milliliters of urine. The Serb felt it running down the leg of his satin pajamas, and he began to whimper.

He finally said, "What do you want, William?"

Kim said, "Money and your car."

Markov said, "The money you have coming is in the account that one of us cannot deplete without the approval of the other. You know that!"

"You get my money tomorrow. I am sleeping here tonight."

"No!" Markov said. "What if the police come here looking for you? William, the murder of the Mexican dancer was all over the news!"

"Yes," Kim said sleepily.

"Why did you walk into a church in broad daylight where you could be so easily seen? That was not smart!"

"I . . . want . . . money . . . tomorrow," Kim said. "But I got to sleep now."

The Korean's speech was slurred and halting, and Markov began thinking furiously about the handgun in the closet of the master bedroom, and of what he might do with it. Finally, he said, "Go into the living room and sleep on the sofa, William. I will go to the bank tomorrow with a letter from you and withdraw all that we have."

"And a car," Kim said.

"Yes, yes," Markov said. "I will get you a car tomorrow. Now go to sleep."

Markov stayed beside the bedroom door and heard Kim shuffling along the hallway to the living room. Still, Markov stayed where he was. After a full two minutes, he turned the knob very slowly and opened the door.

He had drawn the drapes in the living room, and none of the bright light from the full moon illuminated the hallway. Markov kicked off his bedroom slippers and crept barefoot in his pajamas toward the master bedroom. There was only one option open to him. He had to kill Kim and claim that his former business associate had entered his house in the night obviously intending to rob him. Killing an intruder, especially one who was a wanted killer, might even get him accolades from the authorities.

Markov was ecstatic to hear what sounded like a snore coming from the living room. When he reached the door of the master bedroom he ran inside and scrambled to the closet, fumbling around the shelf where he had a Smith & Wesson .38-caliber, six-inch revolver. He got it down and held it in both trembling hands as he crept in darkness down the parquet hallway to the expansive living room. Now he wished he hadn't drawn the drapes. The moonlight would have helped him.

He was only ten feet away from the sofa when he was able to peer over the high back cushions and see that Kim was not there!

"I am here!" Kim said from somewhere to his left, and Markov spun and fired three wild rounds, the muzzle flashes lighting a moving figure who fired back twice.

Markov dove for the floor, crying in terror, but there was not a sound from Kim. No moans, no movement, nothing. Markov heard the neighbor's dog barking wildly, and he knew the shots would have the neighbors on both sides calling the police. He prayed that the police would get there in time to save his life. Even if he was arrested with Kim and indicted, that would be better than dying here in the darkness. Anything would be better than that.

Then he heard Kim chortling again. The Korean wasn't just drunk; he'd come unhinged. Markov realized that he was in a gunfight with a madman.

"I want your car!" Kim said from somewhere in the darkness across the room.

"Take it!" Markov shouted. "The keys are on the table by the front door. Take it and get out!"

"You will shoot me, I think," Kim said, and he fired two more rounds, one of which broke the ceramic lamp on the table behind the sofa, sending shards showering down on Markov.

"William, the police are coming!" Markov yelled. "The neighbors must have called them by now. Get out while you can!"

"Is too late, I think," Kim said. "Too late."

Mount Olympus was not a neighborhood from which "shots fired" calls emanated, not even on New Year's Eve, let alone on a summer night under a lovely Hollywood moon. Shop 6-X-32 received the code 3 call with Flotsam driving and Jetsam unlocking the shotgun rack.

When 6-X-66 heard the call, Hollywood Nate said to Britney Small, "Mount Olympus is where the owner of Club Samara lives!"

Marius Tatarescu, of 6-X-72, asked his senior partner, Sophie Branson, "How fast shall I drive, Sophia? Code two and a half?"

"At least," she answered, unlocking the shotgun rack.

Mel Yarashi and Always Talking Tony were right behind 6-X-72, and Fran Famosa was so close behind them that her new partner was more afraid of her driving than of a murderous Korean fugitive.

Within three minutes the entire midwatch was speeding toward Mount Olympus, hoping that the shots-fired call had something to do with the wanted killer William Kim.

"You are insane!" Markov cried from his place behind the sofa table. "Put down your weapon and run, William! Take my car and run!"

Kim fired two more rounds just for effect and said, "Too late."

Then they both heard the siren wail as 6-X-32 roared up the winding streets, with cypress trees streaming past, ascending a new Mount Olympus where no gods lived.

"Here they come!" Markov yelled, making a dash to the front door, but Kim fired two more rounds and Markov threw himself to the floor again.

He heard glass breaking to his right, but movement came from the left, and then he smelled brandy and garlic and Kim was on top of him, twisting the revolver from his fingers.

"NO, WILLIAM!" Markov screamed, but Kim dropped his own gun and grabbed Markov by the throat with both of his powerful hands.

Everyone on the Job knew that there were two kinds of cops at the LAPD. This, after they'd lived for years under federal judges and outside auditors, following the Rodney King beating and the so-called Rampart scandal. After the chiefs were stripped of civil service protection and bureaucratic autonomy. After the Department was taken over by East Coast carpetbaggers and homegrown hacks. After the LAPD was forced to lower the drawbridge and surrender Excalibur forevermore.

These days, there were plenty of risk-averse cops who wanted to get through their closely supervised careers safely, and be promoted if possible, preferring to work hours and assignments that would let them lead lives similar to those of their middle-class counterparts. But then there were the retro, action-oriented risk takers, who always ran straight to the sound of guns, craving those moments when the belly and brain felt like they were pulling five g's in an F-14. The midwatch was composed of that latter group, which was why they'd chosen to work the busy hours of Watch 5 in the first place.

So when those midwatch cars arrived at the Markov house, nobody talked about setting up perimeters, or requesting a SWAT team, or tear gas, or stinging hot gas, or a K-9 unit, or a hostage negotiator, or a remote-controlled "BatCat" to tear down the house piece by piece, or, God forbid, a *supervisor*! The arrival of a boss could result in an eighteen-hour standoff involving scores of people and a fortune in mechanized assistance, without anyone even knowing for sure if a barricaded suspect was dead or alive. Those Department-approved tactics would deprive the cops of the opportunity to take down the kind of vicious and dangerous killer that they might never get a chance at again.

So they deployed by silently surrounding the house in the moonlight, the only sounds coming from the creak of Sam Browne leather and the ripple of bootsteps. None of the midwatch cops bothered to shout surrender commands, which they thought would be superfluous and foolish in a situation like this. What Watch 5 of Hollywood Station wanted to do was simply handle the matter the same way self-starting LAPD coppers had done during decades past. That is, attack with the zeal of a holy warrior and either capture William Kim or kill him.

Jetsam advanced to the front porch with a shotgun, Flotsam right behind him. Hollywood Nate and Britney Small, toting a shotgun, padded along the side yard to the rear of the house, with the neighbor's security lights going on and dogs barking in a frenzy.

Sophie Branson yelled, "Turn off those damn lights!" when they lit up the cops like ducks in a row.

In the rear yard Nate whispered to Britney, "Bench up, partner."

She took a firing position with her left elbow on the low limb of an olive tree, and Nate deployed thirty feet parallel, behind a jacaranda tree. Both aimed their weapons at a forty-five-degree angle toward the steps leading to the rear door of the house, and they waited in the darkness for William Kim to run outside into a tactically designed funnel of death.

Nobody was at all surprised when Flotsam signaled with his fist raised and whispered to Jetsam, "I'm gonna boot it."

Flotsam took two strides forward and slammed the sole of his boot against the oak front door. The frame splintered, but the door didn't open. He kicked it again, and they heard a single gunshot from inside the house. That made Flotsam leap to the side of the door and wait. After half a minute of silence inside, he kicked the door again, right beside the dead-bolt lock, and it flew open, with one hinge breaking loose while the door dangled from the other hinge.

Both surfer cops peered around the corner of the open doorway and shined their lights inside while keeping their bodies behind the door frame. At that moment they weren't thinking about the resident of the house; they were only looking for a large Korean with a gun.

Suddenly, Jetsam said, "One down at two o'clock!"

"I see him!" Flotsam said.

Jetsam took a few steps inside, holding the shotgun in firing position, with the butt against his shoulder and the flashlight pressed against the gun's receiver, and said, "It's the big Korean. Minus a chunk of skull."

Flotsam lowered his pistol and yelled, "Awww, shit!"

William Kim had cheated them.

TWENTY-FOUR

T HE MURDER-SUICIDE ON Mount Olympus dominated the local news for a week. It was clear that William Kim, the suspected murderer of two Hollywood exotic dancers, had killed himself with a gunshot wound to the head. However, journalists were uncertain as to why the Korean had strangled Pavel Markov before his suicide, until the LAPD—ever conservative with new items and ever fearful of lawsuits and political criticism—revealed the lurid details and background of the case, but only a bit at a time.

Sergeant Murillo defended the midwatch officers against the nitpicking critics at West Bureau, who referred to his coppers as "overamped gunslingers" and "Seal Team Six wannabes" while making air quotes with their fingers. Despite them, the sergeant commended his troops in written attaboys and attagirls for the brave and decisive way they'd attempted to rescue the resident of Mount Olympus, while not knowing that the wanted killer had already murdered him. D2 Albino Villaseñor seconded that with a written commendation of his own.

Madame Tang was subjected to a great deal of questioning until she demanded a lawyer, but finally she could not be connected to any of the events spawned by the thirteen deaths in a cargo container at the Port of Los Angeles.

Hector Cozzo could not be charged for any provable crime after the deaths of Pavel Markov and William Kim. He was forced to give his parents a bonus of three thousand dollars to remain in their house after he was named as a "person of interest" in several news stories, thus bringing shame on an old Italian family that had lived in Pedro honorably for generations.

Dinko and Brigita Babich tried to assist Detective Bino Villaseñor in locating the family of Lita Medina Flores of the city and state of Guanajuato, Mexico. They gave Bino the name and street address of Lita's mother, Luz María, which Lita had written down for them in case of emergency, as well as the telephone number of the woman who Lita had said was a helpful neighbor who would call her mother to the phone.

Bino tried the telephone number, but it was nonexistent. Then he contacted the Guanajuato city police, who informed him that there was no such street of the name that Lita had written down for Dinko and Brigita. Both the city police and the state judicial police checked Lita's name and her mother's against birth records, public health records, and criminal records, but no person was found who could've been the individuals in question. The Mexican police suggested to the Hollywood detective that his information was bogus.

With Bino's assistance, along with a call to the office of the coroner from the city's most powerful politician of Croatian ancestry, the Babich family was permitted to pay the county fees and claim the body of Lita Medina. She was interred at the Catholic cemetery favored by local parishioners, with only a funeral director, a priest, Dinko and Brigita Babich, and Bino Villaseñor in attendance. Brigita wept quietly all through the brief graveside service.

Upon walking to their cars afterward, the detective said to Brigita and Dinko, "I've done everything I can to find the family of Lita Medina Flores. I'm sorry."

"Age nineteen years and four months," Brigita added, wiping tears away. "That's the way Lita would say how old she was."

Bino said, "I think maybe she was just a lost migrant kid who came from nowhere and created a fictitious family and maybe a new name, as a way to deal with her unhappy life. But anyone could see she was a person of quality regardless."

"She found herself a family," Dinko said. "Lita was home at last."

Two months later, summer was officially waning, but the days were still hot in San Pedro. Dinko Babich had thrown himself into his job and worked as many hours as he could on the docks. Every foreman commented that he was a changed young man since coming back from his thirty-day suspension. He'd become serious and taciturn, what the bosses called "all grown up," and he helped less experienced longshoremen whenever he could, even young Latino gang members he'd previously avoided. Everyone said it was only a matter of time until the industrious young man would become a high-paid crane operator like his father.

It was after work on a particularly sweltering day that the ancient Italian widower who lived across the street from the Babich house stood on his porch, leaning on his walker, and beckoned Dinko to come and join him. The old man was in his nineties, and Brigita often took him a plate of *mostaccioli*, which he loved. It was worrisome to see him teetering on that duct-taped walker of his, but he would scrape along the sidewalk for half a block every evening before supper. That was his daily workout.

"Afternoon, Mr. Buccieri," Dinko said.

"Dinko, I got something I keep forgetting to tell to you," the old man said, and Dinko wanted to ask him to sit down before he toppled, but of course he couldn't do that.

"What is it, Mr. Buccieri?"

"There was a man watching your house one night. I saw him standing out there smoking a cigarette."

"When was this?" Dinko asked.

"I'm not sure," the old man said. "Quite a while ago." Then he added, "It was just before the poor girl got killed. That's the reason I didn't tell you back then. I thought he might be a Peeping Tom. But you had so much sorrow and trouble in your house, I didn't want to add more. We got such a bad element all over Pedro nowadays."

"What did he look like?" Dinko asked.

"It was a dark night," the old man said, "and I only got a peek when a car drove by and the headlights hit him, but I still got good eyes. The other tuna fishermen used to say I could spot a sardine on the water two miles from our boat. He wasn't a big guy at all, maybe about my size. A young guy like you."

"A smoker, you say?"

"Yes. Do you know that when I worked on the boats everybody and his brother smoked cigarettes and cigars? Even their mothers smoked cigarettes and cigars." He snuffled at his little witticism.

"Tell me, Mr. Buccieri," Dinko said, "did you notice his hair?"

"Hair?" the old man said. "He had hair, very dark hair. Maybe he was a Mexican. They're taking over Pedro these days."

"What did his hair look like?" Dinko asked. "Think hard. Was it cut . . . different in any way?"

The old man pondered this. "Yes, different from your regular hair-cut. It was short all around the top but not in the back. It hung down long in the back, sort of like the cloth back flaps we wore under our hats on the boats, to protect our necks from the sun when we were hauling in the tuna. Back when times were good."

"That's called a mullet, Mr. Buccieri," Dinko said.

Hector Cozzo had been going to the same bar on Sixth Street since re-turning home to Pedro. It had changed in the past decade, and he was sure that the young Latino customers with shaved heads and total tats were gang members, maybe West Side Wilmas. He stopped there almost every night after he had supper at one of his favorite Italian or seafood spots, and he was already half-juiced when he parked his ten-year-old Ford Mustang a block west. He never noticed the Jeep Grand Cherokee that parked half a block away.

He was working on his second drink when he heard a voice behind him say, "Hey, mullethead."

"Dinko!" Hector said, and felt a preposterous shiver on this very warm night.

"I heard you'd moved back to Pedro," Dinko said as they bumped knuckles.

"Everybody does. That's Pedro pride." Hector gave a forced chuckle. "Lemme buy you a drink."

"Sure," Dinko said. And to the bartender: "A juice of some kind, please. Cranberry, orange, whatever."

"Cranberry?" Hector asked. "What happened to the Scotch drinker and pot smoker I used to know?"

"I think he died," Dinko said. "Two months and three days ago. Now all I do is work as many hours as I can get."

Hector was puzzled for an instant, and then he got the reference. "Yeah, that was a terrible thing about the Mexican dancer," he said. "I guess you were pretty close to her, huh?"

"Lita," Dinko said. "Lita Medina was her name."

"Yeah, Lita. A terrible thing," Hector said. "At least her killer went down for the count. I knew Markov from the club, but the Korean was jist some guy that brought in dancers once in a while. I never really knew the bastard, and may he rot in hell for all eternity."

"That's what happens to people that commit suicide," Dinko said. "Hell for eternity. They taught us that in Catholic school, remember?"

"Those were the days." Hector signaled for another drink with fingers more nicotine-stained than ever.

"Let's talk about happier times," Dinko said. "Seen any of the old pirates lately? What was the name of the Italian chick that Johnny Vidas was always chasing after?"

Brightening up, Hector said, "The one with tits from here to Long Beach? That was Sally Mancuso. Man, I wanted her bad!"

Hector Cozzo talked and drank Scotch, and Dinko Babich drank cranberry juice and listened, for nearly two hours. That's when Hector started turning surly, and gave a contemptuous glance to one of the young Latinos with a shaved head, saying to Dinko, "We call that 'aught bald.' As in zero hair. When these dirts have a little stubble, we call it 'one bald.' A little more, we call it 'two bald,' and so forth. But they're all jist a bunch of greasy onionheads."

He was talking very loud, and one of the tatted-out Latinos turned and looked at him.

"Whoa, partner," Dinko said to Hector. "I think you had enough. Let's pay and take this outside."

"You ain't paying nothing!" Hector said boozily.

"Did you pick a winner at the track, or what?" Dinko asked.

"I made a few bucks working in Hollywood," Hector said.

"I'll bet you did," Dinko said. "Let's get outta here."

Hector staggered as they walked to their cars, and Dinko said, "Maybe you oughta let me drive you home."

"No worries," Hector said, lighting a smoke. "I can drive myself home."

Dinko said, "They got sobriety checkpoints all over the place these days, and you're pretty wrecked."

"Fuck 'em." Hector rubbed his face and had trouble feeling it. When they got to the Mustang he said, "That's my ride."

"What happened to the SL?" Dinko asked.

"I got sick of it," Hector said. "I sold it. That's how I got enough bank to tide me over for a while."

"Yeah, that was a pricey car," Dinko said.

"I'll buy another one," Hector said. "Soon as I get an angle."

"Hector the angle man," Dinko said. Then: "Tell you what, let's get a nice hot cappuccino and then we'll be able to go home and sleep like babies. I'll drive."

"Where's your car?" Hector asked, peering down the dark street.

"Just a little ways behind yours."

"I don't need a wheel man," Hector said.

Dinko said, "I got an idea. How about if I drive you in your car to Starbucks, and after the cappuccino sobers you up, you can drive me back to my car. It's been a long time since I wheeled a Mustang around."

Hector reluctantly took the keys from his pocket and handed them to Dinko, saying apologetically, "The brakes're grabbing, and I hear a transmission whine. I'm gonna buy another cool ride soon as I get an angle."

"Sure you are," Dinko said, unlocking the door of the Mustang.

When Dinko turned the Mustang around, Hector said, "So what's a sober, hardworking longshoreman do for entertainment these days when you ain't working all them hours?"

Dinko said, "Oh, I try to lower my golf handicap, or I go to the movies with my mom. Sometimes I even go to bingo with her."

"What the fuck?" Hector said. "Bingo? With all the boring old Croats?"

Dinko said, "They like me. They tell my mother that I'm a perfect gentleman and she should be proud."

"I'll be go to hell," Hector said, "You ain't the guy I used to know."

Dinko looked at him. "I told you, that guy died."

They were driving for several minutes before Hector tossed his cigarette out the window and said, "Hey! Starbucks is on Western. Where you going?"

"I got something very important to show you," Dinko said.

Hector looked around. "We're headed for Point Fermin Park!"

"Just relax for a couple more minutes," Dinko said. "I gotta take a leak."

"You're going to Point Fermin to take a leak?"

"Be patient," Dinko said. "You'll be surprised."

"What kinda surprised?"

Dinko said, "Don't you think Pedro is beautiful after dark? That's when I can sorta see it the way I once saw it in the daytime through somebody else's eyes. If I could write music, I'd write something about the nights here, and I'd call it 'Harbor Nocturne.' I can almost hear the music in my ears. It sounds melancholy."

"If you say so," Hector muttered. "I jist wanna know where we're headed."

Point Fermin Park was deserted at that time of night, and when Dinko pulled Hector's Mustang to the curb near the highest point of the cliffs, Hector said, "Hey, Babich, what the fuck's going on?"

"I told you I gotta take a leak," Dinko said, removing the ignition key ring and getting out of the car. "Come join me."

"What? You think I'm gonna shake it off for you, or something?"

Dinko walked around the car and jerked open the passenger door, saying, "Get out."

"I ain't getting out," Hector said. "I don't gotta piss."

But Dinko grabbed Hector by his mullet and pulled him out onto the curbside grass.

"Hey!" Hector yelled. "What the fuck!"

Then he was looking at a gun muzzle, and Dinko said, "Do as you're told and keep your voice down or I swear to God I'll kill you on the spot."

"Dinko! What's wrong with you?" Hector cried.

"We're gonna take a stroll," Dinko said, "and whether or not I shoot you depends on your answer to one question. Now get up!"

He dragged Hector to his feet and put the car keys in Hector's pocket, pushing him in a southerly direction toward the Point Fermin cliffs. As they walked, Dinko prodded him in the back with the muzzle of the old U.S. Army–issue .45-caliber pistol that had belonged to his grandfather.

Hector said, "What question? What'd I ever do to you? You and me been friends all our lives!"

"Walk faster," Dinko said.

"Where you taking me, Dinko?" Hector said, but in a few moments he figured it out. They reached the low concrete barrier marking the proximity of the eroding and dangerous cliffs.

"Climb over," Dinko said.

"Are you crazy?" He was answered by a fist to his belly that put him back on the ground, gulping and gasping for air.

Then Dinko shoved the pistol in his belt and grabbed Hector by the shirt collar and the back of his belt and lifted him over the barrier. He leaped across behind him and said, "Get up and walk."

Hector was sobbing now and trying to catch his breath after the body blow, but he managed to say, "No, I won't."

Dinko said, "Hector, I only wanna ask you one question, that's all. Just one. If you answer it truthfully, I won't shoot you. Now get up."

Hector knelt and then struggled to his feet and said, "I swear on my mother and father, I had nothing to do with the death of that Mexican dancer!"

"Her name was Lita Medina," Dinko said. "Why can't you remember that?"

Hector said, "I didn't send Kim down here to Pedro! How could I? I didn't know she was with you! Jesus Christ, Dinko!"

"And yet the Korean found her," Dinko said, sounding most reasonable with the pistol now pointed at Hector's belly.

"Had to be the bitches!" Hector said. "She probably phoned one of the other dancers and said where she was staying and that one told Kim! None of them bitches can keep their mouths shut!"

"Turn around and look at Catalina," Dinko said.

"Please, Dinko!" Hector said, and then wept openly.

"If you answer my one question, I promise not to shoot you," Dinko said. "But you have to answer it truthfully."

"I'm the one that told the cops where to find Kim's old lady in Koreatown!" Hector pleaded. "I helped flush him out!"

"Turn around," Dinko said. "I won't say it again."

Hector turned slowly, hands at his sides, and continued weeping.

Dinko said, "Walk forward a few steps and keep looking at Catalina. Lita loved it over there."

There was no mist to shroud the island, and there was no overcast. This was an uncommonly starry night, the sky looking like fireflies on black velvet, and a platinum quarter-moon hung low over the black island and painted the sea with a silver sheen. They were not alone on that cliff. A ground squirrel scampered from their path, and a lone white gull soared close, unfurling its feathers to hover in the wind over the human silhouettes, as though hoping the human beings would toss a food scrap into the air.

Hector wobbled half a step forward and said, "Dinko! The cliff!"

Dinko said, "Look up, Hector. A white bird watching us. Could it be the Holy Ghost?"

"Please, Dinko!" Hector said, his tears gleaming in the starlight.

Dinko said, "Are you ready for the question that'll decide whether or not I shoot you? This is your road-to-Damascus moment, Hector. Are you prepared?"

The ocean's assault on the shoreline intensified, waves booming against the rocks below, and the wind hissed in their faces, blowing Hector's mullet skyward like a black pennant fluttering. He managed to say between sobs, "Ask it."

Dinko Babich said, "Keep looking out at Lita's island and tell me, did you really pay cash for that Mercedes SL like you told me on the first day I met her or did you lease the car?"

Hector Cozzo stared in the direction of Santa Catalina Island, but he couldn't see anything through his tears except a blur of the great dark ocean and the fearful heavens above it. At last he stopped sobbing long enough to say, "I leased it."

Dinko Babich said, "Hector, you *finally* told the truth about something. God will be so amazed."

Then Dinko stepped forward and, with the heel of his left hand, shoved his former friend over the crumbling edge of the Point Fermin cliffs.

Hector Cozzo screamed all the way down to the rocks below, and Dinko Babich whirled and leaped over the barrier and ran back across the park, still hearing the scream. But as he ran he realized he was hearing the feral South Shores peacock echoing the scream it heard from Hector Cozzo as he was plunging to his death.

Dinko continued to hear it as he ran north, toward his car, not sure if it was the wandering peacock's scream or his memory of Hector's scream, and not even stopping to catch his breath until he'd run as fast as he could run for nearly two miles.

The area patrol unit from Harbor Station made an early-morning check on the unlocked Mustang parked by Point Fermin Park, and when the cops got back to the station they reported it to the watch commander. And because the cliffs of Point Fermin were one of the three favorite suicide locations in southern California, an airship was requested to do a flyover of the shoreline after daybreak. The observer in the police helicopter spotted the shattered body of Hector Cozzo at 9:30 that morning.

There was some press coverage of the recovery, but not much. Nobody from the press connected the deceased to the violent events two months earlier. It was an ordinary suicide from a place where there had been others. But a detective at Harbor Station recognized the name Hector Cozzo as belonging to the man Hollywood detective Albino Villaseñor had interrogated on the day of the church murder. The Harbor detective phoned Hollywood Station to chat with Bino about the Point Fermin suicide.

He said, "I suppose Cozzo coulda been despondent about his connection to all the bad shit that came down from that Hollywood nightclub, and finally just got juiced and spiraled out from a guilty conscience."

"Maybe so," Bino responded.

Then the Harbor detective said, "You don't suppose this could be anything but a suicide, do you?"

Bino Villaseñor hesitated for a few beats before saying, "All the bad guys connected to the case are dead. The murders are cleared. Hector Cozzo's death has to be just an ordinary suicide. Thanks for the call."

The owner of the building in which Club Samara had operated decided to lease the nightclub to a sports bar franchise that expected to do good business at that location. Shanghai Massage closed down, and the building was sold to a real estate broker who only massaged the egos of

Hollywood property owners forced to sell to the bottom-feeders sniffing out real estate steals during the lean years of the Great Recession.

Hector Cozzo's parents were extremely aloof and reticent after the death of their son. His funeral was restricted to family members, and his parents insisted to all that their son's death was the result of a drunken fall, not a suicide. After finding the valise in his closet, the parents bought a new Cadillac Sport Wagon.

It had taken several weeks for the gravestone to be finished and set in place at the cemetery. The lettering said:

Lita Medina Flores
Age nineteen years and four months
She was loved

The cemetery workers noticed that every weekend someone placed fresh sprigs of lilac by the stone.

TWENTY-FIVE

DURING ROLL CALL, the officers of Watch 5 at Hollywood Station could hardly keep their eyes open. They took it as just more political correctness being spoon-fed to them by the geeks at West Bureau. As usual, it involved the care and handling of minority citizens in the ethnic melting pot of Los Angeles, and the need to be ever vigilant about avoiding even the semblance of racial profiling.

After Sergeant Murillo finished droning on with the material he was required to read, he brought an LAPD internal discipline matter to their attention, and this perked up the midwatch considerably. It involved a complaint by an African-American streetwalking hooker in Central Division who had alleged that she'd traded sexual groping for the freedom to ply her trade untroubled by cruising patrol units.

She named four officers in her complaint: two were white, one was Hispanic, and one was Asian. The first three admitted only to watching the hooker expose her breasts for them, but they denied that any touching had taken place and accepted a penalty of a short suspension with the attendant loss of pay. The Asian cop proclaimed his complete innocence and demanded a Board of Rights hearing.

What got the incident repeated at roll calls all over the city was that when the hooker was sworn and gave her testimony at the trial board, the Department advocate, in trying to prove that sexual groping had taken place, asked her if there was something unusual about the officer that could be proven if he submitted to an unclothed examination.

The hooker said, "Oh yeah. I seen bigger pee-nile objects on a doodlebug."

When the midwatch stopped their hooting and chortling, Flotsam said, "Sarge, the moral of this story is that no Asian copper should ever demand a trial board if his pee-nile object is involved."

Mel Yarashi stood and yelled to the sergeant, "That is, without a doubt, the most scurrilous and despicable and absolutely *false* racial stereotyping I have ever heard! I demand that you cut paper on this snarky surf goon!"

Hollywood Nate was without a partner that night while Britney Small was taking a day off. They were so shorthanded on Watch 5 that there was nobody to assign with Nate, so Sergeant Murillo asked if he'd help out at the front desk. Nothing much happened of interest other than when a shirtless young man entered the lobby with his hands cuffed behind him and asked Nate if he could help with "an alternative lifestyle problem." It seemed that the young man and his love partner, who was pacing nervously outside the station, had lost their handcuff key. Nate unlocked the cuffs and sent him on his way with an admonition that a handcuff key should always be kept bedside, next to the handcuffs and condoms.

Before making his exit the young man said, "Thank you, Officer. This has been just *so* embarrassing!"

Nate said, "Think nothing of it. This is just *so* Hollywood."

Hollywood Nate got bored around midnight and asked Sergeant Murillo if he'd like to take a ride with him and grab a burger. They went to Hamburger Hamlet, and after they'd finished their meal, Sergeant Murillo asked Nate to drive along Hollywood Boulevard so he could see what was being done to curtail the panhandling on the Walk of Fame. And it was near Grauman's Chinese Theatre that they spotted the surfer cops jacking up four drunken panhandlers, who were standing in a row facing the street.

Sergeant Murillo said, "Pull over, Nate, and wait for me. I'd like to see my beach boys in action."

"They work in mysterious ways," Nate warned.

The midwatch supervisor got out of the car and made his way through a flock of tourists, approaching unseen by the surfer cops, both of whom had their backs to him and were shaking their heads in frustration. When he got close enough, he watched one of the transients contemplate a question from Jetsam, while Flotsam seemed to be trying to draw out an answer with wild hand waving. The transient suddenly displayed a toothless grin and gave an answer.

Sergeant Murillo returned to the radio car at the curb without having been noticed by the cops or the panhandlers.

When he got in, he said, "Okay, back to the barn."

"What were they doing?" Nate asked.

"You got me," the sergeant said. "It seemed like an audition or something."

"An audition?" Hollywood Nate said. "I'm the only guy at Hollywood Station who goes to auditions."

His sergeant said, "I didn't hear the question from our guys, but only one of the derelicts answered it."

Nate said, "So what was the answer?"

Sergeant Murillo said, "It was *Sesame Street* nonsense. Something about the good ship *Lollipop*. What's up with that?"

Nate pointed toward the Grauman's Chinese Theatre forecourt, jammed with superheroes and stargazers, and tourists surrounding Marilyn Monroe, who displayed her porcelain veneers while cameras flashed.

"Sarge," said Hollywood Nate, "the Oracle always told us that doing good police work was the most fun we'd ever have in our entire lives. But he *never* said that doing police work in Hollywood, California, was a job for grown-ups, now *did* he?"